The
QUEEN'S
POISONER

BOOKS BY JEFF WHEELER

The Kingfountain Series

The Queen's Poisoner
The Thief's Daughter
The King's Traitor

The Covenant of Muirwood Trilogy

The Banished of Muirwood
The Ciphers of Muirwood
The Void of Muirwood

The Legends of Muirwood Trilogy

The Wretched of Muirwood
The Blight of Muirwood
The Scourge of Muirwood

Whispers from Mirrowen Trilogy

Fireblood
Dryad-Born
Poisonwell

Landmoor Series

Landmoor
Silverkin

The QUEEN'S POISONER

JEFF WHEELER

47NORTH

Published by 47North, Seattle

www.apub.com

Amazon, the Amazon logo, and 47North are trademarks of Amazon.com, Inc., or its affiliates.

ISBN-13: 9781503953314 (hardcover)
ISBN-10: 1503953319 (hardcover)
ISBN-13: 9781503953307 (paperback)
ISBN-10: 1503953300 (paperback)

Cover design by Shasti O'Leary Soudant

Printed in the United States of America

First edition

To Lincoln

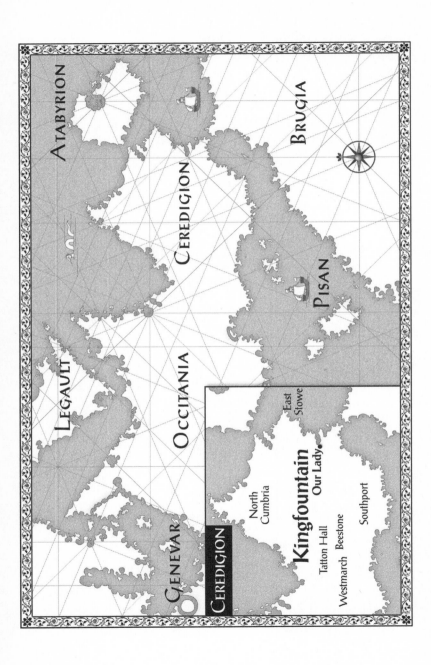

CHARACTERS

ARGENTINE FAMILY

Eredur Argentine: previous King of Ceredigion, deceased under mysterious circumstances

Dunsdworth Argentine: middle brother of Eredur, attainted of treason and executed; has a son with the same name who is ward to the king at the palace

Severn Argentine: King of Ceredigion, youngest brother; usurped throne from Eredur's sons who are missing and presumed murdered

Elyse Argentine: eldest daughter of Eredur

LORDS OF CEREDIGION

Lord Kiskaddon: Duke of Westmarch

Lord Horwath: Duke of North Cumbria

Lord Asilomar: Duke of East Stowe

Lord Lovel: Duke of Southport

Lord Ratcliffe: master of the Espion, the king's spy service

Lord Bletchley: supporter of King Severn's usurpation, master of the Espion, executed for treason

◆ ◆ ◆

There was a battle fought and a battle won. There was much disquiet about the king's odds of victory. Despite his years of battle experience, his faithful friends, and the resources of Ceredigion behind him, many predicted that the upstart would win. There was treachery, of course. There were omens read in the waters. Duke Kiskaddon forbade his men to engage in the battle on either side, even with his eldest son a hostage to the king. A poor decision for the duke. His son was sent over the waterfall after the king's victory. What other vengeance will be wrought upon that treacherous duke, I can only imagine. Though I chuckle to myself. I shall enjoy watching it immensely. Long live the crouch-backed king!

—Dominic Mancini, Espion of Our Lady of Kingfountain

◆ ◆ ◆

CHAPTER ONE

The Duke of Kiskaddon

Lady Eleanor sat at the window seat of her chambers, gently stroking her son's head in her lap. Owen was her youngest child, the one who had barely survived his birth. He was a frail lad of eight, though he looked younger than that. His hair was a mousy-brown color, thick and untameable despite all their efforts, and she loved gliding her fingers through it. There was a little patch of white hair above his left ear. His siblings always asked her why he had been born with such a strange patch of white in his dark hair.

It was a mark that set him apart from his siblings. She considered it a reminder of the miracle that happened after his birth.

Owen stared up at her eyes with his deep brown ones, seeming to know she was fretting and in need of comfort. He was an affectionate child, always the first to come running into her arms. As a babe, he would murmur his parents' endearments while clutching their legs or hugging them. *Maman, Papan. Maman, Papan. Maman, Papan.* He had loved more than anything else to burrow into the sheets of his parents' bed after they had awoken for the day, stealing the ebbing warmth. He stopped doing that finally at age six, but he had not outgrown the hugs and kisses, and he always wanted to be near, especially to her husband, Lord Kiskaddon.

Thoughts of her husband made her stomach churn with worry. Eleanor glanced out the window overlooking the well-sculpted gardens of Tatton Hall. But she found no comfort in the trimmed hedges, the vibrant terraced lawns, or the large foaming fountains. A battle had raged the day before, and she still awaited word on the outcome.

"When will *Papan* come?" the little voice asked. He looked at her with such serious eyes.

Would he even come home?

There was nothing she dreaded more than the battlefield. Her husband was no longer a young man. He was more statesman than battle commander now, in his forty-fifth year. She glanced at the empty armor rack stationed by their canopied bed. The curtains were open, showing the neat folded sheets. He always insisted on the bed being made every day. No matter what troubling news arrived from court, her husband relished the simple rituals of sleep. Though some nights he would lie awake for hours pondering the troubles of Ceredigion, he was still most at peace when they were together, alone, in that canopied bed.

"I don't know," Eleanor whispered, her voice husky. She continued to smooth his thick locks, her finger pausing to play with the tuft of white. Her husband had been summoned to join the king's army on the battlefield to face the invasion, and her oldest son was a hostage in the king's army to ensure her husband's good faith. Word reached her before the battle that the king's army outnumbered their enemies three to one. But this was not a match of mathematics. It was a test of loyalty.

Severn Argentine was a hard king to serve. He had a barbed whip for a tongue and it drew blood whenever he spoke. In the two years since he had usurped the throne from his older brother's children, the kingdom had been fraught with machinations, treason, and executions. It was whispered the uncle had murdered his nephews at the palace in

Kingfountain. The very possibility made Eleanor tremble with horror. She, a mother of nine children, could not bear the thought of such wickedness. Only five of her children had survived childhood, for they were all of sickly constitution. Some of her sons and daughters had died as infants, and each new loss had broken her heart. And then there was her lastborn, little Owen. Her miracle.

Her dear, thoughtful boy was still staring into her eyes, almost as if he could read her thoughts. She loved to catch him playing by himself, to watch at the edge of the door as he knelt on the floor and stacked tiles before toppling them over. She often caught him in the library, reading to himself. She no longer remembered teaching him to read, he had been so young. It was something he seemed to have learned all by himself, like breathing, and he just inhaled the letters and words and sorted them effortlessly in his mind. But, though he was a particularly intelligent child, he was still a child. He loved to run outside in the gardens with his siblings and join the chase for a white ribbon tied to a pole through the hedge maze. Of course, he could start wheezing when he did this, but that did not deter him.

She would never forget the sorrow she had felt when the royal midwife had announced the babe stillborn. There was no cry, no wail like those that had announced the births of Eleanor's other eight children. He came into the world bloody and silent—fully formed, but not breathing. It had devastated her to lose what she knew to be her lastborn, her final child. Her husband's tears had joined her own as they wept over their lost child.

Was there nothing to be done? Were there no words of solace? No skill that could be rendered? The midwife had crooned to the dead babe in her arms, kissing his tender, puckered head, and suggested they mourn with the babe together as husband and wife. Lord Kiskaddon and Lady Eleanor cradled the baby in their arms, burrowing in the sheets of the bed, and wept for the child, hugging and kissing him. Speaking to him softly. Telling him of their family and how much he would be loved and needed.

And then the miracle happened.

It was the Fountain, she was certain of that. Somehow the babe had heard their pleading. The eyes of the dead child blinked open. Eleanor was so startled, she thought she had imagined it at first, but her husband saw the same thing. The eyes opened. *What does it mean?* they asked the midwife.

Perhaps he bids you good-bye, she said softly.

But moments became hours. Hours became days. Days became weeks. Eleanor glided her fingers through her boy's thick hair. He smiled up at her, as if he were remembering it too. He gave her a crooked little smile, pressing his cheek languidly against her lap. His eyelashes fluttered.

"Maman! Maman!"

It was Jessica, her fourteen-year-old, running in with her blond curls bouncing. "It's *Papan!* He rides here with a host!"

Eleanor's heart seized with surprise and swelled with hope. "You saw him?"

"From the balcony!" Jessica said, her eyes eager with excitement. "His head was shining, Maman. He is with Lord Horwath. I recognized him as well."

That made no sense at all.

Lord Horwath ruled the northern borders of the realm. Her husband ruled the west. They were peers of the realm, equals. Why would Stiev Horwath escort him to Tatton Hall? A stab of worry smote her chest.

"Owen, go with your sister to greet your father," Eleanor said. The boy closed his hand on the fabric of her dress, his eyes suddenly wary. He balked.

"Go, Owen!" she bade him earnestly, pushing herself up from the window seat. She began pacing as Jessica grabbed the little boy's hand and pulled him with her toward the doors. There was a great commotion as word of the duke's return spread through the manor house. The people loved him, even the lowliest of scullions respected their kindhearted master.

Eleanor felt as if needles were stabbing her skin as she paced. Her heart raced in her chest. She was her husband's closest advisor. So far her advice had steered him safely through the churning rapids of intrigue that had pitted the noble houses of the realm against each other in several brutal wars. Had that changed?

She heard the sound of boots coming up the stairs. Eleanor wrung her hands, biting her lip as she awaited the news with dread. He was alive! But what of her eldest? What of Jorganon? He had gone into battle with his father and the king. Why had Jessica not mentioned him?

Her husband entered the room, and with one look, she knew her son was dead. Lord Kiskaddon was no longer young, but his face had a boyish look that belied the bald top and the fringe of gray stubble around the sides and back. He was a sturdy man who could spend hours in the saddle without his strength flagging. But now his jaw was clenched and unshaven, and the sadness in his eyes took away from his youthful appearance. Her husband was in mourning. And not just the death of their eldest son. She knew at once he had news that was even worse than the death of their son.

"You are home," Eleanor breathed, rushing to his sturdy arms. But his grip was as weak as a kitten's.

He kissed the top of her head, and she felt the pent-up shuddering inside him.

"Jorganon is dead," she said, hoping it was not true, but knowing that it was.

"Yes," he said hoarsely, his mouth pressing against her hair. He pulled away from her and stared down at the ground.

"What happened?" Eleanor pleaded, grabbing his hand. "Tell me the worst of it! I cannot bear to see you in such anguish, Husband!"

He had tears in his eyes. He—who rarely showed his emotions so nakedly. His cheek twitched. "The king . . . won. The battle is named the Battle of Ambion Hill. It was a close battle, Eleanor. So close. A moment longer, a breath of *wind* could have changed it. A trickling stream could have overturned it. I wish . . . if you had been there to advise me . . . but you were not!" His expression crumpled and he stared at her pleadingly. "Forgive me!"

Eleanor felt her legs quivering. "For what?" she choked.

His lips were pressed so tightly they were white. "Horwath led the battle for the king. His men were hard-pressed. It looked possible that he would fail. The king ordered my army to support Horwath's." He shook his head as if he were still living in that perilous moment when all could be lost or won. "I refused."

"What?" she gasped.

"The king is the last of his dynasty. His only son died a year ago. His wife died next—poisoned, they say. It seemed as if the Fountain had judged him and he was doomed to fail at Ambion. We both believed that or we never would have—"

"Shhh!" Eleanor warned furtively, glancing at the door.

"We *suspected* the new king would be in our favor if we did *not* intervene. In that moment of peril, I believed the king's army would fall. Severn threatened to kill Jorganon on the spot." Her husband knuckled his forehead, his words breaking into sobs. "What have I done?"

Eleanor rushed to her husband and held him tightly. He was a wise and capable man, but such qualities did not aid him in navigating the politics of King Severn's duplicitous court. It was why he so often sought her counsel. She too had suspected Severn's reign would be mercifully short. Yes, she had advised her husband to appear to support the king. But not to support him too well. To be slow, to appear confused by commands. She bit the edge of her finger.

"But the king's army prevailed after all," Eleanor said weakly. "And now he thinks you a traitor."

"From where I sat, it looked like Horwath would be destroyed. The men were fighting slothfully. No one's heart was in it to defend Ceredigion from the invader. But then the king summoned his knights and rode into battle himself. The conflict was raging below them when they made their charge. I watched it, Eleanor. There were only twenty . . . maybe thirty knights in all, but they came like a flood. As if the very Fountain were driving them. They clashed with lances and swords. The king himself unhorsed his enemy and then jumped from his injured horse and killed the man with his own sword. The invaders swarmed him, but he fought as if he had the strength of a dozen men. They fell away from him, and when they saw his triumph, Horwath's men became demons!" His eyes were wide with shock and amazement. "Severn defeated them by himself. Even with his twisted leg and his hunchback, he was unstoppable. I rode hard to join the fray and helped capture the fallen army. The king's crown had fallen from his head during the fighting and I found it in a hawthorn bush. I told him . . . I told him that I was loyal." His face went white.

Eleanor felt her knees losing strength. She clutched to her husband, as if they were alone on an island and the waves of the sea were crashing around them, trying to drag them into the surf. Her ears were ringing with the words.

"The king ordered Jorganon's death. He *mocked* me, saying perhaps I still had sons to spare. And so he sent Horwath with me to bid you the tidings. Thus sayeth King Severn Argentine to the Lady Eleanor Kiskaddon: *Choose you another son to be hostage, to live in the palace of Kingfountain under His Majesty's wardship. Prove your good faith and obedience. Pick the son who will stand as surety for your house.*"

Lady Eleanor would have fainted, but she somehow managed to keep her feet. She looked up at her husband. "I must trust that man with *another* of my children?" Her heart hammered violently in her chest and she quailed under the weight of her grief. "That . . . that . . . *butcher?*"

"Stiev Horwath has come to bring the child to Kingfountain," her husband said, his look full of misery. "If we do not choose, he will execute our entire family for treason now."

Lady Eleanor sobbed against her husband's chest. It was a choice no mother should be forced to make. Should she sacrifice one child so that all the others might live? But King Severn was ruthless and cunning. Would the child she selected be the *only* of her children to survive?

She wept bitterly, swallowed by grief and unable to think. Who could she part with? Why had the choice even been given to her if not to make her suffering more acute? She hated the king. She hated him with all her passion, all her grief. How could she decide such a thing? How would she hand one of her boys over to a man who had murdered his own brother's sons? The king's hands were so wet with blood a trail probably dribbled wherever he went.

In her grief, she did not hear the door open or the soft padding of feet. She did not notice until Owen's arms wrapped around their legs.

He squeezed them both so hard, and though she could not hear any words, she could imagine his thoughts, his childlike attempt to comfort them. *There, there, Maman, Papan. There, there! It will be all right, Maman, Papan. There, there!*

She stared down at her son, her innocent son. And then a memory stirred.

A memory of the royal midwife who had saved his life.

Her chest became tight with anticipation. Perhaps she could get a secret message to the sanctuary of Our Lady, a plea to protect her son, the boy who had been saved once before. She could endure the separation, the despair, so long as she could cling to a thread of hope.

She knew that a thread was all she could expect.

◆ ◆ ◆

The Ceredigic are a highly superstitious people. Then again, so are most of the fools born to women. They have an ancient belief in the power of water that comes from legends no one even knows anymore. It is all chuff and flax. They build massive sanctuaries next to rivers. Our Lady of Kingfountain is actually built within the river, at the gorge of a breathtaking waterfall. These sanctuaries grant men protection from the law. Many a thief lives within these hallowed domains, with their reflecting pools, babbling fountains, and pleasing gardens—stealing by day and sleeping on the sanctuaries' protected tiles by night. These they call fountain-men. All because of an ancient whim that the privilege of sanctuary should last so long as the river flows and the waters fall. It is among these scum at Our Lady where I spend my days watching the king's enemies. I detest my work at times. I am so bored with this.

—Dominic Mancini, Espion of Our Lady of Kingfountain

◆ ◆ ◆

CHAPTER TWO
The Duke of North Cumbria

Owen loved to play by himself and could entertain himself for hours at a time—whether by stacking tiles in a row before knocking them down, marshaling lead soldiers to war, or reading to himself. He was talkative with his family, and when it came to swinging wooden swords with his siblings, he was usually the one who made others cry, even his sisters. But put him in a room with a single stranger, and he would skulk behind a chair and observe the newcomer with wary eyes until he or she left.

That was how he had watched Lord Horwath. Only when the duke left Tatton Hall, Owen was riding behind his saddle, terrified and so stricken by surprise that he could not have spoken to anyone if he had tried. As they rode away from his family, his mother's tears glistening on her cheeks, he wondered if he would ever be able to speak again.

Tatton Hall was his world, and he knew the innermost corners of it from basement to garret. There were some parts of the manor he was afraid of—the wine cellar was dark and had a funny smell—but there were secret places that only he knew, places where he could hide himself away and never be found. The gardens were vast and he had spent countless days enjoying the simple pleasures of running in the grass or resting on beds of leaves to watch the ants and ticklebugs crawl in the earth. He loved how the ticklebugs would coil themselves up into little pebbles that he could roll around on his palm. And then, when he held still, their little legs would start squirming again until they were upright and he'd let them crawl around his hand in circles.

Owen loved nature and the outdoors, but he loved the indoors even more. Books fascinated him, and the effect that letters had on his eyes was much like the thrill of the ticklebugs on his skin. When he read, it was as if he were transported to some dreamland where he could not hear whispers or shouting. He read anything and everything he could get his little hands on, and he remembered it all. His hunger for books was never satisfied, and his favorites were stories about the exploits of the Fountain-blessed.

Tatton Hall disappeared with the sound of clopping hooves. His entire childhood was being banished. Horwath rode stiffly in his saddle, saying nothing to the child as they rode together, except for an occasional question about whether he was hungry or thirsty or needed to use the privy when they stopped to rest the horses.

The duke was not a giant of a man, and he was older than Owen's father. Beneath his black velvet cap, his hair was thick and gray, cut short around the nape of his neck, and he had a thick goatee to match. His face carried a stern, sour expression that told Owen he did not enjoy escorting a boy of eight summers across the kingdom, and wanted the task done as quickly and painlessly as possible. The duke stayed almost as silent as Owen, while the knights of his household joked amongst themselves and were far more interesting companions to observe.

All the nobles of the realm had badges and mottos. Owen was particularly proud of his own family's, having seen it all his life. The badge of House Kiskaddon was called the Aurum, and it was a slash of bright blue decorated with three golden bucks' heads with sharp, thornlike antlers. Horwath's livery was red with a golden lion with an arrow through its open mouth. Owen did not like the look of it, for he could not stop thinking of the lion's pain. The duke had the badge on his tunic, and his standard-bearer, who rode on a horse immediately behind them, carried a flag bearing the image, announcing to everyone who they were and to stay away. Since some of the knights had bows as well as swords, Owen kept his mouth shut for more than one reason.

The boy lost track of time as they rode. Several days had passed. Each morning the duke would jostle him awake at dawn, frown at him, and lead him back to the horse. Owen said nothing. The duke said nothing. It was like that all the way to Kingfountain.

When Owen was three years old, he had come to the royal city of Ceredigion with his family. Enough time had passed that he only had vague snatches of the memory. But as they approached the city from the main road, those little memories began to fuse together and it looked vaguely familiar.

What was striking about Kingfountain was that it had been built around a vast river just at the point where the ground sharply gave way to a raging waterfall. No matter how swollen or low the river was, the waterfall never stopped. There was a large island in the middle of the river where a sanctuary had been constructed—Our Lady of Kingfountain. Huge boulders and rocks emerged from the falls, some with spindly trees somehow clinging to them in spite of the surge of foaming water.

Owen knew the building bore that name because of legends from the past, but none of his reading had been able to explain it to him in as much detail as he wanted. The texts he had tried reading to learn more were full of knights, battles, and disparate kingdoms that no longer existed, but they were written in a style too long and boring to hold his interest. The sanctuary had two sturdy towers and a series of arches that loomed over the back shell of the building. The waterways under the arches always flowed, making the sanctuary a replica of the waterfall itself. On one bank of the river lay the city proper, with its wedge-shaped roofs and smoking chimneys. The noise of bleating goats, lowing oxen, and trundling carts and wagons was barely discernible through the constant roar of the waterfall. On the other bank of the river, on the high ground, stood the palace, and it made Tatton Hall seem like a toy in comparison.

A stone bridge connected the palace to the island and several wooden bridges connected the island to the main shore and the rest of the city. It was a breathtaking sight, and Owen kept leaning in the saddle to get a better view. The rushing of the waterfall could be heard from miles away, the steady churn of waves that sounded like a constant storm.

The palace was built on a green hill full of lush woods and had many tiers and layers, with sharp-edged walls and easily a dozen turrets flying the royal banners. Owen could see gardens and trees rising above portions of the old stone walls, and to his inexperienced eye, it looked as if the castle had stood for thousands of years. Still, the facade was free of ivy or vines, and had been meticulously kept.

So this would be his new home. The king had summoned Owen to live in the palace as his ward. Owen's older brother Jorganon had also lived at Kingfountain for a time. And now he was dead. Was that why *Maman* and *Papan* had wept so much when Owen left? The palace did not feel like a home. It felt like a monument, a relic of the ages, a dangerous place.

As they rode into the city, they were announced by trumpets at the gate and Owen found himself stared at by hundreds of strangers. Some looked at him with pity, which made him even more uncomfortable and shy, and he buried his face in the duke's cloak to hide.

The hooves clopped against the cobbles as they rode through the city and the omnipresent noise from the falls. Eventually Owen peeked out again and stared down at the shops and swarms of people. He soaked in the sights, unable to comprehend the massive size of such a place, his senses overwhelmed by the noise and confusion. He tried to stifle his emotions, but he found himself crying, his heart breaking with sadness that none of his family was there to shelter him. Why had *he* been chosen to go to Kingfountain? Why not one of the others?

Horwath became aware of his little sobs after a while and turned in the saddle to look down at him. "What is it, boy?" he asked gruffly, his goatee bending into a frown.

Owen looked into his eyes, afraid to say anything at all, let alone reveal his true feelings. He tried to stifle his tears, but that only made them worse. He felt the blobs of water rolling down his cheeks. He was miserable and lonely, and though the events of the last few days seemed like a nightmare, he was beginning to realize that the nightmare was his new life.

The duke waved one of his knights over. "Fetch the lad a muffin. Over there."

"Aye, my lord," said the knight, and rode off ahead.

Owen did not want a muffin. He wanted to go back to Tatton Hall. But nothing would have convinced him to say that. He trembled violently, clutching the duke's cloak, feeling sick to his bones as he stared at the arrow-pierced lion on the badge. The horse continued its slow progress until the knight returned and offered Owen a pale brown muffin with tiny dark seeds. Though he did not want it, the boy accepted it without a word of thanks and clutched it tightly. It was soft and bigger than his hand, and the sweet smell wafting from it reminded him of the kitchen at home. Soon his gasping sobs quieted and he rubbed his wet nose on the back of his sleeve. The muffin continued to tempt him and he finally succumbed and took a bite. The bread of the muffin was like cake and the seeds crunched a bit when he bit down on them. He had never had this kind before, but it was delicious, and he wolfed it down.

They reached one of the bridges leading to the sanctuary and Owen perked up, nervous about crossing a bridge over such a mighty river. What if the bridge washed out while they were on it and they were all swept to their deaths over the waterfall? He smiled at the thought, imagining how fun that might be—until the end. The force of the river thrummed against the wooden bridge, causing a giddy feeling of nervousness to twine around the muffin in Owen's stomach. He clutched the duke's cloak more tightly, feeling the tromp of the hooves.

Though they reached the island of the sanctuary, there was no need to enter the holy grounds. Men milled around the fountain yard of the sanctuary, and a few of them rested their arms on the gates to watch the duke's entourage pass. The men were an unkempt, beggarly bunch, and some stared at Owen with open curiosity. He peeked at them before hiding his face once more in the folds of the duke's cloak.

They crossed the small island quickly, heading directly for the stone bridge to the castle. The turrets were so high and sharply pointed, Owen thought they might pop the clouds like bubbles if they came too low. The rippling flags on the pennants featured both the royal lions of Ceredigion and the king's own standard—the badge he still wore after assuming the throne. The white boar. Owen had always considered pigs to be friendly creatures and loved them, but the image of the porcine body and thick tusks against a field of black was chilling.

"Almost there, lad," the duke said gruffly. The horse labored across the bridge and then up the gentle slope of the hill. The brown castle walls looked more friendly than ominous, but the effect was ruined by that white boar presiding over it. There was a tower in the far distance. A tower more slender than the others. It looked like a knife. Owen shuddered.

They reached the drawbridge and portcullis and entered the palace. This was the king's court, but it was not in the heart of the realm, or so Owen had gleaned from studying the few maps and books his father owned. Rather, it was in the east, and the river dumped into the ocean several leagues away. Ships could trundle up the river to a point, and then cargo had to be packed by mules up windy roads to the town. The castle was defended by the river, defended by the hill, protected by the Fountain itself, it was claimed.

Grooms took their horses, and Owen found himself walking along a huge stone corridor. The flicker of torchlight helped dispel some of the gloom. There were not many windows and the place was cool and dark, despite the warmth of the midsummer air outside. Owen looked at the banners, the tapestries, smelled the fumes of the burning oil and leather and steel. He walked next to the duke, his stomach roiling with fear. He had walked this corridor as a toddler. Strange that he remembered it. He knew they were approaching the great hall.

A tall man approached them from ahead, someone much younger than the duke, with golden brown hair beneath a black cap. He was dressed in a black tunic with silver slashes on the sleeves, glittering with gems, and had the urgent walk of a man always in a hurry. He had a very close-trimmed goatee, and although he was a bigger man than the duke, he was not as fit.

"Ah, Stiev! I knew you had arrived when I heard the trumpet. This way, this way, the king is coming down now! We must hurry!"

"Ratcliffe," the duke said with a slight nod. He did not change his pace, but the man's urgent demeanor made Owen want to walk faster.

The man, Ratcliffe, rubbed his hands together in a fidgeting motion. "Thank the *Fountain* we all survived the battle," he said under his breath. "I had my doubts we would, to be sure. This is Kiskaddon's whelp, eh?" He gave Owen a contemptuous look and chuckled almost musically. "The youngest was chosen. As if that will help. The king is in a fury, as you can imagine. His leg still pains him from the battle injury. The doctors say it is healing, but you know he cannot hold still! I wish we could persuade him to stop pacing to and fro so he could rest proper. What news from Westmarch?"

Horwath's expression did not change as they walked. "I will tell the king," he said curtly.

Ratcliffe frowned, his nostrils flaring. "As you wish. Guard your secrets. The king has granted me leave to recruit even more Espion. If a baker's wife complains about the king at breakfast, I will know about it ere nightfall. Ah, here we are." He gestured grandly as they entered the great hall.

As he took in the massive space that had opened before him, Owen nearly stumbled on the carpet trim and had to catch himself. He stared at the huge banners hanging from poles in the wall, the vast ceiling held up by a latticework of timbers, and the gray windows set high in the wall. Some light streamed in through them, but not enough to provide any warmth or comfort. A few servants scurried around the room, carrying dishes and flagons of wine, and a huge fire burned in the hearth. Four fountains gave life to each corner of the throne dais, but the throne itself was empty.

"Where is the king?" Horwath asked.

"Coming, man! Coming! We wait on his pleasure, not ours." Ratcliffe looked almost giddy with excitement, as if he were about to enjoy eating a pie. Owen glanced at him worriedly, half-hidden behind Duke Horwath's cape. Then there was a sound. The march of boots, but the step was uneven, almost halting. Owen crept further behind the duke, watching as one of the servants held open a door. A trumpeter raised a horn to his lips and called out a few shrill tones, announcing the entrance of King Severn Argentine, victor of the Battle of Ambion Hill.

The dread sovereign of Ceredigion.

Everyone in the hall rose to their feet in respect.

♦ ♦ ♦

The king's older brother Eredur—before he died—was a handsome, amiable man. Strong and courageous and, if truth be spoken, quick to admire the beauty of a lady. He was the eldest of four sons, two of whom are now dead. King Severn is the youngest, the last heir of this great house that has ruled for centuries. He was born twisted like an oak root. He equals his brother in strength and courage, but he has none of his softer qualities. They say the king's tongue is sharper than his dagger. Having felt the cut, I concur.

—Dominic Mancini, Espion of Our Lady of Kingfountain

♦ ♦ ♦

CHAPTER THREE

King Severn

A shadow passed over the flickering torchlight when the king limped into the hall. It was the shadow on the floor that Owen first saw, his eyes wide with growing terror. So this was the man who had summoned him to Kingfountain. This was the king everyone feared.

King Severn strode in with shuffling steps, his face grimacing with anger or pain or a mixture of both. What struck Owen first was the blackness of his garb. His long black boots were lined with multiple buckles, and twin ribbons of gold stitching marked the seams with flourishes of holly. His black leather tunic, slashed with velvet and silk, barely concealed a black chain vest that jangled slightly as he limped. A long collar of gold chain denoted his rank. There were thick black leather bracers on his arms, and his hands clenched in strong, tendon-tight fists, one of which gripped the hilt of a dagger lashed to his belt. A thin black cape fluttered as he walked, revealing the distortion of his spine and shoulders. It made his gait uneven, but he walked too quickly for the disfigurement to halt his speed.

He waved at the trumpeter, scowling at him as if the sound bothered his ears, and then mounted the dais with his bold, crooked stride and slumped into the throne.

In the king's determined pose, one could easily overlook that one shoulder was higher than the other. His posture almost concealed it, especially the way he rested his elbow on the arm bar and cradled his chin between his finger and thumb. His hair was long and black, without even a streak of gray, tucked underneath a black cap with a pearl dangling from the royal badge. For some reason, Owen had expected to see a gray-haired and bearded king, and Severn was neither. The king's face would have been handsome except for the brooding anger that seemed to twist every feature. He chuffed, out of breath, and cast a glance at those assembled before him.

"Your Majesty," Ratcliffe said, with a flourish and a bow.

Lord Horwath inclined his head, bending slightly at his waist.

"Out!" the king snapped, waving his hand dismissively at the servants who approached him with silver trays. The servants began scurrying away, clearing the hall.

The king turned his eyes on the duke and then seemed to notice Owen cowering behind the man's cloak. When those dark eyes fell on Owen, the boy's stomach flipped over. He would not be able to speak. He was too terrified.

"She sent her *youngest*," the king said scornfully. His lip curled with disdain. He snorted to himself. "I am surprised. Well, their move is played. Now it is my turn." He shifted himself on the seat, wincing with pain at the motion. With his left hand, he slid the dagger partway out of its sheath and then slammed it back in. The movement startled Owen, even more so when it was repeated.

"Horwath is surprised to even see you walking about, sire," Ratcliffe said graciously. "The wounds still pain you, as we all can see."

"I did not come to the throne to be coddled," the king interrupted. "I would have left my leg on Ambion Hill and crawled back to

Kingfountain with these arms only. I do not need nurses. I need true men. My enemies have all fallen. Save one." He gave Owen a piercing, wrathful look. The boy blinked wildly, fearing for himself. "What is your name, boy?"

Owen's mouth would not work. He knew it would not. He stood trembling in front of the king. His tongue was so dry it felt like sand.

The king's brow furrowed with displeasure as he waited for an answer that could not be pried from the boy's lips with a lever. Owen felt dizzy with panic. His muscles had frozen with fear, making his legs as useless as his mouth.

"The lad's name is Owen," Horwath said in his gruff voice. "And I have not heard a word from him since we left Tatton Hall."

"A mute?" King Severn said with a dark chuckle. "That will be a fine addition to court. It is already too noisy here." He shifted again in the throne. "How did they bear the news at Tatton Hall, Stiev?"

"Very ill, as you can imagine," Horwath said slowly.

The king chuckled. "I can imagine." He turned his eye back to Owen. "Your eldest brother went over the falls because your father would not keep faith with me. He did not die in battle, with honor, as did this noble duke's son."

His parents had told Owen about his brother's fate, and the boy shuddered at the thought of Jorganon plunging off the waterfall strapped in a canoe. That was the form of execution in the realm, though the lad had never seen it happen. It was awful to think it might happen to the rest of his family.

"His son-in-*law*," added Ratcliffe as an aside.

The king gave Ratcliffe a nasty look. "Do you think that distinction matters to me, Dickon? His daughter's husband died at Ambion Hill, and yet he fulfilled his duty to secure this brat instead of returning home to comfort his daughter and granddaughter. His *duty* . . ." he whispered hoarsely, holding up a stiff finger like a spike. "His *duty* rules all. That is why I trust him, Ratcliffe. That is why I trust you both. You remember that little rhyming verse the duke received on the eve of the battle? *Stiev of North, don't be too bold, for Severn your master is bought and sold.* The note was left in his tent by one of our enemies, probably this brat's father, to blacken his mind with doubt and fear. You remember what Stiev did, Dickon?"

Ratcliffe folded his arms over his big chest, looking annoyed. *"Anyone* could have left that note, my liege. I am still investigating how it—"

"Does it matter anymore, Dickon?" the king seethed. "It could have been one of your Espion, for all I know. It could have been the queen's poisoner. Horwath gave me the note at once. Cool as ice from the northern glacier whence he comes. Whence he rules forevermore. Duty. Faithfulness. Those are gems worth more than his gold." He leaned forward and lowered his fingers to his dagger, making that gesture again—pulling it out partway before slamming it back into its sheath. Each time he did it, Owen flinched.

"I was also at Ambion Hill," Ratcliffe said with a little whine in his voice. "It was my Espion who discovered the pretender for you while the battle raged."

The king's mouth curved into a smile. "I'll not forget that good service, my friend. You are loyal, which is why I entrust the Espion to you, but I have not forgotten that some of them tried to murder me." He sneered at the man. "Horwath has always been faithful."

Ratcliffe's face went red with anger. "It is not fair, my liege, to fling that at my face! It was not *I* who ruled them back then. That was the lord chamberlain's doing, and you sent him over the falls for his offense."

"I did that in my *anger*," the king replied, leaning back in his seat. He shook his head. "I should have held a trial." He smoothed his hand across his tunic front, the bracer on his arm winking light from the torches. "Ah, but those were dark days. Treachery around every corner. My brother Eredur kept the tottering dishes from falling. But when he died, they all came crashing down." His face softened a bit, as if the memory of his brother wounded him still. Then his expression hardened and he turned his gaze back to Owen.

"You are my hostage," he said in a cruel tone. "You are the pledge of your family's good faith. Your elder brother was hostage before you and he is dead. If your mother thinks that I will spare a child for *their* disobedience . . ." His voice trailed off, his throat nearly growling with anger. "Then they truly do not understand the determination and *rigor* of their king. You are my ward, Owen Kiskaddon, to do with as I please. You will remain at the palace." He gestured with an open palm, motioning to the vast room. "This is your home now. Drop coins to the Fountain, boy, that your parents keep faith with me." His face twisted with barely suppressed anger. "I nearly condemned your father at Ambion too. But I have been learning *patience*." He chuckled, his mouth twisting into a savage smile. "Rest assured that I will *test* your father, lad. Hopefully he treasures your life more than he did your brother's. Ratcliffe, the boy is yours to guard. Find him a nursery and a governess. I want to see him each day at breakfast with the other children. Without fail."

Owen started in surprise. He had been too terrified to understand everything the king was saying, but one thing was clear: Things were more complicated than his parents had explained them. They had said the king had summoned him to the palace to be his ward. He now saw that he would be assigned to another man, a man who clearly didn't like children. They had told him not to be afraid because there were many kind people at the palace. That was another lie. He was confused, frightened, and homesick beyond enduring.

"He . . . he is *my* problem now?" Ratcliffe said with obvious disappointment and bitterness. "I thought you were giving him to Horwath!"

The king looked up at the ceiling, as if he were searching for his patience in the rafters. "He is duke of the *North*, Dickon! His son-in-law is dead and he must go comfort his daughter and children. The battle is won, man! But I will not rest easy until we have had peace for a season!

I have had naught but troubles and calamity these last two years!" His voice rose to a booming thunder. He started to rise from the throne, but he almost instantly slumped back down. Perhaps his leg pained him. "You oversee the Espion. Pick a man to watch the lad; that is all I am saying. By the Veil, man! Grow a spleen!"

Ratcliffe's expression was black with fury, but he said nothing. The king winced and sagged back in the throne, his mouth tight with anger and emotion.

A big hand rested on Owen's shoulder. The boy looked up and saw the hand belonged to Horwath, who gazed down at him. He said nothing, but his expression seemed sympathetic.

Ratcliffe mastered himself quickly, still burning from the rebuke. "Well, my liege. Let me find a *wet nurse* for the *baby*," he said in a voice dripping with sarcasm.

Owen was *not* a baby, yet to his horror, tears pricked his eyes and he started to silently cry. He had just started trusting Horwath and now the man was going away to the North. Now his care would be in the hands of Ratcliffe, who was exactly the kind of impatient, boisterous fellow that Owen feared most. His own parents had given him up as a hostage to a king capable of lashing out at even his closest allies in a moment.

"He's *crying*?" Ratcliffe said with disgust. "Well, more tears to water the fountains. Dry your eyes, lad. Come . . . stop that at once!"

His little heart was breaking to pieces, and he could no more stop the tears than he could the waterfall rushing outside the palace.

"Stop that!" Ratcliffe chided, stomping forward.

A woman's voice pierced the great hall. Though it was soft, it was commanding. "What needs to stop, my lords, is all this yelling. You've frightened the poor dear out of his wits."

Owen turned to look at her, but his eyes were too swollen with tears to see much beyond her long golden hair. She knelt in front of him and took out a lace kerchief, which she used to dab Owen's eyes. Then she brushed Horwath's hand away from Owen's shoulder and rested her small hand where his had been. The blurry picture of her came into better focus, revealing a girl a little older than Owen's eldest sister, Jessica. She had eyes that were green with blue streaks and the prettiest face he had ever seen.

Of all the myths of Ceredigion, Our Lady of the Fountain was the most widespread. The girl smiled at him kindly, looking into his eyes with compassion and warmth. She was the embodiment of the legend of Our Lady—a woman of wisdom, compassion, and consummate gentleness able to bring even a battle-hardened knight to his knees through the power of her presence. As in the legend, the newcomer seemed to quiet the storm of wrath that had been raging just moments before.

"Uncle," the lady said, glancing up to the man on the throne. "Let me take the boy to the kitchen for a honey cake while Lord Ratcliffe is making arrangements for him. By your leave?"

When Owen chanced a look at the king, he was shocked by the change in his demeanor. His storm of anger was spent, and the tightness around his eyes softened as he gazed at his niece. His hand rested on the dagger hilt, but it did not loosen the blade. The hard frown turned to a small, calm smile. "If you wish so, Elyse," he said, then gestured his approval and a dismissal of them both.

"Take my hand," the lady said, rising slowly and offering hers. Owen took it greedily and relished the softness of her fingers. Her gown was made of the sleekest lavender and blue silk, with a white sideless surcoat and a woven gold front.

Owen gazed up at the duke, wanting to thank him but still unable to speak. It pained him to stay silent.

The duke stared into Owen's eyes, the old man's expression unreadable to a boy so young. His thick goatee helped conceal the lines of his mouth. He nodded once to Owen, as if offering his own dismissal. Owen left the comfort of his cloak and followed the lady out of the hall.

CHAPTER FOUR

The Cook and the Butler

The palace kitchen brought a smile to Owen's face—his first since leaving home. Just like the kitchen at Tatton Hall, it was bustling and crowded and interesting to look at. There were chandelier hooks with rings of sausages hanging from them. There were benches and tables full of fat fish and bowls of greens, and there was a covered area where all the spices hung in thick clumps. The ceilings were vaulted, and there were chairs, benches, and tables spread around. Everywhere there were servants rushing in and out, carrying flagons of wine, dishes of bread and cheese. Even the floor was interesting with its diamond-shaped tiles. There was a crunch of pine boughs on the threshold, but the floor inside was swept and flat, and Owen thought it would be the perfect place to set up tiles to knock down.

"You do smile!" Elyse said with a glow of delight in her voice, squeezing his hand tenderly. "You like the kitchen?"

He nodded vigorously, staring at a woman as she pulled three loaves of bread out of the oven on a wooden paddle. The kitchen was on the ground floor of the palace, so there were thick columns here and there to hold up the mammoth castle, but there were also tall windows, which were open to let in light and air. These gave the place a bright and cheery look, quite different from the great hall.

Elyse guided him through the crowd of servants and maids, leading him to the woman near the ovens, who had set both paddle and bread down on a brick table.

The woman was very short with reddish-brown hair escaping a bonnet, and wearing a flour-dusted apron. She had a little scar on her cheek, but when she turned and saw the princess, her eyes brightened with joy.

"Well, bless me, Princess! You are getting more beautiful by the day. Your mother was a great beauty in her day, and you will shine even brighter. Look at you, lass. Is there a hug for your old cook?"

Princess Elyse was much taller than the cook, but she squeezed her affectionately before kneeling down by Owen's side. She stroked his head, which tickled a bit, and then took his shoulders squarely in her hands as if presenting him to an official audience.

"Liona, this is Owen Kiskaddon. He is a guest at the palace and will be staying here."

The cook's expression brightened even more. "Lord Jorganon's little brother! So grown up a young man, too!" she said cheerily, tapping her chin thoughtfully. "You must be *ten* years old!"

Owen felt a flush of pleasure in his cheeks and shook his head no. "I am only eight."

"Eight! That is a surprise. I would not have guessed it. Would you like a honey cake, Master Owen?"

He grinned, nodding cautiously, and she winked and bade him to follow her. She lifted the lid of a clay jar and pulled out a round flat cake with a hash-mark stamp on it. She offered it to him grandly and then slipped a second one to the princess, winking at her as well.

Owen took a bite and immediately knew he would want a second one. The wafer was thin, crisp on the outside, and chewy in the middle. It tasted of honey and treacle and another strange flavor he could not determine. He ate it hungrily, watching the kitchen bustle around them with big vats of soup, hunks of raw meat, and servants whittling carrots, potatoes, squash, and onions into smaller chunks.

"How be the queen, your mother?" Liona asked Elyse softly, dropping her voice lower.

"She is well, thank you," Elyse said, smiling kindly at the older woman. "I saw her yesterday at the sanctuary."

Liona's expression darkened. "I miss Her Highness," she confided. "What a grand palace this used to be. With parties and balls and so many birthdays to celebrate. The rest of the castle has been downright gloomy since the king came from the North. That is why I refuse to shutter the windows. We need more light. Even a flower withers without sunshine."

Her words made Owen glance at the nearest window, high above them. Through it, he could see one of the thin spires of the castle rising up. It was the thin tower . . . the one that had put him in mind of a dagger. He wondered if that was where the king slept. A little chill ran down his back at the sight of the tower looming so high above them. Before he knew it, he had finished the honey cake.

"And my, what an appetite you have!" Liona said. She was not that much taller than him and he liked it that she was so short. She tousled his hair. "Look at you, Owen. What is this stripe in your hair? Is it flour?" She touched the white spot of hair on the side of his head and he leaned away from her.

"I noticed it, too," the princess said. "Just a little tuft of hair . . . white as snow. I imagine when his hair gets long, you can hardly see it."

Owen himself did not think of it much, but people were always commenting about it. It was just his hair. So what if he had a strange patch in it?

The princess touched the cook's arm. "Would it be all right if he stayed here a little while? When I came into the hall, everyone was shouting and I could tell he was frightened."

The cook shook her head. "Shouting in front of such a young man. The height of bad manners! Owen, you may come to my kitchen as often as you like. Your brother was always welcome here. If someone wants to scold you, well, I will scold him first, be it the king himself! Never upset a cook, or even the milk turns sour. You come this way whenever you are scared or lonely. All right, Owen? Will you keep me company now and then?"

He smiled, gazing around at the arches and the hanging pots on pegs. "I like it here," he said shyly, feeling much calmer now that he was distanced from the king's fury. He did not want to meet him again, yet he knew he would have to share breakfast with him every day.

The princess knelt down again next to Owen. Her eyes were serious and she petted him fondly, as if she had always known him. "Liona will help take care of you. I am going to find Master Ratcliffe to help him choose a governess for you." She stroked his arm. "I will watch out for you, Owen. So will Liona. There are many here still . . . faithful." She hesitated before saying the word. Then she straightened, her dress shimmered with colors in the light, and the beams made her golden hair radiant. She looked like a queen herself.

"Thank you," Owen mumbled, gazing up at her.

Liona's nostrils tightened. "The next round of loaves is nearly done. You can always smell them. I will look after the child, Princess. Fear not. There are so many here, he won't be underfoot." She gave Owen a look of intrigue. "My husband is the woodcutter of the castle," she said mysteriously. "He knows all the best haunts to wander and wouldn't mind a companion on his journeys around the hill. He decides which of the king's trees to keep and which he will cut and make into firewood. He's off tromping in the woods right now, or you'd find him here with a flagon of ale and his feet up on a barrel. But I keep a tidy kitchen, as you see, so he knows to leave his dusty boots outside. Let me fetch you another honey cake!" She winked again and quickly went over to the clay pot to do just that. Another girl had stepped in to remove the loaves from the oven.

"Thank you, Liona," the princess said.

"Anything for Your Highness's family," Liona answered, her look dark and serious. She hugged Elyse again.

"Now I must see to finding a *suitable* governess," the princess said, tousling Owen's hair one last time.

The cook stared wistfully at the princess as she left the kitchen, but as soon as she was gone, her expression changed from wistful to annoyed. Owen's heart sank. Had it all been an act?

"And here *he* comes," Liona said with a huff. "It's enough to sour a pudding. There is the king's butler, Master Berwick. He's from the *North*, Owen. Some men from there are not to be trusted. I pity your lord father. Truly I do. I made my promise and I will keep it. I'll look after you, lad. You will always have a place here in the kitchen." She smiled down at him, buoying his spirits.

The sound of boots jarred Owen's attention, and then an old, wrinkled, leathery man strode in quickly, wheezing as he approached Liona. He was tall with a barrel gut and leathery brown skin. He had a bald dome splotched with liver marks, but there was a wreath of thick, curly hair around his ears and neck. He wore the king's livery, black and gold with the boar insignia.

"Luke at ye," he said derisively to Liona. "Standin' idle at sucha time 'fore supper?" Owen had always struggled to understand people with thick Northern accents. It was as if they were in too much of a hurry to finish all the syllables in their words. "When's the quail egg pie gonna be finished for the master? Aun't you started it yit?"

The look on Liona's face curdled. "Have you not enough to worry about, Berwick, that you must meddle in my kitchen?"

"I wuddun meddle if it were run sharp. The master tain't a patient man, nor doz he brook laziness."

"Are you saying I am lazy?" she asked, her voice hardening. "Do you have any idea how long it takes to feed a palace this size? How many loaves of bread we make in a day?"

"Five hundred and six," he said with a sneer, and snapped his fingers at her. "I tally the flour bags. I know the eggs and yolk. I am the king's butler and managed his castle in the North—"

"Which was much *smaller* than this one, I might remind you, Berwick!"

Owen stared up at the tall butler. He smelled like something strange—cabbage, perhaps.

His stare attracted the attention of the older man. "And whose whelp is this young'un? Another sorry case whose papa won't work?"

"This is the *Duke* of Kiskaddon's son," Liona said, pulling Owen against her apron. "He's not a whelp, you rude man, but of noble blood."

The butler looked at Owen in surprise. "Faw!" he spluttered. "Kiskaddon's brat! I pity him then! His bruther ended in a river."

Liona looked cross. "He's the king's ward. That's nothing to be pitied."

The butler snorted. "Ward? I think not. He's the king's hostage. Just had a little chat with Duke Horwath, a mighty fine lord, on his way back to the North. This lad's days are numbered."

Liona's expression hardened, her face turning pale. "You will stop such talk," she said angrily. She motioned for Owen to go sit on a nearby crate and then walked up to Berwick and started to give him a tongue-lashing in a low voice.

Owen sat on the small crate, his joy in finding the kitchen starting to wane. The king's threats roiled his stomach. Even though the kitchen was comfortable, warm, and had that wonderful yeasty smell, he could not keep his eye from that daggerlike spire out the window. It felt as if the king were watching him even here.

"No, you watch your words, croon!" Berwick said angrily. "My master may call down a new cook from the North, and then what would you do? But if you mind me and do as I say, all will go well for you." He gave Owen a dark look and harrumphed, shaking his head as if the boy were already a cold slab of dead fish.

Liona's eyes sparked with anger as she returned to him, wiping her fingers vigorously on her apron front. She muttered under her breath for a moment.

"I need to get the king's supper ready," she finally said, her voice pitched low. Owen noticed that she would not look him in the eye. "There used to be more children playing around the castle. When the queen and king ruled, it was different. Men like Berwick would watch their words better." Her lips were taut. "If Berwick only knew, if he only *knew*." She cast a surreptitious glance at the boy, and then dropped her voice very low. "Are you afraid, Owen?"

He stared at her and nodded mutely.

She hastily walked over to another table and then brought over a bowl with some flour and other ingredients already inside. She cracked an egg with one hand and emptied the yolk into the bowl. She then began kneading the mixture with her strong fingers. Owen felt she wanted to say more, so he waited for her to speak.

She glanced around the kitchen again, making sure no one else was nearby. "My husband and I walk the grounds often," she said softly, almost in a whisper. "He knows it best. There is a porter door that is always unlocked. Always." She glanced around again, and when she continued, her voice was even softer. "Owen, your parents did not send you here to be killed. You have friends. Like the princess. Like me. The princess's mother is in sanctuary at Our Lady. She has been there for the two years since her husband's brother seized the throne. Mayhap she would help you, Owen. Do you know where the sanctuary is?"

Owen stared at her, his heart pounding fast. "We passed it . . . on the way here."

"You did," she said, kneading the dough as if she were trying to strangle Berwick. "If you go to that sanctuary, not even the king can make you come out. You would be safe there." She glanced back at the crowded kitchen, her eyes darting around worriedly. "If you are a brave little boy."

A little spark of hope lit in his chest. "I'm brave," he whispered softly, gazing hard at her. But as he looked up at her, he saw the knife-like spire through the window again.

♦ ♦ ♦

I am a foreigner to Ceredigion, so I found the political intrigues and bad blood to be almost incomprehensible at first. Let me summarize it thus. The ruling houses of this kingdom can be likened to members of a large family who hate each other fiercely. The grievances go back to the founding of this dynasty, nigh on three centuries ago. These family members make an art out of warring with each other. King Severn's enemies are all in their graves, or should I say all his male enemies are. He is still estranged from the queen dowager, his brother's wife, who continues to plot against him from the sanctuary of Our Lady. But in my assessment, her power and her once-great beauty are now waning. My bets are on the crouch-backed king. Rumor has it he fancies his niece, Princess Elyse. It's a sordid rumor embellished by the queen dowager. Pay it no heed.

—Dominic Mancini, Espion of Our Lady of Kingfountain

♦ ♦ ♦

CHAPTER FIVE

Ghosts

They had assigned Owen to his brother's vacant room, and he found he could not sleep at all. Everything about it, even the smell, was strange and unsettling. He had always been very sensitive to sounds, especially unfamiliar ones, and the palace was full of sounds—creaking timbers, the tapping of boots on stone, the distant murmur of voices, the rattle of keys in locks. There was always some commotion outside his door. So Owen sat up on his small wooden pallet and pulled the curtains wide, letting the moon shine through the window. And as he sat and stared at the moon, he tried to calm the frantic beating of his heart and quell the dreadful homesickness that festered there.

That night, he made several decisions. And he made a promise to the moon.

He knew the world of adults was very different from his own. For reasons he did not comprehend, his parents had abandoned him. He had the vague sense that they'd been forced to offer up one of their children and they had *chosen* him.

In the dark, he wrestled with the feelings that accompanied that realization. He shed more tears, but the tears weren't sad. They weren't angry. They were . . . disappointed. When the tears were finally spent, he ground his teeth and dealt with the harsh truth that his parents were not going to save him. He had the intuition that if he stayed at the castle and did nothing to save himself, he would probably not survive. So he had to figure out a way to change the end of the story and not end up in the river.

Being the youngest in the family, Owen had learned some simple truths in his short life. Because he was the youngest and the smallest in Tatton Hall, the adults around him thought he was weak and could not do things for himself. They always offered to help him, which annoyed Owen and made him even more determined to prove he was capable. He hated it when his suggestions and ideas were not taken seriously, especially when one of his "little speeches" caused his parents or older siblings to laugh at him.

Owen had learned that there was a certain power in being the youngest. He was a strong-willed little boy who'd learned the power of tantrums in getting his way. He used this tactic judiciously, of course, for he was normally soft-spoken and gentle.

It also did not escape Owen's notice that adults fawned over him, especially his sisters. He had learned that being adorable, affectionate, and quick to give hugs and smiles and little kisses earned him treats and stories and attention. By being quiet, especially at night, he could stay up longer because they would forget he was there.

Power. There was power in being able to control how others reacted to you. That reminded Owen of his favorite pastime, the one that he could spend hours and hours doing—placing little tiles in a line and then knocking them down.

He had seen one of his siblings do this once. Maybe Owen had been a baby and the falling tiles had made him giggle. It was one of his earliest memories. Soon he was the one stacking the tiles, and he learned there was an immense thrill in using one tile to topple many. As he grew older, his stacking became more and more elaborate. The lines became crooked. Sometimes he used other objects as barriers and changed the height of the structures he prepared. Sometimes he'd build towers out of his tiles and trigger them to collapse.

Nothing made him more intensely furious than when someone knocked down his tiles accidentally—or purposefully. He even raged at himself when he did it. Stacking the tiles, placing them in exactly the formation he envisioned, helped him sort through his troubles.

Owen made two decisions that night. The first he told to the silver moon. "I will escape from here," he vowed. No matter what his parents did or did not do, he would not give up until he had found a way to flee the king who filled him with such terror. He did not want to join the ghosts of this castle.

His second decision was to make his stay at the castle bearable until he figured out a way to escape. For that, he needed a box of tiles.

Out of all the places he had seen so far, the kitchen was the place he liked the most. It was bright and cheerful. Liona was just the sort of woman he knew would help him. He would ask her for some tiles and for permission to stack them in a corner of the kitchen.

He was so excited to begin that he waited restlessly until the moon faded from the windowpane and the sky began to brighten. Cooks were in the kitchen early. If Owen was to have breakfast with the king, he wanted to at least have something to look forward to after.

Still wearing the rumpled clothes in which he'd traveled, Owen made it back to the kitchen on his own, stealing away soundlessly between shadows. He found the way quite easily, his nose drawing him there as much as his memory of the way. It was still early, and the only two people in the kitchen were Liona and a man he assumed was her husband.

"Look at you, here before the cock crows," Liona said cheerfully. "The Fountain bless you, lad. Are you hungry already?"

Owen looked at the man, suddenly overwhelmed by nervousness. Strangers always did that to him. He was furious at himself when his tongue refused to unknot enough for him to speak. The man had reddish hair and a beard with flecks of gray in it. He wore leathers stained in tree sap, and a gleaming woodsman's axe hung from a hoop in his belt.

Liona noticed his hesitation and patted the man's shoulder. "Drew, this is Owen. I told you of him."

The woodsman turned to look at Owen with a shy smile and a twinkle in his eye. He nodded and then crouched down on the tiled floor. "You are the duke's son," he said in a cheery, soft-spoken manner. "I can see the blood is true. You look like your brothers. My name is Andrew, but folk just call me Drew. Good morning, Owen."

Owen wanted to return the greeting. The man was friendly and easygoing. But Owen still could not bring himself to speak.

"Tend to the fire, Drew," Liona said, briskly warming her hands. "Owen, you will be supping with the king this morning, so I best not ruin your appetite, but no one walks out of my kitchen hungry. There is bread from yesterday."

Owen grinned at her, grateful to have found this ally.

He quietly retreated to a bench to watch her fix him a little plate as Drew coaxed the ashes back to life. Owen had seen men do this before and it fascinated him how a heap of gray ashes, if blown on consistently, could catch fire anew. He stared at Drew as he puffed away, and was thrilled when the crackling sound of the reviving fire met his ears. He wanted to learn how to do that. He thought he could, but he would come back the next day and keep watching to be sure. Then he would try it himself.

Liona tousled his hair after giving him the plate. He ate hungrily, watching as servants began to arrive to prepare the morning meal.

"Liona?" he asked in a small voice. Too small. She had not heard him.

"The lad is calling you," Drew said gently, rising from the ovens.

Liona had dough on her fingers when she approached him. "What is it?"

Owen licked his lips, grateful that Drew had noticed his need. Though he was still nearly tongue-tied with shyness, he was determined to get his tiles.

"Is there . . . is there a box of tiles?" he asked, looking into her eyes imploringly. "That I could play with?"

She looked at him confused. "Tiles?"

"Like these," he said, tapping his shoe against the floor. "Small ones . . . like these. I like to play with them."

Drew gave him a strange look, then said, "I believe there is." Liona needed to deliver instructions to the kitchen help, so she asked her husband to fetch them. Shortly thereafter, he returned with a wooden box that held a substantial number of tiles. Some were chipped and damaged, and there were many different sizes and colors. Owen's eyes widened with delight when Drew handed him the box.

"I'm on my way to the woods," he said in his kind voice. "Maybe you'd care to join me later and I can show you the grounds?"

Owen looked up at him and nodded vigorously. Still his tongue would not loosen. He wanted to thank Drew for the tiles, but a familiar choking feeling had stolen his ability to speak. He gazed down at the box in his lap, trying to force the words to come. The best he could do was to bob his head up and down once.

Drew smiled at him and walked away. Owen clenched his fists for a moment, angry at himself for not speaking. But the wonderful box on his lap was too enticing for him to continue his fit. He abandoned what remained of his plate of food and took the box over to a corner of the kitchen where no one was bustling. He quickly sorted the tiles by size and shape and color and then began placing them in a row.

As soon as the first one went into position, his mind took off as if it were an arrow launched from a bow. The process of taking out the pieces and putting them down was so familiar it was automatic, and he was almost blind to the pattern he was making on the floor. In his mind, he sorted through the details of what he had learned since leaving his family. The different people he had met began to come together in his mind, and as they did, he realized he had feelings about each one. The king, he feared. Duke Horwath, he respected. Ratcliffe, he despised. Princess Elyse, he adored. Liona and Drew would be like his new parents. Berwick was annoying.

Owen had heard a great many things spoken and some of them he did not understand. What he did understand was that the king would kill him if his parents did not prove they were loyal. Every day he stayed in Kingfountain would only increase the danger. If he made it to the sanctuary of Our Lady, the king's sister-in-law might be able to protect him. She was Princess Elyse's mother and had been queen up until two years ago when King Severn had stolen the throne from his brother's heirs. The princes were dead. Owen risked sharing their fate. The solution seemed obvious: He needed to find a way to escape the palace and make it to Our Lady without being caught by the king's men. But how could he arrange that? What would he need to do? He needed to know the grounds. Drew knew the grounds. Drew had even offered to take him for a walk.

Owen set the last tile on the floor. He was sitting amidst a twisting spiral of tiles, which started at his knees and wound farther and farther around him, loop after loop. How many tiles had he placed? A hundred? He did not remember.

Owen noticed that the kitchen was unusually quiet. He looked over his shoulder and saw Liona and the others staring at him, mesmerized by what he had done. He gave Liona a small smile and then tipped over the tile nearest his knee.

The cook startled as the tiles fell, clinking softly and rapidly as they raced around the circles. It only took a few moments for the last one to fall.

"Well," Liona said with surprise. "I'll be *blessed*. That is the most curious thing I've seen a lad do."

Owen flushed at the praise, feeling the pressure of the gazes of the kitchen helpers. And just at that moment, a frantic young woman came rushing into the kitchen, her long dark hair trailing as she ran.

"Has anyone seen a little boy? The duke's son? He's missing. Has anyone . . . ?" She was gasping, almost out of breath, but she heaved a sigh of relief as a few fingers pointed his way. She was Monah Stirling, his young governess he had met the previous evening. "There you are! Owen! The king's breakfast! Hasten!"

The words seemed to remind everyone of their duties. Liona started to call out orders and the servants hurried pell-mell around the kitchen.

Owen had quickly started to gather the tiles into the box, but Monah seized his hand and tugged him away before he could finish, leading him back to his room in the tower.

"There is no time! You must be dressed and ready. Come with me! Lord Ratcliffe is furious!"

◆ ◆ ◆

*There is a great fear of poisoners in any kingdom, but espe-
cially in this one. Think what it must do to the constitution
of a man to live in constant fear that his next sip or mouthful of food may be the very last. The king's brother died suddenly, to the surprise of all. Granted, I was told his revels
of feasting were quite out of control and his consumption of
food and drink gluttonous. I would have enjoyed serving him
immensely! But the very suddenness of his death does incline
one to suspect the use of poison. The question is—who would
poison a king?*

—Dominic Mancini, Espion of Our Lady of Kingfountain

◆ ◆ ◆

CHAPTER SIX

Dickon Ratcliffe

Monah Stirling was not gentle as she helped Owen change into a new suit of clothes. She licked a napkin and roughly scrubbed a smear from his cheek, then stepped back to examine him. "There is no time for a bath, but you will get one later today. What were you doing in the kitchen?"

He stared at her without speaking. His stomach was suddenly upset at the thought of meeting Ratcliffe again . . . and the king. He did not want to breakfast with the king.

Monah mussed her fingers through his thatch of mouse-brown hair and frowned. "Your hair is absolutely wild. What is this pale spot?" She tried to examine the tuft of white hair, but he shrugged away from her.

"None of that, you little brat," she scolded. Then, snatching his hand, she dragged him down the corridor from his room and back toward the great hall. The castle was teeming with servants now, men and women holding pitchers, vases filled with fresh-cut flowers, rolled rush-matting carpets, urns, and silver dishes. The torches along the corridor hissed at Owen as they passed them, casting long and pointed shadows on the floor.

When they reached the great hall, Ratcliffe was pacing, his face furrowed into a sharp frown of disapproval, but he looked relieved as soon as he caught sight of Owen.

"*There* he is!" Ratcliffe said with exasperated relief. "Thought you had snuck out of the castle, lad." His tugged at his fancy collar. "I rather prefer a swim at the baths or the beach, not down a waterfall."

But I do plan to sneak out of the castle, Owen thought firmly, gazing up at the tall man as he continued to pace. Owen looked over the trestle tables that had been set up in the hall. They were loaded with trays of food. Loaves of golden, sweet-smelling bread, tray after tray of smoked salmon, and a variety of pungent cheeses. A tangled skein of grapes was nestled in a silver dish.

Owen noticed that there were no chairs around and also that he was not the only "*guest*." Most were young folk, many were children, and all were part of the king's court. Were they hostages like he was? He didn't know any of them and wasn't sure what to expect. Servants were busying themselves all around him.

"He was in the kitchen," Monah explained wearily. "I found him."

"See you do not lose him again!" Ratcliffe scolded. He rubbed his hands together, searching the faces of those assembled. He gave Owen a pointed look. "Be you on time," he said with an angry frown. "The king is a busy man and must not be kept waiting for fools. Are you a fool, little lord Kiskaddon? Hmmm?"

Owen shook his head but did not speak.

"See that you are not. Ah, the king!"

Owen's stomach wrenched with fear and he felt a little dizzy. In a moment, one of the side doors opened and the king entered, arm in arm with Princess Elyse, clearly in the midst of a conversation.

"No, it would not be proper," the king said in a disapproving tone. "You are a princess of the realm. He is only the son of a duke.

You are cousins, in some degree, but I will not have you looking after my hostages."

The king's gaze swept across the young people assembled in the room, not coming to a rest until it reached Owen.

"The *lost* has been found then?" he asked with a twist to his lip.

Ratcliffe looked shaken. "My lord," he said with a shaky voice, "he was . . . he was . . . where was he, Lady Stirling?"

"Playing in the kitchen," Monah said anxiously, blushing fiercely and curtsying.

The king patted Elyse's arm. "You see? The boy is hale. You worried in vain." Then he turned his gaze on Owen, his eyes smoldering with anger. "You gave my niece concern, lad. She fretted for you."

"Uncle, it is no matter," the girl said, touching the bent arm hooked with hers like a shepherd's staff. "I was only offering to help look after him. It would not be a burden, truly."

The king kept his gaze on Owen. Fear bloomed in the boy's stomach and traveled down through his legs, which felt weak. "You are no nursemaid, Elyse," he said softly.

"What am I then?" she asked him meaningfully. "I am not a princess either. I am a bit of fluff, blown about by the wind. Your guests are hungry, my lord." She gave him a subtle nudge.

The king bowed graciously to her and then gestured that they had his permission to start eating. Owen slowly approached one of the trestle tables, his eyes never leaving the king and the princess. He was curious what would happen, and since Liona had given him something to eat already, he wasn't hungry. As the young people began chatting amongst themselves, some taking slices of bread or a bit of cheese from the table, they ate nervously, anxiously. Some barely finished more than a bite or two.

What Owen noticed next surprised him. The king roamed among the guests, watching their faces as they plucked from the tables of food. He watched them chew their food, occasionally reaching out to take something from a tray that had already been touched. The king was watching the others eat before eating himself. Was that normal for a king? Surely it was his right to save all the best food for himself.

Owen's mind seemed to roll over like a wagon wheel. He did not understand the king at all.

After a few moments, the king poured himself a cup from a pitcher of watery wine. He walked slowly through the gathering, observing his guests with cunning eyes, as if enjoying a private joke.

The king noticed Owen was staring at him and began edging his way toward him. Instinctively, Owen began to retreat, trying to keep space between them. Their eyes locked. The king's eyes were gray with flecks of blue. His cheeks still glistened from his morning shave, and his long black hair was tidy and smooth and fell about his shoulders. He had a sharp nose, angled cheeks, and looked bemused.

Owen stepped around the trestle table, keeping it between them. His heartbeat thundered in his ears. The king was not wearing the velvet cap he'd had on the previous day, a small detail and Owen didn't know why it stood out to him.

Severn continued his approach, almost slithering like a serpent, his fine, gleaming golden chain winking in the torchlight.

Ratcliffe approached the king's shoulder and coughed into his fist. "My lord, a word with you?"

"What is it?" the king asked gruffly, not taking his eyes off Owen.

"How did you know the boy was missing? Did one of the Espion tell you? It was not something you needed to worry about, my lord."

The king broke Owen's gaze to look scornfully at Ratcliffe. "*Should* I have been worried about it? The castle is a maze of corridors and towers. It's no surprise the boy was lost. What surprised me was that he wasn't better watched after."

Ratcliffe flushed with anger. "You would prefer for him to sleep in my chambers so that I might gaze upon him every moment of the day?"

"No, Dickon. I want you to keep your eye on the lad like I asked. I'm trusting you in this. Do not disappoint me."

Ratcliffe frowned, nodded once, and walked away.

The king turned back to Owen, their gazes meeting once more. Owen found he could not look away. The king limped slightly as he approached the table and rested his hand on the tablecloth. "You haven't eaten."

Owen shook his head slowly, unable to loosen his tongue. He quaked with dread.

The king took a heel of bread and pushed it toward him. He nodded slowly to the boy and then turned to face someone else—a young man, probably twelve years old, who was talking with a hunk of bread in his mouth.

The king's tone was sharp as he addressed the lad. "Eat it, Dunsdworth. Don't choke on it."

The boy went crimson with mortification. He tried to chew faster so he could clear his mouth to reply, and the exaggerated motion caused a few titters from bystanders. The king gave the young man a vicious look. Then he turned his gaze on a girl of about ten. "Good morrow, Lady Kate. Your eyes are puffy. Were you weeping already?"

"No, my lord," the girl stammered fearfully. "My eyes were itchy, 'tis all."

"Itchy," the king replied with a chuckle. "It's probably the smoke. This is a smoky hall," he said, his eyes roaming the rafters. "Some fresh air will do you well. Try not to wheeze."

Owen watched as the king prowled around the hall, choosing victim after victim. Age did not spare anyone from his barbed wit. His words were feints and thrusts, always sharp and always ready to draw blood. This was what Owen had to look forward to every day. To be wheedled and teased by a sarcastic king who used children as his royal food tasters.

He felt a soft hand on his shoulder. Turning his head, he saw Princess Elyse standing just beside him. As soon as he noticed her, she dropped her hand and chose a cube of cheese and plopped it into her mouth.

"So you went to the kitchen this morning?" she whispered, giving him a private glance. Though she stood next to him, her body was angled to face the table as if she were only there for the food.

Owen nodded, mesmerized by her presence. It was not just the beauty of her golden hair and hazel eyes. She had a peace about her, a gentleness that seemed totally devoid of any pretense. It was a look that invited Owen's trust.

"You will be safe there," she whispered. "Liona is loyal to my mother. I asked the king if I could be your guardian, but he refused. He thinks it's beneath my dignity." She frowned slightly. "I had two little brothers . . . you see," she said, her voice suddenly thick. "You remind me of one of them. He would have been twelve." Her fingers gently mussed his hair. "I will see you when I can, Owen. But it will not be often. Have courage." Then she stepped away from him to talk to a set of younger girls, admiring their dresses and their hair.

Owen felt a knot of pain in his heart. He wanted to escape. He needed to find a way out.

But first he would need to know the grounds.

♦ ♦ ♦

The palace of Kingfountain was built on a wooded hill alongside the mighty river and near the impressive waterfall. From the outside, it seemed massive—all thick walls and pointed turrets—but Owen quickly realized that it was hollow in the middle. The walls were steep and tall and enclosed an interior garden area with trees and walkways and interesting paths. One could walk around the main corridor of the castle in a giant loop, which made it seem like a never-ending fortress. But once Owen had walked it a few times with Monah Stirling, he began to learn the tricks of the place. It was after a walk with Drew that he learned about the exterior grounds. Because it was built on a hill, there was also a lower level, another series of walls and bulwarks to defend from invaders, and even lower down, a third portion that interlocked with the second set of walls. From one of the tower windows, he could see the different layers, all the way down to the horse masters breaking new stallions in the stables far below. There were yards with the royal coaches. There were towers everywhere, including the knife-like one that had caught his eye the first day.

It would take weeks for Owen to visit every hall, explore every staircase, and gaze at every tapestry. But he had an eye for details, and he quickly made little checkpoints for himself—like the suit of armor holding a poleax that led to a gallery of paintings. Or the iron-railed fountain that led to the sanctuary within the palace where he could hear the sound of lapping waters.

Monah was not used to the exercise of being dragged around the palace, and when he finally returned to the kitchen later to rest and find something sweet to eat, she plopped down on a stool and started complaining to the helpers about how Owen had dragged her tirelessly six times around the castle.

He looked for his box of tiles, but could not find them anywhere. Divining his intent, Liona motioned to a worn leather satchel with a single strap and buckles.

"The tiles are over there," she said kindly. "Drew brought it for you to keep the box of tiles safe. He thought you might want to carry it about. Is it too heavy for you?"

Owen went over and hefted the strap. The satchel was heavy, but he was determined. He grinned at her and shook his head.

"Everyone keeps talking about you and your little tiles and asking where they are. I keep saying, 'Over there, in Owen's Satchel.'"

And that was how the boy from Tatton Hall earned his nickname—Owen Satchel.

Jeff Wheeler

◆ ◆ ◆

The next morning, when he came to the kitchen to play with his tiles, he found the box next to the open satchel. Liona had not yet arrived and he was alone. Some of the tiles were littering the floor next to the box. Upon closer inspection, he realized they had been arranged to form little blocky letters.

O-W-E-N.

It was probably Drew. A little message from a friend. He smiled and then put it out of his mind as he began to build.

♦ ♦ ♦

King Eredur, of blessed memory, experienced all the vicis-
situdes of kingship. He won the crown. He lost the crown.
He won it back. The story is worthy of the epics of any age.
Few have studied his reign as closely as I have, and I know
that Eredur would not have regained his crown if not for his
brother. Not Severn, who was always loyal, but the treach-
erous Earl of Dunsworth, the brother who betrayed him
and then repented. The truce following Eredur's victory was
uneasy. After all, Dunsworth's claim to the crown was what
had made him defect in the first place. There is much secrecy
and suspicion about how the earl met his fate. Some say he
was poisoned. Some say he was drowned in a keg of wine.
No one knows the truth. What we do know is this—he was
declared a traitor. His titles and lands were forfeit, but they
have been promised to his son when he comes of age. I am
certain Eredur had his brother put to death in some fashion
or other, for I saw the corpse. And his only son, the new lord
Dunsworth, is very much turning into the man his father
was. He is a spiteful little braggart and I detest him. The lad
is only twelve, and the castle staff live in terror of him.

—Dominic Mancini, Espion of Our Lady of Kingfountain

♦ ♦ ♦

CHAPTER SEVEN

Dunsdworth's Heir

In the two weeks that Owen had lived in the palace, his days had come to follow a routine. He would rise early in the morning and rush to the kitchen with his satchel to begin laying down tiles in intricate new arrangements. Sometimes, there would already be a design waiting for him—a few tiles arranged into a tower or a wall—but he never got there early enough to catch Drew doing it.

Each morning a meal would be shared with the king and the other children of the realm, full of sarcastic barbs and jests as the king wandered amongst his guests, looking for provocation for a taunt. Then Owen would wander the castle and the grounds with Monah Stirling, who would complain incessantly until he found a tree or wall he wanted to climb, giving her the opportunity to rest. In the afternoon, he would sit in the royal library for hours, devouring the books Monah gave him to read so she could gossip with her friends. Once she mentioned a baker from Pisan who was discovered to be Fountain-blessed. When he baked bread, the loaves seemed to magically multiply. The King of Pisan had learned about him and had the baker seized to serve in the palace kitchen. They spent a long time talking about the rare individuals whom the Fountain had gifted with extraordinary magic.

Owen perked up and listened, for he loved reading about the Fountain-blessed. When he came across such a tale in a book, he would slow down and savor it. There were stories about knights who could not be defeated in battle. Sorceresses who wore helmets instead of headdresses and could summon rain and magic down on their enemies. The magic could manifest in so many different ways. Unfortunately, the stories rarely included enough detail. Even the gossip about the baker boy revealed nothing about how the magic happened.

Owen always spent the final hours of his day back in the kitchen. He was the first one there and the last to leave, and while he lived in a state of fear, he knew that he could find some measure of comfort and calm in that one sacred place.

Until Dunsdworth found out.

Owen was lost inside himself, ignoring the bustle of the kitchen as the cauldrons were scrubbed clean, the floors were swept—except where he knelt and arranged tiles—and dough was left to rise in bowls during the night. He heard none of the commotion, yet the commotion was part of the haze that made the kitchen so comfortable. He could not stand absolute silence, where every rattling lock or clomping bootstep could mean disaster. The noises of the kitchen, particularly Liona's soothing voice and the orders she gave, helped create enough of a lull for him to concentrate on his tile stacking.

He knelt along the fringe, carefully building another section, when suddenly the entire thing came crashing down around him, startling him.

Owen rarely triggered a collapse himself anymore. He sat up, watching as the hours of work vanished in seconds, and then heard the sniggering chuckle behind him. He turned, his face turning white with rage when he saw Dunsdworth standing behind him, arms folded, his boot clearly the offender.

"Awww, poor lad!" Dunsdworth soothed with a wicked smile. "You should be more careful with your *toys!*"

A blistering pain of fury exploded in Owen's skull. He began to shake with rage as he stared at the older boy with undisguised loathing.

Dunsdworth was twelve or thirteen and he was not a small lad. He was easily a head or two taller than Owen and even had muscles beneath his tailored doublet. A dagger sheath hung from his belt. He made it no secret that he longed to wear a sword as the adults did.

The look he gave Owen was provoking, as if he wanted the young boy to rush at him with fists drawn so he could enjoy knocking him down.

His sneer seemed to say—*Well? What are you going to do about this?*

With shaking hands, Owen stared at the devastation around him, at the ruins of his work, and he could barely think from the rage squeezing his heart. But he knew, instinctively, that Dunsdworth could overpower him.

"What? You say nothing?" the older boy scoffed. Then he lowered his tone. "You waste your time here, little Kisky. You should be in the training yard with *me*, earning some bruises that will make you into a man. Your father must be ashamed of you. Quit playing with toys. What? Are you going to cry? Shall I fetch a wet nurse to dry your eyes?"

Owen turned away, humiliated, and began to stack the tiles back into the box with trembling fingers. He would not try setting them up again. It was too late in the day for that. But he could not bear the antagonizing look on Dunsdworth's face. And yes, he was afraid he would start crying.

Owen started again when the heel of Dunsdworth's boot came down on some of the tiles and crushed them. The sound, so out of place in the kitchen, made his heart leap with fear. He turned and watched the older boy grinning at him, defying him to say anything. Staring into his eyes, Dunsdworth stomped again and cracked some more.

"Out! Get out of here!" Liona barked, storming up to the bully with a stern look. "Get you gone, Lord Dunsdworth. Out of my kitchen. Leave that little boy alone."

Dunsdworth gave the approaching cook a disdainful look and hooked his thumbs in his wide leather belt.

"Poor boy, you mean," Dunsdworth said saucily. He ground some more tiles under his heel. "Playing with bits and scraps like a beggar. I came because I was hungry. Give me a muffin, cook."

"I should box your ears!" Liona said angrily. She was a short woman, but Dunsdworth was only twelve, so they were of a size. Though she looked angry enough to thrash him, the bully looked unconcerned.

"You touch me," Dunsdworth warned, "and I'll have my revenge." He raised a hand and closed it around the dagger hilt. "Now fetch me a muffin!"

Liona scowled at him and huffed to herself, but she grabbed a leftover muffin from a tray and thrust it into his hand. Using the older boy's distraction to his favor, Owen dragged his satchel nearer and furiously started picking up the rest of the fallen pieces before they too could be destroyed.

Dunsdworth took a bite, thanked Liona rudely with a wad of it in his mouth, and then sauntered out of the kitchen. Owen's mind was black, but the imminent threat of pain was leaving and his smoldering heart began to cool. Heaving a sigh, Liona knelt by the fallen tiles and helped him collect them.

"I'll ask Drew to find you some more," she offered, touching his hand with her own. "That boy's a rude sort. I hope we did not make an enemy of him today."

Owen frowned and breathed through his nose. "You should see how the king talks to him," he said. "He's treated the worst of us all." .

"True, but that doesn't excuse him to scold and tease smaller children. What sort of life is this?" She mopped her forehead. "Always living at risk of the king's wrath." She stopped gathering tiles, though she remained kneeling by him.

Owen looked at her and saw a strange expression in her eyes. "What is it, Liona?"

"You still wander the grounds with your maid?" she asked him softly.

He nodded, intrigued, as he grabbed another fistful of tiles and stacked them carefully in the box.

"You know the garden with the horse fountains and the hickory trees? It's on the lower ring of walls."

"I do," Owen said, gazing into her eyes. The tiles were cold in his hands.

"There is a porter door in the wall," she confided. "An iron door. They never lock it. The king's Espion use it to get in and out of the palace without the guards seeing. Drew told me of it. I've not told a soul I know." She paused and glanced over her shoulder again, licking her lips. "You cannot tell anyone that I told you, Owen," she said, when she finally returned her gaze to him. "I would lose my place. Or worse. There is a trail leading down to the castle road that goes to the bridge to Our Lady. Get you to sanctuary, Owen." She reached down and squeezed his knee. It tickled, though he knew that was not intended. "Seek out the queen dowager or her daughter, Elyse. Sometimes she is there. Even a child can claim sanctuary." She rose in a hurry and busied herself by the bread ovens, then grabbed a fistful of flour from a sack and spread it on the table nearby. She looked pale and a little nervous and didn't so much as glance at Owen again.

Owen was grateful for her help and excited by the possibility of escaping his life in the palace. He had arrived when the moon was half-full and now it was nearly full. If he managed to claim sanctuary, perhaps his parents could come and visit him? He was heartsick and missed them dreadfully.

After he finished cleaning up, he slung the satchel around his shoulder and started off to find Monah. It was after dark, so he would have to escape the next day. He had just the idea to slip away from his governess.

◆ ◆ ◆

"I don't *wish* to play the seeking game," Monah complained, trudging after Owen down the hill. "There is a groomsman I want to talk to. Let's visit the stables!"

Owen kept a strong pace, and the girl's long skirts made it difficult for her to keep up with him. He was so excited that he had not been hungry all day, but he had still eaten as much as he could and slipped some food in his pockets for later. Worried that his sly thoughts might show in his eyes, Owen had done his best to stay away from the king and Ratcliffe.

"Slow down!" Monah said, tromping through a thin hedge. Owen wove between the shagbark hickories, heading toward the wall. "Can we not go to the stables, Master Owen? I will get you a treat."

"I want to play the seeking game!" Owen said firmly. He could hear the murmuring of the fountain as they came nearer. Soon he could see it, the circular fountain with the huge rearing horse in its midst. Beyond, he spied the porter door, and his heart raced with excitement.

He turned and grabbed Monah's hand as she finally caught up to him. "I will hide first. You wait by the fountain and count to twenty! No . . . fifty! Then find me."

Monah was breathing hard and came to rest on the fountain's edge. Her dark hair was sticking to her forehead. "I don't want to chase you through the garden, Master Owen. I'm weary. Let me catch my breath."

"You won't have to *chase* me," Owen said, straining with impatience. "Once you find me, we'll trade turns. You will hide, and I will find *you*."

She winced and looked around the park, rubbing her arms. "The park is so big," she said. "I don't want to climb any trees. Why do you not wish to visit the stables? You said you liked horses."

"No, I didn't," Owen said petulantly. "Please, Monah? I used to play the seeking game with my sister." He gave her a pleading look and a small pout that always worked on his elders. He put his hand on her leg. "You are so like her."

"How long must we play this?" she asked wearily.

"Four turns," Owen said.

She frowned. "Two turns."

"*Four* turns," Owen insisted. "They will be quick. I won't hide far, and you will be easy to find."

She sighed with exasperation, then covered her eyes and started to count.

Owen sprinted away like a squirrel and took cover behind a tree far from the porter door. He hid in the crook where the branches forked, and he watched Monah as she counted. Over the babble of the fountain, he could not hear her. His heart raced with eagerness. He was going to make it more difficult for her to find him each time and then slip away on the fourth turn.

When she reached fifty, she rose and began walking in his direction. He deliberately let his head poke up from the forked branches so she could find him, though he pretended to be incensed to have been caught so soon. Then he quickly rushed back to the fountain, calling out loudly so that she could hear his counting over the noise of the water.

He spied her resting beneath a tree, her dark hair blending in with the bark, and gave her a little tickle when he found her. She squealed and scolded him before rushing off to the fountain for her next turn. A little pang of guilt threatened him. What would her punishment be for losing him? A scolding from Ratcliffe, probably. Owen's freedom was worth that much.

But the little feeling of guilt still squirmed in Owen's chest. Crushing it down as best he could, he hid in another spot, lying down by a hedge where she would have difficulty seeing him from a distance. His position gave him a view of the porter door and he found himself wondering if he would be strong enough to pull it open. What if the hinges were rusty?

He banished the thought and waited to be found. It took Monah longer this time, and she complained again about the game.

Owen decided he needed to try the door to see if it was too heavy. On his third turn, he quickly slipped away and approached the wall with the pitted metal door. There was a locking mechanism next to the iron handle. If the door was locked, he would be stuck. He glanced over his shoulder and saw Monah sitting at the fountain's edge, her head back, her face angled toward the sun. She seemed to be enjoying herself, not counting at all.

The door was made of wrought iron and had wide slats, some going up and down, others going across. Inside the gaps were decorative iron flowers, so there was no way to see through it. Owen grabbed the cold metal handle and pulled.

The door swung open without a sound.

He quickly peered through the gap, beneath which the forest descended at a steep decline. There was a well-worn dirt trail, marred by horseshoe prints. The opening in the wall was big enough to admit an animal, though not with a rider in the saddle. It was undeniably the secret exit Liona had described. There were no guards posted down below, and the thicket beyond the door was dense enough to hide his passage.

There was no reason to wait.

In his mind, he heard Liona's voice. *If you are a brave little boy . . .*

He glanced back one more time at Monah, sunbathing, her head tilted to one side. Fear painted shadows in his heart, but the thrill in his stomach chased those shadows away. Yes, Owen *was* brave. He was alone in the world now, so he needed to be. If he could find protection at the sanctuary, then it was well worth the risk. They would look for him in the kitchen. They would look for him all over the grounds. But they would not find him quickly enough to stop him.

Owen steeled his courage, feeling his legs wobble with the pent-up excitement. Then he slipped through the crack in the door, gently shut it behind him, and raced toward freedom.

♦ ♦ ♦

The populace of Ceredigion is inherently superstitious, especially in regards to quaint traditions involving the Fountain. When there is a wish or an ambition that a husband, wife, or child wants fulfilled, they hold a coin in their hand, think hard on the wish, and then flick the coin into one of the multitude of fountains within the sanctuary of Our Lady. Coins glisten and shimmer beneath the waters. They return the next day and find the coin still there. Mayhap two days. But invariably the coins vanish and that poor soul believes the Fountain has accepted their offering and will consider their wish. I know for a fact that the sexton of Our Lady dons wading boots, grabs a rake, and harvests the coins for the king's coffers every few days. He always leaves some behind, for a partially full fountain invites more donations to the king's treasury. It is considered the height of blasphemy to steal a coin from a fountain. It amazes me how this superstition prevents even a hungry urchin from stealing a coin that would buy his bread. The children whisper that if you take from the fountain and are caught, you will be thrown into the river and whisked over the falls. The power that tradition wields over simple minds is truly amazing. Whenever some poor fool shows a natural talent, be it baking or growing flowers, how quick people are to announce that person as blessed.

—Dominic Mancini, Espion of Our Lady of Kingfountain

♦ ♦ ♦

CHAPTER EIGHT

Her Majesty

Owen was breathing hard by the time he left the woods and started down the road. Sweat slicked his hair to his forehead, and he joined the carts and wagons and torrent of folk marching along toward the bridge. He worried that he would be spotted by the guards and seized at the gate, so he searched the crowd for a group of people who looked like a family. As soon as he found one, he increased his speed and fell in step with them as they passed the gatehouse. No one paid him any notice.

After leaving the shadow of the portcullis, Owen felt his nervous heart begin to give way to a thrill of excitement. Monah was probably still searching for him, and even after she reported him missing, it would take time before anyone figured out how he had escaped. His plan was simple. Go to the princess's mother in the sanctuary of Our Lady and beg enough coins to hire a coach to take him back to Tatton Hall. He knew of dozens of places he could hide on the grounds, without his parents' knowledge, and he would live among them as a ghost. It was a three-day ride by horseback to Westmarch, which meant a wagon would take longer, but the thought of being back home in a week made him grin with eagerness. He would trick the king and no one would be the wiser. Not even his parents would know where he was, so it would not be *their* fault if Owen was missing. He was still hurt that they had chosen him to go to the palace, but he didn't want them to get in more trouble.

As he crossed the bridge, his confidence began to wane and his stomach started to growl. He broke off a crust from his pocket and chewed it slowly to ease his hunger. Every noise made him whirl around and stare back, as if twenty knights wearing the badge of the white boar might be charging after him. Beneath him he could feel the churn of waves crashing against the bridge and hear the roar of the waterfall. He feared he would never make it, and yet the sanctuary drew closer.

It was a beautiful structure, but he had gazed at it with dull eyes when Horwath had brought him past it weeks ago. Still, he remembered all the grubby men loitering at the gates and felt a shiver of dread. The clomp of hooves startled him, and he moved to the side quickly as a rider passed. Owen felt the panicked sensation that everyone was looking at him. He refused to meet anyone's gaze as he pressed onward.

As he walked, he took notice of the brickwork along the island wall that defended the earth from being washed away. There were patterns in the bricks he had not noticed before, perhaps because huge clumps of hanging ivy covered part of the brickwork, one batch hanging low enough to tease the waters rushing by at great speed. A fence surrounded the entire grounds of the sanctuary, which was on the north side of the island in the midst of the river. Huge trees towered up beyond the fence, and on the side facing Owen, he spied a huge circular stained-glass window in the shape of a sundial. Spikes and turrets rose from the edges, and long gutters and support struts held up the walls. It was narrow and tall and a huge steeple jutted from the crown of the structure, high enough to pierce the clouds.

Owen was so busy gazing at the structure that he stumbled against the backside of a man pushing a cart and earned a quick scolding for his carelessness.

After crossing the bridge onto the island, Owen bent his way toward the main gates. Sure enough, there were feckless men loitering there. Owen mustered his courage and walked through the gates, feeling a jolt of relief once he had passed them. No man could force him from these grounds. Not even the king.

None of the fountain-men, who were muttering among themselves, paid him any mind. Owen gazed at the tall posts with lamps dangling from hooks high above. There were families walking the inner parks and his heart grew sore at the sight of them. He hungered to see his family again, even from afar, and to calm himself, he reflected on where he would hide first when he returned to his estate.

There was a large reflection pool before the steps leading up to the sanctuary doors, which were open, revealing a sunlit entryway. He stopped at the pool, staring into the placid depths, and saw coins gleaming in the bottom. A fat man sat on the edge of the pool, beefy arms folded. He was tossing crumbs to pigeons pecking near his shoes. Owen watched with fascination as the man deftly sprinkled the crumbs, sometimes this way, sometimes that, and the crowd of feathers moved in response, making clucking and cooing noises all the while. The fat man smiled at their squabbling.

Then suddenly the man lurched to his feet and stomped, causing the birds to flap and flee in a cloud of exploding gray plumage. The sudden motion shocked Owen and his heart hammered frightfully in his chest. The fat man laughed boisterously, clutching his girth as he sat back down. He wiped his eyes a moment, still chuckling to himself, and then dug into a pocket for more crumbs and began sprinkling them again on the paving stones.

Sure enough, pigeons began to return a few moments later, flapping down from the trees where they'd fled. They approached cautiously, heads bobbing, and then the braver ones began to peck at the crumbs. Once they did, the others deemed it safe enough and soon the entire area was thick with fowl again.

The fat man had scraggly brown whiskers along his jowls. His hair was thick and wavy, cropped close to his ears, and he had a sad smile, as if he were bored beyond his wits and tormenting the birds was his only way of entertaining himself.

"They keep coming back," the fat man said with a tired sigh. He had not looked at Owen, but his voice was pitched just enough to reach the boy's ears. He had the accent of a foreigner, but his voice was pleasant and he spoke the tongue of the kingdom well. "I can frighten them off a hundred times a day, but they keep coming back for crumbs." He sighed, resting his bread-throwing hand on his paunch. "They cannot resist their need to eat. And I suppose neither can I. It's a sad truth. If I were not so lazy, I would walk over to the muffin vendor and get a tasty morsel. Those would provide tantalizing crumbs indeed! But when you haul around this much baggage, lad, even a little walk is a burden."

Owen stared at the man's mouth as he talked, watching the way he formed his words. He had a gentle, coaxing voice. Then he glanced at Owen and smiled in a friendly way.

"Here to make a wish, lad?" he asked.

Owen blinked, realizing he was formally being addressed. He nodded sheepishly.

The man pitched his voice lower. "They say *that* side of the pool brings better luck." He pointed to the other side of the reflecting pool from where he sat. "But if you *really* want a wish granted, you must toss a crown into the wisdom fountain inside. The statue of the woman with the spear is the true Lady of the Fountain. She'll grant your wish. If you have a whole crown."

"I don't have a crown," Owen said.

The man pursed his lips. "Well . . . that can't be. A lad with such a noble look . . . I thought you'd have a whole bag of crowns. 'Tis a pity.

But if your wish is important, that's where you must make it. Here, I'll lend you a crown." He dug through another pouch, humming a little to himself, and pulled out a fat crown. He put it under his thumb and flicked it, sending the coin spinning in the air toward Owen, who caught it without dropping it.

"Well done, lad, well done!" the fat man said.

Owen stared at the crown and saw it was not from Ceredigion. A different language was scrawled on it and it looked nothing like the coins from his realm. He rubbed his fingers over the letters and spelling he couldn't decipher.

"Can you read it?" the fat man asked, chuckling.

Owen shook his head, turning the coin over in his hand.

"Not many from these parts can. That is called a florin. It's about the same weight as a crown. I'm Genevese—the lake kingdom. Do you know where that is, lad?"

Owen stared at the man. He had never met a foreigner before. "I've seen maps," he said shyly.

The man nodded. "Maps. You looked like a smart one. I bet you can read and know your numbers too."

Owen looked at him in surprise.

"I knew it!" the man said, chuckling and clapping his hands. The birds pecking near his feet were getting angry that he hadn't put any crumbs down in a while. "Well, there is your crown, lad. Go make your wish and run along to your mother."

"Thank you," Owen said, surprised that he wasn't too shy to speak. The man had a way about him that both frightened Owen and intrigued him. He was not like other adults.

"Name is Mancini," the fat man said with a nod.

"Thank you, Mancini," Owen said.

"Someone in your family is sick? Is that why you're making a wish—what was your name again?"

"Owen," the boy replied, only then realizing he should not have said it. He blinked with surprise.

"Well met, Owen," Mancini said. "Go make your wish. I think I might fetch that muffin after all." He groaned and tried to rise, but it seemed to require more effort than he had to give. "Sometimes," Mancini said, breathing hard, "I have to lean back before I can push myself up again. Once I leaned back too far and . . . splash! Went into the fountain!" He gave Owen a wink and a grin and the boy giggled. "Took four men to pull me out. What a mess. Almost drowned."

Owen smiled, enjoying the warmth that came with the laughter. The image of the fat man flailing and spluttering in the water made it even funnier.

Mancini leaned back and then swung himself forward. This time he made it back up to his feet, tottering a bit, and Owen watched him as he waddled away. Once the fat man was gone, Owen walked around to the other side of the pool. He made a wish that the queen would be able to help him and then pitched the florin into the water where it plopped and promptly sank to the bottom. He started to walk around the grounds a bit more, admiring the fountains and searching for the princess's mother. He thought the best place to look would be within the sanctuary itself, so he mounted the wide stone steps. The floor of the sanctuary was made of black and white marble squares, reminding him of an enormous Wizr board, but without the pieces. He loved playing Wizr, and even though he was only eight, he was good enough to beat some of his siblings. His father still bested him every time.

Owen stood on a white square, which was just wide enough for him to fit in without his feet touching the edges. The hall was enormous, and a huge fountain splashed and played in the middle of the chamber. There were higher-ranking visitors inside the sanctuary, as demonstrated by their stylish clothes and felt hats. Owen felt a little more comfortable now, and the effect of the fountain was soothing. There were tall columns and pedestals topped with white marble statues, which looked to Owen like life-size Wizr pieces. Of course, they would be very difficult to move. Not surprisingly, he saw some older men sitting around normal-size Wizr boards and playing matches. He walked among them, looking for a woman who resembled the princess.

It took quite some wandering before he managed to find her, but the time seemed to pass quickly. The princess's mother was talking to the sanctuary sexton, a man with white robes, a black cloak, and a mushroom-shaped hat. The sexton was in charge of the grounds. The deconeus was in charge of performing the water rite for newborn babies. Owen had been around such people his entire life, so he recognized them by their robes. But Owen easily recognized the princess's mother. This was the queen dowager, the wife of the king who had died two years before. She was trailed by a younger woman, probably no more than twelve, who looked to be her other daughter.

Owen waited patiently until the queen dowager's conversation with the sexton was finished, although it took quite a while. Once they were done, the queen dowager took the girl's hand, and the two of them slowly walked back toward the fountain in the center of the huge chamber. Recognizing his opportunity, Owen quickly walked up to her, trying to quell his growing nervousness.

As he walked, the girl holding her mother's hand looked at him curiously and tugged on her mother's arm. It felt as if a cloud of butterflies had filled Owen's stomach.

The queen mother stopped, responding to the tugging, and turned to face Owen. She was a beautiful woman, tall and lithe and regal. Her hair was the same color as her daughters', elegantly styled with braiding and brooches.

Just as Owen was about to reach the dowager, he heard boots tromping into the sanctuary, loud and fervent and very familiar. Twisting around, he watched with horror as Ratcliffe strode into the sanctuary, his face contorted with anger. He marched straight toward Owen and looked as if he would jerk the boy's arm out of its socket and drag him out.

"Come here, boy," the queen mother said to Owen, her voice soft but urgent.

Owen's legs were shaking violently, but he managed to close the gap separating him from the queen mother as the burly man continued his approach. The cap was off Ratcliffe's head, crushed in his fist, and his balding dome looked moist with sweat. He was livid but also flushed with relief to have found Owen.

"There—you—are—young—man!" he barked angrily in a clipped tone. He closed the distance with several long strides, attracting the gaze of everyone in the room, which made Owen cower against the queen mother's gown. She put her hand on his shoulder and he saw the glittering jewel of the coronation ring on her hand.

"This is supposed to be a *quiet* sanctuary, Ratcliffe," the queen mother chastised. "Please . . . you will offend the Fountain. Lower your voice."

His teeth gnashed in fury. "I should have known he would seek refuge *here*!"

"What are you raving about?" she answered patiently. "This boy? I have never seen him before in my life. Who is he?"

"Owen Kiskaddon," Ratcliffe snarled. "The king's hostage."

The queen laughed lightly. "Ah, your anger makes sense now. I was beginning to think you had lost your wits. You think *I* summoned him here?"

"He is standing before you, isn't he?" Ratcliffe said, raising his voice. "How did you manage it, Lizzy? I truly wish to know."

Owen could tell that the name he used was meant as an insult by the way she bridled her reaction.

"Obviously the Fountain led the boy here, Ratcliffe. I heard he was in the palace, of course, but I did not bring him here. We had not even met until just a moment ago. But I will remind you, *sir*, that he has the protection of sanctuary and you cannot force him to leave. Severn wouldn't dare violate it, not after all *he* has done! The people would revolt. Somehow the boy managed to find his way here, and here he will stay, under my protection."

Ratcliffe looked as if he would have a seizure of anger. "The king will not tolerate this!" he growled. "Can the Fountain shield you from his wrath? Your daughter enjoys the privilege of coming back and forth. Shall *she* become his hostage instead?"

Owen's heart quailed at the words, fearing what would happen to the princess. He gave the queen a worried look.

She laughed scornfully. "You and I both know he wouldn't do that. Now be gone, Ratcliffe. Before I call for the sexton. Out."

Ratcliffe's fists trembled with fury. He looked at Owen then, his eyes full of daggers. "Come with me, boy. Now. Come back with me to the castle."

Owen stared at the man and shook his head.

"When the king finds out about this . . ." Ratcliffe snarled, his lips quivering.

"It appears he already has," came a voice from the doorway. It was the deconeus, attended by the sexton. "He is mounting the steps right now, Lord Ratcliffe. The king is *here*." He turned and bowed graciously. "Welcome to Our Lady, sovereign lord."

Owen's eyes widened with terror and he felt the queen's hand tighten on his shoulder.

"No matter what he says, do not let him touch you," the queen whispered in warning.

CHAPTER NINE

The King's Voice

The king was annoyed. Owen could see that emotion burning in his gray eyes, twisting his mouth into a scowl, and twitching in his cheek muscle. The limp from his wound was becoming less pronounced, but it was still there, and Owen could *hear* the distinct sound of his shuffling steps before he saw his face.

The king wore his black and gold. The usual dagger was in his belt, accompanied by a large, scabbarded sword that had seen many years of war. A trickle of sweat fell down the side of his face. His long black hair was windswept, giving him a wild appearance. The queen mother's nails dug into Owen's shoulder, making him flinch.

"Remember," she whispered to Owen.

"My liege," Ratcliffe said with astonishment. "How come you this way? I was going to send word for you—"

"*When*, Ratcliffe? When my hair turned gray? You thought I would not want to know that my hostage had fled? Why is it that I must learn these things from my *niece* rather than from the head of the Espion!"

The king's wrath was focused on Ratcliffe at the moment, but Owen felt his blood turn cold with fear, knowing it would turn on him.

"My . . . my lord!" Ratcliffe stammered. "It was *my* man who told me the boy was here! I had only just learned of it and wanted to confirm the news with my own eyes first!" Ratcliffe wrung his hands, looking as if he feared for his neck.

"Enough excuses, Ratcliffe. Is it too much to ask you to keep my hostages under closer supervision? What will I learn next? That you approved one of his parents' ceaseless requests to see him? By the Fountain, man! He's just a little boy! How could you be so careless?"

"I . . . I . . ." Ratcliffe's cheeks were scarlet and sweat dribbled down them from his brow.

The king made a dismissive gesture with a gloved hand. Then he turned his baleful eyes on the queen mother. His lips pursed angrily. "I should have suspected I would find him here, *Madame*." The hatred in his eyes and tone made Owen shrink.

"You are quite mistaken, Severn, as you typically are when you're upset," the queen mother replied in an icy voice. "I did not summon the lad here. He only just appeared. I haven't even spoken to him yet."

The king snorted in disbelief. "You take me for a fool."

"I take you for one when you *act* like one. This is the Kiskaddon lad then? Your hostage?" There was a shade of meaning in her words that Owen did not understand. "And he found his way to sanctuary. My, but how that must gall you!"

The king's expression hardened. It was clear there was no love between the king and his sister-in-law, and Owen could sense the bitterness that had festered between them.

"You cannot take him from here, Severn. Even *you* have never dared to violate the sanctuary of Our Lady. You've threatened it, to be sure! But the people would throw you into the river if you tried and you'd never survive. The boy stays here with me. I did not send for him, but I will not send him away." She patted Owen's shoulder possessively.

"The lad does not know you as well as I do," the king said with husky anger.

"Nor you, my *liege*," she sneered. "He and I will have great fun together, discussing many things about your lordship. And about my *sons.*"

The king held up a hooked finger, silencing her. His face turned pale with anger and warning. "You will say nothing," he said in a choked growl.

Something peculiar happened then. It was as if the lapping sound of the fountain water had suddenly grown louder, drowning out all other sounds from Owen's ears. The sensation was soothing, and it began to calm his violently beating heart. Then the king's voice slipped in among the waters.

"Owen."

Usually there was a sharp edge to the king's voice when he spoke Owen's name, but this time his voice did not sound angry or accusing. It contained all the tenderness of a loving father's address to his son. He blinked, confused, and peered up at the king.

The sound of the fountain waters grew even louder. He could *feel* them, as if he were splashing in the waters inside the stone railing. In fact, that's what he felt like he was doing, playing and splashing and getting wet and relishing in the deliciousness of being naughty. The feeling of the waters rushed through him, soothing him and calming him and filling him with happiness. He was smiling now. The king was smiling too, as if he felt the same thrill of dancing in a fountain.

"Come away from her, Owen," the king said softly, coaxingly. "She is *here* for a reason. She plots and she destroys. If you heed her, lad, your family will be killed. Because of her. I want to save you, Owen. Come with me."

Owen felt a twinge of pain in his shoulder, but it could not hurt him, not truly. He heard words, the queen's words, but they could not pierce the rushing sound of the waters. A memory tried to intrude, something about the king's touch, but it was as annoying as a buzzing fly, and he brushed it away.

"I would not lie to you," the king said seriously, gently, as if he were inviting a butterfly to land on his palm. "There is danger here. Danger you cannot see. You are being trapped in a spider's web, Owen. Let me free you. Come . . . hold my hand." The king reached out his black glove. The leather looked soft and warm, the gesture so inviting.

Owen shook loose the queen's hand and walked toward the king. It felt as if the very waters of the Fountain were coming from that outstretched hand. He knew without a doubt that he would feel safe and protected if he held the king's hand. More words fluttered around him. Some were sharp-spoken, but they could not pierce the feelings flooding him.

He walked confidently over to the king, who did not look fearsome anymore. He looked tired and pained, but he had a gentle, generous smile.

"My niece is so worried about you," the king said with a warm smile. "Shall we give her a little surprise then? She looked so fearful when she believed you had come to harm, Owen. Shall we find her back at the palace?"

Owen smiled eagerly and nodded. Yes, he would like that. He would like that very much.

"Will you show her how you left the castle, Owen? We were all so surprised you were clever enough to figure it out. But I knew you were a smart lad from the start."

Owen nodded again, anxious to reveal the secret door to Princess Elyse. Perhaps it would be their secret now. His heart was giddy as he finally reached out and took the king's hand. With one touch, it was if he were transported onto a boat, floating away on calm waters. It was the first time he had felt safe since leaving Tatton Hall. Together, Owen and the king walked away from the queen and the bubbling fountain. The boy felt light-headed with happiness as he clung to the king's hand, feeling its strong grip, the warmth of the leather.

Owen turned back to the queen. She was crying. Why? He waved back at her, nodding to tell her all was well. Then he looked down at the black and white tiles on the floor. He only stepped on the white ones. The king only stepped on the black ones. It was as if they were Wizr pieces, he thought, and the notion made him giggle.

"What amuses you, Owen?" the king asked kindly. His voice inspired confidence.

"The squares," the boy said, pointing with his other hand. "The white and the black. Like a Wizr board." It did not dawn on him that this was the first time he had addressed the king. He felt so comfortable with him now, it seemed as if they had always been the best of friends.

"You play Wizr?" the king asked with a surprised chuckle.

"My father taught me."

"I also play Wizr," the king said as they walked. "The game came from the eastern kingdoms. Did you know that?" They approached the huge doors of the sanctuary.

"It came from Chandigarl."

"I knew you were a clever lad. Would you like a Wizr board, Owen? I can have one carved for you."

He stared up at the king's thoughtful face in rapture. "Would you?" he pleaded. "I've never had my own board!"

"Then you shall have one," the king promised. "*If* you stay in the castle. You *must* stay in the castle, Owen."

The boy nodded. It would be worth it if he got his own Wizr board. They left the sanctuary and walked toward the outer gates. Owen saw the reflecting pool and wondered where the fat man was. Mancini. He would have liked to have shared the muffin and watched him throw crumbs to the pigeons again.

A throb of fear nudged his heart. Even though the sun was beating down on them, he felt . . . cold. He adjusted his grip on the king's hand, but the leather did not feel as soft anymore. It was almost as if the king were *clenching* his hand. It was almost uncomfortable. The king's limp grew more pronounced as they walked. Owen heard a stifled gasp of pain and looked up to see the king glaring at the gates, his teeth clenched as if he were concentrating very hard.

The murmuring sound of the fountains began to recede. It felt as if he had been caught playing in the fountains and was about to get in trouble for doing so. A guilty feeling welled up inside his stomach. Something was wrong.

They reached the gate and the sanctuary men parted, allowing them room to pass. Owen looked up at the tall stone arch, then glanced back at the sanctuary. Ratcliffe was just behind them, scowling at him with raw anger and humiliation that made him even more uneasy.

The sexton stood by the gate. "Do you leave of your own free will?" he asked Owen sternly.

The boy nodded, feeling frightened by the man's stern look. The bad feelings ebbed as the king shifted his grip on his hand. Nothing had changed. The king made him feel safe and he wanted his own carved Wizr board and to see Princess Elyse. What else truly mattered? He sidled up closer to the king.

"You heard the boy," the king said with a suppressed groan.

Owen's heart was beating faster now. They walked out the gate together, still hand in hand. Something made Owen glance back once more, and this time he saw the fat man standing by Ratcliffe, taking coins from his hand. Maybe Mancini was paying Ratcliffe to get him some muffins? But that did not make sense.

"Ratcliffe!" the king barked.

They were outside the gate now and had started toward the castle. Owen's heart was like thunder in his chest. Why was he leaving sanctuary? Why had he come there in the first place? There had been a reason, and it seemed important, but he just could not remember it.

"Take him back to the palace," the king said, sounding breathless. "I need to rest. It drained me. The lad has a strong will, thick as tree roots."

"I envy your gifts, my lord," Ratcliffe said tautly, joining them. He seized Owen's other hand, tightening his grip until it was painful.

Then the king released Owen and the fog was gone. Owen remembered everything, like a sleepwalker awakened midstep. Confusion and terror battled within him.

"No need to flatter, Ratcliffe," the king chuckled. "I can't abide flattery. I know what I am. And so do you. Keep this *boy* under better watch, or I promise you that there will be a new Espion master and you will be sent to the North to polish Horwath's boots. I expected better from you, Dickon. If I can't trust you in the little things . . ." He let the threat dangle and then gestured dismissively at them both.

Ratcliffe flushed scarlet again, his jaw clenching with rage. "Come on!" he snarled, yanking Owen's arm so hard it felt like his shoulder would come popping out.

Owen was near tears as he watched the sanctuary of Our Lady start to fade away. He realized, sickeningly, that he had made it there on his own, against all odds, but had been lured out again by some trick. He had been incapable of resisting the king. But why? Then he remembered the queen's warning, and it struck him.

It was the king's voice. It was something in his hands.

Owen had been incapable of resisting.

While they were halfway across the bridge, Owen tried to struggle away from Ratcliffe's hand, wrenching and twisting—anything to free himself so he could flee back to the sanctuary.

A sharp smack on the back of his head put a stop to his resistance.

"*Think*, boy!" Ratcliffe snarled in his ear. "Think about your *family*." He tugged Owen around until he was facing him and then lowered himself down to his height. The head of the Espion spoke softly, but his voice was full of venom. "You cross me again, and they will suffer for it! You escape one more time, and I will have your mother and your sisters thrown into the dungeons to starve and your father and brothers into the river to drown. I will not chase you or hunt you ever again, *boy*! You will obey me or the blood of your family will be on your scrawny little head. It will turn that white patch red! Make a fool of me again, and you will regret it. Am I understood?"

Owen trembled with shock and fright.

"Say it!" Ratcliffe barked.

Owen's mouth would not work.

"Say it," Ratcliffe warned, squeezing his hand until he cried out.

"Yes!" Owen wailed, crumpling to the ground in agony.

◆ ◆ ◆

There is an adage as old as time, but it is universally true: No good deed goes unpunished. In finding Kiskaddon's brat, I have been relocated to the palace to keep an eye on the little devil. I spent several years in the palace before and I hated it. This assignment will, in all likelihood, be very short. The boy is either going to get himself killed or his parents will do something reckless to seal his fate. I'm not sentimental about this and I only hope it happens quickly so I can move on to a more interesting assignment. The only patch of blue in the sky, as they say, is the lad likes to play in the kitchen. I hear Liona can spice and cook a goose like no other!

—Dominic Mancini, Espion of the Palace Kitchen

◆ ◆ ◆

CHAPTER TEN

Ankarette

In the days that followed Owen's escape, it seemed as if the sun had stopped shining. The little boy had been petted and coddled before. Now he was shunned and scolded. Monah Stirling was replaced with a stern old woman by the name of Jewel who did not suffer him to explore the grounds, was too gouty to climb tower steps or walk the corridors with him more than once a day, and kept him on a short leash, predominately in the kitchen, where a new addition had soured the haven.

Owen was surprised to find Mancini had taken up residence in the palace. Liona had explained in hushed tones that the man was a spy for the king, part of the Espion, and that he had been stationed at the palace to keep an eye on Owen. And so Liona and Drew had withdrawn their tenderness, fearful that the king would discover their role in Owen's escape.

Mancini said very little to Owen, but he gave him knowing little smirks and winks that seemed almost threatening, as if he were *daring* the boy to misbehave so he'd have an excuse to report him to Ratcliffe. Occasionally he'd stomp his boot suddenly, like he'd done with the pigeons, just to see Owen start. He would chuckle to himself while Owen stacked his tiles and snort derisively when they all came tumbling down. And he helped himself liberally to the kitchen food throughout the day. Owen could tell Liona resented having to feed such a big man so often, but there was naught she could do.

Owen tried to find Princess Elyse and failed. And she made no attempt to contact him either. It was as if everything good and kind had been banished from the palace after Owen's escape attempt. His wretched heart became a constant torment, and the palace itself felt like a dungeon. After several days of scolding from Jewel, he shrunk inside himself, his appetite waned, and he started at every shadow.

Owen's misery during the king's breakfast grew exquisite. No longer was he spared the king's enmity. On the third day after the botched escape, the king looked almost gleeful as he entered the great hall and advanced on Owen.

"What? Still here, Master Owen?" he said mockingly. He gripped his dagger hilt with his fist and loosed it from its scabbard before slamming it back down—the gesture Owen had always found horrifying. "It has been *days* since my entire household has been frantically searching for you. You cannot imagine what a bother that is in such a spacious fortress as this one. And since then, my kitchen expenses have begun to soar. You have my *thanks*."

Owen shrank from the attention, too frightened to say anything. Dunsdworth coughed a laugh into his fist, which he should not have done, because the king turned on him with delight.

"Shut it, Dunsdworth," the king snapped. "If I wanted your commentary, I would beat it out of you."

"I . . . I was . . . it was only a cough!" Dunsdworth objected in a whiny tone.

"Well, then keep your coughs and your sneezes and your bad airs within, lad. If there was anyone in this hall I *wanted* to escape, it would be *you*."

The young man went scarlet with anger and mortification and Owen could not hide a smile of revenge. Unfortunately, Dunsdworth turned to look at him at that exact moment. The look on his face promised such revenge that the smile cleared away in a blink.

The king hastily ate his breakfast, picking from the trays that others had already sampled. Owen surreptitiously studied the king's face as he put his guests down and made them squirm. He seemed satisfied with the contention he brewed at every meal, as if it fed him more than Liona's fare.

After breakfast, Owen started making his way to the kitchen, but a strong arm closed around his neck from behind. The air vanished from his lungs and a heavy weight crushed against him.

"Laugh at *me*? Who are you to laugh at anyone?" Dunsdworth's voice was low and rough in his ear. A punch to his stomach made him gasp, and he could not breathe. The arm was still choking him.

"You are doomed, Kisky," Dunsdworth jibed. "If you ever laugh at me again, I'll drown you in a barrel of wine. I would be doing the king a favor. You hear me, boy? I'll push you in a wine barrel and hammer down the lid. Don't you *ever* laugh at me!" After delivering another punch to the stomach, he threw Owen to the floor where the boy started to sob.

Dunsdworth kicked Owen's arm with his sharp boot and Owen knew it would leave a huge bruise. He held his stomach, staining the tiles with his tears, as the older boy sauntered away. For a few moments, Owen soothed himself by imagining ways to get revenge. But soon even his fiery anger cooled and he knelt in the passageway, shuddering and trembling as servants passed by him, no one stopping to see what was wrong.

When Owen managed to stumble into the kitchen, no one noticed him except Mancini, who queried if there were any goodies left in the great hall to pluck. Owen nodded, and he was gone. The boy retreated to his corner and sat there in the shadows, his back to the rest of the kitchen, his shoulders slumped, too sad even to stack tiles from his satchel. It took him a moment to notice the scattered tiles waiting for him there. Tears hung thick on his lashes as he edged nearer. Instead of spelling his name, the tiles spelled W-A-I-T. It was a curious message from Drew, but it did not interest him. He suddenly missed his parents dreadfully. No one had ever thrashed him before. His arm throbbed from the kick, and he rubbed it, but the pain did not lessen. Maybe his arm was broken. No one would care if it were.

How had the king talked him into leaving the sanctuary? His memory was a blur. He only remembered how persuasive the king had been, how kind and generous he had seemed. Somehow he had tricked Owen. The boy did not understand how, but he knew it had happened. He gritted his teeth, brushing his tears away on his sleeve.

The day seemed to pass away in a blur and he obeyed the message that had been left with the tiles. He sat and waited and did not eat any food. He did not think he would ever be hungry again. Even when Liona tried to coax him to eat a muffin, he only shook his head.

"By all means give it to me then, Liona!" Mancini said with a laugh. "The boy's not hungry. The man is!"

The butler Berwick snorted. "Yuv eaten as much as sixteen men!" he complained darkly in his Northern accent. "Your appetite is going to bankrupt the king!"

"Your *complaining* is going to bankrupt my patience," Mancini shot back. "If you had the brains the Fountain gave a sheep, you'd know it's not wise to stand between a fat hungry man and his food. I could *eat* you, Berwick."

The butler snorted angrily at the reproof, but Mancini was always joking and no one seemed to pay him any mind.

"He clearly doesn't want the muffin, Liona." Mancini continued his campaign for more food, beckoning with his sausage-like fingers. "Bring it over."

The cook looked pleadingly at Owen, begging him to take it, but he would not.

"See! I told you the lad wasn't hungry today. And it is certainly a sin to let a muffin go to waste." Liona almost threw it at him, but he took it greedily and ate it with little mumbles of relish that sickened Owen. "I am Genevese," he said, spitting a few crumbs as he spoke, to no one in particular. "And I am not ashamed of it! We love our food. This . . . this is the height of deliciousness. I applaud you, morsel! If there are any more, Liona . . . ?"

She gave him a disgusted look and did not reply.

Owen was too tired and hurt to do much that day. He obeyed when Jewel came for him and did as he was told in a listless way. Even her suggestion of reading in the library was met with refusal. He just wanted to sit in the kitchen, to smell the baking bread and try to recapture his memories of Tatton Hall. But his life there was so different from his present reality that the memories were slipping way, dissolving into the air like smoke. He lay down on the warm stone tiles, pressing his cheek against them, and thought about his parents and his siblings. He tried to remember the carefree days he'd spent reading in the library and ambling around the grounds.

He might have fallen asleep there. He dazed and dozed, drifting in and out of consciousness. Sometimes snatches of words, mumbled softly nearby, would linger close enough that he could grab them.

"Poor dear. He misses home," Liona murmured.

"The king is a cruel man. Do you think he will kill the boy?" Drew asked. "He killed his nephews. The man has no qualms."

"Carry him to bed, Drew. It's getting late."

"Let him sleep, Liona. Let him dream of better days. I'll come by early in the morning and carry him to his room."

They left him in the kitchen. The clinking of pots and spoons ended. Mancini grunted as he hiked up the steps. Soon all was peaceful and quiet and warm. Owen's arm throbbed painfully when he turned over on his shoulder. He blinked, feeling some of his mussed hair tickle his forehead. They had all gone. The windows showed the black night sky, and he saw the outline of the knife-blade tower and a single light coming from the upper window. It looked like a star.

He sat up and listened to the deep quiet. It was vast and penetrating. An occasional sound, like the sloughing of ash in the oven, came like a whisper. Owen's heart was a painful thing, almost as sore as his bruised arm.

"I don't want to die," he whispered into the stillness.

There was a grating sound, so soft he almost did not hear it. It took Owen a moment to place it as the sound of polished stone scuffing stone. Then a woman entered the kitchen from a shadowed recess nearby, where the tiles had awaited him with their cryptic message. She was dressed in a pale gray cloak that seemed to match the color of the stone wall. The cowl was up, concealing her face, so he only caught a glimpse of her hair.

His heart started to beat faster. She was slightly taller than Princess Elyse, and for a brief moment, Owen thought she might be a ghost. Then her arms lifted to lower the cowl, revealing a long coil of dark hair that was pinned up around her head like a crown with a single braid coming down and draped across her shoulder. A thin necklace with a brooch hung at the base of her throat. Her elbow-length gloves matched her gown—a light, satin texture that was silver and fashionable. She stood still for a moment, listening to the silence, wrapped in the velvety darkness of night.

"Owen?" she whispered softly.

His heart beat even faster. He swallowed, afraid but hopeful. She knew his name. She was looking for him. It suddenly dawned on him that Drew was not the one who had been leaving him messages with the tiles after all.

He shifted on the floor and her head turned in response to the little noise, her braid slipping down her back. Though he was half-hidden by shadows in the dark corner, that small sound was all it had taken to capture her attention. Aside from the fire embers, only the moon lit the kitchen.

She walked gracefully toward him, and as she came closer, he realized she was beautiful. She was neither as young as the princess nor as old as the queen. Though he could not tell the color of her eyes in the darkness, they were light, like moonbeams—either gray or blue or green—and so very sad. She absentmindedly reached for the braid and began to tease the tips with her fingers. Then she let it rest across her front again, barely touching the laced bodice.

She slowly sat on the bench that separated them, resting her hands in her lap in a nonthreatening way. He thought she was the most beautiful person he had ever seen.

As she studied him, the little frown on her mouth smoothed into a small smile. A welcoming one. "Hello, Owen," she said. Her voice was just loud enough for him to hear her. "Thank you for waiting for me. I am here to help you. The queen sent me."

She sat still, waiting for him to respond, waiting to see how he would react to her presence.

Owen was not sure what he should feel. Her sense of majesty put him a little in mind of the queen herself. She was quiet, her manners very subdued, almost as if she were shy. To his relief, she neither rushed him nor pressured him to reply. She simply waited for him to gather his courage.

It took a few moments for his mouth to work. But it did, which surprised him. "Are you a ghost?"

The smile broadened, amused by his question. She had a pretty smile, with just the hint of a dimple. "No," she answered. "Would you like me to introduce myself?"

He nodded solemnly, feeling more at ease with her quiet manners.

"My name is Ankarette Tryneowy. That's a strange name, isn't it? But it is my name. I am the queen's poisoner. She sent me to help you."

♦ ♦ ♦

Too many people are frightened. They want youth to last. They complain bitterly if sickness comes. But the world is always in tumult, and fortunes rise and fall and fail. It is the ambitious who accomplish things. It takes courage to be ambitious, for never was anything great achieved without risk. I wish to become the head of the Espion. There—I've written it down. A goal not written down is merely a wish.

—Dominic Mancini, Espion of the Palace Kitchen

♦ ♦ ♦

CHAPTER ELEVEN

The Fountain

Ankarette was so quiet, so subdued, that Owen was not as frightened of her as he was of most strangers. But he was not quite sure if being a poisoner wasn't worse than being a ghost.

"Do you have any questions?" she asked him softly.

"What is a poisoner?"

She seemed to have anticipated the question, and it did not trouble her. "Every prince in every realm has enemies, Owen. These enemies try to take away his crown. Being a prince is very dangerous business, you know." She paused. "A poisoner's job is to protect the ruler from his enemies. Sometimes there are dangerous men who need to be stopped. I know how to mix potions that can make someone very sick. Sometimes that is enough to stop the danger. Sometimes, I must make a potion that kills." She glanced down at her hands in her lap. "I don't like doing that, but sometimes it must be done." Her voice was so soft and sad.

"You said you were the *queen's* poisoner," Owen said. "You mean the queen at Our Lady?"

"Yes."

"Do you live in the sanctuary then?"

"No, I live here in the palace." She pointed through the upper window to the spark in the knife-blade tower. "Up there, in that tower."

Owen's eyes widened. "I thought that's where the king lived!"

She smiled again. "No. His back is crooked. It would be too difficult for him to climb the steps every day."

She sat quietly, patiently, looking at him and waiting for more questions.

"Why don't you serve the new king?" he asked. "I'm glad the queen sent you to help me, but she isn't the queen anymore."

"That's a very good question, Owen. I will try to explain so you can understand. When King Eredur died, I was not here. He had sent me on a secret mission to another kingdom. Some terrible things happened while I was gone, and the king's brother claimed the throne. He knew *about* me, but he did not know who I was. I was very loyal to his brother, not to him, you see. He sent men to try and kill me. But I killed them instead." She paused, looking down at her hands. "He does not like me very much."

Owen looked at her gloved hands and then at the brooch at her throat. "Does he think you are going to poison him?" he asked. He remembered that the king ate only from dishes that had already been sampled by others.

She gave him that little smile again. "You are very smart. For one so young. Yes, he *is* afraid I'm going to poison him. But I would never hurt children to stop him. You never need fear that, Owen. I only hurt dangerous men. You went to the queen for help. And so she asked me to help you."

"But you can't help me," he said, shaking his head. "If I leave Kingfountain, my parents will be killed. I must stay here."

She nodded encouragingly. "You're right. You must stay here for now. But I have been giving this some thought. I'm very good at thinking, Owen—a poisoner must be, for a single mistake can be deadly. I'm going to be honest with you, and I hope you will be honest with me in return. Your parents may die. If I can stop that from happening, I will. But the king does not trust them and he will test their loyalty. But know this, Owen. They did not abandon you. It was a difficult choice for them, but they did their best to protect their whole family. Including you. They thought you would be the safest at the palace if I were still here to care for you. And I will do everything within my power to help you. You see . . ." Her words halted, her voice becoming thick. She reached out and smoothed his hair, just as his mother used to do.

"I miss *Maman*," Owen sighed softly. Her shoulder looked soft.

"And I am certain she misses you terribly, Owen," she whispered. She reached up her gloved hand and dabbed it against the tip of his nose. "You are a darling little boy, Owen. So young. The king is wrong to keep you away from your parents."

Owen was getting tired, and he leaned against her arm, resting his head against her shoulder. "Can you really help me?" he asked hopefully.

She put her arm around him. "I think so, Owen. I'm working on a plan."

"Really?"

"Just the beginnings of one."

"Will you tell me?" he begged.

Hugging his shoulders, she planted a kiss on the top of his head. "Not yet. I have some ideas, but I need to ponder them more. Thoughts have a way of growing. If you put your mind to it, you can accomplish surprising things."

"Truly?"

"Truly, Owen. Most people suffer from a lack of imagination. They don't *dare* enough. But I do. I helped Eredur become king. Both times." She nudged his arm. "The reason most people don't arrive at a destination is they never embark. They think of all the reasons why they *can't* do it, so they don't even try."

"I *thought* I could escape," Owen said dejectedly. "I went to the sanctuary, but the king . . . he tricked me into coming out."

He heard a silvery laugh at that. "Oh yes, he did indeed! The king is *Fountain-blessed*, Owen. Do you know what that is?"

He scrunched up his nose in surprise. "He *is*? I've never met one before, but in the stories they are like heroes. The king . . . isn't like that."

She hugged him again, as if she were very much enjoying sitting next to him. "Not exactly, Owen. You know how every baby is taken to a sanctuary so the deconeus can bathe his head with fountain water? That's called the water rite. It marks a *hope* that the child will be Fountain-blessed. But very few are. Only one child in a thousand is Fountain-blessed."

He turned and looked at her, gazing up at her pretty face. "I heard Monah talking about it. She said a man who made bread was Fountain-blessed."

"From Pisan, yes. I heard about him. I know you've heard some of this before, but it will be easier to explain if I start at the beginning. Let me tell you about the true nature of the Fountain. The Fountain is all around us. It's like a rushing of waters that you can feel but not hear. Have you ever lay down and shut your eyes and felt like you were . . . drifting?"

Owen nodded energetically.

"When someone is Fountain-blessed, they can gather the energy of the Fountain. Like filling a cup with water. Then they can use that power to do something. Something amazing! King Severn's power is in his voice. When he uses the magic of the Fountain, when he speaks to you and touches you, he can make you believe what he is saying is true. But as I said, everyone who is Fountain-blessed needs to somehow draw in the magic. The king has an unusual way of filling his cup. Have you noticed it?"

Owen stared at her in surprise and tilted his head. "Is it his dagger? He's always slamming it."

Ankarette smiled fondly. "No . . . that's just a nervous habit. He's restless. Think about his words. He has power with his words."

Owen frowned, deep in thought. "He's always angry, except with the princess."

"I told you that you were clever." She brought her hands together under her chin. "There is power in words, Owen. So much power. When you tell your mother you love her, it makes her feel warm and happy. If you tell her that you *hate* her," her voice became darker, crueler, as one of her hands reached away from her mouth and tapped his chest. "That carries hurt."

Her voice softened again and she settled her hands in her lap. "The king gains his power through insulting others. You cannot be in a room with him without experiencing it. That is how he draws in the Fountain's magic. Every insult, every cutting word, adds a drop to his cup. When it is full, he can use the magic of the Fountain against someone. An individual. And they will believe whatever he says, no matter how outlandish. He did not always realize he was Fountain-blessed. I think he discovered it almost by accident. Once he knew it, he began to use it to make himself king. I warned his brother about it, but he would not listen to me. He thought his brother was loyal."

Owen looked at her curiously. "He doesn't insult Princess Elyse."

Ankarette nodded. "You are right. And observant. I need some time to work out my plan, but if you would like, I will come visit you tomorrow and we can talk again." She paused before continuing. "I've been watching over you since you arrived, Owen. I like playing with your tiles too. Now, you should be abed by this hour." She mussed up his hair again, then her fingers slowed and gently played with some of the feathery tufts.

"How do you know so much about it? About what it feels like? Are you . . . are you Fountain-blessed, Ankarette?" he asked.

She kept her eyes on his hair and then nodded once. "That is another reason the king wants to kill me," she said. "Why don't you head to bed?"

"You are going back to the tower?" he asked.

She nodded with a sad smile. "I must stay hidden during the day," she said. "I do much of my work at night when everyone is asleep."

"Can I see your tower?" he asked, grabbing her hands and squeezing them.

"Of course," she agreed. "If you promise to tell no one how to get up there."

"I promise!"

She patted his cheek tenderly. "There are secret passages throughout the palace," she confided conspiratorially. "I can show you all of them. Would you like that, Owen?"

He wrapped his arms around her waist and hugged her tightly, enjoying her warmth. It had been so long since he had hugged anyone.

Ankarette was startled by his sudden show of affection, but she wrapped her arms around him as well and kissed the top of his tangled hair again.

"I won't let him hurt you," she promised. "Not as he did the others."

"Who?" Owen asked, tilting his face up to her.

"His brother's sons," she answered gravely, and he could see the sadness in her eyes once more.

♦ ♦ ♦

There is a precept amongst us in the Espion. We glory in the tales of our exploits, of our manipulations. We especially love to trick each other. You see, it is double pleasure to deceive the deceiver.

—Dominic Mancini, Espion of the Palace Kitchen

♦ ♦ ♦

CHAPTER TWELVE

Poisoner

Ankarette Tryneowy lived in the highest tower of the palace of King-fountain. As Owen climbed the steps with her, hand in hand, she told him how she was able to keep her presence secret. No servants went to her tower. The butler's servants believed the castle almoner maintained it. The almoner was told that the butler's staff serviced it. The master carpenter thought it was scheduled to be remodeled as soon as the funds became available. It was protected by a web of lies and deceptions so subtle that everyone had a belief about the tower that was just not true. One of the few people who did know the truth, Ankarette explained, was the cook, Liona, who always set aside a tray of food each night.

Not even Eredur's queen knew where the poisoner dwelled.

The stairs were a difficult climb for Owen, and he was breathing hard as they huffed up the narrow tower well the following night, his guide holding a single candle to light the way. His forehead was plastered with sweat by the time they reached the top.

"It's so small," Owen said, panting, after she welcomed him to her private domain.

Most of the space was occupied by a small canopied bed swathed with thick velvet curtains to help her sleep in the daylight. The blankets were furs and Owen went to them and rubbed his hands against their softness. There was a small table topped with a globe, a set of scales, and several vials and tubes containing various potions and concoctions. His eyes widened when he saw them, but he kept his distance. Throughout the room, there were pestles and mortars of various sizes, some on the floor, some on the windowsills. These made him nervous, so he looked away. His gaze fell on a fancy embroidered curtain, and he walked up to it for a better look.

"This is pretty," he said as he touched it reverently.

"Thank you. I made it," Ankarette said. She went to the table with the potions and began mixing up a cup of tea.

"How?" he asked in amazement, but she did not answer as she worked on the drink. Then his eyes narrowed in on the curtains on the bed, done in darker threads, and shot down to the similarly designed carpet. Everything in the room, from the table to the bookshelves, had little ornamented embroideries.

"You did all of these?" Owen declared. His mother and sisters did sewing, but nothing this fancy.

"I like embroidery," she said modestly. "That is my gift. I never tire of it. You like to stack tiles, true?"

He nodded, touching the fringe of a shawl draped over the only chair in the room.

"I normally don't receive visitors," she said. "You are the first to have been in my tower in many years. Here, drink this. It will help with your wheezing. Your lungs are weak and in need of some medicine."

He eyed the cup suspiciously but it smelled fragrant and when he tasted it, he could tell she had added honey. It had a strange flavor, but not unpleasant. As he sipped, his eyes went hungrily to the Wizr board sitting on a small wooden pedestal. The pieces were carved out of alabaster . . . purple and white, with matching squares. The set filled the small round table.

"Do you play Wizr?"

Owen nodded eagerly. "I always used to watch my brothers play. But I like to play as well."

"Would you like to play it with me?"

"Yes!" Owen said, slurping down the rest of the tea. "It's normally black and white. This one is purple. I want to be purple."

"I like to play white," she said. She went over and knelt on the rug by the pedestal and board.

"How do you play it by yourself?" Owen asked curiously, studying the board.

Ankarette moved the first piece. Owen followed, using his normal pattern of moving the middle pieces first. She captured his king in four moves.

Owen's eyes stared at the board, then at her. "How . . . how did you do that so quickly?"

Ankarette smiled knowingly. "I will teach you. There are many strategies in Wizr. If you know them, they can help you win quickly. Would you like to learn them?"

Owen nodded with enthusiasm.

As they reset the few pieces, she asked him another question. "Owen . . . are you afraid of me because I'm a poisoner?"

His head whipped up and he looked at her, his eyes betraying his emotions. He nodded, but did not say anything.

"Owen," she said softly, putting the last piece in its place. "Please understand. I only poison *dangerous* people. And only when it becomes absolutely necessary. I would be a little afraid if I were in your place. But I wanted to show you my tower so you would see that being a poisoner is a very *small* part of who I am. It is one way I serve the queen, yes, but I also serve her by giving her advice and counsel. When I was trained as a poisoner, I was also trained as a midwife. So part of my work involves death and another part involves . . . life." She gave him a meaningful look he didn't understand. Then she brushed her hands together. "I also try to remove threats to the kingdom without resorting to poison. I like to make beautiful things. I do a lot of . . . *thinking* . . . while I stitch. My mind goes this way and that, studying a situation from many angles. That's why I am very good at Wizr."

She put her hands down in her lap. "I want to help you, Owen. But if I am to help you, I need to trust you, and you need to trust me. I brought you to my tower. If you told anyone that I lived up here, the king would send soldiers to kill me."

Owen gasped, feeling a prickle of unease go down his back. He wouldn't do that!

She nodded seriously. "So you see . . . I am trusting *you*. But that is what friends do, Owen. I want to be your friend. Not just because the queen told me to help you, but also because I like you. I will do my best to come up with a plan to keep you safe. I will teach you Wizr. I will teach you all about poisons, so you will know by smell if something is harmful. I will give you potions that will help you breathe better and make you stronger. But Owen, I will never ask you to poison the king or anyone else. That would be wrong of me, wouldn't it?"

Owen nodded vigorously, his eyes wide.

"The queen has not asked me to harm the king, even though he is a dangerous man. He is the last heir of the Argentine family. If he dies, there will be terrible calamity. And Dunsdworth can't inherit because his father was guilty of treason."

"What did he do?" Owen asked with eagerness.

She shook her head. "There is too much to explain for me to tell you everything in one night. We have time, Owen, you and I. Tomorrow, we shall talk again. We will need others to help us if we are to succeed. Liona and Drew will help. I'll speak to them tomorrow, but we will need others to join us as well. You know Dominic Mancini, who stays in the kitchen? He could be a good helper."

Owen gave her a little frown. "But he works for the king!"

She smiled. "He pretends to. He really works for someone else and is spying for them also. I think I can persuade him to be an ally. I can be very convincing. But your role is the most important, Owen. You will need to learn courage. You will need to do things you think are impossible. I believe you can."

She reached out and smoothed his hair, giving him a warm smile. Owen swallowed as he looked into her eyes. Suddenly she winced like the king did when he moved his leg a certain way, but she did not drop the smile.

"Are you sick?" Owen asked.

"Tired," she said. "Go back down to the kitchen. I will meet you there again tomorrow night. Will you do that for me, Owen? I cannot . . . make it back down the steps right now."

He nodded, staring at the little room in wonder again. He was eager to return.

"This is our secret place," Ankarette whispered.

Owen went to the small doorway. "I won't tell anyone. I promise. Can I take the candle?"

She nodded. "Leave it on the table by the tray of food Liona left for me. Blow it out, Owen, when you get downstairs. It was nice seeing you—"

She halted, her words falling into silence. Owen stared at her a moment longer, waiting for her to say more. He had the distinct impression that she was going to say that they had met before, but he would never have forgotten someone like Ankarette.

◆ ◆ ◆

It was midbite of a bowl of blueberry fool that I learned she's still alive. I almost choked. I was handed a note with instructions to wait in the kitchen until after dark. It bore Ratcliffe's seal, so I obeyed and helped myself to the sweet dessert as I waited. But the note was not from the odious Ratcliffe. It was from Ankarette Tryneowy. I jest not. By all accounts, this woman died eight years ago. I remember hearing of it and wondering at the audacity of the king's brother, Earl of Dunsworth, who would judicially murder his brother's poisoner, one of the Fountain-blessed, no less! You can imagine her demise caused no small shock among the Espion, both foreign and domestic. Some say Eredur had his brother killed because of Ankarette's death. I cannot tell you how delicious this is—the news, not the berry fool. She has promised to tell me her story. She has promised me information that cannot be bought, traded, or stolen. She is the penultimate trickster. The cunning hand. The queen of deception. And she is now my teacher. I think I'll take another helping.

—Dominic Mancini, Espion of the Palace Kitchen

◆ ◆ ◆

CHAPTER THIRTEEN

Broken Vows

Owen's world changed the night he met Ankarette Tryneowy. He was part of a secret now—a secret so vast and interesting that he could hardly sleep. Over the nights that followed, she taught him about the secret tunnels and passageways that lined each of the palace's rooms. How to find the hidden latches that would open a door concealed by a painting. How to slip away a panel of wood so he could see and hear what happened in the adjacent room. She taught him how to walk quietly. How to hold perfectly still. She taught him the secrets of torchlight and shadows and how the human eye adjusts to both.

Owen, being an eager learner, soaked it all up.

When Ankarette wanted to visit him during the day, she would slip something into Jewel's tea that would send the woman off into a loud snoring fit. They would always return from their outings well before she snorted herself awake, none the wiser.

The secret gave Owen a sense of power and purpose. When the king jabbed his dagger in his hilt or mocked Owen during the meal, he would look back and think, *If only you knew what I know. If only you saw what I did in your palace.*

The palace was an intricate maze of corridors and towers. But beyond the well-kept halls where everyone walked and ate and slept, there was an underworld teeming with dark hidden places. Places that smelled like musty barrels of wine. Places where the guardsmen diced and drank with the servants and stayed out of Berwick's sight. Owen watched Dickon Ratcliffe's Espion as they boasted and bragged about their exploits when they came in from assignments. As they mocked Ratcliffe behind his back and scorned him for always heaping the credit for their work on himself.

Ankarette did not say much. She would take Owen to new places and let him wander around and explore while she looked on with a smile of affection and warmth and answered his questions. Sometimes she would ask him a question, something to make him think, and think hard. Only after he had exhausted his brain would she provide the clues he needed to teach himself the answer.

"Ankarette?" he asked her one day, as they were playing a round of Wizr at the table in her tower room. She had already taught him the simple ways to defeat any opponent who was untrained. Their games were lasting longer now, but he had never come close to winning yet. "What is the most *useful* thing I need to learn? Is it poisons? When are we starting that?"

She was about to move her next piece, but she lowered her hand into her lap instead. "What do you think the most useful thing is, Owen?"

He scrunched up his brow. "I don't want to kill anyone," he said.

She gave him a patient look and said nothing, letting him tease it out in his own mind.

"There is more useful knowledge than poisons," she said encouragingly.

He frowned, screwing up his nose. "I think it might be knowing *when* to use poison," he said.

"Tell me what you mean?" she asked.

"Well, you said that you only use poison if other things don't work. So, isn't it most important for a person to be able to tell whether a situation is hopeless or not? Like what you did with Mancini. You knew you could trust him to help you."

Ankarette laughed softly. "I wouldn't go *that* far."

"But you trusted him enough to tell him you didn't die. And he's part of the Espion!"

"Many of the Espion know about me," Ankarette said. "He didn't. By giving him that secret, I gave him power. That's what he craves more than anything, so I knew it would make him a valuable tool."

"He craves muffins more than power," Owen said disdainfully.

She smiled again and tousled his mousy hair. "He does indeed. Did I answer your question?"

Owen frowned. "Not really. You're pretty good at *not* answering questions."

"Let me put it another way. Let's talk about it like stacking tiles. You build a tower out of tiles and then you want to knock it down. If you set the tiles too far from the tower, it won't work."

Owen looked at her curiously. "Well, the tower needs to have a weakness. You have to hit it at the right angle to make the tiles fall. If you hit it the other way, nothing will happen."

"Yes, exactly. You have to hit it where it will fall. That's what I did with Mancini. I didn't offer him food. He has *plenty* of that! I offered him knowledge. Secrets." She reached her hand out and moved the next piece, winning the game of Wizr.

Owen scowled. He had already planned his next two moves and had not seen it coming. He didn't think he was ever going to win against her.

"But how did you *know* that?" he pressed. "How did you know that's what he wanted?"

Ankarette folded her hands in her lap. She was quiet for a moment. Sometimes he could tell she was in pain, but this was not one of those moments. Her pain usually started with tightness around her eyes, then her breathing would change and she would tell him it was time to go.

"Owen," she said softly, peering into his eyes. "The most important thing you can learn is discernment. Have you heard that word before?"

He shook his head no.

"It is the ability to judge well. It means not just seeing an action, but the reasons *behind* the action. Many people say things they do not believe. They lie and deceive. They may act one way in public and another in private."

Owen stared at her, still confused. "I don't understand."

"This is hard enough to explain to adults, Owen. It is especially difficult to explain to children because you are so young and haven't experienced much yet. I'll try to help you. You like to talk. You like to ask questions. You like to laugh. But when you are in the presence of King Severn, your voice goes down to a tiny squeak and you cannot speak. It's because he makes you anxious and uncomfortable. Right?"

He nodded.

"If I judged you by how you are in the king's presence, I would not see the whole picture of you. By spending time with you, I've gotten to know you better. I have learned what you are really like. The ability to do this quickly is called discernment. It is priceless, Owen. Let me tell you a story to show you why."

No longer upset about losing the game, he wriggled his finger in his ear to stop an itch, then stared at her eagerly. He loved hearing her stories, for they were rare.

"There was a king . . . almost a century ago. He stole the crown from his cousin."

"Why did he do that?" Owen asked, curious.

"Because the king banished him for having an argument. He was a duke, just like your father. And he had an argument with another man, an earl. They would not resolve it, so the king banished them both. One he banished forever. The other he banished for a time. Then the king needed some money and he stole it from the banished duke's estate. The one who was going to come back in time."

Owen scrunched up his face. "That's not fair!"

Ankarette smiled. "You're right. It wasn't. And the king ended up losing his crown to the duke because of it. One day, years later, some of the new king's men began to rebel against him. They created an army to depose him."

"Why? Had the king done something to them?"

"Yes, but it wasn't over money. What happened was he did not show them enough gratitude. People can be strange sometimes, Owen. They will rebel for small reasons. The king was old and sick at the time, so he could not lead his armies anymore. He sent one of his sons to lead it in his place. When his son arrived, the leaders of the rebels tried to talk to him first in the hopes of avoiding a battle, which would have killed many people on both sides. The prince listened to their complaints and made promises in his father's name. He told them that if they disbanded the army, they would be heard and their problems would be solved. The rebels listened . . . and they believed him because he swore an oath of honor in the king's name. The young prince suggested that both armies disband at the same time. The soldiers would go home and no one would be injured or killed. Do you know what happened next, Owen?"

"No," he said. He had never heard this story before.

"The prince sent his captain out, but he did not disband his army. They waited until the other army was disbanded and the soldiers were leaving. Then they hunted down what remained of the rebels and started killing them as they escaped. The leaders were all taken to the river and drowned because they were wearing heavy armor. This is a sad story, is it not, Owen?"

Owen's heart had filled with horror. "But . . . but . . . the prince *lied!*"

Ankarette nodded, her expression sad. "That is the way of princes and power, Owen. That is the nature of the kingdom of Ceredigion. In truth, it is the nature and disposition of *most* men. So think on this. If you were one of the rebel leaders and the prince promised you forgiveness and reward, it would matter, very much, if you had *discernment*. He needed to make a decision based on what type of man he believed the prince to be. Was he a man of honor? Or was he willing to say anything, *do* anything to help his father keep his crown?" She folded her hands together. "That is why discernment is the most important thing you can learn, Owen. It takes time and experience. Sadly, one wrong judgment can lead to . . . well, you *heard* the end of the story."

Owen had no doubt that King Severn was like the prince who had so ruthlessly killed his enemies. He had made Owen promises and promptly broken them. He would say or do anything to maintain his power. Maybe that's what Ankarette was trying to teach him.

She smoothed her silk skirts. "Why don't you go back? Jewel will awaken soon and then you can have some supper. I hope to see you later tonight."

He smiled and rose, feeling little tingles in his feet from the way he had been sitting. He gave her a hug—she liked it when he did—and she patted his back and kissed his cheek.

"You really are a darling little boy," she whispered, grazing her finger down his cheek.

"Have you thought of a way yet?" he pressed.

"No, but I have some ideas. I'll keep thinking as I work." She reached for her needles and embroidery.

Owen went back down the narrow stairwell and slipped down the secret corridors. He found Jewel in the room, still snoring softly. He waited a moment, listening to her breathing, and then grabbed a book and read it until she awakened with a fitful snort.

"I'm hungry," Owen said, slamming the book shut and putting it away. "I'll meet you at the kitchen."

Without waiting for her reply, he dashed out of the room, hearing her scold and chide him as he went. "Wait for my old bones, lad! Wait a moment! Owen Satchel, you get back here! Owen!"

As he rushed around the corner, he collided with Dunsdworth, who was coming the other way. The older boy grunted, "Watch where—oh, it's you! Kisky!" He seized Owen's arm, clearly intent on giving him bruises.

Owen, almost without thinking, grabbed Dunsdworth's little finger and yanked backward. It was something Ankarette had taught him about the body and its weak points. The little finger wasn't easy to grab, especially if someone was expecting it, but Dunsdworth wasn't. He yelped in pain and surprise and released his grip. Free, the wiry little boy started running toward the kitchen.

"You little *urchin*!" Dunsdworth bellowed, starting after him at a run.

Owen's stomach twisted with fear as he ran down the corridor, cursing himself for not having waited for Jewel. It was a long way to the kitchen, and Dunsdworth's legs were much longer.

Owen ducked around a side corridor. If he could reach the end without being seen, he could vanish through a secret door. The sound of his pursuer's boots grew louder.

"Come back here, little snot!"

Owen's feet were going so fast he almost wasn't touching the tiles. He could feel the vibrations of the pounding behind him. He wondered if he had enough time to trip the latch. But what if Dunsdworth saw him? How would he explain his secret knowledge?

Worry and fear mixed in his bowels.

Panicked with indecision, he veered around the corner and nearly slammed into someone. He caught himself just in time, but a firm and sturdy hand grabbed his shoulder. He twisted around in fear just as Dunsdworth came barreling around the corner, his face twisted with rage.

"Hold there!" Duke Horwath scolded. "Look at you two, racing about."

Dunsdworth's face was red and he was panting. "Lord Horwath!" he stammered as he stumbled to a stop. "I was . . . just . . . trying to catch him . . . he stole something from me."

Horwath's eyes narrowed suspiciously. It was obvious he didn't believe it for a moment. "Get you gone," he snarled at Dunsdworth. The lad's ruddy cheeks paled and he turned on his heel and fled.

Owen had not seen the duke for weeks, and had not expected him to return to Kingfountain so soon. He tried to stammer out his thanks, but his tongue swelled in his mouth and he could say nothing. Frustrated with himself, he wiped sweat from his forehead.

"I just came from the kitchen," the duke said gravely. "I was surprised you weren't there. Everyone says that's your favorite haunt."

Owen bobbed his head, but he still couldn't speak. His jaw was locked and he had no key to open it.

"I brought someone to be a playmate for you. I brought my granddaughter from the North with me."

Horwath's mouth bent into an affectionate smile.

Oh no, Owen thought darkly.

♦ ♦ ♦

I have learned a great deal from Ankarette so far. In return, she asks me for information that is circulating among the Espion. Trivial things, really. She does not want any information that would jeopardize my position. It seems she has been away from court events for several years. I'm curious as to why she's making an appearance now. Perhaps she intends to poison the king. That would not be a loss, and the people would thank her for it. He may be beloved in the North, but the people of Kingfountain believe he's a monster. Ankarette wants gossip about the noble families. Like the Duke of Kiskaddon, for example. I told her the king is using the Espion to trick Kiskaddon into betraying himself by revealing his involvement with the enemy at Ambion Hill. Little things like that. Oh, and we have a newcomer to the kitchen now. Horwath's granddaughter. She's a water sprite if ever there was one! Very obnoxious, never stops talking. It's going to be a pleasure tormenting her.

—Dominic Mancini, Espion of the Palace Kitchen

♦ ♦ ♦

CHAPTER FOURTEEN

Elysabeth Victoria Mortimer

Owen knew he was in trouble when the duke's granddaughter squealed upon seeing him for the first time. Loud noises always rattled the young boy, and she was a force of nature in her own right. The delighted squeal was followed by a hurricane of words, touches, and hugs that nearly made Owen flee the kitchen for his life.

"Oh, it's you! It's Owen! I've heard so much about you that I already feel I know you. Aren't you just the most adorable thing ever! I *love* your hair! Grandpapa, you didn't tell me about how *cute* he is! He's absolutely adorable. Owen, we are going to be the best of friends. Look, we are even the same height! I had imagined you would be shorter than me for some reason. But look, our noses almost touch!"

Owen stood straight as an arrow, feeling overwhelmed by the intensity of the girl. She was holding his hand one second, then mussing his hair the next, then tugging him to stand in front of her, comparing heights.

How to describe the whirlwind?

It was true, the duke's granddaughter was his own height. Her hair, gathered behind a jeweled headband that glinted, was a darker brown than Owen's, and went just past her shoulders. She wore a velvet dress the color of red wine that had sable fur at the wrists and the neck. She could hardly hold still, and he noticed that she wore a sturdy pair of leather boots beneath her hem that swished and swayed as she moved.

She noticed him looking at her feet and grinned, hiking up her skirts. "Do you like my boots? I love these boots! Look at all the buckles and straps. You could try and pull these off, but it wouldn't work. These are my exploring boots. Do you like to climb trees and rocks? I love to climb! There isn't any snow down here at Kingfountain, but up in the North, there is so much snow! These boots keep me warm, but they are also good for tromping in the snow. You don't talk very much, Owen, do you? Grandpapa said you were shy, didn't you, Grandpapa! That's okay, but I've just been so anxious to meet you!" She wrung his hand and nearly yanked it loose with her shakes.

"Give the poor dear a chance to breathe, child!" Liona said with a soft chuckle. "Master Owen, this is Lady Mortimer."

The young girl looked affronted. "No one calls me that!" she chided sweetly. "My name is Elysabeth *Victoria* Mortimer, thank you."

Owen was still reeling from the introduction. He could not decide what color the girl's eyes were. First of all, she did not hold still long enough for him to tell, but they were either blue or gray. Or maybe green. But she had an expressive smile that crinkled around her eyes.

"We'll have so much fun, Owen!" she said, twisting her hands together in delight. "I'm going to live here too for a while. That's what my grandpapa says! You and I will play together and wander the castle together." She gazed up at the rafters, looking all around. "There are so many places to hide!"

"I'll leave you two alone to get acquainted," the duke said, before vanishing from the kitchen.

"My dear young lady," interrupted a sour voice from nearby. It was Mancini, looking more peevish than usual. "You are taking all the air out of the room. Kindly save some for the rest of us!"

Her eyes narrowed when she looked at the huge man on the chair. She did not wilt at all in the face of his rebuke. In fact, it made her a little stern. "You are a fat man," she said decidedly.

Mancini chortled with surprise. "You noticed that all on your own, did you?"

"I spoke the truth," the girl said. "You are the biggest man I have ever seen! In the North, there are animals that are so fat they can only move underwater. They have huge tusks! I've seen the pelts, but I've never seen a real one."

Mancini stared at her in amazement. "What does that have to do with anything?"

"Nothing. You just reminded me is all."

"You're as chatty as a little magpie," Mancini growled. "Do you do this all day or just in the mornings and evenings when people are trying to sleep?"

"I like to talk," she replied eagerly. "I talk in my sleep too. That's what my governess tells me. I can't stop." Then she turned away from Mancini, not giving him another look, and returned her focus to Owen, who was trying to sneak into the corner to find his box of tiles. He was amazed by her fearlessness, but he found himself wondering how she would fare at breakfast with the king. Owen imagined her prattling would quickly earn the king's scorn. His satchel was waiting on the bench, so he set it in the corner and sat down to open the box of tiles.

She followed him and knelt on the floor beside him.

"What are you doing?" she asked him quizzically.

"Owen likes to put them in rows and then knock them down," Liona explained. "He's pretty quiet, Lady Mortimer."

The girl looked at Liona. "Call me Elysabeth *Victoria* Mortimer, please."

"Bless me, child, but that's a mouthful!"

"But it's my name," the girl repeated in a kind way. "I love my name. I love Owen's name too. Owen Kiskaddon. Owen Kiskaddon." She sighed. "It's like 'kiss.' I love saying it!"

Owen shuddered, believing Elysabeth *Victoria* Mortimer was perhaps the strangest and most annoying individual he had ever met. She tried to peer at the box of tiles over his shoulder, so he turned to block her view. He needed to think. If she had come to the palace to be his companion, when would he be able to see Ankarette Tryneowy and learn his lessons? He loved having a secret, and he was absolutely determined to keep it from this *girl*.

He began to lay the tiles, feeling his ears burn hot from the power of the girl's gaze. She craned her neck to look around him, and he kept turning more to block her view, feeling possessive of the tiles and a bit annoyed at her.

After he set up his first row, which looked a bit haphazard because of his discomfort and anxiety, she changed her position and came around in front of him to get an unobstructed view. He ground his teeth and glared at her.

"This is interesting," she whispered, putting her chin on her hands, her elbows on her knees. She grew quiet as she watched him place another row.

"Let me help you, it'll go faster," she said, reaching toward the box. Their hands collided over a tile. Instead of grabbing it, she seized his hand and gave him a sly smile. "We're going to be such friends!" she gushed in a half whisper.

"I don't need help," Owen said thickly, not daring to look her full in the face.

Her eyes widened with surprise, then her startled expression changed into a smile. "All right. I'll just watch then." She planted her chin again and watched, mesmerized, as he continued stacking the tiles.

She was quiet now. That was good. At first he had worried she would chatter so much he wouldn't be able to concentrate. He glanced up once or twice and noticed a light dusting of freckles across the bridge of her nose. The bustle of the kitchen continued around them, and soon Owen could not hear anything—all the background sounds combined into a gentle lull as he lost himself in the tiles once again. Elysabeth Victoria Mortimer was silent and watchful, staring at the intricate arrangements with utter fascination.

He completed the design and sat back on his heels, gazing at it.

"It's amazing, Owen!" the girl said with wide eyes. "What happens next? What happens when you're through?"

He had not solved his problem yet. He wanted to talk to Ankarette and get her advice. She was quiet and subdued, more of a listener than a talker—the total opposite of this wild young thing kneeling in front of him. He wondered what the queen's poisoner would say about Elysabeth Victoria Mortimer. And what the girl would say if she knew who lived in the knifelike tower.

"Push that one," Owen said, pointing to the tile that would start toppling the others.

Her eyes gleamed with eagerness. "Me? That's so sweet of you! You push it over . . . just like . . . this?" She gave the tile a light little tap and it fell over and made a clickety-clack that continued as all the pieces spilled down.

The girl gave a tinkling, silvery laugh of pure delight that was almost pleasant to Owen's ears. Crushing her hands together against her chest, she stared at the collapsed tiles and then shifted her gaze to him.

"I love it! That was so beautiful! How did you . . . ? I love it, Owen! I love it! You are so interesting. I knew you would be. I want to see it again. You must build it again! Let me help clear the space."

Putting away the tiles was Owen's least favorite part, and Elysabeth Victoria Mortimer was only too eager to assist. In moments, the tiles were back in the box and he had started on another design.

"Part of your hair is white," she said suddenly, her fingers tickling his mussy hair. "Why is that? Is it paint?"

He looked at her in annoyance and shook his head.

"You came that way?" she pressed, staring at the little tufts of hair. "That's wonderful. It's like that part of your head is an old man already. You must be really smart then. I love the kitchen. It smells so good in here. Fresh bread out of the oven is divine." She leaned back a bit, sighing contentedly.

"My papa is dead," she said after a while. She reached out and took a tile and examined it with her fingers. "I'm not really sure what it means, but he's not coming back. Mama can't stop crying. I loved Papa. He was so kind to me. He gave me ponies and dresses. And these boots! It's not your fault he died, Owen. I'm not angry at *your* papa."

Owen looked at her, feeling nervous. "My brother . . . died," he said softly.

She nodded matter-of-factly. "He was killed for treason. But that's not your fault either. My grandpapa felt sorry for you. He said you were taken from your family. You were all alone and too shy to talk." She reached out and touched his knee. "We're going to be friends. I like you very much. You are *adorable*!"

Owen wasn't sure how he felt yet, but his ears were burning again.

CHAPTER FIFTEEN

Ankarette's Stratagem

Elysabeth Victoria Mortimer's first breakfast with the king went surprisingly well, much to Owen's chagrin. He had wondered how she would take his taunts and temper. She was absolutely fearless. That was the only word to properly describe her. She loved the idea of picking from all the dishes and gobbled up a hearty breakfast while still managing to talk between mouthfuls. She was eager to meet the king and suggested, rather boldly, that he needed to put a large fountain in the great hall, one with glass walls, and fill it with giant fish so that they could watch them swim while they ate.

Owen was not certain how the king would react to her demands. King Severn looked at her with half annoyance, half amusement and offered her a view of the royal fish pond to placate her. She agreed enthusiastically and rushed over to Owen to share the good news.

In truth, Elysabeth Victoria Mortimer seemed as comfortable in the great hall as if she had lived there her entire life. She wore a new dress. Each day she had a new one. This one was black and silver. Owen stared at her with budding respect, but it frustrated him that he did not share her courage. Why must strangers always leave him so tongue-tied and ashamed? He had always been that way and did not know why.

"And what do *you* think, Master Owen?" the king suddenly said at his ear. "Do you want the hall full of fish?"

Owen's muscles locked up and he felt a coldness shoot through him at being caught off guard. A pit of fear opened up inside him, swallowing everything before it. He could not even stammer a reply. He was powerless to say anything.

The king snorted and then walked away, unsheathing and jamming his dagger as he went.

Owen felt his knees start to buckle and the urge to cry was almost overpowering. Feeling humiliated, he cast his eyes down. Someone approached and he felt a hand on his shoulder. He looked up and saw Duke Horwath looking at him sympathetically. He did not say anything, but his touch was comforting. Then he walked after the king and began speaking to him in a low voice. Owen could not hear their discussion, but he could have sworn he heard the duke say "Tatton Hall" before they were both out of earshot.

Later in the afternoon, Owen was building with his tiles, constructing a tower that was taller than those he usually made. It had tumbled a few times, annoying him, but he continued to work on it. Elysabeth Victoria Mortimer lay on her stomach, playing with several pieces of tile and talking about something to which Owen did not pay much mind as he concentrated on the tower. The kitchen bustled pleasantly, and he could smell the delightful fragrance of a pie cooking in the ovens, making his mouth water. Liona made the best crusts he had ever tasted, and he had been tempted more than once to eat the ring of crispy dough without touching the middle part.

"Well?" the Mortimer girl asked again, and Owen glanced over at where she lay looking up at him. He had started calling her the Mortimer girl in his mind because her name was so long.

He was a little annoyed that she now expected a partner in the conversation. She had been doing so well at it by herself. "What?" he asked.

"When we get *married*, do you want to live in the North or in the West?"

He stared at her in shock. "We're getting married?"

"Of course we are. I think we should live in the North. I love the snow. There are mountains, Owen, mountains so huge they block out the sun until midday. There is always snow up there. There are canyons and rivers and waterfalls." She sighed dreamily. "The North is the best place in the world. I would live in the West, if you insisted. But I would be sad."

"*Why* are we getting married?"

She set down the tiles. "You have to get married *someday*, Owen. Don't be ridiculous."

"I know that, but . . ."

"Everyone has to get married. Even the *king* got married, all bent as he is. His wife was from the North, you know, and she was *lovely*. I'm so sad she died. She used to braid my hair. The prince was ten when he died of a fever. That's only two years older than us. I thought I might marry *him* someday." She shook her head. "I like you better."

"But . . ."

"Really, Owen Kiskaddon, it's not difficult to answer! The North or the West? You must learn to make decisions. I think we'll live in the North first, and then the West. That way, you can choose which you like better. I think I'll always like the North better. But I haven't lived in the West before." There was a dreamy look in her strange-colored eyes as she gazed at the tiles spread out on the floor in front of her. In the light, they were looking greener. It's like they had started off deciding to be blue, then changed their mind and turned gray, and then switched to green just at the very end, around the fringe of her inky black pupils. That was so like her!

"I'm not getting married," Owen said forcefully.

She set down the tiles and looked at him. "Everyone gets married."

"The prince didn't. He died."

"You're not going to die, Owen. The prince was always coughing. I've never heard you cough. You're not sickly at all."

Ankarette's potions had been helping him breathe better. But he knew something the Mortimer girl didn't. Owen looked down at his lap. "The king wants to kill me."

She sat up quickly, her face growing pale with concern. "No, he doesn't. That's the silliest thought I ever heard."

Owen was feeling hot again, his ears burning. She was looking at him with concern and sympathy. She edged closer. "Why would you think something like that?" she whispered.

"I'm his hostage," Owen replied darkly. "That's why I'm here. If my parents do anything to spite him, he's going to kill me. He killed my brother already. It's true."

All the happiness drained from her face. In its place came an implacable anger. "Well, I won't let him do it. I think that's silly. No one kills a little child."

Owen was feeling a little annoyed. "He already has," he mumbled.

"What did you say?" she demanded.

"He has. Everyone knows about it. His brother had two sons. They were hostages, too. He killed them."

"It's not true," she said angrily. "Not everything that's whispered is true, Owen." She reached out and seized his hand, her fingers digging into his flesh. "Don't believe the lies."

Owen gave her a challenging look. "Your grandpapa knows." He glanced around the kitchen, a dark, brooding feeling enveloping him. "None of us are safe here."

Elysabeth Victoria Mortimer stood and marched out of the kitchen, tossing her dark hair back over her shoulder.

Owen was glad she was gone. Mostly.

♦ ♦ ♦

In the middle of the night, Owen was playing Wizr with Ankarette in the poisoner's tower and telling her everything he could about the castle's newest guest, the duke's outspoken granddaughter. Ankarette liked to talk as they played the game, which forced him to speak and think at the same time.

"I don't want to marry the Mortimer girl," Owen said, blocking one of Ankarette's attacks.

"She has decided opinions about many things," Ankarette said, with a hint of amusement in her voice. "It's a trait of those from the North. They tend to be outspoken."

"Her grandfather isn't," Owen said glumly. "He never talks at all." He grimaced when he realized her next move threatened him in two places at once. Since he would lose a piece regardless, he decided to sacrifice the lesser one. But he stopped himself before he made the move. Instead of responding to the threat, he positioned one of his pieces to threaten another one of hers.

"Well done, Owen," she praised. "Counter a threat with a threat. An excellent strategy. Horwath is loyal. He's not as outspoken here at court because this isn't his power base. If you were with him up in the North, there's a chance he would come across differently."

"That's where she says we're going to live when we get married," Owen said bleakly. He looked up at her face. "Can she force me to marry her?"

Ankarette pursed her lips. "No, Owen. It's normal for girls to think about marriage. She really won't have much choice in the matter at all. Girls seldom do."

That gave him some relief. It's not that he didn't *like* the Mortimer girl. But he thought it strange that she was so convinced it was going to happen when they had only just met.

"She is brave," Owen said, responding to her move to block him. Her next move won her the game. He loved Wizr and all the possibilities each game possessed. Even though he'd lost, Ankarette's praise had put him in a good mood, making him feel more generous toward the newcomer.

"She sounds like it. A fish pond in the great hall. What an amusing idea."

Owen helped to stack the pieces again in order. He liked doing that part almost as much as playing the game. There was something about the beginning of a Wizr game, when all the pieces were lined up properly. The world felt . . . *better*.

When he was done, he looked at Ankarette, watching the soft light of the candle play against her pretty face. "Do you think I should trust her?" he asked.

Ankarette considered it thoughtfully. "It's too soon to tell," she answered after a lengthy pause.

Owen thought so too. He had not known her long enough yet. Besides, sharing a secret with someone who so loved to talk would be risky. Owen said as much to Ankarette.

She shook her head. "Just because she talks more than you do, doesn't mean she can't be trusted. She just has a different personality. The question is whether she is trustworthy. And that, my dear Owen, will be determined over time. Who do you think her first loyalty is to?"

Owen perked up. "Her grandfather."

"And who is her grandfather's first loyalty to?" she asked, giving him a knowing smile.

Owen frowned. "The king."

"Best to keep that in mind then, Owen."

"Did the king kill his nephews?" he asked.

Ankarette looked at the floor. "I don't really think so," she answered. "But I was far away when it happened."

"But everyone says . . ." She lifted her gaze to meet his eyes, and his voice trailed off. He swallowed. "But everyone says he did it, so it must be true."

Ankarette smiled, but it wasn't a pleased smile. It was almost a smile of pain. "It's been my experience, Owen, that when everyone agrees on some point of fact, it tends to be the biggest deception of all." She reached out and tousled his hair. "Remember that. Never trust another person to do your thinking for you."

That sounded a little strange to Owen, but he accepted it.

"Do you have a plan yet, Ankarette?"

Her eyebrows lifted. "A plan to save you?"

He nodded eagerly.

She smoothed her skirts, sitting on her knees before him. The jewels of her necklace glimmered in the candlelight. He leaned forward a little, eagerly watching her face.

"I do have a little *stratagem*," she confided.

"What is that? Is it a new necklace?"

She laughed softly. "No, it's not a gem . . . well, in a way it is. It's a gem of an idea. A jewel of a thought. Rough, uncut, and unpolished. But all good ideas start out that way."

"Will you tell me?"

"I need to be careful, Owen. New ideas are delicate. They can be crushed easily. New ideas can be killed by a sneer or a yawn . . . or even a frown."

Owen was not sure what she meant by that. Perhaps reading his expression, she said, "Have you ever seen a seedling grow? A new flower? They are so small and delicate, but they become sturdier as they grow. The easiest time to pluck a weed is when it is little. New ideas can be that way."

"I see," Owen said. He was a little disappointed because he wanted to hear her plan, unfinished as it was.

"Let me tell you what I can," she said, assuaging him. "When you want to accomplish something, you should start out with what you want to achieve and then work backward. Staying alive isn't the goal. What I want to do is change the king's *feelings* about you. He won't want to destroy you if he thinks you are valuable. Like a gem."

Owen's face perked up at that. "Like a stratagem?"

She smiled. "Exactly. Who would be most valuable to a ruler? You already know this."

"Someone who is Fountain-blessed?" Owen answered, and she nodded enthusiastically.

"Yes, and loyal. My stratagem, Owen, is to trick the king into believing you are both."

That was the most brilliant idea he had ever heard. "I think I'd like to be Fountain-blessed," he said.

"I'm sure you would, and for all we know you might be, but most people do not exhibit that disposition until they are eleven or twelve years old at the *earliest*. That's when their gifts start getting noticed by others."

"I'm only eight," Owen said dejectedly.

"Hence why I'm still nurturing this thought. I don't have three years to spare. How does one persuade a cunning prince like Severn that a young boy is Fountain-blessed? I'm still working on it. Give me time." She winced, and though she would never say so, he knew she was in pain. "I'm feeling tired, Owen."

"I am too," he said, though he wasn't very tired at all. He gave her a hug, loving the soft silk feel of her dress against his cheek, her warmth and tenderness. She kissed his brow and sent him back through the tunnels to his room.

Owen's mind was full of wandering thoughts as he slipped down the stairs through the secret corridors leading to his room. He knew the way so well he could have made the journey blindfolded. He paused at a large painting, listening for the sound of footsteps, and heard nothing. The castle was asleep. He loved it that way. The rustle of tapestries, the shouting silence of the blackened halls, the deep shadows perfect for concealment. He did not even need a candle anymore as he stole spiderlike through the passages.

He opened the door of his room and immediately noticed the dim glow from a dying candle on a chest. Had he not doused his candle before leaving?

"Where have *you* been, Owen Kiskaddon?" someone asked in a conspiratorial whisper.

It was Elysabeth Victoria Mortimer, of course.

CHAPTER SIXTEEN
Loyalty Binds Me

"This is *my* room," Owen said in a challenging tone. The girl's eyes lit up mischievously.

"I know it's your room. Why weren't you in it? Where were you? Sneaking something from the kitchen?"

He shook his head and folded his arms. "Why are *you* sneaking around?"

"I hate sleeping," she confided. "It's so boring. Besides, I couldn't wait until morning to tell you."

"What?" he pressed, curious.

She leaned forward on her knees, her eyes almost silver in the darkness. "I spoke to Grandpapa. The king didn't kill his nephews. That's a lie. But he *is* responsible for their deaths. Only, it's not totally confirmed that they're dead. I'm a little confused on that part."

Owen scrunched up his nose. "That doesn't make any sense."

"You told me the king was going to kill you. You said he killed his nephews, but I know he didn't. Grandpapa would not have lied to me."

"He doesn't tell you everything," Owen said flatly. "He's a grown-up."

"He tells *me* everything," she said with a twinkle in her eye. "He's never lied to me. Ever. You know about the coins in the fountains? They don't grant wishes, Owen. That's silly. The sexton shovels them out. Grandpapa told me, and he even let me *watch*. I never throw coins in fountains to make a wish anymore. It's a silly tradition."

Owen frowned. "Just because he said that doesn't mean—"

"Yes, it does," she interrupted. "He doesn't *lie* to me. Here's what he said. I knew you'd want to know. There was confusion when the old king, Cousin Eredur, died. We were only six, Owen. Just babies. Now we're eight and we're more grown-up. My grandpapa said that one of the princes lived in the West. The other lived in Kingfountain. Uncle Severn was named as their protector. You know his badge, right?"

"The boar," Owen said, nodding. Just thinking about it made him want to shiver.

"The *white* boar," she corrected. "You know his motto—'Loyalty Binds Me.' His own brother trusted him with his sons. But the queen tried to steal them away. She summoned the son in the West back to Kingfountain and sent soldiers with him. When Severn went to meet the prince, the queen was planning to have her men ambush and kill him. You see, the queen's manor was on the way there. That's where the ambush was going to happen. But someone warned him."

Owen scratched the back of his head. He was still standing in the doorway. She sighed at him impatiently and waved for him to join her on the bed. He carefully shut the door and climbed up in front of her, kneeling like she was.

"Do you know who warned him?" Elysabeth Victoria Mortimer asked him archly. She had kept her voice low and conspiratorial.

Owen shrugged. "Ratcliffe?"

"No, no, no, Owen! Who was Severn's most trusted man? The one he executed for treason! This was *before* Ratcliffe."

Owen had no idea. "How do you know all this?"

"I *love* stories," she purred like a cat. "Not pretend stories. I love *true* stories. My grandpapa tells me all about them. He's so quiet, but he listens and he watches. He knows who to trust and who is lying. He listens *all* the time."

Owen wondered why the granddaughter didn't follow his example, but he kept that thought to himself.

She squeezed her knees, her eyes lit with excitement. "Lord Bletchley! Cousin Bletchley. He stood a good chance of being on the throne himself. King Eredur never trusted him, but Severn did because he was the one who warned him about the trap. They grabbed the prince as he was going to Kingfountain . . . on the *very same road* you traveled to get here. Isn't this exciting?"

He was more confused than excited, but he did not want to dampen her enthusiasm. "So they grabbed the prince."

"Exactly! That's why the queen went to Our Lady. Her trap failed and she feared Severn's revenge. She stayed in sanctuary and let her other son out. Everyone knows she has stayed in sanctuary so long because she's still afraid of his revenge. The two hate each other."

"I've met her," Owen said softly, rubbing his chin. He would have to ask Ankarette about this.

"Really?" she asked, almost shrilly, grabbing both of his hands and squeezing them hard. He yanked them away.

"I snuck away from the palace," he said. "I went to Our Lady to escape."

Her mouth formed a big O of surprise and she sat up straight, as if all the fragments of a broken jug were coming together in her mind. The look she gave him transformed from eagerness to newfound admiration.

"You didn't!" she whispered in awe.

Owen nodded. "I snuck out of the porter door in the wall and walked there. Ratcliffe caught me because Mancini told him I was there. I don't like Mancini much."

"He's a spy, but he's not very good," she replied in agreement. "So you met her! They say she uses witchery to stay young, but I don't believe any of that stuff. Was she pretty?"

Owen felt a little uncomfortable. "I think so. I don't know."

She waved aside his response. "That's amazing, Owen—you are so brave! I thought you would be too scared to try something like that. So you like to sneak around, too?" Her choice of words implied that she did as well.

He nodded shyly.

She started shaking her hands around excitedly. "We're going to have so much fun together! There's a secret part of the grounds. The cistern. Have you found it yet?"

He stared at her in surprise. "What's a cistern?"

She grinned. "It's like a well, except it catches rainwater from the clouds, not from underground streams. Grandpapa showed me the wall blocking it. He said it's the only place I can't go. Which makes me want to go there even more!"

"Won't we get in trouble?" Owen asked.

She waved a hand dismissively. "I sneak around all the time. So I have to tell you the story of Bletchley. Don't you just *hate* his name? Bletchley. It's like you're throwing up. If your family name was Bletchley, I wouldn't marry you. Kiskaddon, I love! It's not as good as Mortimer, but good enough. Elysabeth Victoria Mortimer Kiskaddon." She shivered with delight. "Oh yes, Bletchley! He was nothing but a lying guttersnipe! He tricked Uncle Severn into giving *him* control of the Espion, which meant he got control of the princes. Then *he* made them disappear. And who gets the blame? Severn gets the blame. It was a nasty bit of work, I tell you. A cruel trick. Bletchley killed the princes, and that's why Severn executed him for treason. Everyone thinks the king did it, but he didn't." She looked into his eyes and then, much more gently, reached for his hand. "You were worried that the king was going to put you to death, but my grandpapa thinks you'll be all right, and I believe him. Do you see why now? The king is upset that his nephews died. He didn't want it to happen. Remember, his motto is 'Loyalty Binds Me.' He took that motto to heart."

Owen was not sure what to think. One thing he knew. The Mortimer girl knew much more than he did. His parents had told him next to nothing about the families of the realm and the troubles between them. He knew his father had gone off to war again because the king had summoned him. He had been surprised to learn that his father was considered a traitor to the king.

How was he supposed to discover what was true and what was tale? Everyone believed the coins vanished from the fountains and granted wishes. But just because they believed it, didn't make it true.

"Goodnight, Owen Kiskaddon!" Elysabeth Victoria Mortimer whispered suddenly, stooping to kiss him on the cheek. And with that, she scampered off the bed and vanished out the door.

◆ ◆ ◆

The following day, the Mortimer girl took Owen on a grand exploration of the grounds. Jewel was not pleased with her and kept demanding they stop and rest, but the girl paid her no mind whatsoever. Grabbing Owen's hand, she led him on a merry romp toward the secret part of the grounds, leaving their elderly guardian lagging behind.

Owen had passed the nondescript wall before and thought nothing of it, but as she brought him closer, she pointed out how different it was from the adjoining structure. There were not any vines, and little moss on it either, which spoke to the fact that it was a new construction.

"My grandpapa said the cistern is just past it," she said eagerly. "I haven't figured out a way to get over it yet, but I think if we had a view from *that* tower," she said, pointing up at Ankarette's tower, "we'd be able to find a way in there." She pressed her palms against the stone wall, as if she hoped to topple it over. "I think there's another way inside—a door maybe. I've been trying to find a way into that tower, you know, but no one can help me."

Owen swallowed guiltily, for he knew the way to the tower and he had no doubt that Ankarette knew the secret of the forbidden wall. He was itching to ask her.

When Jewel finally caught up to them, sputtering for breath, the Mortimer girl grabbed Owen's hand and dragged him away at a run to escape her. It was like playing the seeking game, only better.

After sundown, he waited a long time before sneaking to the tower. He wanted to make sure that his adventure would go unnoticed by his new companion, so he stole into the secret passages and made his way to the Mortimer girl's chamber. He watched from a secret panel on the wall as Elysabeth Victoria Mortimer built a little fort out of chairs and blankets, with only a stubby candle for light. Suspecting she'd be occupied for a while, Owen stole up to the tower.

When he entered the room, Ankarette was lying on the bed, clutching her middle. She looked tired and uncomfortable and he could see she was in no mood to play Wizr.

"Hello, Owen," she greeted, her voice weak. "I left the tea for you on the table." He nestled by the edge of the bed, his stomach growling at the sight of the nearby tray of uneaten food. He was always hungry.

"I'm not feeling well tonight," she said, reaching out tenderly and tousling his hair. "Tomorrow night, perhaps?"

"Are you sick?" he asked her.

She nodded. "Mostly tired. I'll feel better tomorrow, I think. Would you take the tray down to the kitchen for me? I don't think I can make it tonight."

"Of course," he answered, and then took it. "Can I ask you something?"

"You always can," she said with a little gasp of pain.

"I heard about Lord Bletchley today."

"Who told you about *him*?" she asked, her voice showing her interest.

"The Mortimer girl," he replied.

"Elysabeth *Victoria* Mortimer?" Ankarette asked playfully. "What did she tell you?"

Owen knew this was an important moment. He wanted to see if he could trust Ankarette fully. So he decided to test her. He altered some of the story. He said that Severn *ordered* Bletchley to murder his nephews. He wanted to know if that were true.

Ankarette was quiet for a moment, her eyes lost in thought. "No, I'm not certain that's true," she said. "I don't believe the king *ordered* his nephews' deaths. It was Bletchley's handiwork." She frowned, her face troubled. "Many do believe Severn ordered it, so I'm not surprised at the story, only that Duke Horwath did not correct his granddaughter." She shrugged, and Owen felt a surge of relief.

"How do you know he didn't?" Owen stammered. "I was just thinking . . . you told me the king was Fountain-blessed. Couldn't he *persuade* someone that he didn't do something that he did?"

Ankarette gazed at him with a look that reminded him of the one the Mortimer girl had given him. A look of respect and admiration. It made him flush with warmth.

"Are you sure you are only eight?" she asked with a little laugh. "That was very astute, Owen. You will become a great lord someday. How do I know? Because I was there in secret when Severn told the queen what had become of her sons. Their bodies have never been found, you see, but we all presume they are dead. The king came to Our Lady to tell his sister-in-law. He is not a humble man, you may be sure of that. And while he laid the blame for their death on Bletchley, he told her that *he* was responsible. He had trusted Bletchley and given him command of the Espion. It was his fault the boys were dead." She fell quiet. "That took courage, you can imagine. No one made him tell her. And since I was there, I could tell he was not using his Fountain magic. He could have *forced* her to believe him, but he did not attempt to persuade her or touch her. That is why she had summoned me. She wanted to be sure that she had not been convinced against her will. One Fountain-blessed can discern the gift in another. I would have known it if he had used it against her."

Owen adjusted his grip on the tray. His understanding of the king was beginning to shift. He realized that he, like many, might be looking at him in a way that was not entirely true.

"But why does he . . . why does he . . . I don't know how to say this. Why does he *act* as if he did kill them?"

Ankarette's gaze met his. "There is something corrupting about wearing a crown," she answered quietly. "It changes you. I saw it happen to Eredur too. When enough people believe something of you, it can distort your view of yourself. We mimic the judgments of others. It would take a very strong person indeed to resist the effects of so much ill will. So much aversion. I don't think King Severn is all that strong. His older brother was stronger, and yet *he* still succumbed to it. Severn is becoming what everyone already believes him to be. When he was younger, he never limped or stooped, despite being born with a crooked back. He limps now because of his battle wounds. His brother trusted him and he walked straight and proud. Now he's transforming into the monster that his people believe him to be."

◆ ◆ ◆

I did not work for Lord Bletchley when he was the master of the Espion. He coveted the "hollow crown" for himself and thought he could intrigue his way to the throne. The faster someone rises to power, the faster they will inevitably fall. King Severn may prove an exception to this rule, I believe.

—Dominic Mancini, Espion of the Palace Kitchen

◆ ◆ ◆

CHAPTER SEVENTEEN

Discovered

Owen was a curious boy. He had many questions, and when he wanted answers, he could be persistent. The Mortimer girl had pointed out the new wall, and while Owen was not pleased she had discovered it before him, he could not banish it from his mind. Her suggestion about looking from the poisoner's tower—though she had not called it by that name—had inspired him to seek the secret entrance. It would have been easy to ask Ankarette for the information, but he wanted to see if he could find it on his own.

He stole away from the Mortimer girl on the pretext of using the garderobe and then slipped into the secret tunnels that honeycombed the palace at Kingfountain. He couldn't wait until nightfall because then he wouldn't be able to see very well. The tunnels were musty, but the arrow slits in the walls provided some light, and he had grown accustomed to slinking about in the shadows. He was quiet and careful, always listening for the sound of bootsteps coming from ahead or behind. He had a knack for hearing things out of place and for treading softly. The thought of becoming an Espion had its charms.

From an arrow hole in the wall of Ankarette's tower, he had a good view of the walled-off area, though it was overgrown with trees. He could see a giant hole in the center of the enclosure. It was the strangest-looking well he had seen. It had eight sides, each with various rows that narrowed like a funnel the deeper it went. At first he thought it was a series of benches like the small amphitheater in the garden at Tatton Hall, but this wasn't a semicircle, it was a full circle. The center of the well hole was a big eight-pointed star. There were crushed stones and pebbles around it and small sluices that led to the eight points around the perimeter.

It looked like a very interesting place to explore. How to find the way in?

Owen spent some time exploring various tunnels around where he thought the entrance must be, but realizing it would require more diligent searching, he decided to wait until after nightfall. After supper, he spent time in the kitchen arranging tiles in the shape he had seen, earning some curious comments from the Mortimer girl, which he chose not to answer because he wanted to surprise her. He was eager for nightfall to arrive so he could begin his search. He would need a candle if he were going to explore new sections of the tunnels, so he made sure to blow out his night candle early to conserve the wax.

As he walked the dark tunnels between the palace's walls later that evening, he remembered his first nights in the palace and how frightened he had been of all the new sounds. He had grown more accustomed to them and could now differentiate the familiar from the strange. The interior ways were narrow, only wide enough for a single person to pass, but they interconnected the major portions of the palace. Most of the tunnels were as tall as the corridors they lined, and in some places rungs were hammered into the stone to provide access to higher floors. In other places, the tunnels were so narrow a man would have to go sideways through them. Those would have been a problem for Mancini, Owen thought with a smirk, but they were sized perfectly for an eight-year-old boy. At various points, they would connect to the tower stairwells, but some towers had secret ways.

Owen rubbed his hands on the stone walls, feeling the grooves between blocks of stone. He counted the floor blocks too, using that as a measure to help him orient himself. At every junction, there was a symbol carved into a flat stone at the corner, which also provided a way to find something in the dark. He normally kept to the main aisles, running the perimeter of the castle. Tonight, he intended to explore some new ones. His fat candle was impaled on a nail protruding from the stubby bronze candlestick he gripped and held before him as he explored. The normal day-to-day sounds of the castle began to abate as he explored, delving deeper into new tunnels that hopefully hid the secret of the garden well.

Part of him was growing anxious. He did not know how long he had been wandering, but he knew Ankarette would be waiting for him in the tower. He wanted to be able to boast his discovery to her, to prove that he had learned his lessons and could find things on his own. But he could not find any path that led there, and he was getting the feeling that he should turn back and continue his quest another night.

But he was also a stubborn little boy and he really wanted to find it, so he persisted and continued the search despite the nagging feeling in his stomach that increased with each step. He was not entirely certain where he was and thought, with a sick feeling in his stomach, that he might even be lost.

A sound whispered from the corridor behind him. It was a footfall. Not the sound of a boot in the corridor beyond the wall. The sound of someone approaching *within* the tunnel. It was coming from behind him.

The queasiness blossomed inside Owen and a cold sweat started on his brow. Going back was no longer an option. The tunnel was narrow and there was no place to hide, so Owen hurried forward, hoping to find an escape into the main palace corridor. It would be infinitely better to be punished for wandering the hall at night than to be caught in the Espion corridor. His little heart started to hammer wildly in his chest and the blackness in front of him became even darker somehow.

He heard the footfalls again, coming closer.

The boy was starting to panic. Ankarette had warned him this could happen. She had told him it was dangerous to wander the tunnels alone and that he needed to be very cautious and always listen for sounds that were out of place. Such as the footfalls behind him.

The narrow pinch of the corridor suddenly filled in ahead of Owen, the walls closing like an arrowhead. It ended abruptly and finally. It was a dead end.

He gasped with fear and glanced over his shoulder. He could still see nothing, but the steps were getting louder. His mind twisted with regret and shock. He needed to think clearly, but fear had flooded him. He scanned the walls, up and down, looking for ladder rungs to climb. Nothing. Even the ceiling had narrowed, though it was still tall.

His mouth was dry as sand. The wild shuddering in his chest turned into a stampede of horses. He gazed around again, and then he saw the handle latch he had missed. There was a concealed door on one side of the passageway. He almost jerked the latch and flung it wide, and if he had, his time as a poisoner's apprentice would have ended abruptly. Some faint inner voice, probably Ankarette's, cautioned him just in time. All the hidden entrances in the palace were equipped with secret spyholes. The spyhole was almost too tall for him, but they tended to favor crouching people. Owen slid open the cover and gazed through it.

It was the king's bedroom.

Owen knew this because he saw the king inside.

The hearth was blazing, and its flickering light glowed orange off the king's stubbled cheeks. The king was staring into the fire, one hand supporting himself as he leaned against the mantel. His other hand, from his crooked arm, held his crown. He looked as if he were going to toss the crown into the fire and melt the burnished gold.

There were an infinite number of hiding places in the bedroom. A huge canopied bed made of enormous stained-oak beams, carved and sculpted and glistening with the light. There were fur-lined capes and robes. Several stuffed couches and chairs, any of which would have concealed a small boy. There were chests and wardrobes. Even a garderobe! Owen would gladly have thrown himself down the shaft into the cesspit to avoid being caught. But the door might squeal if he opened it, and then the king would turn and see him. He did not want to imagine what he would say. He couldn't let that happen!

Still, the steps were coming closer, and he could now see the shimmer of the light on the walls of the passageway. Owen's options were shrinking with each moment. The first thing he did was snuff the wick of his candle, plunging himself into darkness. Darkness was a blanket in which he could hide. But not from a man with a candle. Who was coming? He prayed it was Ankarette, searching for him, but knew he could not trust to such luck. He quivered with fear.

Then an idea struck. The walls narrowed at the end of the tunnel. He knew he would not be able to climb with the candlestick in hand, so he left it on the floor. Then he wedged himself into the narrowest part of the wall and began using his feet and arms to shimmy up to the tip, pressing against the enclosure to gain leverage. He was small and wiry and quickly began to ascend. His heart was pounding like a blacksmith hammer inside his chest as he watched the glow get closer. Then the candle bearer appeared around the bend.

It was Ratcliffe.

Owen's terror now multiplied. The master of the Espion. The king's sworn man. He walked deliberately toward Owen, and the boy feared for a moment that he was already seen. He was doomed. He was probably level with Ratcliffe's head when he felt the ceiling of the tunnel push against his head. Owen dipped his chin and continued to climb until he felt the tunnel ceiling on his neck.

"What's this?" Ratcliffe chuffed, gazing down at the smoldering candlestick on the ground. He approached faster and stooped to pick it up. The wick was still smoking and the wax was dripping. Owen thought he might faint. He had stopped breathing as soon as he had recognized the man.

Ratcliffe lifted the candle to his nose and sniffed at it. A stern, angry look passed his face. He looked at the concealed door, the slit still clearly open, and then hastily jiggled the handle with the hand holding Owen's candlestick.

"Who's there?" Severn growled as the secret door opened.

"It's me," answered the spymaster. "My lord, were you visiting with someone just now? I found this on the ground by the door."

"I've been alone," came the brusque reply. "Alone with my ghosts."

"My lord, someone's been spying on you!" Ratcliffe said with growing alarm. "The wick is spent, the candle dripping. Were you . . . are you testing me, my lord? Did you leave this here to see if I would tell you?"

"Of course not, Dickon!" the king said with rising anger. "You've proven yourself loyal over and over. Probably one of your *Espion*," he added with derision. "Seeking to catch me fondling the princess or some such rubbish. I don't like those Espion, Dickon. I need them, but I don't like them."

Ratcliffe's tone bridled. "If it weren't for them, you would have *failed* at Ambion Hill, sire."

"If it weren't for them, my nephews would still be alive," he countered bitterly. "I don't need to be reminded. So we have another traitor among our ranks. I didn't set that candlestick there. You didn't. Who do you think it belongs to?"

"It might be *her*," Ratcliffe said in a low, dangerous voice. "I think she's moving freely in the castle again. There are rumors that she's been seen."

The king gave a weary sigh. "With all the power that comes from this golden band, why cannot I find a single woman who haunts my steps and overthrows my designs? Even my brother would not tell me who she was." He grunted with anger.

Owen's arms and legs were beginning to cramp. The door leading to the king's chamber was still open, just below him. If he fell, they would no doubt hear it and then see him.

"She may still be here in the room," Ratcliffe said. "Let me summon the guards to search. The candle was still warm."

"Do it," Severn said. "If you catch this *poisoner*, I want her executed immediately. Do you hear that, my dear? You thought to catch me unawares whilst I slept? Call my guards, Ratcliffe. Make sure all the Espion know that helping her is treason in my eyes. Are you hiding over here, my dear? Hmmm?"

The sound of heavy footfalls flooded the tunnel as the two men began to tromp through the chamber. Owen's fear made him tremble, and his knees and arms were shrieking in pain. Ratcliffe summoned the king's guard into the room, who promptly and thoroughly began examining every nook within the chamber. If Owen had tried to hide in there, he would have been caught for certain. After several minutes of clamoring, the hunt was called off. Owen's muscles throbbed and shook, but he would not give up. He held himself perfectly still, wedged up in the corner above the door in the narrowest part of the tunnel. If Ratcliffe had thought to look up, Owen would have been spotted in an instant.

Another voice joined the sounds, a young woman's voice. "Are you all right, Uncle?" Princess Elyse asked, her voice full of concern. "Someone tried to kill you?"

The sound of her voice sent a surge of relief through Owen. He had not spoken to her in quite some time, and he was grateful to know she was still at the palace. The knowledge did not help his cramping muscles.

Severn's laugh was self-deprecating. "I'm just a crouch-backed soldier, lass. No one tried to hurt me. Get you back to bed."

"Who was it?" Elyse pressed, her voice anxious.

"We think it was your mother's poisoner," Ratcliffe said venomously.

Elyse's voice was firm. "I don't think she would hurt you, Uncle."

"Am I supposed to derive comfort from that?" he said with a chuckle. "Do you know who she is, lass? If you know anything about her, you should tell me."

Owen's stomach twisted with dread. *Don't!* he wanted to call out. *It was me! It wasn't her!*

"I don't know her name," Elyse said hesitantly. "But I have seen her."

"Recently?" Ratcliffe pressed. There was an intensity to his voice.

"No," she replied simply. "Not since before Father died. My mother doesn't want you dead, Uncle."

"Quit listening in on your betters," the king barked angrily. "You are all useless. Be gone. Go outside."

Owen wasn't sure what was happening, but then he realized the king had been addressing the soldiers. The door shut with an audible thud.

Then the king sighed heavily. "Lass, you should not speak so freely in front of people. I could see by the look on your face that you were going to reveal more than you ought to have."

"I'm sorry, Uncle," she replied meekly. "I know you are worried about rumors. I will go as well. It's just that . . ." She stopped short.

"What, lass?" he asked softly, almost tenderly.

"Your Majesty," Ratcliffe said in a warning tone.

"Be silent, man! She's my niece. She is the only colorful thing in this drab world. The only nectar amidst so much poison. Say on, lass."

"You already know," Elyse said uncomfortably. Her voice was quavering. "What my mother suggested you do. I'm not . . . opposed to it, Uncle."

He coughed against his fist. Owen could tell by the sound. "It's not that simple, lass. Things are never that simple. Off with you now. Go." His voice was coaxing, calm.

Owen heard the door open and shut again. Ratcliffe sounded uptight when he spoke next. "There will be rumors again," he said.

"I already know that," the king said flatly. "After her first plan failed, my brother's widow hoped to wed Princess Elyse to my rival so she could become Queen of Ceredigion and keep the line going. That intrigue cost me the wounds at Ambion Hill. By the Fountain, Elyse could be queen in her own right. She or Dunsdworth if they both weren't barred. But that boy is too much like his father to ever entrust with the throne."

"And you won't name her your heir?" Ratcliffe asked prudently.

"I can't," he said softly. "Not after everything that has happened."

Ratcliffe sighed. Owen's arms felt like they were going to fall off. Drops of sweat dripped down his chest. But he would not let go. He held himself up by sheer force of will, ordering himself to be as rigid as one of his tiles.

"Well, the lass certainly cares for you. She came running here straightaway. I know she's your niece, my liege, but there are . . . *precedents* for it. It would give stability to the realm if you married again." He chuckled. "As she said, even her *mother* desires a return to power enough to persuade her daughter to make the match."

"You're wheedling me," Severn snapped. "Stop it. I'll send Horwath to find me a wife when I'm ready. If I'm ever ready again. A nice foreign-born girl who doesn't speak our language or understand our customs. That would be *my* choice. Pity the Occitanian princess is so young. That realm would be a good addition to my power."

"Well, I'll leave you to your brooding then," Ratcliffe said. Owen heard the approaching sound of his boots as he moved to the doorway. He entered the secret corridor and shut the door, securing the latch and slipping the spyhole cover back into place. He marched back down the corridor, and still Owen trembled until he was smothered in blackness.

He waited until there were no more sounds at all. There was also no light. And Owen realized with dread he would have to spend the night in the black tunnel, for it would be nearly impossible to find his way out without a candle.

And he dared not go into the king's bedroom to retrieve it.

◆ ◆ ◆

We should not be encumbered by what we cannot control and change as suits the times. A promise given in the past was a necessity of the past. A broken vow is a necessity of the present. There is no such thing as "honor," or "I give him my word." Words, as you know, are meaningless, and only fools trust in them.

—Dominic Mancini, Espion of the Palace Kitchen

◆ ◆ ◆

CHAPTER EIGHTEEN

Fear

If Owen had experienced fear before coming to Kingfountain, it was nothing compared to wandering the secret tunnels of the palace without a candle. He tried his best to judge the right way, groping with blindness and even crawling on the ground, but his efforts were totally wasted. He was lost, hopelessly so, and the night seemed as if it would go on forever. There were sounds that he understood—the scuttling of rats, the creaking of timbers, and the occasional gusts of wind. But there were also sounds that put him in mind of a person moaning. His imagination supplied the rest—they were the ghosts of the dead princes, the ones whose bodies had never been found.

His courage was utterly spent, his misery complete. Ahead, he thought he saw a translucent shape, a phantom shaped like a man but made entirely of dust motes. The phantom stalked toward him in silence. Owen closed his eyes and buried his face in his hands. He listened for the sound of footfalls. Nothing, not even a whisper of breath. He peeked up again, and it was waiting for him—the shape of a man, all gnats and swirling dust.

Owen groaned with fear and then began to sob. He waited for the being to grab him and carry him away into the void. Terror made him huddle in a ball on the floor and sob in choking heaves that grew louder and louder. He could not help himself. Anything was better than staying lost in the tunnels until morning. He wept bitterly, wishing his parents had never given birth to him.

He did not know how long he lay crumpled on the floor, crying. He waited with anguish and suspense for the worst to happen. And then his eyelids detected light. Ratcliffe! He almost welcomed capture at this point. He lifted his head, still trying to breathe through his tears, gulping, and then he saw Ankarette coming toward him with a candle.

Owen wasn't sure if it was his imagination, but he got to his feet and ran to her with relief. As soon as he reached her, he wrapped his arms around her middle and pressed his cheek against her stomach. He was so grateful to see her, so relieved to have been found.

She set the candlestick down and folded her arms around his head. She stroked his hair, his neck, murmuring softly that everything would be all right. She smelled wonderful. Even in the safety of her arms, he shivered and shuddered, unable to quell the terror.

Ankarette knelt down, bringing herself level with his face, and cupped his cheek in her hand. Not saying anything, she peered into his eyes, her gaze full of sadness and serenity. Then she leaned forward and kissed the corner of his eye, where the tears were still coming. She murmured a word in a language he didn't know, and suddenly he felt peace. His heartbeat began to slow down. The tears stopped. Instead of terror, he felt relief. Warmth and kindness suffused him, putting a stop to his spasms.

Still kneeling, Ankarette took up the candlestick. She then rose to her feet and offered Owen her hand. He clung to it, so grateful to be led away from the darkness.

She took him back to his bedroom and set the candlestick on the table near the bed before helping him under the covers. He could only stare at her with reverence. He would have done anything in the world she asked him to do. Once he was settled, she knelt by his bedside and planted her elbow on the mattress so she could rest her chin on her knuckles.

"There's my little Owen," she whispered with affection, reaching out and smoothing some of his hair from his forehead. "You had quite a scare tonight."

He nodded, feeling a twinge of horror try to well up inside him. It could not rise above the well-being in his heart.

"Was that . . . was that magic?" he asked her simply.

She wrinkled her brow a bit. "Was what?"

"You kissed my eye and whispered something. Was that magic?"

She smiled languidly and then nodded once.

"Can you teach it to me?" he begged.

"You are too young," she answered, tapping his nose with her slender finger.

"Will you teach me when I'm older?"

She pursed her lips, as if his question caused her pain. "If I can," she answered after the hesitation.

"I don't want to be an Espion anymore," Owen said, shaking his head firmly. His eyelids were drooping, and he felt so tired all of a sudden. "I was so afraid."

"You got lost in the tunnels?"

He nodded sleepily. "I found the king's room. And then Ratcliffe came up behind me. I thought I would be caught. I never want to do that again."

"But you weren't caught, were you?"

He shook his head no. "But I was scared. I kept seeing things in the dark."

She laid her hand on his forehead, stroking the tips of his hair. "Courage isn't the absence of fear, Owen. Courage is moving forward even when you're afraid. I've known many brave men who have felt fear the night before a battle. Fear comes and stalks them, like a wolf does a lamb." She paused, sliding her finger down his nose. "But when the dawn comes, they do their duty, and the fear goes away. It only preys on the powerless. Owen, you *have* power."

He stared at her, his eyelids so heavy. "No, I don't."

She nodded sagely. "You do. Your power summoned me tonight. I felt your need. The Fountain whispers to those of us who listen. I had a bad feeling about you tonight when you didn't come. Most people ignore those little feelings. But I've learned to trust them. I didn't know where you were, but I kept looking. Kept searching. And then I heard you weeping." She caressed his cheek with her knuckle.

"Ankarette, will you tell me about the Fountain again?" he asked. He blinked and forced his eyes open. He wanted to listen to her, but he was so tired. He licked his fingertips and then rubbed the wetness over his eyelids. That made it easier to keep them open.

She gently stroked his hair. "The Fountain is everywhere, Owen. It's here in the room with us. It was in your tears. It's likened to water because without water, even a little bit, we would die in days. I can hear its murmur right now, here with us. It carried your fear and despair to me, knowing I could help you. It led me to you. The Fountain is power, like a river current. Even the strongest things must budge to its force, given enough time. The Fountain is magic. We were all born of it. And it was the Fountain that gave me the idea of how to save you."

"By tricking the king," Owen said with a weary smile. "Has the Fountain told you how yet?"

Ankarette nodded emphatically. "It's all so very simple. I don't know why I didn't see it before."

"Tell me?" Owen pressed. He loved staring into her sad eyes, looking at her lovely smile. Ankarette had come to feel like a mother in this place so far from home.

"As you know, I've made an acquaintance of Mancini," she said in a near whisper. "He seeks to do away with Ratcliffe so that he himself might become master of the Espion. I have been helping him with his goal. In return, he will help me with mine. One way to prove that you are Fountain-blessed, Owen, is if you can bring information to the king *before* Ratcliffe does. It won't be easy. Mancini is helping me track down the first tidbits to help build your reputation. Something that will help you without compromising him. Something that Ratcliffe intends to tell the king later, only you will tell him first. You will become a fortune-teller, in a way. Only a Fountain-blessed could have that power of sight."

"I'm . . . I'm not sure I am brave enough," Owen said in a small voice.

Ankarette leaned down and kissed his cheek. "Then you must learn courage, Owen. You must learn it however you can."

The thought of Elysabeth Victoria Mortimer came to his mind. She was the most fearless person he knew. How had she become that way?

He fell asleep while thinking about her.

◆ ◆ ◆

The next day, the two youths were in the interior yard of the palace grounds, arms held out for balance as they walked in the great circle around the rim of the enormous fountain in the yard. Jewel scolded them for risking a fall, but they ignored her. The Mortimer girl was trying to catch up to Owen. He had to keep one eye on the tiles at his feet, and the other on her to make sure she wasn't gaining on him, which she was. He tried to walk faster to widen the distance. The sky was blue and clear of clouds, and the fountain water lapped playfully.

"How come you're not afraid of anything?" Owen asked as they walked.

"Because of my father," the Mortimer girl replied breezily. He could hear the silver laugh in her voice. She was trying really hard to catch up with him. It was obvious she found this kind of play much more interesting than watching him build rows of tiles to knock over.

"How did he teach you?" Owen pressed.

"He taught me to climb waterfalls," she responded matter-of-factly.

"What?" He stumbled a bit and almost fell off the fountain wall.

"Ha! You were about to fall in!" she teased with her silvery laugh. "I'm going to catch you, Owen Kiskaddon!"

Not if I catch you first!

"In the North we have the most beautiful mountains. They're covered in snow all winter, but the water melts in the spring and feeds huge waterfalls."

"Like the one by Our Lady?" he asked, keeping his focus, his arms helping him balance.

"Not like that one," she said, disagreeing. "These waterfalls come off the cliffs. They are huge! They feed the river that flows down here. This one is wide but not as deep. In the North, the waterfalls are beautiful! My father took me for hikes up to the top of one of the waterfalls. There are portions where the mist is so heavy everything is wet and it's easy to slip. But when you reach the top, you can watch the water shooting down. They even built a bridge spanning the waterfall, so you can stand at the very top of it and watch the water come down. It's like watching a snowstorm from a cloud. I can't wait to take you there, Owen! The mountains are steep and hard to climb, but I've done it so long my papa said I'm a billy goat!" She made some bleating noises and then started to run after him.

"You're not supposed—!" Owen stopped, realizing he had one choice: run or be caught. He was getting dizzier with each step, but he was determined not to let her catch up with him.

"Stop running, lass!" Jewel shouted. "You're going to fall in, and bless me if your grandfather won't take a switch to you then!"

The Mortimer girl ignored her, and Owen risked a glance over his shoulder to look at her. There was a hunter's grin on her face as she charged at him, but he kept his balance and ran faster.

Suddenly there was a splash of water, and Owen turned to see that she had stumbled into the fountain water. There was a startled look on her face, and she had landed on her hands and knees. He quickly made it around to her, watching as she rose, sopping wet, her dark hair plastered to her cheeks. She did not look chagrined at all—rather, she seemed to be enjoying herself.

"Mistress Mortimer, you get out of there!" Jewel shouted angrily, hobbling toward the fountain.

"My name is Elysabeth *Victoria* Mortimer!" she shrieked wildly at the old woman. Then she grabbed Owen's belt and yanked him into the fountain with her. Something had warned him she might do that, but he hadn't been prepared. Before he knew it, the cold water was splashing across his face and he was soaked. He got up spluttering and then splashed water at her, which made her squeal with joy.

"Out! You two get out of there!" Jewel huffed, staring at the sopping children with anxiety. To his surprise, there was also the hint of a smile on her face.

"Catch us!" the Mortimer girl called, and grabbing Owen's hand, she began to skip away from Jewel to the other side of the fountain. The water had soaked them both through, but it wasn't so cold anymore and Owen liked the feel of her hand tugging his.

"When your grandfather finds out," Jewel scolded, "it'll be a whipping! You hear me? A whipping!"

"He won't whip me," the Mortimer girl laughed gaily. Then she released Owen's hand and started to twirl around in a circle, looking up at the blue sky. After a few twirls, she slumped down on her bottom, too dizzy to do anything but laugh.

Owen stared in wonder at this girl who was unafraid to dance in a royal fountain. She was sitting down, water running down the dark tips of her hair, smiling at him as if it were only the two of them in the world. Owen pretended to stumble and pitched forward into the water, making a loud splash. She giggled infectiously, just as he had hoped.

Later, the two were huddled underneath blankets to dry off by the bread ovens and Jewel was regaling Liona and Drew with the tale of their exploits. Owen was colder now and shivered under the blanket, not wanting to run upstairs for a change of clothes from his limited wardrobe.

"That was fun," the Mortimer girl said, wiggling her bare toes at the crackling flames. "I don't regret it."

Owen hugged his knees and tried to stop shivering. "You . . . you said your father . . . let you climb . . . waterfalls."

She nodded eagerly. "The water up in the North is so much colder. At the bottom of the waterfall, the one called Mist Falls, there is a little pond. There's a big rock at the edge of the trail and you can climb it and jump in. All the boys and girls from the valley do it."

"You've done it?" he asked, impressed.

She nodded, her eyes wild with the memories. "It's still a little scary, because the stone is so high. But I love the feeling I get in my stomach when I jump. Like I'm flying. I can't wait to bring you there. My papa took me my first time. He held my hand and we jumped together. It makes it easier when you jump with someone else the first time. The water is *so* cold. It's like ice, only wetter. You have to swim back to shore before you get too cold. Papa said you can lose your wits if you're cold for too long. But after we climbed to Mist Falls, we would sit on the edge and eat some wild berries and throw the stems into the mist below. My mother never knew about it. She's afraid of falling. But I'm not. It would get a little windy at times, but that just means you need to be more careful."

"Did you ever jump off?" he asked.

The Mortimer girl looked at him as if he were the stupidest person in the world. "Of course not! Some villagers tried it, but they've all died. Some people break their arms or legs slipping down the trail. But just because you *can* get hurt, doesn't mean you shouldn't climb waterfalls. I'm so grateful someone had the courage to build that bridge. I'm sure it was dangerous work. But they did it, and now everyone can see what it's like to stand on top of such a waterfall! It captures your heart,

Owen." She had a faraway look in her eyes, a brightness and eagerness that made him yearn to see it for himself. Then she looked at him and patted his knee. "When we go up North, I'll take you up to Mist Falls. I'll hold your hand as we jump off that rock, just as my papa did for me. After that . . . you won't be afraid of anything."

The warmth from the ovens made his cheeks burn, but he was still cold beneath the wet clothes. He could picture himself standing on a mountainside with the Mortimer girl next to him. The thought of jumping off a waterfall made his head buzz.

"Owen, guess what!" she whispered, leaning toward him. "I found it!"

"What?" He shook his head to clear it.

"I found where that wall leads from the castle! I saw it out a window. It leads to a small courtyard and there's—"

"The cistern," Owen interrupted, gazing at her.

Her eyes went wide. "You saw it?"

He nodded.

"I think I found the way in," she said conspiratorially.

◆ ◆ ◆

I'm beginning to wonder if the alliance I've struck with the queen's poisoner will be fatal. Ratcliffe insists she invaded the king's bedchamber last night shortly before midnight. That cannot be true because she was, in fact, with me at that time discussing the king's enemies and which nobles are most likely to fall next. It's my opinion it will be Lord Asilomar. The king has set up a trap to test his loyalty. He will fail. I'm wondering when mine will be tested. If Ratcliffe knew that I was working for her, I'd be thrown into the river.

—Dominic Mancini, Espion of the Palace Kitchen

◆ ◆ ◆

CHAPTER NINETEEN

Deep Cisterns

Owen and the Mortimer girl faced each other over a Wizr board in the library. Each move was painstakingly slow. Owen could have won several times already with the tricks he had learned from Ankarette, but the goal wasn't to win the game. The goal was for Jewel to fall asleep. Owen had added some additional ingredients to her tea and the old woman was making a bold effort of fighting off the effects. She sat in a stuffed chair, and the needlework in her hands kept bobbing and dipping.

"I think she's almost asleep," Owen whispered, moving the next piece.

His companion gazed surreptitiously at the old woman in the chair. Jewel's mouth had sagged open and her breath had begun to pull in and out in curt little gasps.

The Mortimer girl almost giggled as she looked back at Owen with her bewitching eyes that were part green, part blue, part gray. She wore a dark green velvet dress with cuffs that matched her hem. Her dark hair was swept back behind her.

"You were right," she whispered in reply. "She normally doesn't fall asleep like this when she's watching us. But choosing a boring game like Wizr, and playing it so quietly . . . just look at her. Should we go?"

Owen nodded. They had several hours before the effects of the tea would wear off. The Mortimer girl grabbed his hand but paused to move one of the game pieces with her free hand. "Threat," she said after the move, indicating a surprise attack he had not expected. Leave it to her to show talent at a complicated game she found boring. "Come on!" she said, tugging him to follow.

The two crept away from the library, their footfalls silenced by the thick carpet. As soon as they were past the doors, they broke into a run. Owen let her guide, as she knew the way. There was always a thrill to being naughty, and he could tell it was coursing through them both. There were servants all around, but everyone in the palace knew about Owen Satchel and the Mortimer girl, and there were only a few grunts and warnings not to get underfoot.

Their destination was a side corridor by the servants' quarters. The level of dust on the floor showed it was not well traveled. A big, sturdy door met them at the end of the corridor. Owen had tried it before and found it locked, so he had never been back again.

The Mortimer girl grinned at him mischievously. "There is a window in the door. I dragged that basket over and stood on it, and that's how I saw the secret place."

"But the door is locked," Owen said, yanking on the iron latch. It rattled but did not loosen.

"I know, but look over there. See the tapestry? Why would there be a tapestry in the middle of a hall that no one uses?"

Owen hadn't noticed it before, and it did look a little strange. The tapestry was suspended from an iron pole fastened into the stone. The Mortimer girl winked and walked over to it, then pulled it aside. The tapestry concealed a curtained window.

"The curtain is thick enough to disguise the light," she explained. "Look how dusty the window is too!"

Owen saw the window had a bar latch and he pulled on it. It was stuck. They exchanged a look and then gripped it together, wrestling with the bar latch. It was tight as a drum.

"I couldn't do it myself," she gasped. "But I thought . . . the two of us!"

Owen squinted and frowned, pulling even harder. The latch finally shifted and swung back, knocking them both to the floor. She landed on top of him and they had to stifle nervous giggles.

"It's open!" she squealed excitedly. Rushing back to the tapestry, she pushed it aside and shoved at the glass. The window groaned open. "Help me up!" she said.

Owen grabbed her around the waist and helped her onto the windowsill.

"It's covered in vines." She scooted around and grabbed a fistful of vines and began lowering herself down.

"How far down is it?" Owen asked, his worry growing.

She let go of the vines and dropped down. Her face was still visible from the window. She beamed at him. "Not far! Come on!"

Owen listened for sounds of anyone approaching in the corridor, but heard nothing. He climbed up onto the windowsill on his own and scooted off and jumped. There was brickwork on the ground outside and the shade from the vines helped conceal him and the Mortimer girl. He reached back and slowly shut the window, making sure to leave it ajar so they could get back in.

There was ivy everywhere, smothering the wall. She had a leaf of it sticking to her hair as she peered at the walled-in courtyard.

There was the well hole in the middle.

"Come on," she whispered, taking his hand and starting to creep forward. They both looked and listened for any warning sounds. Their boots scuffed on the bricks. Owen gazed up and saw Ankarette's tower.

If she was looking out the window, she would be able to see them. The sun was high overhead, making their shadows small at their feet.

"I love wicked ideas like this one!" she said with delight, searching around for any signs they'd get caught.

They approached the well hole. It went down like steps. There were runners and gutters that led to the eight points, and he could discern a slight slope in the bricks. This well made the water run down into it.

"So, this is the cistern?" Owen said. They reached the outer rim and stared down into the huge dark circle.

"That's what my grandpapa said. It collects rainwater during the winter. It goes under the palace quite a ways. That's why there's no dungeon. The palace was built on a cistern!"

Owen had never heard that word before she had first said it to him. The black gaping hole was wide enough that they could have stood across it without being able to reach each other. But he intuitively understood the structure. "It doesn't lead to a water spring, which makes sense since the palace is on a hill. It would be hard to carry water up from the river every day."

"Exactly!" she said excitedly. "The cistern catches the water and holds it." She stepped down into the first ring of stones, trying to pull him along, but he yanked his hand away.

"What are you doing?" he asked, his stomach twisting with fear.

"I want to look down!" She tried to take his hand again, but he stepped back. "Oh, come on, Owen! Let's just look!"

He was curious but cautious. His brush with danger outside the king's chamber had rattled him, and he wasn't feeling very courageous.

"Hold on," he said. He wanted to come down at his own pace. She shrugged and hurried to the edge so she could kneel down and stare into the abyss. Her eyes lit with wonder. "Look how *deep* it is!"

Owen frowned. There was no way he was going to let her enjoy it all by herself. He stiffened his lip and marched down to the edge. "Move over."

She scooted to the side and their heads almost touched as they leaned in. He felt her hair brush against his. It made him feel . . . funny.

The cistern was half-empty. The waters rippled beneath them and he could see their own reflections warped on the placid surface. The chamber was deep, very deep. There were columns of stone and buttresses supporting it. There were numbers and little gashes carved into the column nearest the hole. The numbers meant how deep the water was and he could tell by the numbers at the top of the column that the cistern was just over half-full.

"There is a lot of water down there," he announced.

The Mortimer girl brushed hair over her ear and gripped the edge of the cistern opening before lowering her head deep inside.

"Hello!" she called out, and her voice echoed. Owen thought she was insane.

"Why did you call out?" he demanded.

She pulled her head back up. "I wanted to see if there was anyone down there. Maybe there's a water sprite!"

"Water sprites aren't real," Owen said stiffly.

"Yes, they are," she contradicted.

"Have you ever seen one?"

"Just because I haven't doesn't mean they're not real. Don't be stupid, Owen. Of course they're real. Papa said so. He said there is treasure under the deepest fathoms of the sea. Ancient swords that can't rust. Magic rings. There's another world there that we can't see. The ocean is its own kingdom." She looked him in the face, her eyes wide and sincere. "I'm not making up stories, Owen. It's true. The people who drown are those who try to join the water sprites but fail. They fail because they're afraid." She gave him a determined look. "I'm not afraid."

He looked at her, his stomach doing some twisting and turning. He admired her for her courage. Her fearlessness. And somehow, he knew what she was going to suggest before she announced it.

"Let's jump in!"

Owen hastily rose and backed away. "That's foolish!"

"No it's not!" she laughed. "I've jumped from higher rocks into colder ponds than this. It's fun!"

He could not believe his ears. "But how will you get out?"

She shrugged. "I don't know. The same way they get the water out. This is where the water comes in. I don't see any chains or ropes, so there's got to be another place where the water is drawn."

"But you could drown!"

"I'm a very good swimmer. Can't you swim, Owen?"

"I can *swim*," he said, offended.

"Then jump with me!" she said, eyes blazing. She reached out her hand again.

His heart hammered violently in his chest, and his mouth went so dry with fear he felt he couldn't talk. The fear crippled him, making his ears buzz and his knees weak. He could taste bile in his mouth. His eyes started to water.

The Mortimer girl watched him closely. Her excitement was still evident, but she seemed to sense what was happening to him. She walked around the drain hole and stood in front of him, nose to nose. Then she took his trembling hand in hers. "You're afraid. I know. But you have to *trust* me, Owen Kiskaddon. The water is deep enough. We won't get hurt. I don't know everything that will happen, but we'll find our way out. Let's do it together! Jump with me. That's how I did it the first time. With Papa holding my hand. It's scary! It really is. But we're going to have so much fun. Trust me, Owen! Trust me!"

He stared into her eyes, still unable to tell what color they were. He couldn't speak. His tongue was too thick in his mouth. He was terrified out of his wits, but he didn't want to disappoint her. For once, he wasn't thinking of the risks or the odds of injury. There was just this moment, her warm hand in his, and his trust in her.

"We can do it!" she coaxed.

She led him back to the lip of the cistern. He stared down, and the water looked even farther down this time. It looked as if they were standing on Ankarette's tower. He felt his stomach lurch. He was going to be sick.

She stood next to him, her hand linked with his.

"Are you ready?" she whispered.

Owen nodded violently, trying to swallow.

"Take a breath and hold it. On three."

He felt as if his whole body would shake apart.

"One!"

This was madness. Why was he doing this?

"Two!"

He stared down at the water. He took a huge gulp of air and held it in his chest. He squeezed her hand as hard as he could, hoping it would hurt her.

"Three!"

They jumped.

CHAPTER TWENTY

Secrets

It was a long fall. Longer than Owen had thought possible. He watched the water rush up, but it still felt like they were falling. The buzzing, giddy thrill in his stomach went all the way to his ears before the water splashed and they went under. It was like jumping into a giant blanket. The cold water closed over him, smothering him, until his swelling lungs buoyed him to the surface and he came up spluttering. As he thrashed around, terrified and thrilled, the water began to drain from his ears and he could hear the Mortimer girl giggling.

He wasn't holding her hand anymore, but she was paddling right in front of him, her smile mischievous and full of pride that he had jumped too.

"Wasn't that amazing!" she gasped, kicking the water to keep herself afloat. Owen's tunic and pants were waterlogged, but he had no trouble treading water. Looking up, he stared at the huge hole overhead and the sunlight beaming down on them.

Owen nodded eagerly, feeling the lingering thrill in his blood. He would do that again. He would do it a hundred times.

"I told you it was fun," she chided, splashing him lightly. "You'll love jumping off the boulders by the waterfalls! This water isn't even very cold." She reached up and brushed away wet clumps of hair from her cheek. "You did it!"

Owen smiled shyly at her, knowing he never would have done it without her, then stared back up at the gaping octagonal hole above them. "We need to figure out how to get back up."

"Look! A little boat!"

She was pointing to a series of stone steps leading up to a square. A small boat was sitting on the square, the oars poking over the ridge. The stairs continued up past the square, leading to a wooden door.

"It's a way out!" Owen said, his heart gushing with relief. He observed that the door was about as high as the hole in the ceiling. They swam the short distance and discovered the staircase extended into the water. They were sopping wet and dripping, but that was no concern to them at all as they tromped up the stairs.

Before continuing, they stopped to examine the boat. It was a small canoe-shaped thing, big enough for maybe two adults. There was a pair of oars leaning upright in the interior. The wood was polished and well-worn.

Owen was wondering why a canoe was there, but then he saw that the cistern extended down quite a distance, probably underneath the entire length of the palace, which formed the roof of the cistern.

The Mortimer girl knelt by the canoe, rocking it slightly to see how sturdy it was before she followed Owen's gaze across the shadowed waters.

"They keep this boat here so they can get to the other side without getting wet," she said. "Come on, let's check the door. I hope it isn't locked."

She grabbed his arm and pulled him up the stone steps. The water still rippled and lapped against the lower steps, disturbed by their plummet from above. The noises echoed eerily in the dark cistern, making Owen look back and stare into the blackness.

The door was narrow and wedged into a brace of stone. There was a handle and an intricate locking mechanism that was not operated by a key. The Mortimer girl tugged on the handle, but the door held firm. Owen recognized the lock as an Espion design, one that needed to be released from the outside. He pushed her hands away from the handle and quickly examined the mechanism. In moments, he figured out the triggering part and released the latch.

"How did you . . . ?" she stammered in amazement, staring at him with open admiration.

He shrugged and said nothing, not wanting to reveal anything Ankarette had taught him about the ways of the Espion. The door took some pulling to open and they saw a weave of ivy blocking the way, which explained why they hadn't seen the door while they were in the courtyard beyond. The mouth of the cistern was not far away.

"I'm jumping again!" she declared, and rushed out the door. He followed her and then watched as she rushed up to the edge and made her jump. He could hear the squeal before the splash sounded below him.

Owen's heart hammered with nervousness. He had done it once. He could do it on his own.

"Come on down!" she called to him. "I'm out of the way!"

He stared at the hole, pursed his lips, and then marched up to it. He stared down, his stomach wrenching violently as he stared down at the drop. There she was, paddling just outside the fringe of light in the shadowy waters, gazing up at him, her face beaming.

Owen counted in his heart. One. Two.

He stopped before thinking three and just jumped.

It was even more fun the second time, and he cut through the water like a knife, plunging through the depths. He went down all the way to the bottom until he felt the stone of the floor. Bubbles streamed up around him and he opened his eyes.

And he saw casks of glittering jewels and coins. Strange jeweled scabbards and ropes of pearls covered the floor of the cistern. There was a battered shield, with a huge gouge on its polished surface. None of the metal was rusted. He saw glass vials with stoppers. He kicked off the floor and rose to the surface, spluttering with shock.

"You did it!" the Mortimer girl beamed. "I knew you weren't too scared. I want to jump again!" She started swimming toward the steps.

"Wait!" he said, half choking and spitting out some water. "There's . . . there's treasure!"

She turned midstroke and looked at him, confused. "What did you say?"

"Down at the bottom!" he said excitedly, paddling hard. "I saw it!"

She looked confused. "I can see the bottom, Owen. It's just stone. Stop teasing."

Owen stared down and could only see his reflection in the water. He plunged his head below the surface, blinking rapidly despite the pain in his eyes and the watery view. This time he saw nothing but stone and shadows.

He pulled his face up, dripping. "I saw something! I'm not teasing. When I jumped, I held my arms stiff and went all the way to the bottom. I opened my eyes and saw piles of treasure. There were swords!"

"Swords?" she asked in wonder. "Let me try it." She swam to the steps and slogged up them, hiking up her skirts and pattering water like she was a raincloud. She marched back up to the door, which they had left ajar, and Owen moved away from the circle of light on the water. He wiped his face and waited for her shadow to appear above him.

He kept making circles in the water, paddling slowly to keep afloat despite the heavy feel of his soaked clothes. Then the Mortimer girl was plummeting again, spraying him with water when she struck the surface. She stayed down a long time. He could see her vague shape beneath the rippling waters. Then she was kicking toward the surface again.

When she broke the surface, she splashed water in his face. "You were teasing!" she said indignantly.

"No, I wasn't!" Owen said angrily. He swam back to the steps himself, marched back up them, and returned to the hole. Water streamed from his hair into his face, and he left huge puddles that drained into the small channels leading to the opening of the cistern. The stone was painted with water droplets and wet shapes the size of feet.

He stood at the edge of the cistern, full of confidence this time. When he jumped back in, he held his body rigid again and allowed himself to sink down. He tried to keep his eyes open during the fall, but as soon as he struck the water, he shut them instinctively. Then his feet touched the floor. As soon as he opened his eyes, he saw the treasures nestled on the floor below. He tried swimming toward one of the chests, seeing a golden ring encrusted with gemstones. If he could grab it and bring it back to her, then she would believe him. But as he struggled, he felt himself floating up away from it, as if something were pulling at his foot. His lungs were burning for air.

He came up spluttering again.

Just like before, the treasure seemed to have disappeared when he looked down below.

The Mortimer girl was staring at him, looking concerned. "You . . . you aren't teasing . . . are you?"

He shook his head, wanting to swim back down so he could prove it to her.

She grabbed his arm. "Let's go, Owen. I don't feel good about this. You were down a long time. I don't want to drown. Let's go."

He felt a strong compulsion to swim to the bottom of the cistern again. Maybe if he let the air out of his lungs, he would be able to stay down longer? Or if he let out his breath before jumping, he could—

"Owen!" she said firmly, sharply. "Come on. We'll get in trouble if we're gone too long." She reached out and gripped his shirt and pulled him toward the canoe. He had the urge to shove her away. There was treasure in the cistern. Maybe it was the king's treasure. Was this where some of the fountain coins ended up after a wish was granted? His mind reeled with ideas and possibilities. He *wanted* to take some of the coins. Just a handful. And maybe one of the swords.

In his distraction, the Mortimer girl had managed to pull him back to the stone steps. There was water in his ears and marching up the stone made them feel strange and squishy. She was talking to him, but he could not understand her well. He was seized by the determination to jump back into the water and look again. Maybe he would come back tonight when she was asleep. Then he'd prove it to her.

"There *was* something down there," Owen said sulkily.

She looked at him worriedly. "People drown all the time when they're not careful, Owen. Even little babies can drown in a bucket. Come, let's get dry."

When the door shut behind them, Owen heard the click of the latch closing. This time he saw what he had previously missed—a small wire folded by a stone in the wall. It was the latch trigger; they could use the door from either side.

Then they lay down in the stone courtyard, the sun still high overhead. She squeezed the hem of her dress and he listened to the little sounds of the moisture being squished out. They lay, heads just touching, staring up at the blue sky, which had a few fleecy clouds.

"Don't come back here without me," she said quietly.

Owen wriggled his finger in his ear because of the tickling water. He ignored her request.

"Owen? Please don't come back here without me. It isn't safe to swim alone. My papa taught me that."

"Why?" Owen challenged. "I'm a good swimmer."

"So am I," she said, sounding even more concerned. "But bad things can still happen. Please don't come back here without me. Promise me."

"Why do I have to?" he asked, frowning.

"Please, Owen. Promise me you won't. If you say you won't, I'll believe you."

He felt a darkness brooding in his heart. Resentment. Who was she to tell him what to do? "Will you promise me that you won't?" he demanded.

"Of course!" she said. Then she turned over and got up on her knees so that she was looking down at him. Her eyes were the color of the cistern water now. She gave him a pleading look. "I promise you, Owen Kiskaddon, that I will not come here alone. This is *our* secret place. I won't even tell my grandpapa that we found it. I promise you."

Owen felt guilty now. He had made her promise and now he would have to do the same. He didn't *want* to make the promise. She was always so open about what she thought and felt. Owen had not felt free since leaving Tatton Hall, and his entire life seemed shadowed with secrets.

"Please," she begged, reaching out and taking his hand.

It hurt to be forced like this. But he gave way, as part of him knew he must. "I will," he mumbled with a hint of regret. Why did she have to make things so difficult? "I promise you, Elysabeth *Victoria* Mortimer, that I won't come here alone. This is *our* secret place." Then he smirked. "I won't tell your grandfather, either." She seemed to grin and frown at the same time, which he knew was not possible, and added a shove as well.

"I promise," he finished.

He stared into her eyes, those strange bewitching eyes.

Part of him wanted to go to the North with her to see the waterfalls she had described. To stand on the bridge overlooking the drop. What would it be like, he wondered, to go *over* the falls? It was a punishment given to those who broke sanctuary or broke troth to the king. His brother Jorganon had likely perished this way. He thought of the river rushing past Our Lady and the tumultuous falls just beyond. What would it feel like . . . ?

"Thank you," the Mortimer girl said, and then leaned forward and kissed his cheek. She took his hand in hers.

"Can I call you something else?" he blurted out.

She looked confused. "Something else? What do you mean?"

He wasn't sure how to say it, exactly, and he worried she would get upset. "It's just that . . . well . . . your name is so *long*."

"You don't like my name?" Her eyes were wide with growing surprise.

"I *love* your name. I just don't like saying it all every time I want to talk to you. You call me Owen. That's short. I thought maybe I could call you something short, too. Just between us."

She stared at him, her lips pressed tight, and he could see her consternation. "Like what?" she asked.

"I don't know. It's just an idea. I know you like your middle name, so maybe something that mixes it with your first? I was thinking . . . Evie."

Her expression changed into a pleased smile when he said the name. "Evie. It's a girl's name, first of all. It means 'lively.' Do you think I'm lively?"

He couldn't think of a better word to describe her and nodded eagerly. He hadn't known the origin of the name before suggesting it. She was smarter than him that way.

She tapped her chin, thinking about it, as if it were the biggest decision in her life. "Well, I don't think I'd mind too much . . . but I'd only let *you* call me that. A pet name." She sat a little straighter, even though her clothes were sopping wet and her hair was scraggly. "Very well, Owen Kiskaddon. You *may* call me Evie."

She continued to hold his hand as they walked back to the window from which they'd come. It was still ajar, still waiting for them. Owen helped her climb up, and after she listened at the tapestry for noises, she knelt on the ledge and helped him climb up. They scooted down and shut the window behind them, keeping the secret.

The desire to go back to the cistern and swim for the treasure was fading as they walked. She started chattering about something, her dark hair stringy and damp, her boots squeaking as they walked.

Turning the corner, they collided with a huge, fat man, and the impact nearly knocked them both down.

It was Mancini. Owen's heart startled with fear, but he also felt a thrill—they had not been caught at the cistern.

"What are you doing over here?" the fat man asked in a chuffed voice. "Why are you so wet?"

"You know us, Mancini," Evie said, grabbing Owen's hand and swinging his arm. "We love to play in the fountains!"

"It's disrespectful to play in fountains," he said, his eyes narrowing.

"*You* did it," Owen rebuffed, reminded of Mancini's game with the pigeons at the sanctuary. The boy startled. He had *spoken* to an adult, to someone he normally feared.

Mancini stared at him as if he had suddenly sprouted a second nose. "Have you decided to start speaking at last, Master Kiskaddon? Is Lady Mortimer's banter contagious?"

"It's Elysabeth *Victoria* Mortimer," Owen said challengingly. He felt a little naughty, defying a grown-up.

Then he gripped her hand and pulled her away before Mancini could ask any more questions.

♦ ♦ ♦

The kingdom of Ceredigion has an interesting method for burying the dead, involving its rivers and waterfalls. When a person dies, they are not laid in a tomb or a sarcophagus— they are laid in a narrow boat or canoe with a few worldly possessions and set loose into a river near the falls. According to superstition, they are transported to the world of the Deep Fathoms after tumbling off the falls. This is why coins are tossed into fountains. They petition the dead for miracles in our world. Not only are the dead handled this way, it is also a form of justice for capital crimes. Someone guilty of treason is tied up in a canoe and shoved into the river. Vigilante justice dispenses with the boat altogether. If someone survives the fall, they are deemed innocent by the Fountain. You can imagine that only a few ever survive such an ordeal. I heard from Ratcliffe that Lord Asilomar failed his test of loyalty to the king and he, along with his children, will be "disembarking" from Our Lady tomorrow at noon. There is always a crowd at such events.

—Dominic Mancini, Espion of the Palace Kitchen

♦ ♦ ♦

CHAPTER TWENTY-ONE

Pinecone

Ankarette did not want to play Wizr that night. Instead, she taught Owen about potions and herbs and explained the properties of wound-wort, feverfew, and wisteria, and how to recognize the various plants. He had noticed an improvement in his wheezing since drinking her tea each night, and he was curious to learn more. She taught him about harmful plants, like nightshade, which—depending on the dosage—could either help a mother during a difficult pregnancy or kill a man. While they talked, she listened eagerly to his tales of adventure with Evie, but he omitted the story about the cistern because he'd promised to keep it secret. He even told her about being rude to Mancini. He longed to ask her about the treasure he had seen, but he could not do that without betraying the secret.

The queen's poisoner listened carefully, watching his face most intently. There was something about her keen interest that intrigued him. From the look in her eyes, it was as if he were sharing the most interesting story imaginable. She waited patiently until he was done, and then she grew serious.

"Owen, time is running short," she said. "The king will start destroying those who were disloyal to him before Ambion Hill. I wanted to have more time to prepare, to practice with you, but we just don't have it."

His heart lurched and he felt a sick, dark feeling bloom in his chest.

"Many families will fall during the purge," she said. "Maybe even your own. The thought of such a loss would be difficult for anyone, Owen. But especially for a little boy. Know that whatever happens, your parents would want you to live. To be safe. That is why they sent you here. Why the *Fountain* may have sent you here."

Owen shuddered, feeling miserable. Would he never see Tatton Hall again? His world had become Kingfountain palace. The thought of not playing with Evie made him feel awful. What about Liona in the kitchen? He was already forgetting what home was like, for he had been away for so many months. This new world, this dangerous world, had become familiar. He squeezed Ankarette's hands worriedly.

"Now is the time to act, Owen." She reached out and smoothed some of his hair, then gently stroked the side of his head, as if she were petting him. "Time to trick the king. You must do this. The idea was mine, but you must be the one to act. Are you ready to hear more about the plan?"

He nodded nervously, trying to quell the budding panic in his stomach. "The king is clever."

She nodded appreciatively. "But not as clever as I am. Listen to my idea. In the game Wizr, which is the most powerful piece? Is it the one marking the king?"

"No, it's the Wizr piece. It can move in any direction as far as it wants."

She nodded in agreement. "There will come a day when people forget what the Wizr piece represents. Perhaps they will even remove it from the board. The Wizr piece exists because it reminds us of the very first king of Ceredigion, King Andrew, the one who bound all the disparate chiefs and kings together under one crown. You see, that king had an advisor, someone who was Fountain-blessed. He was a great man, could move leagues away with his magic. That is why the piece can move the farthest. He was unique among his kind. He was called the king's Wizr. In other lands, the title is Vizier. His name was Myrddin. He has an interesting story, but I won't tell it to you now. Some Fountain-blessed are gifted with archery. Some with music. Some even with running. There's the story of an ancient man who ran for three days without stopping and then died after delivering his message. Myrddin's power, his magic from the Fountain, was his ability to see the future. They say it nearly drove him mad. It is the most rare gift that a Fountain-blessed can have, Owen."

"I don't understand," Owen said, blinking with confusion.

"This is the gift that you must trick the king into believing you have," she said with a wry smile. "Now lay your head on my lap and close your eyes." They were both sitting on the edge of her bed. It was late, but Owen was not sleepy yet. Although he was still unsettled and confused, he did as she asked.

Once his head was settled in her lap, she began stroking the hair away from his forehead. "Keep your eyes closed and listen to my voice." Her hand lightly stroked his forehead, smoothing away his hair. Her voice was soft, coaxing, melodious. "I had a dream last night. It was a strange dream. I was in a high tower. It was as tall as a mountain. I could see everything. Even the birds. As I looked from the window, I saw Our Lady. At Our Lady, I saw a branch with a swollen pinecone amidst the needles. The pinecone was fat and heavy. It fell off the branch into the river and went over the falls. That was my dream."

"I like that," Owen said, smiling. "I like pine trees, except for the sap."

"The sap is sticky, isn't it?" Ankarette said, a smile in her voice. She kept stroking his hair. "Let me tell you the story again. You must remember it." Then with an even softer voice, she repeated the story, not deviating from a single word. She had memorized it. As she spoke, and as he listened, he felt the distant shushing noise of the river. It was the sound of the waterfall at Our Lady. Ankarette was a great storyteller. He could imagine the waters rushing and falling like an avalanche of snow. He could hear the far-off roar of the falls, even from the poisoner's tower. And he could imagine a big, fat pinecone plopping into the water and being carried over the falls.

"Can you remember it?" she asked him. "Can you remember the story?"

"I think so," Owen said.

"Let me tell you again," she said. He felt her body move and shift and she stopped stroking his hair. Then she started again on the story, using the same words as before, the same lulling tone of voice. The churn of the water grew louder. Ankarette pressed something into his hand. It was hard and jagged and pointy. A pinecone. He did not want to squeeze it too hard, but he held it in a firm grip. Then he heard the sound of little things snapping. Ankarette put something in front of his nose, and he smelled the scent of pine needles. When she finished the story, he opened his eyes, still gripping the pinecone and smelling the scent.

"This is your dream, Owen," she said, helping him sit up. She put a hand on his shoulder. "You must tell the king about it in the morning during breakfast."

Owen stared at her in surprise. "Me?" he asked.

She squeezed his shoulder. "It's better that you *don't* understand what the dream means. He will. You *must* tell him this morning, Owen. The next day will be too late. Have courage."

He stared at her solemnly. "This will trick the king?" he asked.

She nodded, eyes deep and serious.

"What will he do when I tell him?" Owen asked, excited and nervous at the same time.

"I don't know," she answered. "I can only guess. But it will be his move next. And I'm very good at Wizr."

◆ ◆ ◆

Owen fidgeted nervously in the breakfast hall. He had stayed up quite late talking with Ankarette, but he was not sleepy at all. She normally sent him to bed when she felt pain, but for some reason, she had felt better, and they had stayed up talking.

Evie was chattering away next to Owen, but he was having a difficult time concentrating on her words.

"I hope Jewel falls asleep again today, but it might be too much to ask," she said conspiratorially. "I would love to jump back into the cistern again. Especially in the afternoon when it's so hot. But two days in a row would be suspicious. The servants may discover us. Let's not go back today. I really don't think it would be wise. Where else would you like to explore? We haven't been to the stables in a while. How about there?"

She waited a moment and then tugged on his arm. "How about the stables?"

"What?" he asked, turning to face her.

There was a mischievous look on her face. "You weren't even listening! How rude, Owen Kiskaddon. I don't think I'll marry you after all, if that's how you're going to behave. You're probably daydreaming about the treasure."

He saw Dunsdworth approaching and quickly warned her to be silent.

"What treasure?" Dunsdworth asked, coming closer. "What were you saying, Elysabeth?"

"It's Elysabeth Victoria—"

"I know your *name*," he sneered. "You've reminded me enough times, haven't you? No one wants to use so many words when they talk to a person."

"At least she has a *pretty* name," Owen said, only then realizing his thoughts had spilled out of his mouth before he could think through the wisdom of sharing them.

Evie went into a hysterical fit of shocked giggles, but the blood rushed into Dunsdworth's face and his mouth twisted into an angry frown.

"What?" the bigger boy said coldly.

Owen was saved by Ratcliffe's sudden entrance into the breakfast hall. He glanced around Dunsdworth, almost sighing with relief. Seeing his look, the older boy whirled around as the Espion master strode into the room. He turned back to give Owen a look that promised future vengeance and stalked away.

Ratcliffe clapped his hands. "The king is coming, the king is coming!" he said with his hasty breath. "Much is happening today, so no dawdling."

"You were brilliant," Evie whispered in Owen's ear. She gave him a light kiss on the cheek.

It was Owen's turn to flush. "He's a bully," he said brusquely, his insides starting to squirm.

Ratcliffe made a few curt announcements and then Owen heard the shuffle-step portending the king's entrance into the breakfast hall. As he came inside, a dark claw seemed to reach out and pierce Owen's heart. Even after jumping into the cistern, even after talking to Ankarette almost all night, his courage wilted from the mere sight of the king and the dagger hanging from his belt.

"Ooh, the thimbleberries are ripe!" Evie crooned, tugging Owen toward the table. She loved the fresh berries from the palace gardens. Everyone began to sample the delights of bread, fruit, and cheese that the kitchen had prepared. The king, as he usually did, lurked amidst the guests and ate sparingly.

"You're dropping half those berries on the floor," the king chided Evie as he passed. "Slow down. The cook will make the leftovers into jellies."

"They are delicious, my lord!" she said with a grin, impervious to his criticism. Then she grabbed a wafer and crammed it into her mouth.

"Ah, a respite from her tales," the king said mockingly, but his expression was pleased. Besides Princess Elyse, who happened to be there that morning, Evie was the only person in the breakfast hall who wasn't intimidated by him. Although the king teased her, he seemed to respect her courage and never aimed to wound her.

Severn looked at her with his gray eyes, and Owen noticed the dark smudges in his hollows. He was fidgeting with his dagger again, making the boy's courage shrivel even more. This was the best opportunity Owen was going to get, but his tongue felt swollen in his mouth.

Evie grabbed a goblet and quickly gulped down some drink as Owen stared at the king, willing himself to speak. The king's gaze met his own, and there was a moment of curiosity, of interest. He seemed to realize that Owen wanted to speak to him, and so he paused, just slightly, his look observant and interested.

Owen just stared at him, his legs like rocks, his stomach churning like butter. His throat was so dry he wanted to snatch the goblet away from Evie and drown in it.

The king, narrowing his eyebrows with a flicker of disappointment, turned away from them and took a halting step toward Ratcliffe, who was approaching rapidly.

Owen felt the sickness of defeat encase his heart, dragging him down. He had failed.

He felt Evie's hand clasp his own.

"What is it, Owen?" she asked him. "You look . . . sick."

Her hand.

They had jumped together into the cistern.

Holding her hand, he could do it. He squeezed her fingers hard, before he could shrink with fear.

Ratcliffe was almost to the king when Owen's little voice croaked out, "My lord, I had a dream last night. It was a strange dream."

◆ ◆ ◆

I am caught in a web. How did I get entangled? I convinced myself that Ankarette was harmless, that providing information to her would aid me. How could I have been so blind? She has wrested secrets of the Espion from me and is using them to preserve the life of the Kiskaddon boy. I know it, and yet I dare not confront her. She is in the kitchen often now. And one does not double-cross a poisoner without pain.

—Dominic Mancini, Espion of the Palace Kitchen

◆ ◆ ◆

CHAPTER TWENTY-TWO

Fountain-blessed

As Owen finished telling the king about his dream, the look on the older man's face completely transformed. Gone was the snide hostility. The king seemed thunderstruck, and he grabbed the table edge to steady himself. Ratcliffe, who had overheard the whole thing, stared at Owen incredulously as well, his mouth gaping.

"Ratcliffe, did you tell him?" the king whispered hoarsely. "Is there any . . . is there *any* way he could have known?"

Ratcliffe stared down at Owen with open distrust. "My lord, I don't see how. It's incredible."

"Your Espion in the kitchen . . . was he talking? Was he blabbing secrets?"

"I . . . I don't think so," Ratcliffe said. "It doesn't make any sense."

"It makes perfect sense," the king said, his voice distant, his eyes intense. He stared down at Owen, his expression changing to one of pleasure. "So this was a dream you had, was it? Last night?"

"Yes, my lord," Owen answered meekly, still clinging to Evie's hand to keep from drifting away in the current of fear that wanted to extinguish his voice.

"A pinecone," Severn repeated thoughtfully. He gave Ratcliffe a knowing look. Ankarette was right, there was no confusion at all, though Owen was still baffled.

"Well, lad," the king said, resting his other hand on Owen's shoulder and giving it a playful nudge. "You will be sure to tell me should you have any other such dreams?"

"If it pleases you, my lord," Owen said with a small bow.

"It does indeed, Owen. It pleases me much. How old are you again?"

"He's eight," Ratcliffe said, fidgeting with great energy. "Shall we continue with our plans then?"

"The Fountain has blessed it," Severn said with a mocking laugh. "See it done, Ratcliffe. Immediately." Then he turned his attention back to Owen. "Well, lad. Enjoy your breakfast."

As the king limped away, Owen realized the eyes of everyone in the room were fixed on him. There were servants and children, nobles who had come to petition the king. He had announced his dream in front of a hall full of witnesses. Many of them were beginning to whisper behind their hands, openly curious about the boy who had spoken.

"You didn't tell me you had a dream," Evie said, pulling Owen aside. "Have you had these before?"

He shook his head. "It was the first time. It was like a . . . a vision." He felt guilty lying to her, but he could not reveal the truth, certainly not without Ankarette's permission.

The meaning of Ankarette's story became tremendously clear later that morning when Lord Asilomar, from the east coast of Ceredigion, and his wife were trussed up on canoes and launched into the river from the island of Our Lady to plummet to their deaths over the falls. This was the first public execution Owen had attended in his life. They watched from the lower walls of the palace, and even from such a distance, they could see the thousands of people who had gathered to watch the canoes gain speed before charging off the falls. There was a collective gasp as the two vessels reached the terminus and pitched off. Owen stared, wondering again what it would be like.

When Duke Horwath returned from Our Lady, he clutched something in his hand, a banner. Owen had not seen the duke for several days. He had left the palace on an assignment for the king, which was almost certainly related to today's proceedings. And then Owen understood. The banner held the badge of House Asilomar. The badge of House Asilomar was a large pinecone stuck on a branch with pine needles. The pinecone had fallen into the river and run over the falls. Just like in Owen's dream.

"Look at it, Owen!" Evie said, when her grandfather showed her the crumpled banner. She stared at it in wonder before turning to look at him. "You saw it! You saw it in your dream!"

Horwath's eyes were narrowed at him, his face a mask devoid of emotions. "Everyone is talking," he said in his quiet way. "They are saying young Kiskaddon may be Fountain-blessed."

"Of course he is, Grandpapa," Evie answered with a glint in her eye. "I've always known that." She grabbed and clung to Owen's arm possessively.

There was a peculiar feeling in Owen's stomach. A shy smile crossed his face, but he said nothing.

Later, as he knelt in the kitchen arranging tiles, he found it difficult to concentrate because of all the visitors coming in and out, wanting to see him. There were whispers and comments, and even though he was trying not to listen, he could pick out some of the words. Liona took the time to explain what he was doing to the visitors.

"Yes, he's in the kitchen every day playing with those tiles. My husband Drew found them for him. He stacks them up and then knocks them down. No, he makes different patterns. Sometimes straight rows. Sometimes circles. It's the oddest thing you've seen, I'll warrant. Bless me if he doesn't come here every day. He's a clever lad. He's always been shy and clever."

"Ignore them." Evie was lying on her stomach with her chin propped on her wrist. "I've always believed you were Fountain-blessed, Owen. Do you know how rare that is? There was a Fountain-blessed boy in North Cumbria once who could talk to wolves."

He felt a prickle of apprehension that made him knock over one of the tiles and collapse the tower he was building. He frowned with anger and started building it again. All the attention made him feel good, but at the same time, he was lying to his best friend. *He* knew he wasn't Fountain-blessed. This was Ankarette's trick. He didn't mind tricking the king. Or Ratcliffe. Especially not Dunsdworth. But he did not like the thought of tricking *her*.

"I wonder how many of our children will be that way," Evie sighed dreamily. Grabbing a tile, she examined it closely before setting it back down. "It's not impossible, but sometimes more than one child can have it. But usually just one in a family. One who is special. Your mother had many children, so odds were good that one of you would be. I think it's that tuft of white hair that marks you. It was a sign from the Fountain."

The feeling of discomfort wriggling in his stomach was growing worse. He wanted to tell her very badly. It was eating away inside of him.

"It's almost as rare as surviving a waterfall," she continued. She was always prattling, even when he didn't feel like speaking. "About one in a hundred survive. There are always soldiers down at the bottom of the falls to see if anyone makes it. Lord Asilomar and his wife didn't. They drowned."

"That's awful," Owen said softly, working on the tower again.

"It's the punishment for being a traitor, Owen. The king didn't kill their boy. They had one son, who is four. The king sent him to be ward to Lord Lovel in Southport. I wouldn't want to marry someone younger than me. That would be disagreeable. I'm glad we're the same age."

Owen was amazed at how many people continued to come through the kitchen that day. The old gray-haired butler, Berwick, entered several times and complained loudly about the ruckus and how meals were not going to be served on time because of all the talk and nonsense.

"Yud think the lad sprootid wings and tuck a turn in the sky," he said brusquely. "A heap of bother. A lucky guess. Every'un knew Asilomar was a traitor. He's from East Stowe!"

"None of us here knew it," Liona said challengingly. "Being from the East doesn't make someone a traitor, Berwick. Hold your tongue."

"Hoold my tongue? You should hoold your tongue! Yuv been blabbing all day to visitors and such. Not an honest piece of work done all day long. It'll quiet doown. You'll see."

"I don't like Berwick," Owen said softly.

"I enjoy hearing him talk," Evie replied. "I love our quaint accent from the North. My father liked to hear me speak it."

Owen looked up at her. "You can talk like that?"

She grinned. "Forsooth, young lad, 'tis but the only prooper way amongst countrymen." She winked at him and returned to her normal way of speaking. "It's for the lesser born, really. My grandpapa is quiet because he was raised in the North and his accent comes out more often. He trained me to speak like the court. I like hearing it, though. It's musical."

"Berwick's always complaining," Owen mumbled.

"Everyone complains," she said, waving her hand. "Have you had any other dreams, Owen? About . . . us?"

The hopeful look in her eye made the guilt twist more deeply. He blushed and stared down at the tiles he was arranging. "I don't control it," he said limply.

"If you had a dream about *me* going into the river, you must tell me!" she said eagerly. "You know, some people have to be bound up because they're so frightened. I wouldn't want that. If I were condemned to die over the falls, I would want a paddle! Think of how it would *feel!* We'd go down together, you and I. Maybe we could hold hands from across our canoes? Papa said the people who survive point their toes down and keep as straight as a stick. Most of them die, though. I thought it would be fun to go over the falls with a big rope and have someone pull me up again from the bridge. But Papa said the falls would be too hard to pull against and I'd be dashed to pieces." She had a dreamy look in her eye as she contemplated her death over the falls.

He dropped his voice lower. "Don't you think it's awful, though? That the king tries to trick people into being loyal to him?"

She gave him a curious look. "That's just gossip, Owen. The king wouldn't do that."

"I think he does," Owen said, growing more uncomfortable. He wanted so much to tell her about Ankarette.

She shook her head. "I'll ask Grandpapa."

Owen frowned. "What if it's true?"

She shrugged, unconcerned. "Then I'll tell the king he must stop it." And Owen did not doubt for a moment that she would.

◆ ◆ ◆

When the castle was finally dark and fast asleep, Owen slipped out of his room to visit Ankarette. He was eager to see her again, and he hoped to get her permission to share at least part of his secret with Evie. He walked on cat's feet down the dark corridor and tripped the latch to enter one of the secret doors of the palace. He started down the corridor without a candle, for he knew the way even in the dark. When he reached the tower steps, he halted in his tracks and his heart started to hammer with fear.

There were men's voices coming from Ankarette's room.

Slowly, he crept up the stairwell, his body tense and low to the ground. He was ready to flee at a moment's warning. Had Ratcliffe discovered her hiding place at last? No, it wasn't his voice.

As he drew closer, he heard Ankarette. "It is as simple as that, Dominic. I want the boy to survive. And I need your help. Give me another bit of news. Something not even Ratcliffe knows. Nothing pivotal—nothing that will harm *you*. But something that will lend credibility to the rumor that Owen is Fountain-blessed."

"You are asking me," Mancini growled, "to risk my life, trusting *your* word."

"What she is askin'," came a third voice, and Owen recognized it immediately as the butler Berwick, "is that you stop eatin' in the kitchun and actually *doo* what Ratcliffe pays ya to *doo*! Look at yur flesh, man! You are lit'rally eatin' yourself to death!"

Ankarette's voice interrupted. "Patience, Berwick. You cannot coax a man beyond his willingness to suffer. If our friend wants to meet his end through his stomach, I have sympathy for that. We should not condemn him."

"*He's* increased the househoold costs of the palace fourfold!" Berwick complained.

"It's a trifle," Ankarette soothed. "When he becomes the head of the Espion, it will no longer matter."

"That is still your plan?" Mancini demanded in a wary voice. "I may be fat. I may be lazy. But I am not often called a fool. When the boy spouted off about pinecones, you can trust every Espion in the palace began pointing fingers at each other. I was actually startled enough that my defense seemed plausible. I didn't *tell* the boy anything!"

"Nor will you," Ankarette said placatingly. "You will tell me, and I will tell him. And in such a way that it cannot possibly come back and hurt you. In such a way that it will ultimately *benefit* you."

Owen heard the scratching sound of fingernails against whiskers. "I cannot believe I've been duped this easily. My pride is wounded."

"Your liver is wounded," Berwick taunted. "This woman is the queen's poisoner. She's the wiliest person in the kingdom, Fountainblessed herself! I owe quite a bit to her, and I have kept foolk from wanderin' up these steps for years. When she gives her word, she means it."

"No one *means* it," Mancini grumbled. "Trust is an eggshell. Bah, I'm going to get myself killed. If I could run away, I would. My legs would protest, unfortunately."

"Still he complains," Berwick muttered darkly. "Finish him now, lass. A little drink of that black vial would rid you of him."

"That's supposed to *inspire* my confidence?" Mancini wailed.

"You must pardon Berwick," Ankarette said. "He is loyal. I've kept his secret for years and he's been rewarded for turning a blind eye to my movements. I've helped him, just as I've offered to help you. Now . . . repeat again what we need from you."

"My unflinching courage," Mancini snapped.

"Goch, he's tiresome!" Berwick complained.

"Let him speak," Ankarette soothed.

"I need to provide you with some news that is going to reach the king through Ratcliffe. But the king must hear it from the boy first. So the tiding must hearken to something slightly less interesting than treason but more important than the rising cost of butter and treacle in the palace kitchen. Something short and easy to remember. Something that will make the boy look more *mystical*." He sighed wearily. "I'm going to regret this. I'm *already* regretting this. Why did you make me come up all these steps? Maybe you thought to kill me by exercise."

"No, Dominic," Ankarette said. "It's to show that I trust *you*. This is a delicate dance. You trust no one. But I promise you, when this is done, the king will value you so much that he will name you head of the Espion. And you'll be worthy of the post. I haven't forgotten my promise to teach you my history. How I came to live in this tower. But that will be another night. Go find us your news, Dominic. Give it to Berwick, who can reach me faster."

There was a deep, troubled sigh. "Very well, my lady. Is it true that you were hung from a gibbet? That is the legend anyway. That you survived?"

"It wasn't a gibbet," she answered softly. "It was a waterfall."

◆ ◆ ◆

It is a dangerous thing to try and grasp a snake by the tail. If you are not fast enough, it will bite you. If you are too fast, you will kill it. If it is dead, you cannot harvest its venom or use it to frighten someone else. I wish I were ten years younger. My hands are trembling.

—Dominic Mancini, Espion of the Palace Kitchen

◆ ◆ ◆

CHAPTER TWENTY-THREE

Wizr

There was a little space beneath the stone steps of the tower where Owen hid himself as Mancini and Berwick descended from Ankarette's room. He was as quiet as a mouse, listening to their conversation as they passed. Mancini was winded from the descent, but he was bubbling with queries and intrigue like a stew pot.

"And how did she lull *you* into service?" Mancini wheedled. "I never would have guessed you were part of her ring."

Berwick's reply was thick with sarcasm. "Isn't that the point? No, I'll be thrushed, man. She's a cunning one, but caring too. Hooked me like a fish in my heart pulp. Me daughter's womb was thick with twin bairns. The birthing was like moore than not to kill 'er and the babes. Ankarette is a midwife. Not only does she knoow all the poisons, but she also knoows all the remedies of feverfew and hypericum. She helped my lass, and the twins survived. She did it without me begging. She only said she might need a favor. And she did, and she does, and soo I am loyal to her more than the king. Because the king would have shrugged and let them all die. But the king's brother was king back then, and he cared about a butler and his family. He told his wife and she told her poisoner. And soo help came. I thaynk her for it."

"But she's *using* you, man, surely you see that?" Mancini's voice was low but sharp.

"Aye. But instead of years of grief, she's given me years of glee. That's worth something to a man with gray hairs like me. Spying and sneaking is not about coins. Coins can be stolen. They can be lost. But good memories . . . aye, they be the stuffings in the pie."

"That made no sense to me," Mancini grumbled.

"I'm surprised it did not, considering your girth," Berwick teased.

"My girth and I are boon companions, thank you. I eat so that I don't *have* to remember. The past is pain and best forgotten. Tomorrow is a day that may never see the sun. There is only now. I'm hungry, Berwick. I'm going to the kitchen."

"You do that," Berwick said with a laugh, and Owen heard the sound of a hand clapping against a back. The two ambled off down a side tunnel, their voices growing distant. The boy scampered up the stairs again.

When he entered the tower room, Ankarette was leaning against a table, gripping its edge with one hand and holding her stomach, as if she might vomit, with the other. Sweat trickled down her cheek and she breathed in and out quickly. Owen shrank with worry.

Some of her hair had straggled down from its braided nest, and when she turned her gaze on him, he could see the suffering in her eyes.

A tender smile twitched on her mouth. "Hello, Owen," she said, lips tight with suppressed pain. "Our little plan worked. So far. Tell me how it went." She took a hesitant step toward her bed, looking almost like a puppet dangling on strings.

Owen walked up and reached for her hand, but she rested it on his shoulder instead. She leaned her weight against him, but it was not burdensome.

"Thank you," she whispered, using Owen as a crutch as she hobbled to her bedside. Once they reached the bed, she seated herself delicately on the edge and folded her hands in her lap. She blinked a few times, and then her face looked peaceful and serene. She looked like herself again, pretty and gentle and caring, but his heart cringed in pain at the evidence he'd seen of her suffering.

"Are you very sick?" he asked.

"I am a little tired tonight," she said dismissively. "That is all. Tell me about what happened. The palace was buzzing like a beehive today!"

Owen quickly related what he had done and how he had summoned the courage to tell the king about his "dream." She listened attentively, waiting for him to finish the story before asking questions.

"How did Ratcliffe look?" she pressed.

"He looked frightened. Like he was scared of me."

"He's not scared of you, Owen," she said. "He's scared for himself. His first fear is that someone in the Espion has betrayed him. Which is what has happened. He will seek to discover who it is, but I don't think we'll have any trouble outmaneuvering him. What about the king? How did *he* look?"

"Almost . . . pleased," Owen answered. "He seemed to like me for the first time."

Ankarette nodded with satisfaction. "It is rare for a young boy to demonstrate aptitude with the Fountain. It bodes well for the king if he is able to find people who are Fountain-blessed to serve him. This is what I suspect will happen next. Ratcliffe will keep you on a shorter leash. He'll start leaking information to different spies to see if your next dream reveals it. Then he'll know which Espion betrayed him. That's what most people without vision would do. What you will reveal in your next dream is something Ratcliffe doesn't even know yet." She grinned playfully. "It may take several attempts for us to win the king's trust completely. Do you understand now what the dream meant?"

Owen was amazed at her level of thinking. He would never have been able to come up with such an idea on his own. "I think so. Lord Asilomar's badge was the clue."

She nodded affectionately and reached out and took his hand. "I need rest, Owen. Mancini will help us with the next clue."

"I know," Owen said shyly. "I heard him from the hall."

"I'm glad you did," she answered with a wink. "You were clever to stay hidden. The next clue will be tricky because it may not come in the night. You must be ready to act quickly. Like before, you won't know what it means. Just trust the words I tell you. Each is chosen deliberately. There may be many more deaths in the near future. The king defeated his enemies at Ambion Hill, but he is still unsure of his throne. He now has absolute power in the realm, and his enemies at home are quaking with fear that what happened to Lord Asilomar is just the beginning."

"I wanted to ask you something," Owen said. "I want to tell Evie about our secret." He bit his lip, looking at her worriedly. "I think she would help us. The only reason I had enough courage to speak to the king was because she was with me."

Ankarette's expression hardened. It was almost imperceptible, but Owen knew her well enough to notice the tightening around her eyes and the little dip in her smile.

"I see," she said softly, then looked down at her hands, which still held his. Owen could tell she was thinking very hard, very quickly. After a long pause, she squeezed his hand lightly and peered into his eyes.

"It is difficult for you, for anyone, to keep a secret," she said in a very serious tone. Then she released his hand and tapped her own heart with her fingers. "A secret squirms inside of us. Like a chick wanting to be free of its egg. Or a moth quivering inside a cocoon. Secrets *want* to be told, don't they?"

He stared at her, not sure if she was pleased with him or not. Her serious manner made him fear he had made a mistake. "Yes," he agreed, because he *did* want to tell Evie. Especially considering the way she had reacted to his dream. It felt . . . dishonest keeping it from her.

She reached and put her hand on his shoulder. "You want to tell her because you feel a sense of loyalty toward her. She is your friend, your playmate. She is pretty and she is kind. You two share confidences. But remember the nature of secrets, Owen. If you share yours, it will stop wriggling inside your chest. And it will start wriggling inside hers. Secrets always want to come out. She feels loyalty to you. That is clear. But is her loyalty to you greater than her loyalty to her *grandfather*?" She raised her eyebrows. "Who has she known longer? Who has shown her more love and devotion?"

She sighed deeply and dropped her hand back into her lap. Then she looked at him with her luminous eyes, her gaze imploring. "When you share a secret, Owen, you take a great risk. I am who I am, I became who I became, because I *don't* share secrets very easily. I make sure I can trust someone fully *before* I do. I have trusted Mancini with only a portion of my plan. The same with Berwick. I need to tell them things in order to accomplish my goal, but either one of them could betray us. Before you share the truth with Lady Mortimer, I need to know if I can trust her. That means I must meet her and look her in the eyes. I must discern her. That is a risk, of course, but I am willing to take it if it will help you have courage."

Owen nodded firmly, understanding what she meant. "I trust you, Ankarette Tryneowy," he said. "I also trust her. I think . . . I think she's like us."

"Then watch for me in the kitchen," Ankarette said, stroking the white patch of hair above Owen's ear.

♦ ♦ ♦

The next morning in the great hall, Owen found that his world had changed overnight. When he and Evie walked into the room, he noticed that attendance in the hall had increased dramatically. There were noble families there who had never attended the king's breakfasts before. Fathers and mothers with children clustering around their legs. Hushing noises heralded his entrance and people eyed him with open curiosity and interest. Additional food had been gathered to the trestle tables—huge trays of fried bacon, muffins, breads and cheeses, vines of grapes, and green pears.

The commotion subsided for only a moment and then people began talking again, wondering aloud if the lad had had any more dreams. Owen had predicted the fall of House Asilomar. People wanted to know if another family would be named.

"They are like carrion birds," Evie whispered disdainfully in his ear. "They want to peck at the lands and farms that will be left behind if other traitors are named. Where were they all before?"

The rumble of voices quieted when the king entered, with Lord Horwath at his side holding a wooden crate in his arms.

"I wonder what *that* is," Evie said curiously, nudging Owen's ribs.

The king slowed when he saw the multitude in attendance. He cast his gaze around the crowd, looking perplexed, but then understanding seemed to dawn on his face. "Ah!" he said in a loud, strong voice. "My meals have suddenly become very . . . popular! Well, I cannot give credit to the excellent cooking, which has gone unchanged for years. I cannot give credit to myself, because I am, as you all know, a rough soldier and not a gallant with fine plumes in my cap. Black suits me best, I think. No, you are not here for the tasty treats. You are here because of a little boy." He sneered at them, his expression full of disdain. "Thank you all, my lords and ladies, for gracing us with your presence this morning. I will not send you all away, although I am tempted! The palace has ever been a place to assemble and gather. Eat! Do not let this mountain of a meal go to waste! Eat! And may your guts sicken of it before mine does."

He waved his hand in a sweeping gesture, granting those in attendance permission to begin the meal. The children sprang from their parents' legs and quickly mobbed the table, which seemed funny to Owen, especially since he knew the king was not the only one who feared the morning feast might be poisoned. The king quickly picked out his meal, joining the melee of children. He chuckled to himself as one of the tables was almost overturned by the crowd.

"Hold there, Bowen! There is enough for all! If the table breaks, my hounds will snarl and snap at the food too! You are all a bunch of greedy hounds! Why, Lady Marple, do you hesitate to join the feast? You let your son gorge himself quickly enough. Lord Tanner . . . a pleasure truly! Why, I do not think you have darkened this hall since my coronation. Why so solemn, sir? What has changed?"

The king seemed to take a perverse delight in tormenting everyone. As he flung his barbs and jests around the hall, Owen could hear the faint trickling sound of water, as if a cup were being filled. The king's elation only grew with the increased number in attendance. His eyes were almost feverish with delight as he made his way through the crowd. His tongue was like the knife at his belt, always sharp and always sudden, ready to strike at any opportunity.

Owen grabbed some food himself, feeling uncomfortable with the knowledge that Ankarette's scheme—and his part in it—had prompted the change.

"Well, my little lord Kiskaddon!" the king suddenly said, calling attention to Owen in front of all the gathered feasters. "Look what you have done. I am sure many came here to see if you had another dream last night. But that could not have happened, or else you would have fetched me right away. But please put these miserable creatures out of their discomfort."

Owen shook his head, and he could see the looks of disappointment, the crestfallen glances. Parents began summoning their children to them, scolding them for indulging in the feast.

Many began to retreat from the room. The king ridiculed them. "How quick you are to leave, Lord Bascom! Lady Tress, please don't snap a garter in your haste to flee! There are crumbs left on the plates still! Look at them," he said in an undertone, mockingly. "Look how they run." Then he glanced back at Owen and snapped his fingers, so suddenly and so loud that Owen flinched.

The commotion in the hall quelled in an instant.

"Lord Horwath, if you would," the king said dramatically. Some of those who were fleeing halted, seemingly intrigued by his announcement. The king folded his arms imperiously, his look contented and smug. Although his shoulders were crooked, the way his arms were folded made him look regal, impressive.

Lord Horwath approached Owen with the wooden box. He dropped to one knee in front of his granddaughter and Owen, and set the box down on his angled leg. Then, with a weather-beaten hand, he lifted the top of the wooden box.

"Ooohh!" Evie cooed with delight.

It was a Wizr set, the most beautiful one Owen had ever seen. The tiles were violet and white, like Ankarette's, made of stone. The gleaming pieces were carved and polished out of matching colors, resting in little felt nooks along the edges of the box. Owen stared at it breathlessly.

"I promised you a Wizr set," the king said with a twist in his voice. "I ordered this to be made and it recently arrived from Brugia. I was only looking for the opportunity to gift it to you, boy." Owen pried his gaze away from the dazzling pieces and stared at the king in confusion. This was no ordinary Wizr set. It was one meant for a king.

Severn's eyes were full of meaning. "It is my *gift* to you, Owen. When I make a promise, I honor it. And I expect the same in return."

The children in the room shuffled forward to look at the expensive, custom-made pieces. Even Dunsdworth stared at it hungrily. It was clear he had never been favored by the king before.

Owen felt a guilty smile tug at the corner of his mouth.

"Let's play!" Evie gasped, her interest in the game miraculously renewed.

◆ ◆ ◆

Ratcliffe is shrewd. He doesn't believe the boy is Fountain-blessed at all. It's too suspicious, too convenient. He is on the hunt, like a wolf searching for a promising scent. I think he wants to destroy the boy. There is anger in his eyes. If the poisoner isn't careful, the lad might end up like the princes. Wasn't it the last head of the Espion who had the two boys murdered?

—Dominic Mancini, Espion of the Palace Kitchen

◆ ◆ ◆

CHAPTER TWENTY-FOUR

Lord Dunsdworth

The novelty of the new Wizr set had galvanized the kitchen, which was almost as bustling as it had been the day Owen had predicted the fall of House Asilomar. The Wizr set was pristine, polished to a glassy shine, and each piece was thick and handcrafted. Owen's satchel remained undisturbed while the king's gift dominated.

Owen was careful as he showed Evie some of the strategies Ankarette had taught him. It wasn't fun playing someone who could be defeated so easily, but she was more eager to learn with a new set, and she had found new relish in the idea of defeating adults in a game meant for them.

"How did you learn all of these moves?" she asked him in wonderment, and Owen felt the wriggling moth of the secret in his chest again. His lips burned to tell her, but he remained silent.

"I've always loved Wizr," he said, completing a series of movements to win the game.

"Do you know why they call the game Wizr?" she asked, as they both began to settle the pieces back to the starting position.

He nodded and quickly explained the origin of the term.

"I wish Myrddin was real," she said with a sigh. "Some people say it's just a story. There aren't any *true* Wizrs anymore. But I like to imagine that Wizrs *are* real, that the Fountain truly can bless people with magic. There are so many stories, some of them must be true. Like with you," she said slyly. They stared at the board and started another game.

"Your Highness, so lovely to see you," Liona said. Her voice was one of many in the background, but Owen had especially cunning hearing. He jerked his head up and saw Princess Elyse speaking softly to Liona. He had not spoken to her in a while and his heart sighed wistfully, remembering how gently she had welcomed him to the palace. He felt tenderness toward her and hoped she would stop to greet him.

"Why are you staring at her?" Evie asked with a taunting voice. "She's so beautiful. I wish my hair was gold like hers, not dark as wood. She's very lovely, Owen. You *should* admire her. She's ten years older than us and she *still* doesn't have a husband. I pity her, truly. Her last betrothed was killed at Ambion Hill by the king. Did you know that? My grandpapa told me about it. He led the vanguard."

At her words, Owen felt worry and regret. Perhaps Ankarette was right, and Evie would not be able to keep a secret from her grandfather. Maybe it was not fair to ask it of her.

She was oblivious to his inner turmoil. "There was fighting and arrows and crossbows. I wish I could have been there. I would love to learn how to fight, but they will not let ladies into the training yard. When you learn how to fight, you must *promise* to teach me. The king remained on the hill, watching as Grandpapa was losing the battle down below. Then he saw his enemy cross the field, unguarded. So the king took his household knights and they charged them. The king himself! I wish I had been there! They slammed into the rebels' men and the king took down the standard-bearer with his own lance. His horse was cut down beneath him, but still he fought, surrounded only by his most loyal knights. And he struck down his enemy with his own sword. After he fell, the battle ended. There was no one left to fight for." She sighed, fidgeting with a particular piece of the set. "Are you . . . afraid of going into battle?" she asked him.

Owen looked at her, perplexed. "I'm too young."

"Not now, silly boy. When you are *older*. You start training when you are ten. It's hard work, but I know I would love it. Like the Maid of Donremy at the siege of Lionn! When King Severn was young, he was sent to his uncle's castle in the North to be trained in war." She gave him an eager look. "Maybe the king will send *you* to the North! Wouldn't that be wonderful, Owen Kiskaddon? Then we could have all the adventures we've talked about. Maybe Grandpapa would let me train too. Or you and I could do it in secret! It would be just like a dream." She sighed contentedly.

Owen heard the sound of someone sitting on the bench next to them and felt the shadow spread over him. He smelled her—Ankarette. The scent like a rose pressed into the pages of a book. He glanced surreptitiously at her, feeling his stomach wriggling again. There were so many people around.

Elysabeth Victoria Mortimer lifted her head at the newcomer. She was completely unafraid of meeting new people, and it didn't bother her in the least that an adult had come so close to their game. "Hello," she said with a bright smile. "I'm Elysabeth *Victoria* Mortimer."

"What a lovely name," Ankarette said, returning the smile. "Please, don't let me disturb your game."

"We weren't playing exactly," Evie replied confidentially. "Owen is teaching me how to win. He's very clever. Do you know who this is? He's Owen Kiskaddon, the king's ward. He's my friend." Her eyes crinkled as she reached out and squeezed Owen's hand.

"I can tell you are very close," Ankarette said, her smile warm and inviting.

"What is your name?" Evie asked.

Owen swallowed, wondering what the reply would be. His stomach was churning with the newness of the situation. Ankarette had never come down into the kitchen before when others were around. It made him worry for her safety.

"How thoughtful of you to ask," Ankarette said with a winning smile. "I used to come here often, back when the queen dowager lived in the palace. There were always so many children running about back then. They had a large brood."

Evie nodded. "She lives in the sanctuary of Our Lady now. How sad it must be to go from being a queen to being a prisoner in a sanctuary. My grandpapa says she is never going to come out. My grandpapa is Duke Horwath. Do you know him?"

"I do," Ankarette answered. "You must love him a great deal."

She nodded vigorously. "Oh yes. He is dear to my heart. I love my grandpapa. But he brought me here to Kingfountain to meet Owen." She patted his leg. "We're going to be married, you know. He's *Fountain-blessed*."

"So I've heard," Ankarette said smugly. "You best play your game. I'm sorry to have bothered you. I love playing Wizr myself."

"Would you like to play with us?" Evie said. "What was your name again? I thought you had told me, but then I realized you hadn't. You're very pretty. I like how your hair is done up like that. It's so beautiful. Mine isn't long enough yet, but when I'm older, I will wear it like yours. What was your name?"

Another sound reached Owen's ears, one that caused a jolt of alarm. It was Dunsdworth's voice, and from the tone, he had come looking for trouble. Owen glanced at the door as the older boy came swaggering into the kitchen, disdainful of the crowds, and began elbowing his way over to the very corner where they sat.

Ankarette's face went white. "I must go," she whispered softly. Rising from the bench, she started away from them and headed toward the bread ovens. It was all happening so quickly, Owen could only take note of his own alarm and hers before Dunsdworth came close enough to see her. As the older boy gazed upon Ankarette, his expression altered into recognition.

"You?" Dunsdworth said in shock and surprise. Ankarette took advantage of the commotion to try and slip away, but the boy barged through the crowd and cut her off.

"I think he knows her," Evie said with concern. She rose, a frown forming on her lips. "Who was she?"

Dunsdworth's face was livid with rage. "You . . . you're alive? But how can this be? What trickery?"

So Dunsdworth knew Ankarette Tryneowy. He recognized her. The dread thickened inside Owen, almost choking him.

"I'm afraid you're confused," Ankarette said softly, trying to escape, but the young man barred her way and reached out to grab her arm. She deftly avoided the hand, retreating deeper into the kitchen. Owen knew she could easily best Dunsdworth, but this was not a contest of skill. Too much attention had already been directed at them.

If Ankarette were caught, Owen had no doubt she would be killed. It was *his* fault she had come down into the kitchen at all. He needed to help her. But how? His mind worked furiously to solve the problem. Then he felt a little gush bloom inside him, followed by a flowing sensation, and suddenly his mind was full of ideas. He saw all the possibilities laid out before him. And he acted.

He grabbed one of the Wizr pieces, jumped over the bench, and rushed toward Dunsdworth. Distract him. Draw him away so Ankarette could escape through the secret door.

"Look what the king gave me!" Owen said loudly. He rushed up to Dunsdworth and shoved the piece beneath his nose.

"Who cares about your toy!" Dunsdworth thundered, trying to shove Owen out of his way.

Owen thrust the piece into his face again. "It's not a toy. It's the king's gift! You probably don't even know *how* to play Wizr."

The rebuke was enough to wrest Dunsdworth's attention away from Ankarette. "Why would I care to play that silly game? Life is not like Wizr. Two pieces of stone aren't two men, one trained more than the other." He yanked the piece out of Owen's hand and gave him a rough shove.

"That's mine!" Owen shouted with pretended rage. "You're jealous because the king gave me a gift and he only teases you. Give it back!" Owen grabbed Dunsdworth's belt and yanked it hard to try and propel himself upward. As he yanked, his fingers began to deftly loosen the belt buckle. "It's mine!"

"Give it back!" Evie shouted angrily. She had rushed up to them and was standing nearby, her fists clenched and her cheeks pale with anger. "It's Owen's!"

"Get off!" Dunsdworth barked. He waved the piece over his head with one hand and gave Owen a hard shove with the other, sending him crashing to the ground.

With Dunsdworth's belt.

Without the belt, Dunsdworth's pants dropped down to his ankles, revealing his linen braies, which were hitched up high. There was a spattering of laughter throughout the kitchen, but it was the tittering of the ladies that made the lad's face turn purple. Owen's arm hurt from landing on the hard tiles, but his plan had worked. Ankarette had used the commotion to slip away.

Suddenly Dunsdworth's purple face twisted with wrath and revenge. He threw down the piece and leaped on top of Owen. Snatching his belt, he started to thrash the smaller boy with vigor.

The explosion of pain made Owen gasp in shock and roll into a ball like a ticklebug.

"Stop it! Stop it!" Evie shrieked, launching herself at Dunsdworth like a cat. She yanked his hair and clawed at him in a frenzy. Freed from the onslaught for a moment, Owen could only look on in awe, surprised at how the girl had turned into a fury.

To protect himself, Dunsdworth shoved her away too, sending her sprawling, which caused the witnesses to gasp.

Owen, curled up on the floor, saw his opening. Without even rising, he kicked out his foot and caught Dunsdworth in his most sensitive area. The purple angry face went milk-white as the young man tottered over, clutching himself and whimpering.

And it was in that precise moment, as Elysabeth Victoria Mortimer was about to hurl herself at the older boy again in rage and eat his heart, that her grandfather, Duke Horwath, stormed into the kitchen. He saw his little girl on the floor, her face wet with tears of fury. He saw Dunsdworth with no pants. And he saw Owen curled up like a beaten pup.

The duke was not gentle as he hauled the young man to his feet and nearly threw him out of the kitchen ahead of him. Owen almost pitied the condemned, but then his body began to tremble with all the pent-up fear, pain, and shame of the last moments. He didn't feel the cut on his cheekbone from the belt buckle until Evie was kneeling in front of him worriedly. She was so angry she was sobbing.

"Are you all right?" she pleaded, using the hem of her dress to mop the blood from his cheek.

He glanced at the doorway from which the duke had left with Dunsdworth. And he saw Mancini slip back into the kitchen, a satisfied smile playing on his flabby mouth. The Espion gazed down at Owen on the floor and gave him a little nod of respect. Owen returned the gesture.

"I'll be all right," he groaned, clutching his stomach, making his injuries look worse than they really were.

Together, he and Mancini had helped save Ankarette. Something had shifted between them. It was as if they now shared an alliance of self-preservation.

Owen let Evie nurse him. And in a moment, the Princess Elyse was kneeling by him as well.

"Well done," she whispered in his ear.

Her praise was worth the pain.

CHAPTER TWENTY-FIVE

Secrets of Wine

Ankarette came to Owen's room that night, much to his surprise. After dark, he tracked the passing hours by how low his candle burned. It was still high and bright when the hidden door opened and she emerged, soundless as a shadow. He would not have left to seek her for some time.

"Ankarette!" he whispered, rising from the floor where he had spread his Wizr board. He had been playing with the pieces while he waited.

"There's a little cut on your cheek," she said, with a wrinkle in her brow.

He nodded. "Liona put some goose grease on it. It doesn't sting that much."

She knelt in front of him so that their eyes were level. As he stood before her, she reached out and smoothed the hair on his forehead. "You saved me this afternoon, Owen Kiskaddon. Despite all our plans, things happen that surprise us." She paused, giving him such a serious and tender look that he flushed. She placed her hand on his shoulder and gave it a squeeze. "Thank you, Owen. I'm so grateful."

He swallowed, feeling his ears burn pink. "You're helping me. I *had* to help you."

She then took his hands in hers and kissed them before letting them go. "Bless you for it. Thank you. Now come with me."

"It's early still. Part of the castle is still awake."

"I know. We're not going to the tower. We're going to Elysabeth's room."

Owen stared at her in shock. "You mean . . . we're going to tell her?" he asked excitedly.

Ankarette gave him a knowing nod. "When I met her in the kitchen, I studied her closely. I believe she is trustworthy. Now we'll prove if I'm right. Better to know sooner than later. Come with me."

She rose and held out her hand, which he gratefully took. He was used to walking the secret corridors alone, but going with her added a secret pleasure. "What will you tell her?" he asked in a whisper, knowing that voices could carry.

"You'll see," she replied softly, squeezing his hand.

"She talks a lot, Ankarette. She talks *so* much. She's chatty. Are you sure?"

"Yes, she's *loquacious*. That's the proper word. But I like that about her. When I saw what she did after Dunsdworth's boy started flogging you—how she attacked him like a cat—that earned her my respect. You want someone like her on *your* side. And how you tricked him out of his pants? Oh, Owen, you've made an enemy for life. I hope you realize that. But he and his family have been my enemies for years. I will tell you of it tonight . . . with her to hear the story."

When they reached the secret door leading to Evie's room, they paused. Ankarette secretly slid open the spyhole and gazed into the room. Candlelight streamed into the corridor from the interior of the room, and the light exposed Ankarette's luminous eyes and the skin of her cheeks. She looked so hauntingly pretty at that moment, and Owen felt lucky to know her.

"She's still awake, good," Ankarette whispered. She slid the spyhole shut and then crouched by Owen so she could whisper into his ear. Her breath tickled him. She had the scent of roses about her still. "You go in first and tell her that you'd like her to meet a secret friend. Someone who has been trying to help you. Tell her you are about to entrust her with your greatest secret. I'll listen and see what she says. Can you remember that?"

"Yes," Owen whispered. He was so excited to finally tell Evie the truth that he nearly barged into the room.

Ankarette released the hidden latch and Owen pushed the door open and slipped inside the room. He left the hidden door ajar.

"How did you get in here?" Evie gasped. She was kneeling on her bed in her nightgown, brushing her dark hair. She scooted off the bed, her eyes gleaming with surprise. "Is that a secret door? Have you come in here before? Why didn't you tell me?"

"Ssshhh!" Owen insisted, holding up his hands to try and stop the flow of questions. He put his finger to his own lips to show her she needed to be quiet. She was almost bouncing with excitement, her eyes glittering.

"Tell me!" she said, her hands flapping.

"I want to. Ssshh! Someone will hear us. I want to tell you my greatest secret. But first I need to know I can trust you not to tell."

She looked at him with exasperation. "Of course you can trust me! I haven't told anyone about the cistern. Do you think Grandpapa would like to know that? There are some things you just don't tell adults. What is it? I'm about to burst!" She gripped his arms and shook him just a little.

"Quiet!" he said urgently. "I want you to meet someone. A friend. Someone who is trying to help me escape."

"Why do you need to escape?" she asked.

"Because I don't want to get pushed off a waterfall like my older brother!" Owen said, getting frustrated. "Look, will you keep this a secret? If I can't tell you—"

"Of course I will!" she said indignantly. "I would never betray you, Owen Kiskaddon. Never." She put her finger on her brow, thinking hard. "You can . . . you can cut off all my hair if I do!"

The thought of her bald made him giggle. But then her eyes widened with surprise as she looked over his shoulder. Ankarette had come into the room.

"The lady from the kitchen," she whispered in awe.

Ankarette came and sat on the edge of Evie's bed. The soft candlelight highlighted her silk gown and perfectly coiffed hair. She looked like such a fairy creature that Elysabeth's mouth formed a lovely O as she stared at her. For the first time, Owen noticed there were some similarities between them—the color of their hair and their eyes almost matched. If Elysabeth Victoria Mortimer grew up looking like Ankarette Tryneowy, he would have no problem marrying her.

"I'm pleased to meet you again, my lady," Ankarette said, bowing her head respectfully. "Owen tells me you are Elysabeth Victoria Mortimer, daughter of Lord Mortimer and granddaughter of Lord Horwath. You have esteemed parentage."

A small smile came to Evie's face. "Who are you?" she asked, looking intrigued but also a little wary.

"My name is Ankarette Tryneowy. I am the queen's poisoner."

If possible, the girl's eyes seemed to light up even more. "Truly? That is so interesting. You make poisons? But you said you're the *queen's poisoner*. The queen died. Did you . . . did you poison her?"

Ankarette suppressed a smile. "I served a different queen than King Severn's wife. And no, I did not poison her. She died from a sickness. I have been teaching Owen Kiskaddon many things, but most importantly, how to become Fountain-blessed. *I* am Fountain-blessed."

"You are?" she asked eagerly, even more involved if that were possible. Owen was so grateful that he did not have to carry the burden of the secret alone.

"I am. Owen is very special to me. I know he is to you, as well. I don't want the king to hurt him or his family if I can help it. I came here tonight to tell you both a story. Owen wanted so much to tell you about me. He's been pleading with me to trust you, so I came by the kitchen today to see if I dared. When you defended your friend against a much bigger boy, I knew that I could give you my confidence."

Evie smiled with self-satisfaction. "Grandpapa said I should leave flogging to him. But I couldn't stand by while Dunsdworth beat Owen with a belt. Did you see what it did to his cheek? It wasn't Owen's fault his pants fell down!"

Ankarette suppressed a smile as she gave Owen a pointed look.

"Actually, it was," Owen admitted.

Evie covered her mouth, stifling a laugh. "You *are* wicked," she said, laughing softly. "He deserved it." She turned her gaze on Ankarette. "If you are trying to help Owen, then I want to help too."

"I thought you would," Ankarette replied sagely. "So I must tell you both a story. It is a secret that very few know about. But even though it's a secret, it is still true. Why don't you both sit on the floor and listen? It is the story of how I died."

Owen's eyes widened. He sat on the floor next to Evie, his knees touching hers. His companion was so eager to hear the story, she was fidgeting slightly. Owen felt just as anxious, but for a different reason—he was concerned by the ominous beginning.

"This is a story about four brothers," Ankarette said simply. "Three of them are dead now. Only the youngest has survived. He is the last of the brothers. His name is Severn. He is your king." She folded her hands in her lap, bending closer so she could speak more softly. "The eldest brother was Eredur. His father and the next-eldest brother died rebelling against their king. That happens a lot in Ceredigion, and this was *many* years ago. Eredur was tall, strong, and handsome. The people liked him. With his uncle Warrewik's help, he defeated the king and claimed the crown. While the war was still raging, he sent his two youngest brothers to live across the sea in the kingdom of Brugia. Severn was eight years old when that happened. He was *your* age, Owen. His father had just died in a terrible battle. Just like yours did, my lady. He was very sad."

Evie nodded, her countenance darkening, betraying the pent-up grief she felt over her loss. Owen looked at her, surprised. He reached over and covered her hand with his. She smiled at him, but there were tears in her eyes.

"King Eredur began to establish himself in the realm. His uncle Warrewik, the one who had helped him gain the throne, was his chief supporter, and he ran the king's network of Espion. I was very young back then. Sixteen. I was a servant in Warrewik's household, but I was part of the Espion. I served his eldest daughter, Isybelle. We were very close. But as often happens in families, the king and his uncle grew angry with each other. The uncle didn't get his way when he thought that he should have. There was a misunderstanding about the king's marriage. And so Warrewik decided to topple the king. He had his daughter, my mistress Isybelle, marry the king's younger brother, Lord Dunsdworth, and he promised his son-in-law the kingdom of Ceredigion. My loyalty was to the king, not to the uncle. When I learned of his plot, I tried to warn the king of his brother's treachery, but I was too late to save him. He was captured and almost thrown into the river. The uncle should have done away with him. The decision cost him his life later."

Owen swallowed, keenly listening to the story unfold. He was too young to understand the ways of kings and kingmakers. He didn't know any of this history.

Ankarette continued. "King Eredur escaped his confinement and fled across the sea to Brugia with his youngest brother, Severn. They were in exile, living on the grace of others. After biding his time, Eredur returned with a trick he had learned from one of his ancestors."

"What trick?" Evie asked with keen interest.

"The trick was this. He returned and went to the North. Rather than reclaim his crown, he said he merely wanted to be Duke of North Cumbria again. Your grandfather's role, my dear. It surprised everyone, and the uncle was furious, of course. Very quickly, King Eredur gathered enough supporters to fight his uncle. Warrewik and Lord Dunsdworth fled Ceredigion soon after. What a turn of events! King Eredur wasn't secure, though. His enemies were abroad, causing trouble. And so the uncle made an alliance with the wife of the king he had helped Eredur depose, promising to restore *that* king to power. It was a cowardly act. To preserve his own power, he forsook his entire family. How do you think his son-in-law, Lord Dunsdworth, felt about that? And here is where my part comes in."

Owen and Evie looked at each other.

"King Eredur sent me on a secret mission. I was very young, not even eighteen years old. He sent me across the sea to find Lord Dunsdworth. The king asked me to persuade the younger man to relent and join forces with his king and brother. If I could not persuade him, the king ordered me to *poison* him. That was my first assignment as the royal poisoner. It was a difficult thing to do." She bowed her head, breathing softly. Then she looked up at both of the children. "But I succeeded. I had the badge of Warrewik's house still, so I was able to infiltrate my way to Lord Dunsdworth. I persuaded him to rejoin his family loyalty. When the uncle returned to Ceredigion with a huge army, he was shocked to learn that his son-in-law had betrayed him and joined his forces with King Eredur's. The uncle fought in a battle and was killed. The brothers were reconciled. For a time.

"I still worked for Lord Dunsdworth's wife after that," Ankarette said. "To keep an eye on the brother and make sure he remained loyal. During that time, the brother grew more and more upset that he was not going to become the king his ambition demanded he be. He did some things in his own household that were terrible. He was not a gentle man. He beat his wife and his son. But then he learned something. He learned from rumors, from men who fed his itching ears, that King Eredur had married someone before wedding his queen. If that were true, then all the king's children were bastards and *he*, Lord Dunsdworth, would be in line to be the next king. You can imagine how the bad blood between the brothers grew after this. I do not know whether the rumors were true or not. Dunsdworth *believed* they were. He began plotting his own rebellion."

She stopped, rubbing a hand along her arm, and shook her head. "This part is difficult to talk about. Only the queen in the sanctuary of Our Lady knows the whole story." She sighed. "The king, fearing another rebellion, ordered me to poison his brother."

Owen stared at her. It was so quiet in the room they could hear her every breath.

"It was not the only time the king had asked me to act against his enemies. I knew by then that attempting to reason with Lord Dunsdworth would be a waste of breath. He was so ambitious, so determined to take the throne for himself. When I began to prepare myself to finish this hard task, I poisoned his cup of wine, knowing that he loved to drink it. Unfortunately, he did not get the cup. His pregnant wife did."

Ankarette's shoulders slumped. "The poison"—she swallowed, trying to master her emotions—"was subtle. Even I didn't realize what had happened until it was too late. It brought on her contractions early. I was trained as a midwife, but I could not save the child . . . or the mother. My mistress died in my arms." Her eyes were haunted, her mouth grim. Owen had always wondered why Ankarette was so sad. Perhaps this was the reason.

"Lord Dunsdworth was devastated. I returned to my family to grieve. I could not bear to tell the king how I had failed him, but I told the queen. She promised to protect me. It was to protect her children and their rights that I had been commanded to act as I did." She sighed deeply, smoothing her skirts. "Lord Dunsdworth went mad with grief. He sent his officers to arrest me, accusing me of poisoning his wife.

Before the king could find out, I was tried and found guilty of murder. I assumed the royal guard would come for me in time, which is why I allowed myself to be arrested." She shook her head sadly. "I was tied up in a boat and thrown into a river at the head of a waterfall."

She looked from Owen to Evie and back again. "Only one in a hundred can survive such a plunge. It was not the Fountain's will for me to die. It broke my neck and much of my body, but I survived. My fate was kept a secret. The queen cared for me herself and helped me to heal—not just my body but my heart as well. The king charged Lord Dunsdworth with treason for executing me on his own authority. He was locked away in a tower here at the palace. They tried to drown him with wine, giving him so much that it would kill him, but he lingered and lingered." She paused again, shuddering. "When he did not die, the king ordered me to poison him again. And so I did. Mine was the last face he looked upon in this life."

Owen felt so strange and conflicted he didn't know what to say. He only stared at her, trembling slightly.

Her voice ghosted from her bowed head. "His son, the boy you know as Dunsdworth, saw me in the kitchen today. He recognized me because I used to serve his family. He has believed for many years that I was dead and that his father was put to death because of me. Now you two know a truth that no one else in the realm understands. King Severn doesn't know who I am. Nor does Ratcliffe. Not even your grandfather knows the truth, my lady. I still serve my queen, in her own prison, but I am not here to poison anyone. I never want to do that to anyone again if there is no need."

She raised her sad face to look at the children. Owen's heart ached for her. And as he had done for his mother so many times, he went to her and embraced her, resting his head on her shoulder and patting her in comfort.

"Does that mean," Elysabeth Victoria Mortimer said, her voice trembling, "that if the king dies, *Dunsdworth* could rule us?"

Ankarette looked at the girl for a long moment before giving a firm nod.

"What have we done?" the girl moaned.

Owen felt sick to his stomach as well. But his ears picked out a sound he hadn't been expecting. The sound of many boots coming down the hall. Toward them. He felt the thrum on the stone floor.

Ankarette saw his look and unsheathed a dagger.

♦ ♦ ♦

Ratcliffe is determined to discover the leak. He's been snooping around even more lately, always asking questions, prying for secrets. I can't trust any news I hear from him, for anything he offers has either already been shared with the king or is a trap to ferret me out. I need to learn of something before Ratcliffe does if the poisoner's plan is to work. The best place for news has always been the sanctuary of Our Lady. I can always tell when an Espion is riding toward the palace with something to report. What I need is a poison, something to stall the rider with stomach cramps, delay his arrival by even an hour. This is so risky. I'm not assigned to the sanctuary anymore. Why am I even considering this?

—Dominic Mancini, Espion of the Palace Kitchen

♦ ♦ ♦

CHAPTER TWENTY-SIX

Feathers

"They're coming," Owen whispered to Evie. He thought Ankarette would hurry to the secret door, but instead she rushed to the headboard of the bed and plunged her dagger into one of the pillows, ripping the case open. She tossed the pillow to the girl and a cloud of feathers came trailing out.

"Hit him with it!" Ankarette gasped, and Evie needed no more coaxing than that.

A plume of white feathers exploded into the room as the ruptured pillow smashed into Owen's chest. A half moment later, another torn pillow was sent spinning at Owen. He caught it, and suddenly the two children were filling the air with goose down as they clubbed each other with the sagging pillowcases.

Ankarette ducked to the floor and rolled under the bed as the bedroom door jolted open and Ratcliffe entered with four soldiers, swords drawn.

He started choking on the feather fluff immediately. It was like a blizzard from the North had settled on the room.

Giggling uncontrollably, Evie whopped Owen on the side of the head with a well-placed blow. She came at him again, but he held up his featherless pillow hood to block the blow and then whipped it around to catch her in the face. She gasped with pretend outrage, but her gasp was drowned out by a thundering roar.

"What in the *devil* is going on!" Ratcliffe bellowed.

Feathers were everywhere, sticking like leaves to Evie's hair, her nightclothes, Owen's tunic. The swirling swarms of feathers started to settle as both children froze in place and stared at the new arrivals.

A bit of fluff landed on Elysabeth's lip and her mouth squirmed as she attempted to blow it off. The face she made was so funny that Owen grunted, trying to suppress a laugh.

Ratcliffe stomped on the feathers, his balding head wet with sweat, and the feathers clung to it, making him look completely ridiculous.

Evie stared up at him, her jaw quivering with subdued laughter.

It only made Ratcliffe angrier. "You think . . . you think this is amusing, Lady Mortimer? Amusing? I come to hunt down this missing *brat*, only to discover you both destroying His Majesty's *pillows*? I ask you, I *ask* you!"

But she was giggling uncontrollably now, pointing at Ratcliffe's snowy head. Owen felt a twinge of fear, but there was nothing he could do, he couldn't stop laughing either. It only made matters worse that some of the soldiers were trying to smother *their* smirks and failing.

"Out! Out!" Ratcliffe shouted. "You little scamp, back to your room. I'll report this to Berwick and make you both pick up every, single, f-f-f—" His scolding was interrupted when a feather went into his mouth, just at that very word, and started to choke him.

One of the soldiers guffawed, and then they were all laughing. Ratcliffe's color went red as a tomato as he roughly grabbed Owen's shoulder and propelled him out of the room, kicking up another plume of feathers. Owen looked back at Evie. She was smiling mischievously, and when their eyes met, she gave him a wink. He winked back at her.

Goose down swirled in the room, and Owen felt a pulse of warmth. Ankarette was hidden beneath the bed, safe. Twice in one day.

She truly was a clever woman.

◆ ◆ ◆

The next morning, Owen was arranging tiles in the kitchen before breakfast when Evie arrived, later than usual. She wore a dark green gown with a wide, braided girdle paired with her favorite boots, of course. Owen knew she had arrived by the sound of her walking, but also because of what Liona said.

"Ah, here's the other *guilty* one. Bless me, but both of you children were up to wickedness last night. There are evil feathers floating in the air all the way to the throne room, you two. The king will not be pleased. Look at you, lass, you have one stuck in your hair still!"

"I did it on purpose," she replied without even a hint of remorse. "Owen has a white patch in his hair and now I do as well."

He looked up swiftly and nearly knocked over the tower he was carefully building in his surprise.

Liona laughed and shook her head as she continued slaving at the ovens. Evie grabbed two round muffins from the table and wandered over to where Owen was kneeling, her eyes gleaming with the shared secret. When she reached the bench, she set down the muffins and crossed over to him.

Owen turned back to his tower, trying to finish it so he could topple it. He noticed the white feather in her hair, just over her left ear. She had done a little braid on that side and stuck the piece of goose down through the upper part of it.

"We were almost caught," Owen whispered conspiratorially.

"I don't think I've ever laughed so hard," she answered with a grin. "I'll never forget Ratcliffe's face. That crown of feathers stuck to his balding head! I still want to laugh when I *think* on it!" She held her stomach a moment, her smile infectious.

Owen added another part of the tower. This was one of the tallest ones he had built, and it was starting to sway, which was a bad sign.

"What did Ratcliffe say after he dragged you out? Did he hurt you?"

Owen shrugged. "Not really. I think he expected . . . her . . . to be with us." He placed the next tile delicately and it stayed up.

"When she pulled that dagger," Evie whispered, "I was afraid for just a moment. But what a brilliant idea! I don't mind cleaning up all the feathers. It was worth it." Her hand snaked over to touch his. "Thank you for telling me," she whispered. "You are my dearest friend."

He gave her a sideways smile and then prepared to place the final pieces, moving very slowly and with painstaking gentleness as he put them on. He was at it for quite a while when she drew closer behind him and offered him one of the muffins.

Then she picked up the other one and nibbled on the edge. "Pumpkin . . . my favorite! I love pumpkin muffins and pumpkin soup and pumpkin tarts. Have you had oyster stew before? Oysters are rare, but we have them in the North. Mussels, too. We usually harvest them in the fall. Our cook would make pumpkin muffins and we'd eat oyster soup in trencher bowls to go with them." She smiled dreamily as she took another bite from her muffin. "Are you ready to knock it down?"

"You can," Owen said, backing away from the tower. He set up the final trail of tiles that led to it.

"A kind gentleman!" she praised. After taking another bite of muffin, she set it down on the bench and knelt in front of the tiles, gazing at the structure with admiration. "Do you know where she lives?"

Owen nodded. "I'll . . . I'll take you there sometime."

Jewel waddled into the kitchen, her expression sour, and she was muttering something about two children in desperate need of a willow switch to their backsides. Liona began repeating the story of their night-time adventures. It seemed the whole palace had heard about it.

"I wish Jewel would go away. She's fat and she smells like . . . like a garderobe. Ugh. I'm going to ask Papa to send her away."

Owen stared at her. "You mean Grandpapa."

Her finger paused before it could topple the tile. "Yes. That's what I meant."

"Do you miss your Maman?" Owen asked gently.

She scrunched up her face a little. "She's still . . . sad. She grew sick of all my talking. I was only trying to help. Grandpapa thought it best if I came with him to the palace. I think she's grateful I'm gone."

She nudged the tile with only enough force for it to start the first wobble, and then the whole structure came shattering down in a rain of tiles. She clapped her hands with wild eagerness, her smile dispelling the shadow that had been there only a moment before.

"I love it when they fall!" she breathed.

"There he goes again," Jewel moaned. "Owen Satchel and Evie. I tell you, Liona, I cannot keep up with those two. I think I'm going to visit Brad the blacksmith to see if I can borrow some ankle fetters to clap on them."

"She's so rude," Evie whispered, giving Owen a devious look. "We might lock her in the privy, you know."

"We'd only get in more trouble," Owen said.

Together they started picking up the pieces of tile and stacking them in the box by Owen's leather satchel. It was nearly time for break-fast with the king and face his scolding for the fate of the pillows.

"Do you like your nickname?" she asked him amidst the cleanup. "I've been meaning to ask you since the cistern. I like it, but if you don't, I won't use it."

He gave her a sincere look. "Owen Satchel?"

She nodded vigorously. "What did you think I meant—*Kisky*?"

"Don't ever call me that. I don't mind if people call me Owen Satchel."

"To me, you'll always be Owen Kiskaddon. Elysabeth Victoria Mortimer Kiskaddon. It sounds very important."

Owen smiled and sighed.

"What?"

"Have you gotten used to 'Evie' yet?" he asked.

"Only when you say it."

"I *am* the only one who says it!"

She set her hands down on her lap. "I hate being called Lady Mortimer. That's my *mother's* name. I'm not the lady of anything right now. I've never had a nickname, though. Until now. I always make people say my *whole* name."

"When I was a baby, my sister called me Ugwen. They still tease me with it."

She giggled at the name. "I like it better than Kisky! But people have pet names for each other. When we're older, you can change mine to something like *darling* or *dearest*. Do you know what Ankarette means?"

He looked at her in surprise. "No."

She nodded with enthusiasm. "It's a Northern name. It comes from a different language. Ankarette is how we say it in Ceredigion, but the name comes from the Atabyrion name Angarad. Let me say it again. An-GAR-ad. It means *much loved one*. It's a girl's name. It's so pretty." She reached out and touched his little white tuft of hair.

"Where are thuh troublemakers? Ovur there, makin' another mess? Another spill?" It was Berwick's voice, and it was full of wrath. "Get you two over here. By the Fountain, what a mess! Come on. You two are thick as thieves. I'm in a *fine* feather today at the mess you've made!"

Owen and Evie glanced at each other, feeling the laughter starting to bubble up inside them at his choice of words.

Berwick had a mean scowl on his face. He looked full of thunder. "Come hither, you two," he grumbled as he towered by the bench. Only then did Owen notice that beyond the anger he seemed fearful. "Come with me now. We've not a moment to lose."

Their smiles faded.

◆ ◆ ◆

The news will catch everyone at the palace off guard. It will secure the boy's status as Fountain-blessed for certain. Everyone in the kingdom knows about the Deconeus of Ely, John Tunmore. He was a member of the privy council under King Eredur. The man was born to run the Espion, but no one dedicated to the Fountain ever can. He is cunning, wise, and cold as winter's ice. King Severn sent him in chains to Brakenbury Dungeon in Westmarch for his complicity in the plot to prevent Severn from becoming king. He was undoubtedly part of the plot that led to Ambion Hill. And now he's been caught by the Espion. Will Severn execute a man of the Fountain by the waters? I wonder.

—Dominic Mancini, Espion of the Palace Kitchen

◆ ◆ ◆

CHAPTER TWENTY-SEVEN

The Eel

Berwick walked with a slight limp, his face agitated and nervous, his gaze continually glancing back the way they had come.

"Move along, you two. Hurry now," he growled. Owen's heart was racing. Evie looked excited at the opportunity for intrigue.

They reached a locked servant's door and Berwick removed a huge ring of keys that had been flapping on his belt and quickly unlocked it. He gestured for them to enter, but he did not go with them. Owen heard the lock click fast behind them.

Ankarette and Mancini awaited them in the room. The fat spy was pacing, his cheeks dripping with sweat. His tunic was stained with huge circles of perspiration at his neck and under his armpits. He wiped his mouth on a kerchief as he gazed in wonderment at the two children.

"You brought them *here*?" Mancini whined. "If we're all caught together—"

Ankarette held up her hand. "Berwick is guarding the corridor. He'll rap twice if anyone comes. There is no time for hesitation. What is your message?"

Mancini looked flustered, as if he expected intruders at any moment. "One of the Espion just passed Our Lady," he said gruffly, chafing his meaty hands. "I recognized the fellow. Gates. Sharp young man. I saw his lathered stallion and realized he'd been riding hard and riding fast. He accepted a muffin, which he shouldn't have because it's made him ill. His innards are exploding down the privy well of the garderobe at the moment."

"The message!" Ankarette insisted.

"Yes! Apologies! Ratcliffe caught another one on his hook. A big fish. A really big one. The Deconeus of Ely."

"Tunmore," Ankarette breathed in surprise. By the look of concern on her face, Owen could tell that she admired the man. "I wonder how he was trapped."

Mancini shrugged, mopping the back of his neck with the rag. "I only know he was caught by the Espion abroad. Whatever news Gates has brought, he will share it with Ratcliffe immediately. You only have moments to get this lad in front of the king with another dream!"

Ankarette started pacing, her brow furrowed.

Evie frowned. "My grandpapa and my papa don't like Tunmore. He committed treason."

Ankarette's gaze turned to her. "You are right," she said softly, gently. "He was guilty of treason. Other men paid for theirs with blood, but the Deconeus of Ely did not. I'm surprised he allowed himself to be trapped. He was one of the wisest men I ever met . . . a mentor of mine." She shook her head. "What is done is done. Without knowing the full news, we must not guess at it. Just the news of his capture will be enough."

"What am I to say then?" Owen asked nervously. There were so many names. He did not understand them, and he wasn't sure he could say them all.

Ankarette turned to Mancini. "Do you have any suggestions?"

Mancini looked at her, startled. "I did my part!" he complained angrily. "This is just the sort of gossip you wanted from me. I had to run . . . *run!* . . . from Our Lady. I won't catch my breath for another week." He groaned and jiggled his joints. "I even tossed a coin into the Fountain for good luck, which shows my utter desperation that Gates won't think to connect his violent diarrhea with the muffin I gave him! If he does, I'm a dead man."

"You've done well, Dominic," Ankarette soothed. She stopped pacing and turned quickly. "Owen, do you know what an eel is?"

He blinked at her.

"They're like snake fishes!" Evie chimed in.

Owen nodded but grimaced. "I don't like them," he said, shaking his head. "They taste funny."

Ankarette beamed. "The blessing of talking to the children of nobles! Yes, an eel is like a water snake. This is what you must say, Owen. You were in the kitchen this morning. You heard Liona say she was planning to make eel for the king's dinner. That made you think of eels, and then you felt like you *were* an eel. An eel that was caught by a fishhook. You struggled against the hook, but you were dragged out of the water. There was a rat with a fishing rod on the shore. You were the eel. Can you remember this, Owen?"

Evie frowned. "What does it mean? Oh! Ely! That's the eel!"

Ankarette winked at her. "Clever girl."

There was a firm double knock at the door.

"This way, Dominic," Ankarette said, motioning for him to follow her. Ankarette waved at Owen to go to the door and then slipped through another doorway with Mancini and shut it behind her. Moments later, Berwick had unlocked the door and was standing in the frame, his face dripping sweat.

"Look at you two! Always gettin' into mischief! The king's at breakfast noow, don't you know! Come along, come along. I'll be bruised if I get in trouble for you being late."

Owen and Evie marched out and followed him. She squeezed his hand as they walked, but Owen's stomach was indeed wriggling like a hooked eel. Berwick's limp became more pronounced. As they walked, a man turned the corner ahead of them, wearing the badge of the king— the white boar. When he saw them, his eyes narrowed and his expression changed.

"Found 'em!" Berwick said, giving Owen a little jab to his head with his fist. "These two are naught but trouble. Someone younger and more limber needs to watch after them. Goch!"

The man did not respond, but after they passed him, he continued down the hall the way they had come. He went straight to the servant's door and rattled the handle, but Berwick had locked it.

When they turned the corner out of the man's sight, Berwick offered a puckered sigh of relief. They strode into the great hall where breakfast was already underway. King Severn was making his rounds of the tables, jabbing at his youthful guests, while Ratcliffe stood fidgeting in the corner. When the head of the Espion saw them enter, a look of relief quickly passed over his eyes, followed promptly by blazing anger.

"Ah, you've come at last!" the king said with a sardonic look. "Normally one waits on the king, but I see that I must wait on two wayward children. How pleasant of you both to join us."

"Pardon, my lord," Berwick said sheepishly. He bowed several times. "My pardon, my pardon. These two made a royal mess last night and I was chiding them—"

"You were chiding them?" the king interrupted, a wry look in his eye. "I think a piece of white fluff made it all the way down to my bedchamber this morn. But then again, the bit of down *may* have come from my own pillow." He chuckled to himself, his face brightening a bit at the mischief. He already knew.

"Again, I beg your pardon," Berwick said, bowing meekly as he slowly retreated. Ratcliffe caught him before he could escape and began snarling in his ear.

"Ease off, Ratcliffe," the king said with a twinge of annoyance. "But their escapades last night do not condone such behavior from the rest of you," he added, wagging a finger at the other youngsters in the room. "Why so sullen this morning, Lord Dunsdworth? Is the fare not to your liking?"

Owen's stomach roiled with nerves as the king's attention focused on the older boy, who was sulking from the humiliations of the previous day. His cheeks were ruddy and he grunted something under his breath. Owen wondered how Lord Horwath had cowed him so much.

"Go," Evie whispered in his ear, nudging him.

He would rather have jumped into the cistern again than face the king. Ankarette's words were all jumbling inside his head. Before, she had taught him precisely what to say. They had practiced it several times. There had been time to think on it, to practice it in his head. This was very different, extremely urgent.

"Go!" she insisted, butting him harder.

He sighed and started toward the king. A man he didn't recognize came into the hall, looked around a moment, and then started walking toward Ratcliffe and Berwick. There was a queasy look on his face and one of his gloved hands held his stomach. Owen had the distinct suspicion that this was the man who had just arrived, the one Mancini had poisoned. Time was running out.

Owen's stomach began to thicken in his mouth. He glanced back at Evie and saw her eyes boring into his. *You will do this!* her look commanded. Her eyes were very green at that moment.

Owen took a few more steps, feeling as if all of his bones had become unhinged. He was trembling and fearful. Dunsdworth glanced up, saw him, and his face tightened with pent-up anger. It was nearly enough to make Owen lose his resolve.

"What is it, lad?" the king suddenly asked him, his voice dropping low. He was giving Owen a serious look, as if he were concerned about him. He walked up to him, and Owen hardly noticed his limp. He saw the hand gripping the dagger hilt, loosening it from the scabbard. In his mind, he saw a blizzard of white feathers, set free by Ankarette's blade. He blinked rapidly, trying to calm himself.

"Are you unwell?" the king asked, pitching his voice softer. He set a hand on the boy's shoulder, and the sudden weight nearly made his knees buckle. He wanted to flee, to dash away, to find a dark tunnel and curl up and start crying. How could someone so little be asked to do this?

His eyes were watering, which was embarrassing. He wasn't crying. They were just watering. He looked up at the king's face, saw the pointed jaw that was so freshly shaved it still gleamed with shiny oil. He had a smell about him too, a smell of leather and metal. Owen nearly fainted.

But he noticed that Evie had come around behind the king, so that she could meet Owen's eyes. She willed him to speak, her eyes fierce and determined and utterly fearless. It was like she was pouring her courage into his cup through her look.

Just tell him! she seemed to say.

"Do you . . . do you care for . . . for eels?"

Owen didn't know why those words popped out of his mouth.

The king looked at him in confusion. "Do I care for eels?"

Owen nodded.

"Not really," the king said. "Do you fancy them?"

"Not really," Owen said, trying to master himself. "I was in the kitchen this morning. Liona said she was making eels."

The king snorted. "You don't have to *eat* them if you don't care for them, lad. I thought . . . well, never mind." He lifted his hand away and frowned with disappointment.

Owen was losing his nerve and his chance. "When she said that about the eels," he forced himself to continue, "I started to feel . . . strange." He blinked rapidly.

He had the king's attention again. "You did? Like another vision?" He seemed eager, almost hungry, when Owen nodded.

"Ratcliffe!" the king barked, gesturing for him to hurry over. Ratcliffe frowned with annoyance and made his way to them. Evie beamed with pride at Owen.

"Go on!" the king implored, his voice low and coaxing, his eyes shining with interest.

"It was like a dream, except I was awake," Owen said. "I was an eel. And there was a hook in my mouth, like a fisherman's hook, tugging me out of the water. I was wiggling and trying to get free, but the hook kept pulling. It hurt. And when I came out of the water, it wasn't a fisherman at all. A rat was holding the pole. A grinning rat." Owen swallowed, feeling relief that he had gotten it out.

The king stared at him in confusion. "That is a *strange* thing, Owen. Peculiar." He glanced at Ratcliffe for clarification.

Ratcliffe shrugged, totally perplexed. "I make no sense of it. The boy doesn't like eels. Not many do. Did you know the second king of Ceredigion died from eating too many eels?"

The king's expression hardened. "That was *lampreys*, you fool." He turned back to Owen and patted his shoulder. "You don't have to eat them. Have Liona make you a roast capon or another fish that you prefer."

Owen nodded, very hungry now, and grabbed a muffin from the table. It had little seeds in it and reminded him of the one he had eaten while riding into the city for the first time.

Evie butted into his shoulder, just slightly, as she stood next to him by the table. She gazed across the assortment of food, carefully decided, and then chose a pear.

"You did it," she whispered, not looking at him.

He wanted to collapse under the table in relief.

The king's sharp voice echoed in the hall. "What?"

All eyes turned to him. The queasy-looking man Owen had noticed earlier was standing by the king and Ratcliffe. He looked like he had just said something.

Then, in unison, the king and Ratcliffe turned and looked at Owen.

◆ ◆ ◆

I've learned this above all else. You must bind men to you by benefits, or else make sure of them in some other way. Never reduce them to the alternative of having either to destroy you or perish themselves. I fear that Ratcliffe, in his efforts to secure his master's throne, may be risking it all the more. There is never anything more tenuous than peace.

—Dominic Mancini, Espion of the Palace Kitchen

◆ ◆ ◆

CHAPTER TWENTY-EIGHT

Loyalty

Ankarette had predicted, correctly as it turned out, that the king would immediately assemble his councillors after such a miraculous demonstration of Owen's gift. So when the men started to gather in the king's council chambers, Owen and Ankarette were already poised by the spyhole in the secret door, ready to watch and to listen. She held a finger to her lips, warning him to be absolutely still, but her eyes gleamed with the thrill of bearing silent witness to such a meeting. Owen shifted so his legs wouldn't get too tired as he watched and listened.

He recognized some but not all of those in attendance, and Ankarette quietly whispered in his ear whenever someone he did not know entered the room. The king had called in Ratcliffe, Horwath, and his chancellor Catsby, along with two religious officials representing the sanctuaries. In the months following his victory at Ambion Hill, he had not yet replenished all of the council seats, Ankarette explained quietly. Owen's father, for example, had not been restored to his previous role and was awaiting his fate in his own lands. The council was small and getting smaller.

Some of the council members had seated themselves, but the king was pacing, keen displeasure and more unnameable emotions playing in his eyes.

"Everyone is here, Your Grace," Ratcliffe announced, after shutting the door. There was a wary look on his face.

"You are wondering why I've summoned you," Severn said in a low voice. He cast his gaze over the men. "You all look like men who are about to be shoved into the waters. Are you feeling guilty? Did any of you know of this news before it arrived?"

There was a moment of awkward silence. "Know of *what* news, my lord?" said the man Ankarette had identified as Catsby.

"Tell them," the king said gruffly, waving a hand at Ratcliffe. That directive delivered, he turned away from the council and started to slip his dagger in and out of its sheath.

Ratcliffe assumed an authoritative posture and advanced to the head of the table. He planted his palms on the gleaming, waxed surface. "News from Southport. We have John Tunmore in custody."

There were startled gasps around the room. Only Horwath, who was always unflappable, did not react with open shock.

"How could he . . . ?"

"The knave!"

"Be silent!" the king reprimanded. "Hear the news first before you begin babbling. Go on, Dickon."

Ratcliffe cleared his throat. "He was caught, you may be sure, in the port of Brugia. He was never very far from Ceredigion. A boat was waiting for him in case he needed to escape quickly. A boat paid for by the King of Occitania, if my suspicions hold true. The Espion used it to smuggle him back here."

"Facts, Dickon," the king scolded. "Let's keep to the facts first. Tell them what you found with Tunmore."

"Yes, my lord. Of course." Ratcliffe's anger was stirring, but he kept his tone civil. "He had a book on his person. A private history, to be precise. I have it here." He withdrew a black leather-bound book, small enough to fit in his hand. "Entries, dates, scribblings, musings. Lots of nonsense about the Fountain, really. But it is clear he was plotting something. He's been in hiding for nearly two years and played a complicit role in the attempted usurpation. I believe—*we* believe—the information in here will implicate many." He waggled the book.

"Only two years ago?" Severn said, his voice cold. "I'd forgotten. It feels so much longer than that." He pushed away from the wall and strode to the table, limping slightly, an angry frown on his mouth. "Yes, two years ago he plotted to murder me, my wife, and my son. My wife is dead. My son is dead. No doubt he wishes to *finish* what he started when he seduced Bletchley into treason. For all we may *suspect,* he was likely behind that pretender's claim to my throne as well. Tunmore is an eel. The lad was right about that."

Ankarette, listening keenly, flashed Owen a secret smile.

"What lad?" asked one of the prelates. "The Kiskaddon boy? Was there another prophecy?"

The king's countenance softened remarkably and his eyes took on the same shining look Evie's got whenever she talked about the cistern. "Indeed."

Ratcliffe held up his hands. "Let's not be hasty, Your Majesty, in ascribing the boy's powers to anything beyond coincidence or cunning."

"Twice he's done it," Severn said. "Twice! The first you could ascribe to coincidence, if a fantastic one. But the second? He knew something before *you* did!"

There were grumbles of concern and interest amongst the councillors, one of them begging to know what had happened.

The king silenced them with a wave of his hand.

"The boy had another vision," Severn said, pacing slowly along the table's edge with his hobbled gait. "This was not a dream at night like before. It was a day vision. He saw an eel caught by a hook. A *rat* was holding the fishing pole." He gave Ratcliffe a meaningful look. "And then news arrives that Tunmore, the Deconeus of *Ely*, was caught in Brugia—on a *hook*—by the Espion. The lad is blessed, I tell you. He is Fountain-blessed with the gift of foresight!"

Ankarette smiled and squeezed Owen's hand. He smiled back at her, giddy that her plan was working out so well.

"The question, I ask you," the king continued, "is if I have the authority to execute a prelate of the realm. A man purportedly sanctioned by the Fountain. This man has been a raw blister on my heel for these many years. Lest we forget, he was the one who helped write up the truce terms with Occitania ten years ago. Truce terms that shamed my brother—shamed us all!—when Occitania repudiated them. He was a member of *this* council two years ago." He tapped his forefinger on the table. "Others more noble than he have paid for their treachery with their lives. Yet he has been immune from the consequences of treason. What say you, council? Do we see if the Fountain will pardon this man when we throw him into the river?"

One of the lesser nobles raised his hand. "What does the child say?"

The king looked at him, confused.

"The child's last prediction. You recall it! He said the pinecone fell into the river. In this vision, the hook saved the eel from the river, did it not?"

"A good point, Rufus," said one of the prelates, seated on his left. "It did indeed! It saved the eel from the river!"

The king turned to look at Ratcliffe, who had rushed up to him. "My lord," said the spymaster, hardly able to contain his agitation. "My lord, you cannot look to a *boy* as your source of knowing the Fountain's will! You would risk far too much, it would be—"

"A miracle?" the king interrupted softly. The room settled down, but Owen's stomach churned in anticipation.

"You don't believe the boy's Fountain-blessed, Dickon, do you?"

"I do not," Ratcliffe responded angrily without a pause. His voice was low and urgent. "I think he's a tool being used to dupe you. My liege, if you hearken to him, she will have you. She will have tricked and deceived you. The woman is *alive*. I tell you, she is. I didn't know her name until I heard Dunsdworth speak it, but he swears he saw her in the kitchen. The kitchen! Where else does the boy play his silly games but there? My lord, my *friend*, you must trust me on this! That woman is the most dangerous person in your realm. Even more dangerous than Tunmore. Ask Horwath. Even he fears her."

A spasm of worry shot through Owen as he realized they were talking about Ankarette. The euphoria turned into nausea in his stomach.

"And what do you say, Stiev?" the king asked, turning his attention to the grizzled duke who was lounging in a stuffed chair within view of the spyhole.

There was a long moment of silence. He stared at the tabletop and slowly drummed his fingers. "According to the official records, Ankarette Tryneowy plunged to her death in a boat. If she lived, your brother never told me, Your Majesty." Ratcliffe's face twisted with impatience, but the king's attention was wholly focused on the old duke.

"But?" Severn prompted.

"But," continued the duke. "I have harbored some suspicions of my own. In the North, we throw the condemned off the mountain falls. In all our histories, only the Fountain-blessed have survived this test. If the queen's poisoner is Fountain-blessed, as we suspect, perhaps she did not perish in the falls." He fell silent again, plucking at the gray hairs at the end of his goatee.

The king's voice was serious. "Do you believe the boy is Fountain-blessed?"

Horwath lifted his eyes and nodded once.

Ratcliffe scowled. It was his word against the entire council. Even Owen could see that. And yet the king still heeded him.

The king walked back to the mantel and rested his arm on it. "What do you advise, Dickon?" he asked. "You know that I trust you."

Ratcliffe was at the king's elbow in a moment. "One thing, my lord. One thing that solves all your problems at once."

Ankarette frowned, her expression serious and concerned, and Owen felt his chest tighten. Sometimes their plan felt like a game of Wizr, but at moments like this he was reminded that it was not. It was a match of wits that would impact all their lives.

"Bring the boy with us when we go to the West to dispense the king's justice at the Assizes. Take the boy away from the palace and all the intrigues here. We need to separate him from those who may be influencing him. If he's Fountain-blessed, his powers should work beyond the palace grounds. That would be proof sufficient to satisfy even me."

The king smirked. "And what if he *is* Fountain-blessed, Dickon? Do you know how *rare* this particular gift is? Not the rarity of being Fountain-blessed, but seeing the future!" His eyes glittered with eagerness. He *wanted* to believe it. "If it's true, this lad will become the greatest noble in Ceredigion. Think of it! You are right to be wary and cautious. But my heart tells me this boy is special. My own power hardly works on him."

Ratcliffe looked like he was about to argue, but he changed his tack. "My lord, then my plan will only help you decide if he is legitimate. This news from Tunmore is an opportunity in disguise. I believe I have a way of testing the loyalty of the boy *and* his parents. I must arrange something first, but we will know the truth of things once my plan is in motion." He smiled, a great wolf's smile. "Believe me, my lord, I would like nothing better than to have a Fountain-blessed who can see the future among us. Even if he's a Kiskaddon. I hope you are right and my concerns prove false."

"He's a wily one, my lord," said Catsby with approval.

"You picked the right man to lead the Espion," concurred another man Owen couldn't see.

The king looked satisfied. "What is your plan, Dickon?"

The spymaster smirked. "It would be best, of course, if no one knew of it except myself. But let's just say that the boy will soon be seeing his old home of Tatton Hall again."

Ankarette's frown did not leave her face as the councilmen trailed out of the room. She slowly and gently secured the spyhole and then rested her hands in her lap, giving Owen a thoughtful look.

"What's going to happen?" he asked her.

She shook her head a moment, trying to find words that would not alarm him. He could read her clearly, and her need to comfort him made him worry even more.

"When a man feels threatened," Ankarette said in a voice as quiet as feathers, "he is apt to do terrible things." She shook her head. "I don't think the king has noticed that his spymaster is no longer serving *his* interests."

♦ ♦ ♦

Men rise from one ambition to another. If there was ever a man born to lead the Espion, it was John Tunmore. I'm frankly startled that Ratcliffe managed to capture him. The rat has a gift. His book would be priceless. I wonder if there is anything in it that incriminates me?

—Dominic Mancini, Espion of the Palace Kitchen

♦ ♦ ♦

CHAPTER TWENTY-NINE

Deep Fathoms

In the months Owen had spent at Kingfountain, the season should have started turning to autumn, but instead, it decided to retreat back to summer. The day the eel was smuggled back into Ceredigion, a heat wave struck the kingdom and turned the castle into a brick oven. It lasted for days.

Sweat dripped down Owen's nose as he lay on the kitchen floor, fidgeting with the tiles. He had stacked a row up on the bench so that they would fall and instigate a group down lower to collapse as well. His designs were getting more and more complicated.

"It is *so* hot!" Evie complained, scooting away from him, her back to the wall. She stretched and yawned lazily. "It is never this hot in the North, Owen. Even this late in the year, there is still ice up on the mountains. Did you know there are ice caves up there? Huge ice caves. I have not seen them yet. Papa said I was too young to climb up to them."

"Mmm-hmmm," Owen mumbled distractedly. The salty sweat stung his eyes, and he wiped it away furiously. He hated being so hot and irritable.

The windows of the kitchen were fully open, but it did not help against the sweltering heat. Liona was still responsible for baking bread for all the meals, and after hours of standing in front of the boiling ovens, she was snapping at her underlings impatiently. Everyone was upset and short-tempered.

"I wish the king would take us with him when the court moves. It's moving West, I hear. Grandpapa told me. Would you like to see Tatton Hall again? What is your manor like? Would you like Grandpapa to give a message to your family for you?"

Owen stared at her, his heart suddenly clenching. "Why is the king going West?" He felt a prickle of apprehension. Had this Deconeus of Ely somehow compromised his parents? Worry began to wriggle in his stomach.

"The king always travels, silly. He must administer justice and order throughout the realm. There are always disputes that need resolution. Laws to be enforced. Taxes to be collected, of course. He usually picks a place for his winter court. It takes several months to make all the arrangements, you know. I hear he's going West this year. Maybe he'll spend winter court at Tatton Hall? Or perhaps the royal palace Beestone."

Owen was not sure how he should feel about that. It had been months since he'd seen his family. He was still upset with his parents for abandoning him, whether they'd had a choice or not, but his life had drastically changed in the months since he'd left home. He no longer felt like the same boy he'd been.

"I have an idea," Evie whispered. "It's so hot, let's go jump into the cistern again!"

The idea was absolutely wonderful and Owen grinned his agreement. He toppled the lead tile and they watched the pieces collapse in a dazzling explosion of sound loud enough to awake Mancini, who had been snoring in a chair.

Then Evie grabbed Owen's hand and the two started across the kitchen, running.

"Where are you off to now?" Liona asked over her shoulder. Jewel was suffering with gout from the heat wave and had asked the cook to watch them that afternoon.

"To dance in the fountain!" Evie yelled back mischievously.

"That's not proper, young lady!" Liona hollered.

But the two children were both too eager to care about propriety. Owen felt a little twinge of nervousness about jumping into the cistern again, but not only did the cool water sound inviting on such a humid day, he also remembered seeing the treasure, and he wanted to see if he had been imagining it.

The chair squeaked as Mancini got up and started after them. "Hold on, you two!" he said curtly.

"Run!" Evie whispered, tugging hard on Owen's hand, and the two escaped out the kitchen door and started down the hall, the fat Espion shouting after them. Owen felt laughter bubble up inside him and spill out his mouth. They ran through the halls, nearly colliding with sweaty servants who glowered at them in annoyance. The race only added to their excitement as they went one way and then another, their feet pounding on the polished tiles of the immaculate palace.

Their pace slowed when they reached the rarely used corridors where the window leading to the cistern yard was concealed. They were listening for sounds of pursuit and, hearing none, they approached the familiar tapestry. Evie glanced back one more time and then pushed aside the fabric of the tapestry and shoved at the window, raising it. After helping her scramble up, Owen followed her through the opening.

The sun was beating down on the yard, the heat shimmering on the hot stones. Owen and Evie quickly traipsed to the huge gullet of the cistern and peered down inside. Given the brightness of the light, they couldn't see very well down the shaft. They heard the water lapping against the columns below, but the markers identifying the depth of the cistern were masked by the glare.

Evie scratched her head, squinting. "Let's make sure it's still deep enough."

They walked over to the ivy-covered door they had found last time, but when Owen stooped to trip the latch, he found it was already ajar. Had they not closed it last time? He couldn't remember. They pulled the door open and started to descend the steps to the water's edge.

"It's lower than it was," she murmured. "It's down several notches. See?"

"Where's the boat?" Owen asked. He'd noticed immediately that it was missing.

She whirled and looked to where it had been. "I don't see it. Is someone down here, do you think?"

"Shhh!" Owen said, holding a finger up to his lips. He listened for any sound of trouble, anything out of the ordinary. There was nothing, and the only sight ahead of them was the empty water of the cistern brightened by the pillar of light from above. Who could have taken the boat?

"I think it's deep enough," Evie said after a while, growing impatient. She started back up the steps.

"Wait!" he called, running after her. He wanted to figure out the answers to his questions before they risked a jump, but he could tell she was eager to start swimming.

They reached the large hole looming above the cistern. The water was indeed lower, and Owen could see their shadows shimmering on the choppy surface.

"Ready?" she asked, reaching out and clasping his hand.

Owen nodded and let her count.

"Go!" she said, tugging on his hand and pulling him with her.

The wild frenzied feeling of plummeting reminded him partway down that he should be terrified, but then the shock of cold water met his face and he plunged into the depths. His feet touched the bottom of the cistern. His hand still gripped hers.

Owen opened his eyes and found himself surrounded by a pile of treasure. He felt a huge burst of excitement in his ribs as he stared at the sword hilts, the jewels, and the necklaces. Evie was tugging at his hand and trying to swim up, but he pulled back, not wanting to lose sight of the treasure. There was so much! But then he noticed something awry. There was a gap in the treasure, as if someone had dragged a rake through it. No, that wasn't it. One of the chests appeared to have been dragged back toward the stairs. The dragging motion had cleared a path through the bounty and knocked other bits over.

His companion was yanking hard on his hand now, and when he looked up, he saw bubbles were coming out of her mouth, obscuring her face.

Owen wanted to stay down and figure out what had happened to the treasure, but they both needed to breathe. He pushed with his legs and they started toward the surface. As they moved through the water, a loud grinding noise filled his water-soaked ears.

When Owen's face broke the surface, he gulped in a chest full of air to stop his lungs from burning. Evie was spluttering and paddling on the waters.

"Owen! Did you hear that noise?"

Owen looked and saw they were farther away from the stairs. In fact, they were gliding away from it at a fast pace.

"What's wrong?" Owen asked, kicking around. The water was tugging them deeper into the dark cistern.

"Swim!" she shouted, and started paddling her arms and kicking with her legs. Owen began to swim as well, trying to reach the safety of the stairs, but the current was too strong. They were being sucked deep into the throat of the cistern. Fear made him forget the treasure he had seen down below.

There was light coming from the far end. He hadn't seen that before. Was there an opening in the cistern? Then he heard the sound of rushing water, the sound of a waterfall.

"Owen!" Evie shrieked, realizing it at the same time he did.

The cistern was draining into the river.

The stairs were far away now, and the shaft of light from the opening was a pale spear in the darkness that was growing larger as the current pushed them farther and farther from safety.

"Grab a column!" she shouted. She reached for the nearest one, but her fingers slipped on the wet stone.

Owen tried to grab one too and his fingers managed to stick. He grabbed Evie's wrist and clung to her, but the force of the waters pulled him away from the column and they were both swept into the current once more.

The maw of the opening loomed closer and they could hear the water spilling over its edge. Would they be able to stop themselves from going over? He didn't think so, not with how fast the water was moving them.

"Owen!" she said desperately, grabbing his waist in terror.

There was nothing to hold on to. There was nothing to grab. The boat was gone. His mind whirled frantically, but then, with the shushing sounds of the water, he felt a stab of peacefulness. His mind opened to the possibilities, quick as lightning. He needed something heavy. Something so heavy the waters couldn't move it.

The treasure.

"Hold on to me!" he shouted at her fear-stricken face. "Hold tight!" Instead of swimming against the current, he swam with it and went down. Flailing, his foot struck against something hard on the bottom. It was too dark to see, but he felt with his hands and discovered a handhold, the rung on a chest. He grabbed it tightly with one hand and felt himself slipping, so he grabbed it with both. Evie clung to his belt, holding on for dear life. He was running out of air, but at least they weren't moving. The chest was saving them from being swept away. Why was there treasure on the floor? Who had left it there? How had someone dragged one of the chests away? Why?

His lungs burned painfully. He wanted so badly to breathe! He felt Evie's hands slipping away. He needed to act quickly if he were to save them both. He pulled on the ring and dragged himself over the chest, so that he could plant his feet on either side of it. The chest was big, probably up to his waist. It slid a little on the ground when he jostled it, but it was too heavy to be dragged away.

Breathe.

The thought came to his mind and he started to panic. He felt he should just breathe in the water, but he knew he would die if he did. As Evie had told him, children drowned all the time. He needed air! He wedged the chest between his legs, freeing his hands, and then grabbed Evie's arms and pulled her away from his belt. He pushed her up toward the surface, holding her by her boots. He felt the current tugging her away, but he held on fiercely, determined not to lose her.

She was screaming. Even under the water, he could hear her voice. Bits of blackness drifted in front of his eyes. He was fading. Falling asleep.

He was drowning.

He felt his muscles tingling and burning. They were near the opening where the water spilled out, he realized. A big square of light could be seen overhead. Owen felt peaceful as he stared at it. His lungs stopped burning. Everything slowed down and he felt one with the waters.

Breathe.

The thought didn't sound so frightening now. Owen opened his mouth.

Evie was gone. He blinked in confusion. When had he let go of her? He heard the pattering of a fountain, could almost smell the scent of honeysuckle and other garden flowers. Strange that he could smell so deep underwater.

Then strong hands grabbed him beneath his arms and pulled him up. His face broke the surface and then air was suddenly filling his chest again. Delicious, yeasty air that made his bones sing.

"Up, lad! Up!" It was Mancini's voice.

Owen spluttered dreamily and saw Evie clinging to the fat spy's neck, her hair dripping into her face. Her dress drooped as well and she hung limply, looking too tired to move. She stared at Owen in relief and he could tell she was struggling not to cry.

Mancini hauled Owen up under his arm and started tromping back toward the stairs. The waters rushed around him, but enough had drained that it was down to his middle, and it appeared to have lost some of its power.

"Why the devil I should risk my life saving you two," the Espion muttered darkly as he marched. "Reckless. Careless. Stupid little urchins. I thought you were a water sprite, girl, but you're clearly not! A water sprite wouldn't have almost got herself drowned. How did you even know about this place? It was walled off for a reason!"

Owen ignored the man's rant and stared at the water. It was draining past Mancini's knees now. Soon the treasure would be seen. He would prove to them it was real.

They reached the bottom of the stairs, and Mancini dropped Owen like a heavy sack before turning around and sitting on the steps, breathing roughly. "Too much work. This is too much. Goodness, children are always trying to kill themselves for naught. Why I should bother saving you is beyond me. We're all wet and drippy now. Ugh!"

Evie rushed over to Owen and wrapped him in a tight hug. "How did you? How did you save us? What were you holding on to? It was like you had a boat anchor!"

"It was the treasure," Owen gasped, wiping water from his face. He stared down at the draining cistern. The water had drained even lower than the steps.

"Treasure?" Mancini said eagerly, looking at the water.

There was nothing. Owen stepped off the stairs and searched the spot where they had originally landed. The cistern hole was above them.

He kicked at the waters, splashing them, and saw nothing on the shimmering floor. Nothing.

"His wits are addled," Mancini said, still chuffing for breath.

Owen turned and looked at Evie pleadingly. "I saw it!" he insisted. "I felt it."

She stared at him, her face wilting. Then she rushed over and hugged him again and started to cry.

♦ ♦ ♦

I think Ratcliffe intends to murder the boy just as the princes were murdered. When the two brats ran off, I felt uneasy about them, so I hastened to follow. They had apparently discovered the way to the palace cistern. Ratcliffe found me observing them, and when I told him what was going on, a strange gleam came to his eye and he hurried away. That made me even more uneasy, so I tried to call the children back, but they couldn't hear me. Shortly after, I heard screaming and broke down the door. The cistern waters were being drained into the river. I saved the children, dragging both of their soggy carcasses out of that pit. It took an hour to catch my breath afterward. I don't think it's a coincidence that it happened not long after Ratcliffe left me. And he meant, I think, to put the blame of their deaths on me. Well, two can throw the dice in a game of chance.

—Dominic Mancini, Espion of the Palace Cistern

♦ ♦ ♦

CHAPTER THIRTY

Cursing

The entire palace was in an uproar when it was discovered that John Tunmore had escaped his cell. A search of the castle had been conducted throughout the night, and it was impossible for Owen to sleep amidst the torchlight and the racket of marching boots. His room was searched for the fugitive not once, but twice. He dared not visit Ankarette that night, for even the spy tunnels were being thoroughly searched.

The king was in such a rage that everyone was on tenterhooks. Owen and Evie were both feeling the aftereffects of the deadly peril from the previous day, and it was the first time Owen had ever known Evie to be quiet and soft-spoken. The two children stayed near each other during breakfast as the king ranted and raved, filling the air with blistering curses about the incompetence of his trusted servants, who stared at the king with open shock.

"And what have you learned thus far?" the king demanded hotly, his cheeks flushed, his nostrils white with anger. He hadn't been shaved that morning, as he usually was, and his dark hair was untidy beneath his black felt hat.

Ratcliffe looked almost desperate. "From what I understand, Your Grace, he *walked* out of his cell on your orders."

The king's visage grew even fiercer. "And why, by the bloody Fountain, would I command his release, Dickon? Your people had him in the tower. Obviously one of them let him go!"

"That's not true!" Ratcliffe said. "There was a paper given to the guard with your seal on it. A note written in your own hand, as they said, demanding the release of the prisoner, explaining that he was on a secret embassy from you and his capture was all part of the ploy. My lord," he said, his voice lowering. "I have four men who *swear* they read this note!"

"Then where *is* it, Ratcliffe? Show it to me!"

A crumpled frown preceded the response. "It was thrown into the fire. But four men—!"

"I don't care if a dozen men all swore they saw pigs fly!" the king thundered. "I did not order his release. My signet ring is on my hand, as you can see, and I assure you, Dickon, that I ordered no such thing! Why do I bother having an Espion if you bungle everything? This palace is riddled with rat holes. Tunnels and scratching claws. I detest it. And I've learned from Berwick that the cistern went dry and we'll be hauling water from the river for days to refill it since the rains haven't started." He wiped sweat from his face, his mouth twisted into a brooding scowl. "Why am I surrounded by such ineptitude? Is there no man who can be true to his king?"

Ratcliffe's face blackened at the king's harsh words. His voice was thick with anger when he spoke again. "I am doing the best I can!" he seethed.

The king glared at him. "It's not enough, Dickon. We've known each other for a long while and I consider you a friend. Even our wives were friends. But friendship is not enough. This duty is beyond you, man. This is a load on the halter you aren't strong enough to pull!"

"Am I . . . an ox then?" Ratcliffe stuttered, coming dangerously close to losing control of his tongue. "You are whipping me like one!"

King Severn muttered something under his breath. Owen and Evie were close enough to see his face, but not close enough to hear the words. He looked up at his Espion lord with daggers in his eyes. "I'm going to call on another man to take on the job, Ratcliffe. This blunder is too visible, too humiliating. I'll be the laughingstock in every court from here to Pisan. I had success at Ambion Hill, proved my right to rule through blood and the blessing of the Fountain. But losing a notorious traitor from my own towers?" He extended a gloved hand. "Give me his book. I want Tunmore's book. I want to read his lies about me with my own eyes."

Ratcliffe's face contorted with fury. "I beg you, Severn," he said in a groveling, impetuous tone and tried to draw the king away from all the witnesses. His voice was angry but pitched low enough not to be heard by the entire room of onlookers. "Do not cast me aside like you have others. I'm not Hastings. I'm not Bletchley. I'm not Kiskaddon! You can *trust* me."

Owen stared at the king, hoping he did not believe the spymaster. Owen had seen Ratcliffe when the king wasn't around. He knew the disdainful way he treated others. When a man led others, he needed to earn their respect, not lord over them because of his rank. It was a lesson he'd learned from his father, who always treated his men with respect. In his head, it sounded like tiles were being set up to fall. He could almost hear the clicking sound of them.

"Give me the book," Severn insisted.

Ratcliffe's face twisted with fury. "I will fetch it."

"It's in your *belt*," the king snapped, his hand outstretched.

Ratcliffe tugged it loose and thrust it into the king's hand. He was sulking now, his looks so dark and stormy that Owen feared him even more. "What about your journey? Are we still going into Westmarch as I planned?"

"We leave tomorrow," the king said, mollified somewhat. He turned the black-bound book over in his hand, examining the binding with curiosity.

"Tomorrow? It will take weeks before the household is ready to move!"

"I'm a soldier, Ratcliffe. You know that. I don't care how long it takes the household to follow us. I'm bringing an army with me to the West. Soldiers from the North are riding down even now. We will surprise Kiskaddon with our numbers. The last time I ordered him into battle, he balked and refused to come to my aid until the bitter end. If he balks about joining us, it'll cost him dearly. I think I've learned enough lessons from Ambion Hill. It's time for me to do what I should have done months ago."

Owen didn't catch the king's meaning, but he could tell by his tone of voice that his parents were in trouble. He glanced nervously at his friend and saw her eyes darken with worry. They were doing their best to conceal themselves behind one of the food tables.

"You won't . . . like . . . what you read in it," Ratcliffe said, nodding at the book as if it were a living snake. "You won't care for it. Not at all."

"I am used to slander, Dickon." His mouth began to twist with suppressed anger. "I've been accused of seducing my niece. Murdering my brother's sons. Poisoning my wife." He grunted with disgust. "Remember the eclipse, Dickon? The eclipse that happened the day my wife died? I was blamed for that, too." His voice had shrunk to almost a whisper. "That, however, may have been my doing. My soul was black that day. And I *am* Fountain-blessed."

A silence hung between the two men as they shared memories like a cup of bitter wine.

"My lord," Ratcliffe said, his voice so humble it was almost convincing, "if you will but give me one more chance. Let me prove my loyalty to you. I have no doubt that Tryneowy was behind Tunmore's disappearance. I wouldn't put it past her to have stolen your ring off your finger in the night."

The king looked at him coldly. "That would be impossible," he said. "For I did not sleep. I will not announce the change yet, Ratcliffe.

But I will soon." He tugged off one of his black gloves and stuffed it in his belt, then reached out a hand and clapped Ratcliffe's shoulder. His voice changed in pitch and tone. "You've been loyal, Dickon. I value you, truly I do."

Owen felt a ripple in the air, heard the murmuring churn of waters. He watched with fascination as the king opened himself up to the Fountain, willing it into their presence, summoning it as he might summon a horse to be ridden.

"You will step down as head of the Espion when I command it. You will curb your resentment and think on what you have learned from the experience. My brother always taught me that men should be lifted up to the point where they fail, but no further. You have ambition. You have many good capacities. You are a loyal advisor and friend. But this task is beyond you, and I must find another more capable to stand in your place. You will assist me in finding your replacement. This I charge you. This I command you."

Owen remembered how the king had used his power to command him to walk out of the sanctuary of Our Lady. He had felt the flow of the Fountain all around him then, and he felt it now, too, even though the words were not directed at him. This time he was removed enough from the situation to observe the king's use of his power without being pulled into the current. He was impressed with how the king had dealt with the situation. He hadn't said anything untruthful or insincere. And he had not done it scoldingly or harshly.

"Look," Evie whispered in Owen's ear. "Mancini!"

Owen turned and saw the fat Espion approaching the king and Ratcliffe. He was gazing hungrily at the piles of food on the trestle tables, but he approached deliberately, one hand resting on his enormous belly.

Ratcliffe's eyes were still clouded, but he was staring fixedly at the king, and he looked to be near tears. The king folded his arms and gave Mancini a shrewd look as the big man made his approach.

"Ah, the man who has increased the expenses of my kitchen," he said.

Mancini bowed with a flourish. "Your Grace honors me by noticing such trifling details," he said graciously. "I do have an appetite, it is true. But what I hunger for more than honeyed bread and sack wine is gossip and secrets. And what I have just learned I thought Your Majesty would wish to know straightaway."

Ratcliffe whirled at the sound of Mancini's voice, his face flushed with anger. It was known throughout the palace that he preferred for his underlings to report their news to him—and only him. Mancini was breaking protocol, and everyone in the room knew it. The king looked intrigued.

"What news, Master . . . ?"

"Mancini, Dominic Mancini. I'm Genevese, if you didn't know it. We love our food!"

"I didn't," he said, giving Ratcliffe an unidentifiable look.

"Well, Your Grace, I thought you would wish to hear this straightaway." The big man took another step forward, pitching his voice softly so that it would not carry through the hall. Ratcliffe leaned forward, straining. Owen and Evie sidled a little closer.

"I thought it would be worth mentioning," Mancini continued, "that John Tunmore was spotted in the sanctuary of Our Lady conferring with the old queen. Well, she isn't that *old*, but she is the *previous* queen. I used to be stationed at Our Lady, Your Majesty, and have some acquaintances there who are not part of the Espion. They thought I would be willing to . . . ahem . . . *pay* for such news. Of course, I keep a purse of florins on my person for just such a moment." He jiggled his coin purse and wagged his eyebrows at the king.

The king's expression changed to wonderment and respect. He completely ignored Ratcliffe. "How did he manage to get through the gate?" the king demanded. "Did he sneak away in disguise? The gatekeepers did not see anyone matching his description."

Mancini grinned, cocking his head conspiratorially. "I understand he was seen disembarking from a little boat, Your Majesty. It is dangerous, as you know, maneuvering boats so near the falls, but that is what my contacts told me. There are many secret places here in the palace, as you know."

"I do," the king agreed briskly with a hint of anger. "Well, that explains the disappearance. What remains is to decide what we should do about it."

"He's claimed sanctuary," Ratcliffe interjected, shouldering his way into the conversation. The look of resentment on his face was implacable. "There is nothing that can be done except guard the gates and wait for him to try and slip away. He'll hunker down there for months to try and lull us—"

"This may be presumptuous," Mancini said delicately, interrupting Ratcliffe, "but I have a suggestion."

The king chuckled and put a hand on Ratcliffe's shoulder. "Let's hear him out."

"Your Grace, let me speak with him first. It would—"

"This is where you lack in understanding," the king cut him off. "When you fear having underlings who are better than you, you drive away the most capable men. If you claim credit for their efforts, they resent you. Too often, you keep your Espion to yourself. This man clearly doesn't lack in ambition or presumption. Let him speak. Trust me, Dickon. I have my own opinions and always will. What is your advice, Mancini?"

Owen saw a fleeting smile on Mancini's mouth, but it was gone faster than a blink. "My lord, the master who trained me put it this way. Men ought either to be indulged or utterly destroyed. If you merely offend them, they take vengeance. If you *injure* them greatly, they are unable to retaliate, so the injury done to a man ought to be such that vengeance cannot be feared. There are *ways* of removing people from sanctuary. I know men there who would . . . how shall I say this delicately . . . ?"

"Then don't say it delicately," the king said with a snort.

"I know men who would pizzle in the Fountain of Our Lady if you gave them a coin. If you say the word, my lord, Master Tunmore will be groveling before you in time for supper."

The king brooded on Mancini's words.

"The risk is too great," Ratcliffe hissed. "If the people found out . . ."

"The people are always supposing one thing or another," Mancini said with a shrug.

"I like him," the king said. "But I will not give you the order. Not yet. What is your current assignment, Mancini?"

Owen stared at him, seeing the change unfold before his eyes. The king didn't even realize that Mancini was part of Ankarette's plot to deceive him. Ratcliffe had the king's trust, but he had lost his confidence. Mancini was seen as having the capability to lead the Espion, but he was not trustworthy.

"An important role, I assure you," Mancini said stiffly, rocking on his heels. "I'm overseeing the custody of that little boy. The one who has been listening in on this very conversation." He gave Owen a little wave.

The king turned and saw Owen and Evie hovering just behind his sight. Severn looked at Owen with surprise . . . and could that be approval?

"A timely coincidence," the king said. "Owen, you will join us when we leave tomorrow for Tatton Hall. We ride at first light. Be ready."

CHAPTER THIRTY-ONE

The Assizes

It was after darkfall and most of the kitchen had emptied, except for Liona and Drew, Berwick and Mancini, and Owen. Duke Horwath had taken his granddaughter with him earlier to another room in the palace for some reason. The boy's stomach was twisting with confused feelings as he considered how it would be to return to Tatton Hall. To soothe himself, he had been stacking an elaborate series of tiles for hours as he listened to the conversations ebb and flow in the kitchen. All anyone would talk about was the king's decision to hold the Assizes in the West.

Evie had explained to him, since he did not know, that the Assizes was the annual event at which the king's justice was administered. Formal charges of treason would be debated by the lord justices of the realm, and Evie's grandfather, Duke Horwath, had been named the chief justice and would be presiding over the evidence and the court. While the lords and earls would offer recommendations to the king, it was King Severn who would decide the guilt and punishment meted out by the Assizes.

"I don't see why I can't just ride in a wagon," Mancini complained to Berwick. "It is not healthy for a man to get too much exercise."

Berwick snorted with derision. "The king said yoo'd ride at first light, and you will. I've heard the stable master has fetched old Ribald from the mews to seat you, Mancini. It's the only broot *big* enough, I think. But you're like as not to bounce off!"

"My parts are very tender," Mancini replied, holding his paunch. "I haven't ridden horseback in years. A wagon would suit me just fine, Berwick. Come now, you're the butler. Surely you can arrange something?"

"My advice to you is to stop drinking sack wine from the cellars and start riding more horses," Berwick replied sardonically.

"I don't want your advice. I want a cart! A wagon! Something!"

"Pfah! You'd best be doown in the courtyard before the cock crows. It may take the drawbridge winch to get you seated, but seat you we will. I have enough troubles of my own." He waved the spy aside. "Liona—the stable hands have provender for the beasts, but the king will be eating his breakfast in the saddle."

"I thought of that and will have something ready—"

"No need. He'll stop for a pie from a local vendor as he rides out. Keep carting in water to refill the cistern. It won't rain for another month, at the least, but the king plans to winter away from Kingfountain. Time to put things in order, dismiss the extra staff, and prepare to hunker down for the snows."

Liona's husband, Drew, coughed into his fist. "There is a stock of firewood already prepared for the winters and a few more trees to cut down, besides. We'll be ready in case His Majesty changes his mind."

"Good man," Berwick said with a sniff.

"Now really, Master Berwick," Mancini said in a whining voice.

"I dun't wunt to hear it, man! I've got troubles enough of my own! An entire household to move, and only a fortnight to move it in. We thought the Assizes would happen at Kingfountain, but there's been a change and now we all must obey. Be there before the cock crows, man. Dress warmly."

Mancini scowled. "I'll remember this, Berwick. Don't think that I won't."

"Aye, I grant you will. Any more threats from you, and the staff will forget your feathered mattress. Or to empty your filthy chamber pot. Beware who you threaten, Mancini. Now I'm off." He glanced at Owen, fidgeted a moment as if he wanted to say something, then nodded curtly and stalked out of the kitchen.

Drew came over and tousled the boy's hair. "I'll miss you, Owen. Everyone talks about you, you know, even outside the palace. The people know that you're Fountain-blessed. It will count for something." His look was tender and sympathetic, which made Owen worry even more about what would happen at Tatton Hall. After giving a little pat to Owen's shoulder, Drew left the kitchen. It was late, and Liona had already concealed the tray with Ankarette's dinner, but she stayed in the kitchen to do some final tidying.

Suddenly the noise of footsteps rushing down the hall stairs broke the quiet of the room. Evie came running in, her dark hair wild, tearstains on her pink cheeks. Her nose was dripping and she wiped it on her sleeve. It was already past time for her to be abed and he hadn't seen her in hours. She looked frantic and worried, and the sight of her upset made Owen tremble with concern.

In moments, she was kneeling at his side and pulling him into a frantic hug, half sobbing on his shoulder.

"What happened?" Owen said, pulling back a bit to look at her face.

Her green-gray-blue eyes were filled with tears. "Grandpapa says I can't . . . can't come to the Assizes!" she wailed. "He's sending me back North! Owen! This isn't fair! I want to be there when you see your parents. I want to help give you courage when you face the king! Owen!" Her face crumpled with misery and she grabbed his hands, squeezing them so hard it hurt.

He hadn't imagined that she wouldn't be going with him. Dread flooded him from head to foot. This would make it all so much worse.

"Grandpapa said," she sniffled, "that you'll be riding with him, as you did when you came here. He doesn't want me to see . . . not after Papa . . . Owen! What are they going to do with you?"

Owen felt tears in his own eyes. He'd never seen her so vulnerable.

"Not after Papa. I can't lose you, not you too!" Her fingers tightened, their knuckles locking together. "We're to be married. I thought that's why Grandpapa brought me here. But he said . . . he said no. That the king might send your entire family over the falls." She hung her head, sobbing uncontrollably. "It's not fair! You didn't betray the king at Ambion Hill. It wasn't your fault! Owen, I couldn't bear it! Losing Papa was hard enough. I've tried so hard to be brave, but I can't lose you too! And I won't even be there to see what happens to you! This isn't fair!" she shrieked.

Liona had rushed over to them, and began clucking and cooing softly as she wrapped her arms around Evie's shoulders. "There, there, my little girl. There, there. Shhhh! You must be brave. We must all be brave. Ankarette will help. You'll see. You're upsetting Owen, lass."

Owen felt his own tears streaming down his cheeks. His longing for his parents had been like an underground stream in his time at the palace—an undercurrent to all his other emotions, even though he resented them for letting him go, even though he had formed attachments to other people. But seeing Evie's grief made him feel selfish and stupid. He'd never even talked to her about her own troubles for more than a moment. And what she was saying . . . well, it was as if he and his family were suspended over the edge of a waterfall. They could go under in an instant.

The sound of boots came again, sturdier and heavier, and Owen recognized the set as her grandfather's and Ratcliffe's. Both men entered the kitchen together, one looking somber and grave, the other looking betrayed and aggrieved when he caught sight of Mancini.

"No!" the girl shrieked when she saw her grandfather. She looked betrayed and miserable, yet she still had her spark of defiance and iron will. "I'm going too!"

Ratcliffe sighed at the spectacle of emotion. He snorted to himself and folded his arms over his big chest, giving Horwath a pitying look. "You deal with the water sprite. That's your concern."

Horwath's brow furrowed. "She's my *granddaughter*. Mind that." Horwath approached slowly, as if she were a skittish horse ready to bolt.

"It's not fair, Grandpapa!" she wailed. She tugged on Owen's arm, as if he were the anchor that would prevent her from being swept away.

"Come, Lady Mortimer," Liona said. "Don't shame your grandfather. Obey him."

She rounded on Liona as if she were an enemy. "My *mother* is Lady Mortimer," she said passionately, with a hint of malice. "*I* am Elysabeth *Victoria* Mortimer!"

"Come," Duke Horwath said tenderly, kneeling down by the bench. He held out his hand to her, palm up, entreatingly.

"Is Owen going to die?" she squeaked, her voice full of sorrow. She looked up at her grandfather, tears spilling from her eyes.

The duke had a brave face, stern and calm, but his eyes were full of pain. He glanced at Owen and then back at his granddaughter. "I know not," he whispered.

That made it even worse. A black hole seemed to have opened up below Owen, threatening to swallow him. He remembered when he had first come to Kingfountain, riding behind the duke on his horse. The sense of abandonment, the loneliness, the fear of speaking to anyone.

"Come, lass," Duke Horwath prodded gently, his hand poised to accept hers.

She stared at her grandfather, unable to resist his gentleness. He wouldn't force her. But if she did not obey him, a man born to rule, there would be consequences. There would be freedoms revoked.

Perhaps even estrangement. Owen saw the battle in her eyes, the guilt and anguish in her quivering pout.

She finally stood and took her grandfather's hand. Ratcliffe snorted to himself and strode from the kitchen first. Owen thought his heart was going to break as he watched Evie start away from him. She glanced back once, her lips trembling. Liona, who was wiping her own eyes, patted Owen's shoulder comfortingly as another tear rolled down to the tip of his nose.

Then suddenly Evie did something that startled them all. She grabbed her grandfather's dagger from his belt and yanked it loose. Then she pulled her hand free and marched back to Owen. Using her empty hand, she took the braid she had woven on the side of her head, the one with the white feather stuck in it, and sawed through the hair before anyone could stop her.

She dropped the dagger and then gave Owen a final hug, pressing her moist lips to his cheek, thrusting the severed braid into his hands.

"Be *brave!*" she hissed defiantly into his ear. Gone was the misery and despair. When she pulled back, her eyes burned into his with urgency, a will strong enough to crash into his own and topple his pieces. She squeezed the braid into his hands, her fingers digging deep into his flesh. Her lips were taut and fierce. She was wild with emotion.

Then she kissed him one more time, turned, and marched back to her grandfather, kicking the dagger with her boot to send it clattering across the kitchen. Even Mancini stared at her in awe and respect as she left.

♦ ♦ ♦

Ratcliffe hates me, it's clear enough to see. His power is end-ing and another will rise to take his place. Myself, if all goes well. When a man is tottering on a ledge, sometimes a little push is all that's needed. He said the Espion will be gathering at Holywell Inn when we reach Beestone. He told me because he did not believe I would be able to keep up with the oth-ers. I have no intention of keeping up with the others. He also implied there is news about the Kiskaddons—both of the brat's parents—in Tunmore's book. If only I could get my hands on it to learn what it was. I have no doubt that Ankarette will expect me to steal it. If she hasn't already done so herself.

—Dominic Mancini, Espion of the Palace Kitchen

♦ ♦ ♦

CHAPTER THIRTY-TWO

Weakness

After dark, it was only Owen and Mancini in the kitchen. The dim light in the room came from the flickering coals in the bread ovens and a single lantern hanging from a hook. Owen had finished building his masterpiece, but he did not want to knock it over. He felt that if the tiles did not fall, perhaps he would not have to leave in the morning for the West. Perhaps he would not face his fate—and his family's. He stroked the braid of hair, feeling its softness and warmth. The little white feather reminded him of the time Ratcliffe had stormed into the sea of swirling goose down they'd unleashed in Evie's room. The memory of the feathers stuck to Ratcliffe's head almost made him laugh. But not even that could make him smile more than fleetingly, given the gloom of his predicament.

Mancini sat where he always sat, his hands over his belt, his boot tapping slowly to some song on the floor. He was waiting for Ankarette. He looked rather pleased with himself.

"I've never really cared for children," Mancini said, either to himself or Owen, while nibbling on a fingernail. "I would be a terrible father."

"I agree with you," Owen said darkly, just loud enough for the big man to hear it.

"My father used to whip me when I got my letters wrong. He was always pushing me to excel in languages, in law, in scholarship. I only wanted to please him." He sniffed, shaking his head. "I only drink when I am bored, you know. When I lack things to engage my mind. I may return to Genevar when this is done. You would like it there, lad. There is lots of water for swimming. I used to swim." He sighed again. "Maybe I should have just let you drown."

Owen felt his stomach squirm as he stared at the man. Their eyes finally met when Mancini glanced at him. Neither of them spoke.

It was nearly midnight when she finally came.

The secret door slid open and Ankarette emerged holding a candle, like she had done that first night months ago. Owen rose from his seated posture and walked over. She looked pale, drawn, and weary, almost as if the small weight of the candle was burdensome to her.

"Did you get the book?" Mancini asked her, a wry smile on his face.

Ankarette shook her head and set the candle down. She ignored the tray of food completely. "The king is reading it right now. He read it all last night, too. He has hardly set it down."

Mancini grunted. "I suppose then that you want me to try and steal it."

Owen felt his insides twist with anger as he looked at the lazy spy.

As if reading his thoughts, and perhaps she was, Ankarette gave him a sad, weary smile, and gently stroked his hair. She smelled like faded roses.

"What's going to happen?" Owen whispered. "They're taking me home tomorrow, but I'm afraid to go."

She cupped his cheek. "I told you I would help you, Owen."

"You told *me* you would help *me*," Mancini quipped. "I don't know, boy. I think she's out of tricks this time." He grunted and huffed and made it to his feet ponderously. "If you couldn't steal the book, how am

I supposed to do it? Your game is about played out. There are too many pieces still on the king's side of the Wizr board. Not enough on yours. Best to realize this one is over. You can't save the boy."

Owen turned and gave Mancini a blistering look. But he saw the cunning in Mancini's eyes. He was trying to provoke Ankarette into admitting or revealing something.

A small smile flickered on her mouth. "You no longer want to help me then? You think you can step into Ratcliffe's place on your own?"

Mancini shrugged. "Actually, I do. The king pretty much dismissed him today. And what I know about foreign courts will be much more useful to him if all his enemies at home are dead." He scratched the corner of his mouth.

"His trust must be earned, Dominic," Ankarette insisted. "He's been betrayed too many times. You are Genevese. It would take something incredible to change his opinion of you. But I am helping you, as I said I would. I need a conversation with John Tunmore, but that can't happen while he's in sanctuary."

Mancini chuckled. "I thought you were behind his escape?"

Owen was surprised when she shook her head no.

"Not directly. I just helped him unlock the door. And because of you, the king has Our Lady under constant guard. Deconeus Tunmore has merely shifted his prison from one cell to another. He won't last long in there. He needs freedom. Are you ready for your next assignment, Dominic? Or will you quit now?"

He squinted, looking puzzled. "I think I am done," he said ominously. "If you are pushing Tunmore to lead the Espion, then our interests no longer align."

"The king will not trust Deconeus Tunmore," Ankarette said. "Have no doubt of that. We need to get that book."

Mancini shook his head. "Impossible."

She knelt down by Owen's side and rubbed his shoulder. She glanced over at Mancini. "You can never fully earn the king's trust, Mancini.

There are too many barriers. But someday *Owen* will lead the Espion. And he will need you, and you will need him. Your fates are entwined together. You must help the boy when I am gone."

Mancini looked shocked, his mouth hanging open. "But I thought . . . we agreed . . . that *I* would lead the Espion!"

"And you will!" she said smiling. "Through Owen. The king is sending you with him. Don't you see? It gives you permission to be near him, to advise him. To help him gain the information he needs to survive. I've wrapped your fates together in silk threads. You need each other to be successful. I won't be able to come with you."

Owen started in surprise. "You're not coming?"

"I can't, Owen," she said. "I'm very sick. It is difficult even coming down the steps into the kitchen. Mancini is going. He will help you, and you must help him."

Owen blinked back tears. "I don't want him to help me."

"You should have mentioned that down in the cistern, boy," Mancini said sharply.

"He already has," Ankarette said. "Owen, he saved your life. He was the one who rushed down to save you. He was there for you. He pulled you and Elysabeth Victoria Mortimer from danger."

Mancini came closer, looming over them both. "I don't want to be saddled with this brat!" he chuffed.

She looked up at him. "He will not always be this small, Dominic." She stroked Owen's hair again. "Do you remember the last time the Fountain touched someone so young?"

Mancini snorted. "That Maid of Donremy was a trick of the King of Occitania!"

"No, Dominic," Ankarette said. "She *was* Fountain-blessed. She was just a little girl, but she led the army that overthrew Ceredigion's influence in Occitania. There are many who remember her. Duke Horwath remembers her. Her legend will last for centuries to come. Owen . . .

our *Owen* will be like that. Remember the Battle of Azinkeep? The King of Ceredigion defeated twenty thousand and only lost eighty of his own men. He became the *ruler* of Occitania when he married the princess and her father died. *He* was Fountain-blessed."

Mancini shook his head. "But we've only been *pretending* the boy is! You expect me to keep up the ruse forever? To continue to deceive the king into thinking the boy is something he's not? I couldn't possibly . . . !"

Ankarette closed her eyes, breathing softly, as if she were in great pain. "You must, Dominic. Because I tell you, I tell you truly, the boy *is* Fountain-blessed!" She opened her eyes, piercing the spy with her gaze. "I know what I speak of. He can hear it. He can sense it. He must learn how to become what he has the potential to be, and for that, he will need help. It really takes one who is Fountain-blessed to teach another. Tunmore trained me. I won't be alive long enough to teach him that." She turned to Owen, running her hand along his arm. "That is why the Fountain sent me to you. From the very *moment* of your birth. Owen, it takes *years* to learn about your powers. To be able to control them. To *fuel* them. It takes a rigor of will and self-discipline that most simply do not have. That you can already tap into this, even slightly, is a sign you're just as special as I've always thought you were." She gazed at the structure he had made out of the tiles, unable to hide a pleased smile. "But for someone like us, the rigor of it is not even work. We enjoy it."

Owen's heart was on fire. He grabbed the silk fabric of her dress, the lacings at her front. "You have to come! I . . . I can't do it without you! Please, Ankarette! Please! I can't do this!"

She gave him a sympathetic but firm look. Her hand rested on his shoulder. "You must, Owen."

Tears leaked from the corners of his eyes. "No! I've lost Elysabeth Victoria Mortimer. I've lost my parents. I can't lose you too! I need your help! I won't know what to do if you are not around to tell me what to say!"

"The boy is right," Mancini said darkly. "I'm a poor substitute for your cleverness. Besides, you have not upheld your end of the bargain. You promised me your story! You promised me the tale."

She sighed and patted Owen's shoulder with a trembling hand. "I gave *him* the story," she said to Mancini. "If you want to learn it, you must keep him alive."

Mancini ground his teeth in frustration. "You tricked me."

"No," she said. "I always deliver what I promise. In my own way. But you of all people know it is a double pleasure to deceive the deceiver."

He gasped when she said this and Owen didn't know why. The look he gave her was full of incredulity . . . and respect. Something she had said had shot straight into his heart, leaving him flummoxed. Ankarette slowly rose.

Mancini was stuttering. "You are the most duplicitous, the most conniving, the most scheming . . . the best spy I have ever met!" He gave her a grudging smile. "You've read my journal. Even though it's written in Genevese ciphers."

She gave him a slight curtsy and a triumphant smile.

"I'll be blessed," he replied with a belly laugh. "Well, lad. I hope Tatton Hall has a decent kitchen and a wine cellar. I'm off to bed." He chuckled to himself as he staggered to the steps.

When he was gone, Ankarette knelt again, looking Owen directly in the eyes.

"There is something I didn't tell you," Owen said nervously. "About the cistern."

"What is it?" she asked, smoothing the front of his tunic in a motherly way.

"I've been there before with Evie. When I jumped into the water, I saw a treasure." He told her of the treasure he had found—how at first he could not reach it, but then he clung to a chest to keep himself and Evie from being swept away in the flood.

The queen's poisoner listened carefully to his story, watching his face most intently. There was something about her keen interest that intrigued him. From the look in her eyes, it was as if he were sharing the most interesting story imaginable. She waited patiently until he was done and then she grew serious.

"Was the treasure real, Ankarette?" he asked her at the end of the story, hoping she would say yes.

She reached out and rubbed the sides of his arms, holding him fast. "That you can even see it means many things, Owen. People see many things in the water. Sometimes glimpses of the future. Sometimes of their own death. I don't know what you saw or why. I don't know if it's real or not. But I do believe the Fountain is trying to speak to you. Your powers are blossoming even faster than I expected they would. Your *life* is about to change."

He wasn't sure he was ready for it.

"*Please* come with me," he begged her.

She licked her lips, then let out a painful breath. She gazed at the floor for a moment. "I will try," she whispered, and Owen felt his heart jump with a thrill.

"You will? Oh, Ankarette!" he gushed, throwing his arms around her neck and squeezing her in the biggest hug he had given her yet.

She leaned into the hug, patting his hair. The panic he had felt rising all day began to subside.

◆ ◆ ◆

A wagon. A wagon—this bloody kingdom for a ride in a wagon!

—Dominic Mancini, Espion of the Ribald Horse

◆ ◆ ◆

CHAPTER THIRTY-THREE

Strawberries

There was a great deal of mirth and amusement in the torch-lit yard as everyone watched Mancini try to mount his enormous horse. Owen wanted to stay and watch, but Duke Horwath had other ideas and the boy could hardly insist otherwise. The final embers of the late-summer heat wave were barely cooling. The night was dark but still muggy and Owen's jacket and hood were uncomfortable as he got situated behind the duke's saddle.

The king maneuvered his steed close to Horwath's.

"Where is Ratcliffe?" Horwath asked gruffly.

The king tugged one of his black gloves on more snugly. "He rode ahead last night with several of the Espion to secure the way."

"What village are we stopping in tonight? Stony Stratford?"

The king snorted. "I wouldn't dare. The queen dowager has a manor near there. That was where Bletchley warned me of her treachery two years ago." His expression soured with the memory. Then he gave Horwath a pointed look. "You must do your duty at the Assizes, my friend. Be ready."

"Loyalty binds me," replied the duke, dipping his head in a nod.

Owen wondered what the king had meant by duty, but even thinking about it made him sick with worry for his family. The clash of horseshoes on stone nearly drowned out the rushing noise of the waterfall as the king's men crossed the bridge to the island of Our Lady. Firelight gleamed in the sanctuary, but the new day was still hours from dawning. As they passed the gigantic sanctuary, Owen saw dozens of soldiers wearing the badge of the white boar, patrolling the closed gates. Many dipped their pikes in salute to the king as he passed. There were no street vendors, no smoked sausages for sale, but Owen could see a few timid faces peeking at the entourage from behind drawn curtains.

Soon the island and the city of Kingfountain were behind them and the world opened up into hills, woods, and roads. When Owen had traveled from Tatton Hall, the scenery had passed him in a blur. It was different now. Many of the men they were with carried the badge of the Duke of Horwath, the lion with the arrow piercing its mouth. And the symbol of the white boar was ever present. These were the king's soldiers, men who had fought with him at Ambion Hill. There were swords strapped to saddle harnesses. There were armor and shields. The host looked as if it was prepared to make or rebuff an attack.

The pace was brutal and bone-jarring, and Owen kept fading in and out of consciousness as he clung to Evie's grandfather. At midday, they stopped in a copse of massive yew trees to rest their mounts and eat the provisions collected earlier from one of the many towns along the way.

The trunks of the trees looked like they were made of massive cords wound up together into a huge rope that jutted straight up and sent out spear-like branches. Owen remembered from his reading that yew was the favored wood for making bows. This was what he thought of as he sat under the shadow of the giant tree and nibbled on a mincemeat pie that was cold and too peppery.

Duke Horwath was next to him, silently gnawing on his meal and offering no conversation. He took a large gulp from a leather flask and then offered it to Owen, who accepted it gratefully to ease the burning of his tongue.

Owen kept looking up at the massive trees, for there were many, and the smell was interesting. He liked being outdoors and was a little jealous that Elysabeth Victoria Mortimer's father had taken her into the mountains of the North so often. Owen's father had lavished most of his fatherly attention on the older boys, treating Owen as if he were too delicate for hunting.

"How old is this tree?" Owen asked the grizzled duke.

Horwath seemed surprised, not by the question, but that Owen had possessed the courage to ask it.

"Older than Ceredigion," he said gruffly.

Owen crinkled his nose. "How can that be? How can a tree be older than the land?"

The duke gave him an amused smile and brushed some crumbs from his silver goatee. "Not the land, my boy. The kingdom. The tree is older than the kingdom. The Occitanians came to this land almost five hundred years ago and earned the right to rule by the sword. Less than a hundred years ago, we did the same to them in their realm. Beat them bloody. And then they drove us out again." He sighed and shook his head.

"The Maid of Donremy," Owen said softly, earning another curious look from the duke.

He frowned at the words and then nodded. "I was a young lad myself. Your age. I still remember her."

"How did she die?" Owen asked, though he thought he knew. He had heard her story before Ankarette mentioned her.

The duke looked down at the ground, almost as if he were ashamed. "They couldn't trust her fate to a waterfall, lad. Some said if she were put in a boat, she would step off it and walk back up the river and away from the falls. No, she met a winter's death. The only thing that can tame water is cold. It's the only thing that can make it sit still." He wiped his bearded mouth again, lost in the distant past. "She was taken to a high mountain and chained there. With only a shift. She lasted a few days, but then she died."

Owen wasn't hungry anymore. The thought of perishing on a frozen mountaintop made him shudder.

The sound of boots crunching fallen detritus roused his attention. King Severn had joined them against the huge trunk of the muscled yew tree. The hours in the saddle seemed to have reinvigorated him and he looked less sullen, more at peace.

"Telling the lad stories of the Maid?" the king asked with a wry smile. He unhooked his leather flask from his belt and tilted it high. After finishing his drink, he wiped his mouth on his forearm and gave a satisfied sigh. "You are an old man, Stiev. You lived those days. When a half-mad boy ruled Ceredigion. His uncle, though, he was the one with the power. There is always an uncle in these stories," he added with self-deprecating humor.

Horwath chuckled softly. "Aye, my lord. Are we truly staying at Tatton Hall?"

"No. I wouldn't trust the lad's father so much. We'll be staying at the royal castle, Beestone. And we will summon Lord Kiskaddon to attend us. And when he comes, well . . ." He paused, giving Owen a smirk. "We shall see, won't we?"

"You aren't going to trust the Espion to that Genevese man, are you?" Horwath asked, after a long pause.

"I've considered it," Severn said with a shrug. "Would I had a man as crafty as Tunmore to serve me." His face began to darken, his jaw tightening with anger. "I've been reading his book, you know." He dangled the water skin from one of his gloved fingers, letting it sway back and forth until it almost clapped against his leg. "This is the title. *The Occupation of the Throne of Ceredigion by King Severn.*" He frowned as he said the words. Owen watched his face closely. "As I read that screed, I swear I almost started *believing* it. He tells an eloquent tale and comes across as a philosopher, not a . . . a deconeus. He was writing it to be published, I think. That city where we caught him is a major trading hub. Imagine how far he could have spread his lies." He tugged his dagger loose in the scabbard and slammed it down. "But what truly makes me furious, Stiev, is how he covered his own part. His own crimes."

"What do you mean?" Horwath asked.

Severn leaned forward, wincing as if his back were paining him. "I won't even tell you all he said about *me*. That I was born feet first, with teeth, and only ever kissed those I meant to kill. That I plotted my nephews' deaths from the start." His breath hissed out with frustration. "Never mind the lies. How can you expect otherwise from a man who lives on the graces of others, one who has committed high treason not once, but twice? No, what angers me most is his complete denial of his own complicity. Remember the plot Catsby told us about, how Tunmore conspired with the others to murder me the morning when we met at privy council? How I charged Hastings with high treason and he confessed all in front of the council?" He clenched his fist with his pent-up emotions, bringing it to his mouth in frustration. "You were there, Stiev. Yet in the book, the saintly Deconeus of Ely says I asked him to fetch strawberries from his garden! His garden!" He looked nearly apoplectic. "I was nigh on being murdered, my son and wife were to be put in the river or worse, and I asked him for *strawberries*? And he says that when he went to fetch them, I turned on Hastings and murdered him. I never sent Tunmore away for fruit. He was there the whole time! It's a bald-faced lie, and from a man of the Fountain, no less." He seemed so uncomfortable that he rocked forward and stood, then began pacing. "And the thing is, Stiev. The fact of the matter is that while *reading* it, I *wanted* to believe it." He grunted with contempt. "I wanted to believe those lies about myself. Is this what men think of me, Stiev? Truly? Not just my enemies, forsooth. But do the common people believe I murdered my nephews? That I conspired and connived for my nephews' throne? I took it. Yes. But only after the Deconeus of Stillwater told us—*us!*—that my brother's marriage to his wife was invalid. That would make all of his children illegitimate. Can I believe that of my brother? Of course I can! He was a rake! He had our brother Dunsdworth killed because he learned of it. By the Fountain, does everyone see me this way? That I would murder my brother's sons after snatching the throne from them?" His face was a rictus of frustration. He never looked down at Horwath. He wasn't truly seeking an answer.

"My lord, my hair and beard are quite gray," Horwath said in a low, coaxing tone. "So I suppose it entitles me to some wisdom about the nature of men. It has been my experience that while it's easy to persuade most men of some new thing, it is more difficult to *fix* them in that persuasion. In the end, the truth will out eventually."

The king folded his arms imperiously and gave the old man a curious look. "The truth will out," he said, his tone showing he was not fully convinced.

Their attention was diverted with the arrival of a horse, a lathered monster of a beast holding the panting, disheveled, and thoroughly exhausted Dominic Mancini.

"You've arrived just in time to leave," the king snorted contemptuously.

"My . . . my . . . lord . . ." the man wheezed, trying to catch his breath. "You keep a . . . hazardous pace. Horseflesh . . . was not intended . . . to work this hard. I implore . . . Your Majesty . . . to slow down."

"Or do you mean *your* flesh?" the king said with a chuckle. He clapped Horwath's shoulder. "Onward, lads. I've ridden nearly every corner of this kingdom on my brother's orders. He said a soldier should always know the ground he travels. Where are the fens and fords. Where are the falls. Over yonder," he added, pointing, "is an estuary called the Stroud. At the head of that muggy estuary is a little castle called Glosstyr. My brother made me its duke and the constable of that castle on my ninth birthday." He looked down at Owen, his face scrutinizing the young boy, who was nearing his ninth birthday. "Loyalty bound me. And it still does."

The king slapped his thighs. "That's where we will be spending the night."

Horwath whistled through his teeth. Owen had the sense that it would be a long journey.

The king smirked. "Try to keep up, Master Mancini. Or at the least, try not to kill the horse or *yourself* getting there."

◆ ◆ ◆

I don't think the princes of the various realms fully appreci-
ate that King Severn Argentine is first and foremost a soldier.
Or maybe they do and that's why they fear him so much. We
rode thirty-five leagues in a single day, changing horses three
times at various castles. We did not make it to Glosstyr until
well after midnight, but the king's energy only improved as
the day waned. I am nearly fainting with fatigue. If I were
to guess, the king intends to swoop down on Westmarch unex-
pectedly, for we are traveling faster than pigeons can fly. Even
if Ankarette left before us, I don't see how she can reach Tat-
ton Hall first.

—Dominic Mancini, Espion of the Piebald Nag

◆ ◆ ◆

CHAPTER THIRTY-FOUR

Beestone

The royal palace in Westmarch had been dubbed Beestone Castle, although it was not clear why. The reason for the location was much more apparent, for it had been built on Castle Hill overlooking the city of Knotsbury and its surrounding valleys and farms. It was an impressive castle, a royal castle, with squat round towers on each side of the main gate and drawbridge, and the entire hill was enclosed by thick, sturdy walls. Sharp, stony cliffs surrounded the circumference of the hill, making the castle impregnable to attack and able to withstand sieges. It was not opulent, but it was safe and secure. Right now the main bailey was teeming with horses and soldiers bearing the colors and badges of the white boar. Archers strolled the ramparts, and Owen spied the king's flag fluttering from pennants overhanging the walls.

Amidst such confusion, no one took much notice of the small little boy sneaking around and exploring the castle from one end to the other. It was much smaller than Kingfountain, he soon realized, and the wind here was sharp and cool. The view from the bulwarks was impressive, but Tatton Hall was too far away to see.

Owen felt uneasy and wondered how Ankarette was going to find him. The royal retinue would not be arriving with the baggage carts from Kingfountain for several more days. As a result, there were mostly soldiers around the grounds. A woman would surely stand out among them, but Owen was confident that she would find a way.

While he was wandering the battlement walls, a squire bearing the badge of Duke Horwath found him and took him to the royal apartments where the king was meeting with the duke. There were knights and servants coming in and out of the sitting room, heralds waiting to bring messages. Owen looked at all the tall men and felt out of place as the only child among them. He missed Evie and wished she were here to explore the castle with him. He missed his tiles too, and the serenity they gave him. While the adults were talking, Owen found a Wizr set by the table near the king's luggage and began playing with it and admiring the pieces.

Then he noticed the black book on top of a chest. It felt like his stomach was suddenly full of worms, all wriggling and twisting. The book seemed to call to him, whispering to him to open it. He glanced over at Duke Horwath and the king, but the king was doing most of the talking and his back was to Owen. The king's hand tugged on his dagger hilt in his habitual nervous gesture. He looked tall and strong, and while one of his shoulders was slightly higher than the other, his posture and gestures seemed to hide the fact.

Owen glanced back at the book. He had a craving to start reading it. If he stole it, he knew it would be missed. But what if he could learn something about his family in it, something that could help them?

He knew what Elysabeth Victoria Mortimer would do. He reached into his pocket and rubbed his thumb on the braid she had cut off and given him. Then, steeling himself, he inched his way over to the bed, as if he were merely curious. His fingers shook a little as he reached out and touched the book's binding.

He glanced back one more time, and when he saw everyone else was still thoroughly engrossed in conversation, he carefully opened the book and started reading.

The Occupation of the Throne of Ceredigion
by King Severn (unfinished),
written by Master John Tunmore.

> *King Eredur, of that name the Fourth, after he had lived fifty and three years, seven months, and six days, and thereof reigned two and twenty years, one month, and eight days, died at Kingfountain the ninth day of Averil, leaving much fair issue . . .*

—He was poisoned—

Owen started when he heard the whisper in his mind. A tremulous feeling began to unfurl inside him. As soon as he had started to read the little black book, a gentle murmuring sound began to fill his ears, so subtle he had not noticed it swelling. Then the thought struck him with the force of a blow. King Eredur had been poisoned.

Owen blinked, feeling giddy and worried at the same time. He kept reading.

> *That is, to wit: Eredur the Crown Prince, a lad thirteen years of age; Eyric Duke of Yuork, age ten. Elysabeth, the eldest, fairest princess of the realm, whose fortune and grace are those of a queen. Selia, not so fortunate as fair. Bridget the virtuous. This noble prince of great fame, Eredur, deceased at his palace of Kingfountain, and, with great funeral honor and heaviness of his people, was put in a royal barge and commended to the river in the hopes that he would become the Dreadful Deadman prophecy*

fulfilled, and return from the watery grave. His body was
taken by the Fountain, not seen hence.

—*Eredur was not the Dreadful Deadman*—

Owen started again when the voice whispered to him. His stomach clenched and twisted, his heart feeling like the burning coals in the brazier nearby. Owen was so wrapped up in reading, he could hear nothing else in the room. His eyes were fixed on the page.

He read next about how Eredur had taken the throne and the wars that had happened along the way. Much of this history he had learned from Ankarette.

> *Many nobles of the realm at Wakefield were slain,*
> *leaving three sons—Eredur, Dunsdworth, and Severn. All*
> *three, as they were great princes of birth, were great and*
> *stately, greedy and ambitious of authority, and impatient*
> *of partners. Eredur, revenging his father's death, attained*
> *the crown. Lord Dunsdworth was a goodly, noble prince*
> *and at all points fortunate, if his own ambition had not*
> *set him against his brother and the envy of his enemies had*
> *not set his brother against him. For were it by the queen*
> *and the lords of her blood, the king was persuaded to hate*
> *his own brother or the proud appetite of the duke himself,*
> *intending to be king, Lord Dunsdworth was charged with*
> *heinous treason, and finally, attainted was he and judged*
> *to the death. Not thrown in the river, but drowned in a*
> *keg of wine. Whose death King Eredur, when he knew it*
> *was done, piteously bewailed and sorrowfully repented.*

—*Dunsdworth was poisoned by Ankarette Tryneowy. His craving of*
power and wealth made him go mad chasing the treasure in the cistern
waters. Dunsdworth was not the Dreadful Deadman—

If the walls of the palace crumbled around him, Owen would not have noticed. He was so engrossed in the book he could not pull his eyes away. He read on.

> *Severn, the third son, of whom we now entreat, was in intellect and courage equal with either of his brothers, in body and prowess far beneath them both: little of stature, ill-featured of limbs, crook-backed—his left shoulder much higher than his right—hard-favored of visage, and warlike in his demeanor. He was malicious, wrathful, envious, and, from afore his birth, ever perverse. It is for truth reported that the duchess his mother had so much ado in her travail that she could not be delivered of him uncut, and, as the fame runneth, also not untoothed. Able captain was he in war, for which his disposition was much better met than for peace. He was close and secret, a deep dissembler, lowly of countenance, arrogant of heart; outwardly companionable where he inwardly hated, not refraining to kiss those whom he thought to kill; dispiteous and cruel, not for evil, but often for ambition. He slew with his own hand—*

The book was suddenly snatched out of Owen's hands and Ratcliffe waggled it over his head. "Do you *see* what the lad is reading, my lord? Look at him, he was transfixed!" He then whapped the side of Owen's head with the book and gave him a shove.

Duke Horwath stepped forward, putting himself between Owen and Ratcliffe.

"He was *reading* it, you say?" the king asked, suddenly interested and concerned.

"Did you not see him?" Ratcliffe said sharply.

"I saw him," came another voice, much younger. Owen glared at

Dunsdworth, who had appeared in the doorway and was giving him a malicious smile. In Owen's mind, he saw a man inside a bucket, clawing at the bottom as if trying to reach a treasure he could not grab. The vision was enough to make him shudder.

But the king stepped forward, blocking his view of Dunsdworth. "You were reading my book?"

Owen had been caught. There was no denying it. His tongue felt like it was sticking to the roof of his mouth. Fear made him want to cower, but he reached inside his pocket and gripped the braid of Elysabeth's hair.

"I wanted to play Wizr," Owen said, his mouth finally able to move. "But everyone was talking, so I started playing with the pieces. Then I saw the book."

"Did you understand it?" the king asked incredulously.

Owen nodded.

"There are hard words in there, lad. It's not a child's book. Did you truly understand its meaning?"

Owen stared at the king, whose eyes were now boring into his. "I . . . like books," he said sheepishly.

The king snatched the book from Ratcliffe's hand and then thumbed through it. "I like books under normal circumstances. But this book . . . there are *falsehoods* written in it. Falsehoods about me."

"I know," Owen said, nodding.

The king's brow wrinkled. "What do you mean you *know*?"

Owen blinked, feeling more and more confused. How did he know? How could he describe the voice he'd heard while reading it?

"I . . . I felt it. As I read," Owen said simply. "I *felt* the parts that weren't true."

The king's eyes narrowed. "We will speak of this later," he murmured, then stuffed the book into his belt. "Dunsdworth! Play Wizr with the lad."

The older boy scowled fiercely at the command, and Owen groaned inwardly as he walked to the Wizr board. Dunsdworth sulked as he took up the white pieces and set them up, incorrectly. It hurt to watch him, but Owen gritted his teeth, knowing Dunsdworth wouldn't care the pieces were in the wrong positions.

"What news from Tatton Hall?" the king demanded of Ratcliffe in an undertone. Owen had clearly not heard the spymaster or Dunsdworth enter the room earlier, for he had been too caught up in reading the book. As Owen silently began moving pieces, he kept his eyes on the game board while his ears listened keenly to the king's conversation.

"I hate this game," Dunsdworth seethed.

I hate you, Owen almost said, but managed to bite his tongue in time.

"As you requested, my lord, I delivered your summons to Duke Kiskaddon at Beestone Castle. As you can imagine, he wanted to know the nature of the summons. I explained that you were holding the Assizes. He then had the temerity to ask whether he would be participating in the Assizes as a justice." Ratcliffe chuckled.

"And what did you tell him?" the king asked with amusement.

"I said, of course, that Duke Horwath was the chief justice and he would learn more when he obeyed the summons."

"Do you think he will come, Dickon?" the king asked softly.

"If he doesn't, he's guilty of treason. If he does, he'll be found guilty of treason. Either way, we have him."

"There are three estuaries with ports in Westmarch," the king said. "Mold and Runcin in the South and Blackpool in the North. No one sails from any of those ports without my approval. And the King of Occitania would not want his territory to help Kiskaddon."

"The only place he can go is sanctuary. And you can be sure, we have Espion watching all of them and watching the estate. He won't be able to use the privy without us knowing."

There was a smile in the king's voice. "Thank you, Dickon. You've done well. It's time for the lad to see his parents again. You told them I brought the boy with me?"

"Indeed, my lord. They know the price for open treason."

"He was guilty of *that* at Ambion Hill. Stiev, how long would it take for him to summon his retainers and an army from the borderlands?"

Duke Horwath's voice was gruff. "Do you think he will, my lord?"

"Beestone has a thousand men, and more have been arriving all day. A thousand more will join us from the North. How many can Kiskaddon summon, and how quickly?"

"Only a few hundred men by tomorrow. Maybe half of that. It would take him a fortnight to collect the rest of those who owe him service, and I doubt they would join him against you now that you are already established here. You didn't give him enough time to react."

The king chuckled. "That was my intent. The wolf is at the door. The sheep are bleating. What will you do next, Kiskaddon? It's your move."

Owen made his final move, having defeated Dunsdworth in five turns. His stomach was twisting into knots. Dunsdworth grunted with disgust at the loss and swore under his breath.

♦ ♦ ♦

When Owen made it to his bedchamber after the evening meal, his thoughts whirling with both what he had read and what he had overheard, he realized that his parents had failed their test of loyalty and his own life hung in the balance.

He stopped in surprise.

On the floor in his room was the satchel he had left behind at Kingfountain. Tiles on the floor spelled his name: O-W-E-N.

◆ ◆ ◆

My master taught me certain maxims. A prince ought to inspire fear in such a way that if he does not win love, he avoids hatred. He can avoid the hatred of his people as long as he abstains from the property of his subjects and from their women. But when it becomes necessary for him to proceed against the life of someone, especially one of the nobles who hold so much power, he must do it with proper justification. But above all things, he must keep his hands off the property of others, because men will more quickly forget the death of their father than the loss of their patrimony. History teaches this plainly, and many a king has lost his crown after stealing what belonged to another man. It's ironic that even though it causes more trouble to take away land than to kill, it's more difficult to find justification to take someone's life. That's why it's best to strike your enemy down after he's given you the opportunity to do so. The Assizes of Westmarch are just such a pretext.

—Dominic Mancini, Exhausted Espion of Beestone Castle

◆ ◆ ◆

CHAPTER THIRTY-FIVE

Well of Tears

It was after nightfall, but there were enough torches to illuminate the castle bailey as if it were day. There was no end to the clattering of wagons as arrivals from the king's court continued to ascend to Beestone Castle throughout the night. Soldiers wearing the badge of the white boar were everywhere, but Owen made his way through the bailey yard anyway, careful to keep away from adults who might send him to bed. After seeing his name spelled with tiles, he had been searching for Ankarette.

In the center of the courtyard was a raised well made of stone and mortar. Owen clambered up onto the edge of it and stared down into the black depths. He could hear a faint gurgling, but it was too deep for him to see the shimmer of water.

The sound of boots coming up behind him warned him that he was no longer alone, and he scuttled back from the edge as Mancini approached, holding a gleaming florin in his hand.

"Ready to make another wish?" the fat man asked with a grin. He offered the coin to the boy, putting Owen in mind of their meeting long ago at Our Lady.

The boy shook his head.

Mancini pursed his lips and nodded knowingly. "I agree. It's a waste of a good coin. I mean, look at this piece. I could buy several muffins with it and gain an hour's satisfaction. Or I can plop it down a well shaft and never gain a single thing from it. If wishes were horses, beggars would ride, eh?" Mancini sat on the edge of the well, next to Owen, folding his meaty arms over his chest. He clucked his tongue softly. "Frankly, lad, I don't see how she can pull this one off. The guards at the gate are letting only Espion pass back out. The baggage continues to arrive, but naught are leaving. Word amongst us is your lord father has ridden down from Tatton Hall with an escort of a hundred men. He's camped about a league away from the city. Doesn't look good for him."

Owen's twisting nerves grew worse. "I trust her," he whispered softly.

"Trust is a pretty dish, lad. But this is the *king's* trust we are talking about. If *I* were in Severn's place, I'd use the Assizes to my advantage to destroy a threat known to me. A dish may be a pretty thing, but it's easily broken. Even if you fit the pieces back together, it won't hold a meal. Your father broke the king's trust at Ambion Hill. Your brother already paid for that with his life. Bets are being waged among the Espion that your father will go into the river tomorrow." He clapped Owen on the back. "I hate to bear bad news, but I just don't see how Ankarette can change his mind."

Anger churning in his heart, Owen gave Mancini a sulky look. "She's more clever than you, though. She'll think of a way."

Mancini snorted. "Well, if she's slipped into the castle, she won't be slipping out, I can tell you that."

"You sound very sure of yourself." It was Ankarette's voice, ghosting up to them from the lip of the well. Owen startled, and Mancini had to lurch forward to keep from falling backward into the well in pure surprise.

Owen's faith in the queen's poisoner had been vindicated once again. He leaned over the edge of the well, staring down into its dark throat. "Are you down in the well?" he whispered, his voice echoing down the shaft.

"I am," she replied, her voice kind but tired.

"I can't see you," Owen said.

"But I can see you," she answered. "All is well."

"I'm beginning to believe in all this Fountain nonsense," Mancini grumbled nastily, having partially recovered from his shock. "Where are you?"

"There are tunnels honeycombing beneath the castle," she whispered. "It's one of the reasons that castle was named Beestone. This is a famous castle, Owen. Or an infamous one. Several kings have started their reign here. Studying the past sometimes helps us make the future. Dominic, have you found what I asked you to find?"

Owen gripped the edge, his heart afire with hope.

The spy frowned distastefully. "Yes, but it's not good news, Ankarette. It would seem the king means to execute the lad's family tomorrow. I was just telling him that. The Espion are all betting on it, coins changing hands."

"Thank you. Yes, it does seem very likely that the king will make an announcement tomorrow. This is the bit of news I needed to confirm. Do you know what time the Assizes will start? When must Kiskaddon arrive before he's guilty of treason?"

Mancini frowned, his arms folded. "Tenth hour. I heard he's camped a league away."

"Dominic, I need you to go to him. I can't ride that far and be back in time. You must go to Lord Kiskaddon and you must tell him to come to the Assizes tomorrow. He cannot be late."

"Why would he listen to me?" Mancini said.

"Because I sent you. He will trust you because his wife trusts me. Believe this. You must persuade Owen's father to come without a retinue. Without arms. He must put himself completely at the king's mercy."

Owen shivered.

The incredulous look on Mancini's face said it all. "Are you serious?"

"Quite so. You must deliver this message for me. Tonight. If you leave now, you can be at his camp and back before dawn. See if you can persuade him to come with you. He cannot be late to the Assizes. Will you do this?"

"I'm risking my neck," Mancini grumbled. "Will you not tell me your plan? I haven't been able to get the book. The king keeps it with him at all times."

"He's struggling to understand what is written in it. I need to know what's in that book."

"But the king won't let go," Mancini said.

"He's not the only one who's read it. Where are the Espion staying? Where is Ratcliffe?"

"What?"

"Where is Ratcliffe?" More insistently this time.

"The . . . all the Espion are staying at the Holywell in town. It's near Castle Hill, on the—"

"I know it," she said, cutting him off. Her voice sounded more tired, more pained. "Go, Dominic. Go warn Kiskaddon."

The spy grunted as he leaned away from the well and marched off toward the torchlight. Owen was grateful he was gone.

"Are you feeling sick?" Owen whispered into the well.

There was a long pause. "I'm very sick, Owen. And we're running out of time."

He fidgeted nervously. "I wish there was a way *I* could help," he said miserably. "I saw the book on the king's bed today. I started reading it, but Ratcliffe took it away."

"That was clever of you," she said, sounding pleased. "You could tell John Tunmore is Fountain-blessed just from reading it, couldn't you?"

"Yes," Owen said. "Ankarette, what is the Dreadful Deadman?"

She was quiet a moment. "How do you know about that name?" she finally asked. "Was it in the book?"

"In a way," he answered, feeling confused. "While I was *reading* the book, I heard the name. I heard it twice. The voice said King Eredur wasn't the Dreadful Deadman. Then it said Lord Dunsdworth—not the boy, but his father—was also not the Dreadful Deadman. What is it?"

"I don't know for certain," Ankarette said, her voice soft and subdued. "It is a superstition, mostly. One that is whispered about late at night. It is a legend of the first king of Ceredigion, the one who ruled before Occitania invaded our lands. I told you before of his Wizr. Myrddin was Fountain-blessed and could see the future. There are stories that he left a prophecy. Before he disappeared, he said that the first king of Ceredigion would return someday. He would come back from the dead to rule Ceredigion *and* Occitania. This prophecy was named the Dreadful Deadman, for when he returns, there will be much war and bloodshed. This legend is not written down, but the people believe in it. It is rumor ladled on gossip and served in a trencher of lies. King Eredur claimed he was the Dreadful Deadman. It's a ploy many have used to become king. But that is the nature of prophecies. They are much speculated about. I know the Occitanians *fear* this prophecy. To them it is certainly dreadful. But in this case, Owen, I cannot tell you what is true and what is false. I do not know."

Owen rubbed his hand over the cool, smooth stone of the well. He kept staring into the depths, wishing he could see her. "Are you truly down there?" he asked.

"I am," she answered, a smile in her voice. "Now, you said you wished you could help."

"Can I?" he asked, growing more hopeful.

"Owen, you are the biggest help of all. You are the one who is going to save your family."

He leaned forward so far he almost fell in. "Really? How?"

"You are going to tell the king your family is guilty of treason."

His hope suddenly wilted. "Ankarette?"

"Listen to me, my boy. The verdict of the Assizes has already been determined. There must be enough evidence in that book to condemn your parents. I cannot do anything about that. The king has already made up his mind. He will use Duke Horwath to execute his will and deliver the king's justice. No matter what is said tomorrow at the Assizes, your family will be declared guilty of treason and will be attainted. Do you know that word?"

"No," Owen groaned miserably. He wanted to be sick.

"Attainder means the forfeiture of land and rights as a consequence of a sentence of death for treason or felony. It means the king will strip away Westmarch from your family and put them to death. Then *he* can claim the duchy as royal lands or give them to another person. That is what happens. That is what is *going* to happen tomorrow. What I need to know is what is in that book. Because you are going to have a dream tonight, Owen, and you are going to share it with the king before the Assizes begins. You will confess your family's treason. That exhibition of your power will not only astonish the king, but the fact that you used it to benefit him will put you in a position of trust. The Assizes, Owen, is *your* test of loyalty. Your parents have already failed theirs. They failed it months ago when your father didn't fight for the king at Ambion Hill until it was too late. Your father is useless to the king now, for he can never trust him again. What Severn needs to know is if *you* will be faithful to him."

Owen felt tears stinging his eyes. "But I don't want my family to die!" he gasped. He felt utterly miserable.

"I know, I know," Ankarette soothed, her voice thickening with pain. "But you can save them, Owen. Listen. Don't let your grief run away with you. I'm doing the best I can to help you." Her voice trailed off and Owen stifled his own sobs, wanting so much to reach into the black hole to comfort her.

"Listen to me . . ." she whispered, her voice so soft. "Your dream will reveal your parents' treason. I will find out what's in the black book so I can tell you tonight. It will solidify your reputation as one who can see the future."

"But how?" Owen asked, confused. "What my parents did was in the past. Why would knowing that convince the king I can see the future?" The sound of approaching boots met his ears, and when he looked up, he saw Duke Horwath approaching, a look of concern on his face.

"He's coming," Owen whimpered nervously.

"Listen carefully," Ankarette said. "Even if someone is attainted, found guilty, the king can show mercy and pardon them. We will *make* the future. Your dream will predict that the king will pardon your family and banish them from the realm. Exile. That is what your dream must tell him. I will work out the details tonight. I'll find you before dawn."

"He's almost here!" Owen warned.

"And in your dream," she whispered, her voice ghosting up from the well hole, "the rat dies."

◆ ◆ ◆

Lord Kiskaddon is a broken man, a husk. He's a man stand-ing on the brink of a waterfall, seeing the rushing waters whisking him toward his doom. Flail as he might, he cannot escape the current. He was almost too willing to speak to a total stranger—a Genevese, no less! His greatest regret? That Tunmore's book reveals his wife was his partner in all things. She helped arrange and receive the messages from the pretend king who was slain at Ambion Hill. Their entire family is going to be shoved into the river after the Assizes. Well, all except one. Kiskaddon has come to Beestone Castle to beg for a pardon he won't be getting.

—Dominic Mancini, Espion of the Assizes

◆ ◆ ◆

♦ ♦ ♦

I'm in shock. When I got back to the tavern, all was in an uproar. Ankarette is dead. Apparently she went after Ratcliffe at the Espion stronghold. I've heard only snippets, but she blew powder in his face to drug him. She was discovered by my colleagues and stabbed to death. There were easily a dozen men with blood on their shirts and daggers. Ratcliffe survived a neck wound—unfortunately—and has gone to the king in triumph. They've taken her corpse to the castle. What was she trying to accomplish? I have no idea. I saw her body myself, lying on a cold stone slab in the doctor's chambers. Everyone is afraid to even touch her. Pale as marble, she is. Pale and beautiful in death.

—Dominic Mancini, Espion of the Doomed Boy

♦ ♦ ♦

CHAPTER THIRTY-SIX

The White Pig

Owen was awakened by the touch of a woman's fingers on his hair. The room was dark, but it was the birth of dawn. It was the time just before the birds started to sing, the cusp of a new day, the deep breath before the plunge.

The royal apartments in Beestone Castle were furnished and unfamiliar. As Owen blinked awake, it took him a moment to place himself. Was he in Tatton Hall? Kingfountain? He saw Ankarette kneeling beside the bed, her cheek resting on the mattress, her fingers playing absently with tufts of his hair. She had a languid smile on her pale face. A shudder rippled through her, and she bent her lips to the mattress to muffle a little cough. Then she gazed fondly at him again.

"Ankarette," Owen whispered, feeling his heart lighten. He rubbed his eyes on his hand. "I tried to stay awake. I fell asleep waiting for you."

"It's all right, Owen," she soothed. "I was . . . late." She smiled.

"You're quite pale," the boy said, feeling concern.

She looked as if that didn't matter at all. "I feel tired. I need a long sleep. Like you've had." She pinched his cheek tenderly and grazed it with her thumb. "Shall I tell you about your dream? Will you be able to remember it?"

He nodded eagerly and stared into her eyes, lost in them for a moment.

"After I've told you," she said softly, "you need to go to the king. Right away. You need to be brave, little Owen. Can you do that?"

"I have Evie's braid. I can be brave like her." Owen sat up, and noticed that she did not. She was kneeling at the edge of the bed, holding herself up on her arms.

"Very well. Listen carefully. You had a dream tonight. In the dream, three golden bucks came to Beestone Castle. The bucks all knelt before a white pig. You saw their antlers touch the ground before the pig. Then a rat with a knife walked up to the bucks to kill them and eat them. But the white pig shook its snout. It wouldn't let the rat hurt the bucks. The pig walked to the river and the bucks followed. All of them boarded a boat except for one. The smallest of the bucks stayed with the pig. The boat went against the current of the river—upstream instead of down— and sailed away to a land of flowers."

She stiffened and let out a soft breath of pain. She blinked, her eyes growing dazed. "Owen, then the pig sniffed the rat. When it did, it found a gold coin in its fur. The pig turned into a boar and grew tusks. With the tusks, the boar threw the rat into the river, and it drowned."

Her fingers, which had been playing in his hair, went limp, and her wrist sagged to the mattress blanket. Her head lolled to one side.

"Ankarette?" Owen asked worriedly.

"So sleepy," she whispered. She blinked rapidly, then lifted her head. Her eyes seemed to sharpen and focus. "Now go tell the king about your dream. This is important, Owen. This is how you can save your family." She gave him a tender look, so poignant and full of love. Her weak fingers lifted and grazed the white patch of his hair. "Go. Then tell me what happens."

"Will you be here when I get back?" Owen asked, his worry growing.

"I promise," she answered, smiling sadly.

Owen scuttled off the edge of the bed and quickly threw on his clothes. He made sure Evie's braid was in his pocket and he walked away from his room, wandering the halls.

He saw Mancini slumped in the corridor, a jug of wine crooked in his arm.

"Take me to the king's room," Owen told the Espion, tugging on his sleeve.

Mancini looked haggard, depressed, and irritable. His eyes opened slowly. His breath was awful. "You?" he said, looking pained.

"Where is it? I need to tell the king about my dream."

"What dream?" Mancini said in confusion. "There are no more dreams. There is no more hope. It's all been ruined. All is lost." He shook the empty jug a little, listening to see if there was any liquid sloshing around inside. It was empty.

"Ankarette said I must!" Owen insisted, gripping the man's shoulder.

Mancini's face crinkled with confusion. "Who said?"

"Ankarette!" Owen seethed, frustrated at the man's blockheadedness.

Mancini leaned forward. "You've . . . *seen* . . . her?"

"She's in my room." Owen hooked his thumb and pointed.

The expression on Mancini's face transformed. He shoved away the empty jug and broke it in his haste to get back to his feet. "She is? At this very moment? But how?"

"Sshh!" Owen said, for he heard the sound of boots coming.

Mancini grabbed the boy's hand and marched him down the hall. He swayed a bit as he walked, but he knew the way. Coming toward them were several night guards wearing the badge of the white boar and carrying torches.

One of the soldiers challenged them. "Who goes there?"

"This is the Kiskaddon brat—*boy*! He had another dream and must tell it to the king!"

The soldier looked at Owen in surprise. "Follow us, boy."

Mancini's cheeks were pink and rosy, and he looked elated. They marched back the way they had come and quickly went to the king's bedchamber. As soon as they walked into the room, Owen saw Duke Horwath. Ratcliffe was also there, a bloody bandage around his neck, along with several other men who were talking angrily amongst themselves. To Owen's surprise, Princess Elyse was also present, wearing a robe over her nightdress, her hair straggling as she paced the chamber in her slippers, her face pinched with worry.

"My liege," the soldier announced, stamping his boots as he halted. "Found these two in the corridors. The boy has had another dream."

The king, looking furious, turned when he heard the soldier's announcement. His face was flushed with emotion, but he calmed when he saw Owen.

"Another one?" the king asked, his voice suddenly interested and concerned. He started walking toward Owen.

"My lord," Ratcliffe broke in. "That can wait. You promised my reward. I have served you faithfully. I want Tatton Hall!"

The princess glowered at Ratcliffe, her face showing her absolute disapproval. Horwath looked angry too, his stern lips pressed hard together.

"Give it a rest, Dickon!" the king snapped. "This is important!"

Ratcliffe seethed with fury. "If you are still taking the Espion away from me, I deserve something in return! Something that won't be a loss of reputation. If this is how you reward loyalty . . ."

The king was in no mood to hear him. His cheeks were full of stubble and he looked as if he hadn't slept well or at all that night. It reminded Owen of the night he had found the secret tunnel leading to the king's bedroom. The king's face was full of weariness and agitation. But it softened when he dropped down on one knee in front of the boy, putting their eyes on a level.

"What is it, lad?" he asked in a kindly voice. "Tell me of your dream."

Everyone was staring at Owen. The soldiers. Duke Horwath. The princess. Ratcliffe. The king. All their eyes bored into him, all their ears listened, and he realized he had power over these men. A king was kneeling in front of *him* because he believed Owen was Fountain-blessed and could read the future. He was convinced.

All Owen needed to do was speak.

His tongue grew thick in his mouth. The pressure of being the focus of so much pointed attention unearthed his hidden terrors and fears, which came popping up from the ground like worms after a rainstorm. Owen dug his hand into his pocket and felt the reassuring touch of his friend's hair. He wished she were there. He could almost see her in his mind's eye, standing behind the king with an impatient look. *Just tell him!*

"My lord," Ratcliffe interrupted, suddenly nervous. "It's so early. Wouldn't it be better to hear the lad later, during breakfast? The queen's poisoner is dead, so you need not fear your meals now. It's nearly dawn. Surely this can wait."

The queen's poisoner was dead? Owen's stomach took an uneasy flop.

The king's hand rested on the boy's shoulder. "Tell me," he said.

Owen licked his lips. He tried to speak, but his tongue wouldn't work. A worried spurt of panic enveloped his gut. Was Ankarette dying? No! She had said she would wait for him to return. She was tired, that was all. Owen forced himself to concentrate.

"Go ahead," Princess Elyse said coaxingly.

"My lord . . ." Ratcliffe whined.

"Shut it!" Horwath barked at him.

"I did have a dream," Owen said, looking into the king's gray eyes. A wavering smile hovered on the king's mouth, encouraging him to continue. "In the dream, I saw three golden bucks. They had big antlers, though one of the bucks was small. They came walking across a field. There was a white pig in the field. A happy pig. The bucks knelt before the pig, their antlers touching the ground. While they were kneeling, a rat with a knife approached them." Owen swallowed, feeling the hate burning at him from Ratcliffe's eyes. He focused on the king's face. "The rat wanted to slaughter the bucks. To eat them."

"This is intolerable!" muttered Ratcliffe desperately.

The king held up his other hand, cutting him off. "Go on."

"The white pig shook its snout. It would not let the rat hurt the deer." Owen swallowed again, squirming. He understood the dream. He understood what Ankarette was trying to do. "The white pig . . . the white pig couldn't *trust* the bucks, though. And so he went with them to the river." The king's grip on his shoulder tightened, almost painfully. His eyes stared into Owen's eyes with a look of shock.

"Listen to him, my lord!" Ratcliffe said suddenly, his tone changing.

"The pig could not trust the bucks," Owen went on. "They had not defended the pig when hunters were trying to kill him. So the pig, the *white* pig, put the bucks on a boat in the river. And he sent them to another land, a land full of flowers. The boat sailed upstream, away from the falls. Only one of the bucks stayed behind. The littlest buck stayed by the pig. It stayed right next to the pig." Owen's voice trailed off, almost to a whisper. The king was hanging on his every word.

Then Owen lifted his voice again. "What happened next was the pig sniffed at the rat. I think it was smelly. And there, in the rat's fur, was a gold coin. The pig grew tusks, like a boar. And with the tusks, it threw the rat in the river. The rat . . . drowned."

There was a series of gasps when he spoke the final part.

The king was astonished. His eyes were so curious, his expression so moved with emotion that he pressed several fingers against his lips, but he kept his other hand on Owen's shoulder. Suddenly, Owen heard the rushing of the Fountain. The sound filled his ears and the king's hand tightened on his shoulder. Owen felt the magic rushing down the king's arm.

Can you hear me?

It was the king's voice, in Owen's mind.

Yes.

The king blinked, but did not seem surprised.

You know what your dream means, don't you, Owen?

Yes. It means my parents are guilty of treason. I know that now.

The king quivered with suppressed emotions. His eyes were fierce. *You know then, that I have to punish them. I cannot trust them. I cannot let your father serve me. Owen, you must understand this. I must destroy them or risk an even worse betrayal. Owen, please understand. I don't wish to hurt you. But I cannot let them escape, not when I have power to stop further mischief. A prince must make difficult decisions betimes. A prince must destroy his enemies when he has the chance.*

Owen felt the power of the Fountain rushing through him. The king was using his power to convince him that his parents must die. He could tell that the king truly believed he had no choice. That wisdom and prudence demanded justice for his parents' involvement at Ambion Hill. Owen was utterly convinced it was just.

But he also realized the king was using the magic of the Fountain on him. And so he turned it back against him.

But a king can pardon an enemy, Owen thought in response. *You have that right and that power. My dream tells you the Fountain's will for my parents. And its will for me. I will serve you. I will take their place.*

Owen looked deep into the king's eyes.

I know you didn't murder your nephews. I know you care for your niece and would never hurt her. And I know you won't hurt me. You are not the monster others pretend you are. I trust you.

The king let go of Owen's shoulder as if it burned him. He rose to his feet, staggering backward in surprise and shock, his face totally unmasked of pretense and cunning. Owen's words had cut him to his very center, had tapped into the secret need of his heart—the need to be loved and trusted by a child after the loss of his own son and his nephews.

"Uncle? Are you unwell?" Elyse said, rushing to him in concern. He was trembling, his entire body quaking with emotion. Tears trickled down the king's cheeks. And then, falling to his knees in front of them all, the king wept.

♦ ♦ ♦

The wish to acquire more is admittedly a very natural and common thing; and when men succeed, they are praised rather than condemned. But when they lack the ability to do so and yet want to acquire more at all costs, they deserve condemnation for their mistakes.

—Dominic Mancini, Espion of the Palace Kitchen

♦ ♦ ♦

CHAPTER THIRTY-SEVEN

The Queen's Midwife

"What is the meaning of this, Horwath? Unhand me! Unhand me, I say!" The voice was Ratcliffe's, and the attention of those gathered in the royal chamber shifted from the grieving king and his niece to the master of the Espion. On Horwath's barked command, several soldiers wearing the arrow-pierced lion had marched forward and seized Ratcliffe.

Horwath's face was impassive, cold, and very menacing. "Search him," he ordered brusquely.

"This is outrageous!" Ratcliffe snarled, struggling against the soldiers, but he was quickly overpowered. "What do you hope to find? A bag of gold? Of course I have a bag of gold! This is preposterous!"

"My lord duke?" one of the soldiers said, bringing forth a folded scrap of paper, the red waxy seal already broken. "It was in his pocket."

Ratcliffe's eyes widened with shock. "Where did you get that? I did not have that in my pocket. You must . . . you must have put it there!" He bucked against the soldiers, trying to free himself, and one of them clamped an arm around his neck to subdue him.

Owen stood by the princess, watching with building interest as Elysabeth's grandfather unfolded the note and started reading it aloud.

"Master Ratcliffe, long has my master desired to earn your good opinion. Rumor crosses our borders that your master has a new Fountain-blessed. A little brat from Kiskaddon. Please arrange an accident to remove this threat to us. In return, you will inherit the lordship of one of our many pleasant estates on your borders with income received from the king's coffers annually. Be quick, Master Ratcliffe. Your prompt cooperation will be amply rewarded." Horwath's frown and boiling anger intensified as he read. "Yours et cetera, Grey."

Ratcliffe's face turned as white as milk.

The king rose to his feet, his look so full of wrath and disappointment that it made Owen cower.

"How could you—*you*—turn traitor, Dickon?" the king said in a husky whisper. "You, above all, know my heart. You, above all, have shared my history. I am not sure I can trust anyone now. For greed or gold? Was it worth it, old friend?" His hand closed against his dagger hilt, and for a brief instant, Owen feared the king would plunge the blade into Ratcliffe's heart.

"My lord," Mancini said politely.

The king turned his savage gaze to the Genevese man.

"There was an incident—quite recently—when I discovered little Owen and the duke's granddaughter at play. Well, to be honest, they were being rather *naughty* and had found their way into the palace cistern. I happened to tell Master Ratcliffe this fact shortly thereafter and . . . well, rather coincidentally, the gate winches of the cistern drain were tugged on. That's why the palace ran out of water. The two children were nearly swept into the river. I had no proof it was not an *accident*, of course. Until now. I thought I might mention it."

Ratcliffe's face turned green and he hung his head as if all his strength had failed him.

The king stared at Owen in mixed surprise and horror. "Is this true, lad?"

Owen stared at the king purposefully. He nodded and then looked at Duke Horwath. "Mancini saved both of us. He broke down the door and caught us before we went over the falls."

"By the Fountain!" the king exclaimed. He knelt in front of Owen and mussed the boy's hair, looking at him with wonder and the utmost relief. "Is this true? Were you spared the horrors of it? I almost cannot bear to look at you without weeping anew."

It took him a moment to master his emotions. Then the king rose like a thunderhead, and when he next spoke, his voice was full of menace and warning. "You desire wealth and fame like a sick man craves his drink. But you were not meant for so much power, Dickon. You are as inept as you are ambitious. This message reeks of the smell of Occitania, the nation that has always sought our overthrow and humiliation. For this, you would have murdered two innocent children . . . just like Bletchley. How could you, man? How could you?" His jaw was clenched with rage. "My lord duke of North Cumbria, acting as chief justice, arrest this man of high treason and commit his body to the waters. May the Fountain spare his life if he be innocent or bury him in the Deep Fathoms with all the moldering treasures of the world for him to feast his greedy eyes on without being able to touch once his skin turns to bones. Out of my sight!"

The soldiers hauled up Ratcliffe, but his legs no longer seemed to work. His face dripped with so much sweat that he looked like a melting candle.

Duke Horwath, stiff and imperious, stood in front of him. "I arrest you on grounds of high treason, by the name of Dickon, Lord Ratcliffe of Brent." He grabbed the chain of office around Ratcliffe's neck and snapped it, then hurled it to the floor like refuse. That done, he smacked Ratcliffe across the face so hard it rocked his head back. He nodded curtly to the soldiers to drag him away, and as they did, Owen heard the man sobbing.

The king's frown was fierce and determined. He stared after Ratcliffe, his heart closing with another wound.

"Uncle, I am so sorry," Princess Elyse murmured. "But in truth, I am *not* surprised. I have had fears for Owen's life since he came to Kingfountain." She came and stood behind Owen, resting her hands on his shoulders. "That is why I asked if *I* could look after him."

The king nodded at her words. "I should have listened to you, Niece. I should have heeded your counsel. I would have you near me to always give me your advice. To help me steer this ship of state. You are wise beyond your years. I would value your suggestions."

The princess smiled, pleased. "I would like that, Uncle." She squeezed Owen's shoulders. "So may I look after him now?"

The king smiled wanly and then shook his head. "No, Elyse."

"But why not? What are you going to do with him?" Her voice had an edge of worry.

"Indeed. What will I do with him?" the king muttered calmly. His gray eyes were serious and intense as he looked into Owen's. "I will make him into a duke. A lord of the realm. He will need to be taught. He will need to be trained. When I was nine, my brother made me the Duke of Glosstyr, and I was sent to the North to be trained by my uncle Warrewik. After the Assizes, I will name Owen the Duke of Westmarch, and he will be sent to the North under the wardship of my faithful friend, who knows the price of loyalty. There is a little granddaughter, I believe, who was recently sent back to Cumbria?"

The duke's stern mouth broke into a smile. "She is, Your Grace. She *was*. I think a season or two up in the North would strengthen this little pup. Make a man out of him."

"Then I give his wardship to you, Stiev. Make a man out of him. Make a lord out of him." The king stared at Owen with kindness. "For your parents' treason, I *will* pardon them. For your sake, Owen. They will never be permitted back to Ceredigion on pain of death. But I will not forbid you from seeing them. My lord duke, when you draw up the attainder, please be sure that Owen is excluded."

"I will, Your Grace." The duke was still smiling, and Owen could imagine why.

The king knelt down on the ground and picked up the broken chain and badge that Horwath had thrown down. He rose, staring at the fine workmanship of the badge, the symbol of the rose and star made of gold. Then he looked warily at Mancini.

"For now," the king said with almost a threat in his voice, and offered the medallion to him.

"Your Grace," Mancini replied meekly, bowing.

◆ ◆ ◆

Owen hurried back to his bedchamber, and his heart gave a shiver and a lurch when he found it empty. His heart was boiling inside, ready to burst with relief. He had to tell her.

"Ankarette?" Owen whispered, carefully padding to the other side of the bed. He found a bloodstain on the floor.

His heart was hammering faster and faster. "Ankarette?" he whispered again.

She was gone.

"Owen."

Her voice was so soft, muffled, he almost didn't hear it, but it came from under the bed. Owen dropped to his knees and looked and found her curled up under the bedframe, her head resting on her arm.

Afraid, he crawled under the bed beside her. Her face was pale, her eyelids purple and bruised. She looked so weak and tired, as though she lacked the strength to even move.

"Are you hurt?" he asked.

"I'm very sick, Owen," she whispered, her voice so faint that he had to bring his ear near her mouth to hear her. "I've been sick for months."

"But you will get better now," Owen said, his mouth tightening into a frown.

"No, Owen." She sighed deeply. Very slowly, she lifted her fingers and grazed his hair. "Tell me . . . what happened."

He swallowed some tears before they could spill. His throat was thick and tight. He burrowed himself against her. She felt cold. Her hand limply stroked his hair.

"I'm going to be a duke," he stammered. "Duke Kiskaddon, like my father. The king is giving me Westmarch. But I'm going North first. To be with Evie and trained by her grandfather. I'm . . . I'm not going to see you again, am I?"

"Sshhh," she soothed. "I'm going to the Deep Fathoms now. Where I can rest. Where I can sleep without pain. Sshhhh, don't cry."

He was crying. The tears were hot against his cheeks. "I don't want you to go," he moaned. "You need to keep teaching me. I can't do this without you. I *am* Fountain-blessed, Ankarette. You were right about me. The king tried using his magic on me and I . . . I turned it back on him. I felt it. So did he. Someone sent Ratcliffe to kill me. I . . . I need you, Ankarette!"

She was quiet for a while, so still it felt as if she wasn't breathing. Her hand still stroked his hair. He sobbed quietly into her, burying his face in her gown. She let him grieve, gently patting his back.

"I know about Ratcliffe's message," Ankarette said, her voice quiet and distant. "I put it in his pocket last night at the inn. It was hidden among his papers." She paused, struggling for breath. "Owen, remember how I said that secrets always try to get out? Do you remember that?"

"Um-hmm," he said, hardly able to speak through his tears. He looked up at her face, and the loving smile he saw there made his heart hurt even more.

"There's one more . . . in my heart, trying to get out. I think it's been . . . keeping me from dying. But I need . . . to let it out now." She sighed, her eyes closing as if she were falling asleep. Or dying. "I was trained . . . to be a poisoner . . . from a midwife. That's common, actually." Her hand strokes were getting slower. "So many of the herbs . . . and medicines that can save . . . can also kill. One of my favorites . . . is nightshade. It's used . . . in childbirth . . . when the mother has too much pain." Her voice trailed off again.

"Ankarette?" Owen pleaded, shaking her gently.

Her eyes fluttered open. "Nightshade . . . has many purposes. I used it on Ratcliffe . . . last night. He told me his secrets. He told me about the letter. But when it . . . when it wears off . . . you can't remember what you did . . . what you said. That's how I tricked Ratcliffe into forgetting. That's how I learned what was in the book. But that's not my secret." Her voice thickened with pain. "When you were stillborn, I was . . . the midwife . . . who helped your mother. For you. You've always been precious to me, Owen. I had to give you . . . some of my magic . . . for you to live. I learned . . . when you give of the magic . . . it grows stronger. Remember that. I've tried to help you the best . . . I could. Now you . . . now you must use your magic . . . to help others. Remember."

Her hand slipped down. She had no strength left.

"Ankarette!" Owen moaned, taking her hand and squeezing it.

Her eyelashes fluttered. She stared at him, blinking dreamily. The sad smile was gone. Her expression was full of peace.

"I love you," he whispered, kissing her cheek.

"I . . . love you, my little prince," she whispered back thickly. Then her eyes shut and her last breath sighed out.

◆ ◆ ◆

"Where is that little brat?" Mancini muttered from the doorway.

When Owen heard the voice, his little heart shriveled like a prune. "Down here," he called, pulling himself from under the bed. He rose disheveled, but the tears were all gone now.

"You've been crying?" Mancini said aghast. "After all the king has given you, you've been *crying?*"

"Ankarette is dead."

Mancini frowned. "It's a miracle she was not dead hours ago. She was knifed several times after she snuck into Ratcliffe's room at the inn. To think, it was all part of her plan."

Owen glared at him. "She's under the bed, Mancini. I need your help. I can't lift her on my own. She needs to go back to the Fountain. We need to get her into a boat."

Mancini sighed. "Lad, that's just out of the question. I just became the temporary head of the Espion. I'm not about to lose it on some risky gamble with a corpse!"

"No!" Owen said. "She needs to go back to the Fountain. A boat, Mancini. You need to arrange for a boat. She needs to go back to the Fountain!"

Mancini stared at Owen as if he were being childish. "I am not superstitious, boy. All this talk of gurgling waters and dreams is a bunch of nonsense. We *both* know that. Ankarette Tryneowy was the most cunning woman living, as far as I'm concerned. But she's dead now, and I wash my hands of her."

Owen was furious. He wanted to command Mancini to obey him, but he knew that people forced against their will were not persuaded. He needed to outthink Mancini, to maneuver his actions as if this were a game of Wizr. He felt a little trickle rippling through him. An idea came.

"If you will do this for me, I will give you a stipend from my duchy independent of the king," Owen said flatly, folding his arms.

The fat man stared at him in surprise. "A stipend, you say? How much would this stipend entail, to be precise?"

A number came to Owen's mind. "Fifty florins a year. In Genevese coins."

Again Mancini looked startled. "My young man, you have yourself a bargain. I like how you think. You and I are going to be great friends from now on."

It was a tender farewell between the Kiskaddon brat and his family. Even I found myself dabbing an eye with a kerchief. The Assizes were a dreadful affair, with evidence brought, witnesses testifying, and verdicts rendered. There was a collective gasp of fearful breath when Duke Horwath read the guilty verdict against Lord and Lady Kiskaddon, followed by much weeping and anguish. They were beloved in Westmarch. But they gambled that King Severn would fail when they supported the pretender before Ambion Hill. When you gamble, you often lose. Now imagine, if you will, how the despair turned to joy when the king pronounced the punishment. Lord and Lady Kiskaddon and their sons and daughters would be banished from Ceredigion instead of meeting their fate at a river like Dickon Ratcliffe. And then the king proclaimed that their youngest son, the little brat, would inherit the duchy at eight years old. The tears of anguish turned to tears of rejoicing. Not a dry eye when the lad hugged his parents and kissed them in farewell. Except for Horwath—that man is made of stone! But what was even more pleasurable was knowing the outcome before the masses did. This is the way of politics and power. This is what I was born for!

—Dominic Mancini, Master of the Espion

CHAPTER THIRTY-EIGHT

The North

Owen had never been to the North before, and he was unprepared for the sights awaiting him. He rode on the back of the duke's horse, as he had many times before, clutching the duke's cloak. Owen's toes were freezing in his fur-lined boots, and despite several layers of tunics, he still felt like shivering. His cheeks were pink, his nose hurt, but he stared in awe at the snowcapped mountains that rose in majestic plinths as far as the eye could see. This was a land with few farms, many rocks, and wild goats. And waterfalls! Owen was amazed at the huge waterfalls that roared down from the icy peaks, the sound a welcoming anthem to his senses.

The horses of the duke and his men lumbered into a mountain valley, wedged between colossal shelves of rock and ice, exposing a huge castle and town in the heart of it. A mammoth waterfall cascaded from behind the castle, spellbinding in height and majesty. Even from their position, Owen could see a bridge at the crest of the falls, putting him in mind of a story Evie had once told him.

"Ooohhh," the boy uttered reverently, seeing the sights, feeling a prick of pain from his freezing nose.

"It's a tranquil place," the duke said with a chuckle. "Except when my granddaughter is around."

Owen turned around and saw the soldiers accompanying them. Some bore the banners of the arrow-pierced lion. Some bore the blue shields and golden bucks of Kiskaddon. They were Owen's men, his captains and ancients and councillors who would bear his orders back to the duchy and bring word to him in the mountains when his orders were fulfilled.

The mountain air was absolutely delicious. As the horses reached the outer walls of the town, the trumpets from the castle sounded and the townsfolk began to crowd around them, cheering the two dukes they had heard were coming. Owen wore the glittering collar of his rank, the symbol of his power. He wore the badge now. He was the youngest duke in the realm. And it was all Ankarette's doing. In the weeks that had passed since her body had been entrusted to the waters, he had thought of her often. He would *always* remember her. And with those memories, he had feelings and secrets he could share with no one else.

No one except the girl waiting for them at the castle ahead. Owen reached into his pocket and felt her crumpled braid and squeezed it.

As they reached the drawbridge of the castle, she could contain herself no longer. Owen saw Elysabeth *Victoria* Mortimer running down the wooden planks, squealing with happiness as she saw her grandfather and Owen riding up to meet her.

"Go lad," the grizzled duke said to Owen, giving him a wink.

And by the time he had dropped down from the saddle, Evie had reached him and hugged him so hard he thought he might start crying for the first time in weeks.

"Owen! Owen Kiskaddon! *My* Owen!"

AUTHOR'S NOTE

As Ovid once said, "a new idea is delicate." The idea for this story has been in my mind for several years and has many sources for its inspiration. During my college years at San Jose State, I focused a lot on the War of the Roses in fifteenth-century England. I read many if not most of the histories written by contemporaries of the time and often took notes when discovering something interesting. The Kingfountain series is loosely based on the events of 1485 following Richard III's ascension to the throne of England. In preparation for writing, I watched several versions of Shakespeare's play and reread many of the histories I studied in college to help provide some of the details.

One of the tiny details that I stumbled across in college regards Ankarette. In the sources, there is mention of a woman who sailed to Calais to persuade Edward IV's brother George, Duke of Clarence, to rejoin his brother's side and help him reclaim his lost crown. This girl is never named, but she is given credit by the chronicler for Edward's success. I was curious about who this woman was and came to suspect that she was probably part of the Earl of Warwick's household. Warwick was George's father-in-law. She is never mentioned again, but I wrote a note about her in a spiral notebook, which I still have today.

Following the life story of the Duke of Clarence further, I discovered that after his wife died giving birth, he accused the midwife of poisoning her and wanting to murder him. This woman did have a name—Ankarette Twynneowe. George had her arrested, illegally tried, and executed for murder, which he did without the approval of his brother, King Edward IV. It was this act of judicial murder that likely led to George's own execution. As Shakespeare puts it, he was drowned in a barrel of malmsey wine.

What if, I thought, George was telling the truth?

The persona of the queen's poisoner started to come together in my mind based on the historical person and some unrelated facts I tied in. The cast of this novel is primarily based on real people in history who participated in real events. What would have happened if Richard III had won the Battle of Bosworth Field on August 22, 1485, instead of losing to Henry Tudor? Richard III has been in the news lately—his bones have been discovered in England, and he finally has been given a proper burial.

Now a quick word on the Fountain. As I did the research for this book, I continued to stumble across references to fountains and water as I developed the magic system of this world. I read *Little Lord Fauntleroy* by Frances Hodgson Burnett, who has always inspired me. It's the story of a young boy who softens the hard heart of his grandfather, the Earl of Dorincourt. The name Fauntleroy can be translated as "Kingfountain." In Shakespeare's play *Richard III*, the condemned George of Clarence has a nightmare in which he's fallen overboard a ship. While drowning, he sees the magnificent treasures of the deep. The constable of the Tower of London, who is talking to him, is surprised he had the presence of mind to note the treasures while drowning. As I looked through other events of history, including the tales of the Mabinogion in Wales, I saw other references to the Fountain in there too. All these pieces helped come together.

Last but certainly not least, I was inspired for this book by E. B. White's *Charlotte's Web*. I'd often thought it very moving and inspiring how Wilbur and Charlotte became so close.

I've never written a book from the perspective of a young boy. I based the character of Owen on my youngest son. Many of his antics and traits were leveraged for Owen, including his penchant for reading at a young age and knocking down tiles. And yes, he does have a streak of white in his hair.

In the second book of the Kingfountain Trilogy, you will find that seven years have passed and the world has changed. I hope you continue to enjoy Owen's and Elysabeth *Victoria* Mortimer's adventures in *The Thief's Daughter*.

ACKNOWLEDGMENTS

I told a few people about this story before actually sitting down to write it. One was my daughter Isabelle, and I could see by the look in her eyes that she thought it was special. So thanks, Isabelle, for listening to my brainstorms and talking through them with me. I'd also like to extend my gratitude and thanks to the folks at 47North for their amazing partnership and support. And to my loyal cohort of early readers for their input, enthusiasm, and encouragement, I offer my continued thanks (and freebies!): Gina, Emily, Karen, Robin, Shannon, and Sunil.

And also to my fantastic editors—Jason Kirk and Angela Polidoro—whose early input and direction helped a palsied crew quit trembling!

ABOUT THE AUTHOR

Photograph © Kim Bills

Jeff Wheeler took an early retirement from his career at Intel in 2014 to become a full-time author. He is, most importantly, a husband and father, and a devout member of his church. He is occasionally spotted roaming hills with oak trees and granite boulders in California or in any number of the state's majestic redwood groves.

Visit the author's website: www.jeff-wheeler. com. Be sure to "follow" Jeff through his Amazon.com author page to be notified of his latest work.